Duality

The Duality Series | Book One

Becca Fogg

Duality

Book One, The Duality Series

By Becca Fogg

This is a work of fiction. Names, characters, places, and incidents either are the product of the author's imagination or are used fictitiously. Any resemblance to actual persons, living or dead, events, or locales is entirely coincidental.

Unless you're Hillary—you know what you did and why you're in here. Also, why are you reading the copyright page? It's weird, even for lawyers. Love you, hon.

Cover in coordination with rebecacovers.

Editing by Susan Barnes Editing and Mary-Theresa Hussey

Proofreading by Nice Girl Naughty Edits

First paperback edition November 2021

ISBN 9798461714963 (paperback)

ISBN 9798753308276 (hardcover)

ASIN B09JFVZNKC (ebook)

www.beccafogg.com

Dedication

---

for Logan,
and for anyone who has been told they can't

Track List

"Fell In Love With A Boy," Joss Stone
"Goodbye Earl," Dixie Chicks
"Rodeo," Lil Nas X, Cardi B
"Sin Wagon," Dixie Chicks
"7 Rings," Ariana Grande
"Don't Know Why," Norah Jones
"Boss Bitch," Doja Cat
"Slow Hands," Niall Horan
"Freak," Doja Cat
"Ice Cream," BLACKPINK ft. Selena Gomez
"Havana," Camilla Cabello ft. Young Thug
"Welcome to the Jungle," Guns N' Roses

These songs and more for this book (and the next) are arranged on the Duality playlist on Spotify.

Book Description

Jex thought she was an average, post-college girl—until she crippled a drunk and nearly incinerated a gas station. When her elemental powers manifest, she's torn from her placid life and shoved into the war between good and evil. Forced to rely on new allies, including the sweetheart Captain of the Guard and her alphahole Valen, Jex must come to terms with her newfound ability before her enemies succeed in capturing her.

I am made of extremes. Normalcy was key, before. I'd have a normal life, with a normal job, and a normal white-picket fence. That was before I crippled a drunk and torched a gas station.

As it turns out, normalcy lives in the average gray, but I do not. Instead, I am made of extremes. Of fire and water. Of light over darkness. Of good over evil. Well, *mostly* good over evil, apparently.

Now I have no choice but to embrace the not-normal before my world comes crashing down a second time—to piece myself back together with the family I found when I needed it, with the support of two men dragging me (kicking and screaming) to my full capability.

But the bad guys are coming, and they're coming for me. ***He's*** coming for me. *Ain't that some shit.*

A Letter From Jex

Six Months From Now

Hey, so welcome.

You're about to embark on a story about how I got to where I am, and it can get rough. I've been through a lot—a lot of woo-woo magic (good and bad), a lot of fighting (verbal and physical), and a metric fuckton of turmoil (particularly about my family, and my own issues).

It could be fun to work through, to get out my aggression in more ways than one, but mostly . . . not.

That's not to say everyone else had it easy, or that I made it easy on them. Rivals don't become besties overnight. If you had any idea of the gargantuan effort to get my unconventional little circle on the same page.

Well, I suppose you'll find out if you keep reading.

Understand that I don't pull punches or give you the rose-colored version. It's my story, and I'll tell it how I want to. If that's not for you, that's okay. My friend writing all this down won't take it personal if you turn back.

I just hope you'll have the patience to deal with my fuckups, or at least more patience than I had for myself.

Or than Eli had. *Fucking Eli.*

Anyway, you've been warned. Explicit stuff inside, and it only goes downhill from here. I'll circle back in a couple of weeks to check in on 'ya.

Content Information

This book contains on-page sexual content and violence, including death. It discusses or includes abandonment, disownment, grief, adoption, kidnapping, stalking, and infidelity (not among the main characters). There is discussion of dubcon but no dubcon. Duality is medium-burn MF and slow-burn RH/why-choose.

Chapter One

The creature roared in my ear, the blast razing my sanity like a steamroller. My head lolled at the assault as I tried to regain control of my senses.

I admit that might be *slightly* melodramatic.

"Jex, are you even listening?" Anna scolded through the cell phone.

Pedestrians, huddled in their coats against the brisk April air, hurried around me as I paced at the street-level entrance to the Arlington T-station. Rush-hour commuters brushed by in the race down the stairs for prime spots on the subway platform. There was no way I could follow them down while trapped by Anna's rambling.

"Yeah, yeah, I'm here," I mumbled. Attempting to focus on her tinny voice was harder than doing long division while drunk. It happened a lot when my sister was involved.

"So, are you coming?" she asked, irritation plain in her voice. I sighed.

"Where am I going again?"

"To my baby shower! I swear you haven't heard a word I've said. This weekend? Mom bought you a plane ticket."

Admittedly, I'd rather jump *in front of* a train if it meant I could escape this call. Knowing Anna, it wouldn't save me, even then.

Frustration tightened my chest. I'd been struggling to live in Boston—an expensive city where what you get and what you paid for were two vastly different things. I hated when my parents had to chip in for flights but loved living here too much to concede and move home to Orlando.

"Anna, it's already Tuesday. You can't ambush me and expect me to drop everything to come home, and you really shouldn't have gone to Mom and Dad."

My sister had developed the habit of regularly calling me home, often for the most random events. It could be our cousin's birthday, the Epcot Flower and Garden Expo, or a friend's graduation. She even flew me home once, on two-days' notice, only to find out it was a blind date.

She also routinely "forgot" to tell me until the last minute. If Anna could channel her pushiness for Good, every terrorist organization would have surrendered. She already had most of our hometown on her whichever-now MLM mailing list.

"I'll have to check my calendar," I said hesitantly, fidgeting with the phone. My palms started to sweat.

"Is this about your electrician?"

"This has nothing to do with the electrician," I grumbled. "I broke it off with him months ago."

"You were having an affair, big sis."

"He had the affair. I was having fun," I huffed.

Of course, she'd use it to guilt me into submission. Post-college living had been a lot harder than I'd imagined. You spend your entire life in school surrounded by a group of easily accessible peers, then they shove you out into the world and expect you to be fine all on your lonesome.

We don't all make good choices when we're struggling.

"Don't give me that, Jessica Eve Kantor. You will be here, in three days, because you are going to the shower of your niece!" Her voice shrilled, the pitch and volume bordering on screeching. It was like nails on a chalkboard, even over a cell phone and fifteen hundred miles away.

Her point-of-no-return tone meant that nothing I said or did could change this outcome. If I didn't cave, she'd go nuclear and get Mom to shame me or have Dad scream at me. I didn't have the energy for *all that* right now.

"Fine, but please, *please*, talk to me before you do anything like this again."

Was it still surrendering if you included a command? Was it still a command if you said "please," twice, with emphasis?

"Oh, you know you love it. See you Friday night!"

The line went dead. *Shit.*

Anna and I had always been close, and she hadn't coped well with my failure to remain in her proximity. I'd moved from a tiny town south of Orlando years ago, ostensibly for a job, but really I needed to experience something other than the beach or Disney. Anna knew why, even understood it, but it didn't stop her from trying to change my mind.

Slipping the phone into my purse, I headed down the grimy subway stairs. I'd have to remember to screen her calls from now on.

Pacing on the platform, I combed my fingers through my long curls. How had my baby sister outmaneuvered me so seamlessly? When we were kids, it was so easy to resist her demands. All I had to do was sit on her and she'd yield. Was I losing my touch? Going soft? My verve was one of my best attributes.

I mentally noted to weave the word "fuck" into more of our conversations, for the intimidation factor and because her reaction was priceless.

Exhaustion dragged me down as I shuffled inside my "garden-level" apartment in one of the mini-cities that composed the greater Boston area. Having a secluded entrance was a blessing; very few people knew of it, and drunken passersby or street noise rarely woke me up.

The day had stretched on for an eternity and was only going to be extended by the need to prepare for the trip home. After changing into PJs, I sorted laundry, refilled Georgia's automated cat food bowl, and dumped ancient food containers into the garbage.

Living in the city had its pros, but trash collection was not one of them. Garbage bags had to be lugged around the building into a back alley straight out of an old horror film. I regularly waited until I had multiple bags—it was about risk limitation, and maybe a little laziness.

Cold air slapped my face as I stepped out, carting the stuffed bag with me. I was tempted to leave it by the door a few days, but if I did, it'd sag there until it reeked, leaked, and I tripped over it as I tried to leave. Better to hustle.

Hurrying past the gate separating the main street and alley, I hoisted the heavy bag into the bin. Light from the streetlamps splintered through the mesh fence and disintegrated as it took the turn, casting a glow barely enough to see with. Not a single breath escaped as I sped back toward my apartment.

As I turned the corner, a man with a scruffy beard lurched from the shadows and rushed me.

Soiled clothes stank of urine. His body crowded close behind me, with an arm slung around my shoulder. The asshole's hands were crusted in dirt, his touch oppressive on my already icy skin. The sharp pinch of a knife threatened to split the skin on my neck as he forced me down the alley.

"W-what do you w-want?" I stammered. My mind reeled with the possibilities as my throat refused to vocalize more than a whisper. I fought the panic, but tears formed at the corners of my eyes.

"Just keep walking," he barked in the gravelly tone of a two-pack-a-day smoker. His breath stank of stale alcohol. The knife-wielding hand moved to brace my shoulder as he shoved me along faster.

My breathing ratcheted up to hyperventilation, and I forced myself to draw a few deep breaths. What did he want? I had no purse, no wallet. I was wearing pajamas, for fuck's sake.

Fear and anger rose as a churning heat in my chest. With every shuffled step, burning waves crested and flooded in more, like a rising tide never truly receding.

My mind failed to produce a plan. I didn't know how to fight; I had a hard enough time jockeying for seats on the subway. My thoughts flipped from trying to incapacitate him, to calling for help, to attempting escape, and all competed for control.

The white-hot rage built and intensified until it grew painful on its own. My head pounded from the roiling anxiety, and the world lost focus.

We neared the gate when the searing pressure burst.

It was a moment of pure clarity.

I could sense each of his movements—feel the hobble of his feet, smell his shallow breaths as he exhaled, felt his fingernails digging into my left shoulder and the blade at my right.

Hot blood rushed to the tips of my fingers, to my toes, and my thoughts righted themselves.

In that moment, the world regained sanity.

Resolve settled in my gut, a balm comforting and certain.

Having a plan of action does that, although I had no clue what the fear had decided on. Muscles contracted at the sensation, and I felt myself exhale and shift reflexively.

My body turned on its own as it grabbed the man's unarmed hand with a crushing grip. My hand twisted his wrist and heaved with more power than I thought physically possible. Strength surged from the blaze out through my arms. His wrist cracked, and he howled in pain.

The sudden movement spun him, the knife slicing across my back before flinging away. The weapon took flight and hit the brick wall with a muted *clink*.

The drunk whirled ten feet into the alley. I looked to the gate at the street, and knew I should escape. He no longer stood between me and safety.

Still, something made me stop and eye the attacker with quiet resolve. My body, propelled by that bizarre heat, repositioned itself with my weight balanced perfectly between both feet.

My limbs coiled as tense aggression emanated from my spine. That scorching heat accelerated, climbing to its apex immediately, waiting for the gasket to blow.

The rest of the world shifted out of focus—it was just him in my sights, with nothing else to threaten the assessment. A snarl rumbled from deep in my throat.

My muscles contracted again, and I sprinted toward the now-terrified drunk. His eyes, once cloudy and unfocused, cleared. He staggered, fear reflecting in his pupils so thickly I could almost see it wafting off in wispy waves.

On the approach, my feet took a few gracefully twined paces, controlling and directing the momentum. They did a quick, two-step turn and threw a sideways foot through his chest that sent him flying into the neighboring building's facade.

The offense continued as he bounced off the wall. My fingers seized his shoulder and elbow, my arms pivoting around and over as I knelt. I watched in amazement as his body flew overhead and landed on the brick pavers with a *thud* that reverberated in the narrow passageway.

Stunned, I realized I'd flipped him four feet in the air without even recognizing my hands had done it.

He lay on the ground, unmoving. His chest still rose and fell, but he didn't make a sound.

My whole body unwound, the fear and anger cascading away like water wrung from my limbs.

Suddenly, the world seemed very quiet.

The burning sensation in my chest withdrew, leaving a cold, dull ache in its place. I remembered to breathe and inhaled.

I froze in horror at what I'd done—I'd hurt him, another human being. I had never so much as laid a hand on anyone in aggression in my life. I'd taken a self-defense class when I first moved, like any woman living alone in a city should, but had never set out with the intention of seriously harming someone.

I supposed I still hadn't. I hadn't intended my actions, my body just . . . reacted. It lasted mere seconds. I couldn't even accurately describe it, but I'd moved so quickly and effortlessly as though I'd performed the motions every day of my life.

In a panic, I ran into my apartment, slammed the door, and called the police.

* * *

The paramedics carried the drunk away on a stretcher.

I watched from my window, curled into a quilt with the door firmly locked.

My limbs *ached*, my whole body trembling with a bone-deep chill. The altercation left me shaken—not just from the attack, but also from my inexplicable response. I refused to leave my apartment, even after the police arrived.

The officers were standard-issue PD—the term stereotype didn't even do them justice—but I'd still insisted the pair show their badges. I wrote down the numbers and called to confirm they were valid and, even then, only reluctantly let them in.

None of us were in an amiable mood.

The officers argued with me to allow a medic to look at the gash on my back. It throbbed and bled in short, cold streaks. My attacker left me a nice little gift, probably with a side of tetanus. How sweet.

Perched precariously on the edge of the couch, a smallish woman in EMT gear assessed my injury. She pronounced me likely to live, then told me she'd return after loading my attacker into the ambulance.

My fingers fidgeted with my pearl-and-obsidian ring throughout the entire ordeal. The calming distraction soothed my mind as I methodically slid the ring onto one finger, took it off, put it on the next finger, turned it.

Focus, Jex. Get this over with.

Their questions began innocently enough, but quickly nose-dived and plummeted toward dumpster-fire status.

"Ma'am, we need to know what happened," officer one huffed, "it's a criminal offense to lie to the police."

He seriously *ma'am*'d me! I delivered my absolute best fuck-all-the-way-off face.

"I'm not lying," I snarled. "I've sat here—patiently, I might add—answering the same question five, six, seven times. What more do you want from me?"

In fairness, I'd left out how I could have run inside. BPD would surely frown on the fact I could have gotten away without causing further harm.

Still, they seemed very interested in how I'd incapacitated a knife-wielding attacker. Officer Krupke, as I thought of him, considered my five-foot-four height and curvy frame and his assessment was obvious—he didn't think I could deal damage to a paper bag, let alone an armed drunk with a hundred pounds on me.

It's not as if I'm a lightweight. I shouldn't complain, since my hourglass bumps me up a notch on the hot-or-not scale. I could probably lay-off the soda and zebra cakes, but no one's perfect.

Krupke's interrogation tactics escalated, the menace intensifying until his face splotched with every shade between white and red. His partner only passively watched while Krupke imploded.

The EMT returned with a package of butterfly strips and braced a shoulder with one hand while she worked.

"Ma'am, I don't appreciate your tone of voice," he said. My temper flared, and I gave a pointed look.

"I'm nobody's *ma'am*, first of all," I retorted. "I'm twenty-four, so save the snide *ma'am*'s for someone else."

Contempt bubbling over, I sneered at him. Officer Krupke wasn't causing any fuzzy feelings, and I felt little need for tact. No chance I'd let pass the opportunity to disabuse him of his entitled attitude.

"Maybe you should talk to Chester Molester out there. I'm sure he can verify no one else was there. My knowledge may be limited to *Law & Order* reruns, but shouldn't you question the guy with a knife and advanced cirrhosis?"

"You're lucky we're not doing this in an interrogation room," he thundered, looking hard at his partner, "and I still think we should take you in. That 'guy with a knife' has a broken wrist, two bruised ribs, and a cracked vertebrae. How do you explain that?"

"Oh, I'm sorry. Did the boozer get a boo-boo? In that case, maybe *I* should apologize to *him*."

I snatched the pad and pen from beside me on the key table and read as I wrote.

"I'm . . . so . . . sorry . . . you . . . couldn't . . . kill . . . me. Next . . . time . . . try . . . sober." I peeled the page off and waved it around with my index and middle finger. He hulked over me, so I took the opportunity presented.

"Help a girl out and deliver this to him?"

My smile twisted as I folded the page in half and tucked it into his breast pocket.

As he reared back, returning my sneer, the second officer edged between us.

"Ah, Bill, why don't you go check on the medics?" Officer Two told his partner.

Krupke broke his death stare to glare at Two before stomping outside, hands balled into fists. It was satisfying to watch his sulky retreat. I pay the rent; I'm the only one allowed to have tantrums in my house.

"We need to know exactly what happened," Officer Two continued. His worried face seemed sincere, and my anger ebbed a smidge.

"I told you what happened. I took the trash out. As I came back, he grabbed my arm and put a knife to me. I swung him around, and he hit the wall and fell over."

Officer Two appeared unconvinced as well.

"No one was there to help you? You did all that damage by yourself?"

"It must have been adrenaline, I don't know, but no one else was around. He attacked me. I defended myself."

I folded my arms and winced as it caused the skin on my back to separate. *Ouch.*

The medic grunted and yanked my shoulders into position, then began reapplying the butterfly tape.

Officer Two surrendered and handed me his card. He gave an obligatory, "Give us a call if you remember anything else. We may ask you to testify," before following his partner outside.

The medic finished by pressing medical tape halfway across the length of my back. Great, how was I supposed to change that? Being un-coupled is great, until you decide on an unfortunate back tattoo or need someone to zip your dresses.

"You're pretty lucky," the medic said, "most knife wounds are much worse. Like they say, assume you'll get cut if you're confronted with a knife. Which class did you take?"

"Class?" I looked at her blankly.

"Yeah, isn't that how you disarmed him? Self-defense classes? I hear the Kenpo class at the Y is great." The confusion must have been plain on my face because she continued, "The broken wrist? The damage looked like it was from a wrist lock."

I paused, trying to detect any hint of humor. Her face reflected only wide-eyed innocence. She hadn't done anything to draw my ire, but with the way I felt, casualties could abound.

"Yeah, that's it," I hedged, and looked away to foreclose further conversation. What else could I say? *Why, yes, I went Karate Kid on his ass even though I have basically no training and, of course, I can explain what I did with perfect clarity.*

The medic left extra dressings and care instructions and disappeared into the ambulance.

As I sank into bed, my whole body felt tender. It was nearing three in the morning, and I had to be awake and alert in four hours. My head throbbed, and it was difficult finding a comfortable position that wouldn't irritate the slash across my back. My calico, Georgia, jumped onto the bed and licked at my arm.

Life would be so much simpler if I were a house cat.

Chapter Two

MacGyver himself would have been proud of the long-handled kitchen tong technique I devised to change the dressings on my back.

The rest of the week mercifully whizzed by. I didn't attack anyone and, thankfully, the heat never burned through my chest again. I told no one about the incident. It was ludicrous, and not the fun Ludacris that made me dance and drink too much when it came through the speakers.

If ignorance is bliss, then willful denial is at least somewhere around making-it-through-the-day.

By the time the end of the week rolled around, the slice on my back had at least stopped stinging every time I moved. Tuesday was on its way to being a fading memory.

On Friday morning, with Georgia safely ensconced under my neighbor's couch, I gathered my rolling bag and headed to the airport.

As I edged out of the Orlando airport rental car lot, heat drifted from the asphalt, making the landscape waver and my eyes glaze. The sun's too bright in Florida, too sweltering. Sweat stuck to my skin, despite the car's blasting air. The stark shift from frigid north to boiling south always threw me. The locals still thought this was *cold.*

Visits home were bittersweet. I'd developed a strong independence young, which strained my relationship with my father. I'll never forget the look on his face when I accused him of "a clinical case of self-righteous assholitis"—a phrase I'd managed to keep in my head to that point. The disorder entailed roaring his statements, really commands, along with the phrase "because I said so," while that vein in his neck bulged.

Why didn't parents understand that "because I said so" was a terrible response to anyone over the age of six? Thoughtlessly following authority without understanding the reasoning or consequences never got you anywhere.

Blind faith, one; critical thought, zero.

The return trip home began uneventful, but an ominous cloud planted the first seeds of apprehension during the drive. I'd been on the ground for just half an hour and was already edgy and anxious.

As if they knew my destination, my cheeks flushed under the stress of the literal and emotional hostile climates. A regular side effect of my father's assholitis included my face swelling from crying and screaming. Many a Kleenex were slaughtered on the altar of teenage angst.

If I were entirely honest, the move to New England was not solely about the job and adventure. I'd bit my tongue so often on these trips it was a wonder I still had taste buds.

In the driveway, I stared at my parents' home and tried to prepare myself for what waited inside. Awkward relatives. Inadequate junk food. Anna's school friends, who'd seep disappointment when I explained that life in Boston was not a Matt Damon movie. And my father . . .

Maybe if I sat there long enough, I'd gather the courage to drive away?

Nope, can't do that. Anna would be *very* unhappy. She undoubtedly knew my plane's ETA and probably signed up for rental car notifications. Even if I tried to escape, I could envision the carefully worded Amber Alert.

As if she instinctively knew I was avoiding her party, Anna came out the front door.

My sister and I looked almost nothing alike. She's two sizes smaller but taller by several inches. The phrase "chicken legs" was a staple of my vocabulary when we were younger. I'd matured, though. Now I screamed it mentally.

As kids, I'd teased Anna for her "pixie pretty" smooth skin and rosy cheeks. She seemed delicate and breakable, like a tanned Kewpie doll and about as threatening. That is, until she opened her mouth. At that point, the hardest gangster would cower.

I'll admit I've been called pretty, even beautiful, by people who were not drunk at the time. Probably didn't help that half my personality came from the movie *Clue*.

Still, my sister was the envy of every girl in school, and very used to the people around her indulging her whims.

She walked toward my car with a playful hop-skip that made her dress swish. Her soft curls had been cut into a blunt bob, the ringlets bouncing as she moved. Hints of hibiscus perfume wafted into the car when she sat in the passenger seat.

Anna's pale pink sundress showed off the slightest baby bump. She'd only found out she was pregnant a few weeks ago and was clearly going to milk it for all it was worth.

"Hey, Jex," she said with a toothy smile. She fussed with my hair and brought out a cherry lip gloss.

Uh oh, danger ahead.

"What did you do?"

Her smile morphed into a mischievous grin. She held out the pause after my question until I thought the Cheshire Cat might explode from her head.

"There's a boy in there for you," she proclaimed.

I sighed. Twenty-one, married, and pregnant, and Anna still obsessed over my romantic matches. Couldn't she just get me a kitten? I'd excel at the cat-lady lifestyle.

"No, *hello, so nice to see you*? Thank you for flying cross-country for me? So glad you could make it. It means a lot?"

"Hello, so nice to see you. Thank you for flying cross-country for me. It means a lot, especially to the boy I brought for you."

Exhaling yet another exasperated sigh, I repeated to myself how much I loved my sister and did, in fact, want to see her. Didn't mean I couldn't poke at her, as required by the Rules of Sisterhood.

"I'd rather fucking not, dear sister," I replied with a grin. "I just landed, and this isn't a swoon-worthy ensemble."

She winced. *Point to me.*

"Mom bought you a dress. Come on, you need to get over your electrician."

"Not my electrician," I replied.

"Perhaps if that had been the case, there wouldn't be a boy here for you."

Point to her.

There was no use arguing, really, and it would make her happy. I could last the few days and flee to the solitude of my northern escape. If she wanted to torment me, well, it was her party.

"Let's get this over with," I mumbled. Putting on my big-girl pants, I pushed open the car door.

Sweat collected on my hairline, and the slightest ache of heat nipped at my chest as I dragged out my luggage.

Shit. I hesitated at the odd sensation. Was I about to kung-fu someone?

Nope, only normal social anxiety and the Florida sun's hatred of an acceptable comfort level. I hadn't felt that bizarre burn all week, so perhaps it'd been an exhaustion-induced hallucination.

The party was getting into the swing while Joss Stone crooned how she "Fell in Love with a Boy." Decorations shaped like pacifiers were strung along the walls. Pink, fuzzy teddy bears perched on each step of the staircase. Everywhere I looked, something was bubble-gum pink.

A Pepto Bismol factory had exploded in what used to be my parent's sleek and elegant home.

My sister married Seth, a real estate agent, about six months ago. The two had known each other for exactly ten months as of now, but they seemed happy.

I carried my bag up the steps, kicking a bear for good measure, and went into the room I'd occupied since I was two. It still held my high-school paraphernalia and brought back echoes of memories. Pictures of friends, leftover college texts, several books—including a fantasy series I never got around to reading—and various other young-adult accouterments covered the walls and floor.

Even my nightly To-Do list was taped to the ceiling over the bed, pinned up as a reminder to myself after falling asleep one too many times without cleaning the cat box.

With as much as Anna demanded my return trips, my parents never changed my room. Still, I knew my father was desperate for a private study. I surveyed the jettisoned bits of life that had once been so important.

"The place is a pigsty. It's good you're home to sort the mess." I whirled, surprised by the sound of my father behind me. He stood in the doorway.

"Hi, Dad, it's good to be home."

He grunted a response. He looked so much older than the last time I'd seen him, even though it had only been two months. His hair grayed a little more, the line receding.

My mother stood beside him. Anna got her waifish figure from our mother, currently donning pearls and a pale pink pantsuit that would do Barbie proud. The decor downstairs was undoubtedly her doing.

"We're so glad you came, Jessica," my mother's sing-song voice cooed.

Everyone and their mother was "Jessica," and I loathed it. Only three people close to me used the name. Jex was unique and interesting, and it made it easier to pick out the creditors and telemarketers.

Granted, my grandmother once awkwardly told me she would never accept my chosen moniker, which she insisted in a hushed tone was too much like the word "sex" for polite company.

I gave my mother a look that conveyed how I felt about Anna's recent shenanigans.

"Like I have a choice, Anna's nearly perfected her push-until-agreement-or-death method. She'll make an excellent mother."

Hearing my mother's hearty laugh warmed my chest. You would never put her, with her slight frame and mild personality, and that laugh together.

"Speaking of which, you can't go to her party dressed like that!" She appraised my holey jeans and hoodie that told the world, *I'm never lost—people always tell me where to go.*

"It's fine, Mom, really, not that big of a deal."

"Well, I left something special for you. Freshen up and come down to see everyone," my mother added, motioning to a box on the ancient sleigh bed.

My father rolled his eyes, muttering about girls and parties, but they left me in peace to change.

Parting the tissue paper in the box revealed a navy dress with matching shoes. The A-line silhouette fluttered lightly as I brought it out. The neckline and hem were made of an intricate lattice that blended effortlessly so that you couldn't tell where satin charmeuse ended and lace began.

The cut would hug my curves and cinch my waist exactly right to show off the hourglass. I might not be squeal-level girly, but even I had weaknesses.

Sighing, at least a little of the stress siphoned away.

The dress gave a nice burst of energy, and I twisted my hair into a messy bun and plucked out a few wispy curls, then paired it all with a drop pendant stolen from my mother's old jewelry box.

The cake had been cut by the time I made it downstairs. Starving, I beelined for the buffet, only to be intercepted by my hormone-ravaged sister.

Anna towed me by the hand toward a small group of people. A woman with long, blond hair and legs up to her neck wore the tiniest patch of fabric that would cover her. She leaned close to a wiry man in a sweater-vest with wavy hair and glasses. Neither of them noticed us.

The third member, however, immediately looked up and tracked our approach. His physique was all baseball player, tall with wide shoulders and powerful arms. Dark, wavy hair framed intense green eyes and a strong jaw. A forest-green shirt amplified the effect as he stood casually with his hands in his pockets.

Clark Kent, eat your heart out.

"Matt, Kim, Ryan, this is my sister, Jex." Anna became Vanna, complete with a hand wave.

Sweater-vest Matt ogled my "new dress," but Kim only sniffed her dismissal. Ryan, Mr. Magnificent in green, leaned over to shake my hand. His grip was firm and considerate, despite callouses on his palms. Too hot, too cold, and just right. The classics never die.

We must have held hands a moment too long, because Kim wrapped garishly manicured fingers around Ryan's shoulder. She glared at me.

He pulled his hand back, replacing them in his pockets and avoiding eye contact.

Right, already made an enemy of the banded-bombshell just by shaking her apparent-boyfriend's hand.

"Jex," prompted my sister, "Matt is an assistant manager of the bank in Seth's building. You share a lot of interests, so you should talk. Matt, did I tell you Jex has an accounting degree?"

She made the barest shove in sweater-vest's direction. I glared at Anna and suppressed the urge to smack her. Someone should hide the butter knives. The law had to have a loophole for overzealous siblings.

"Banking and accounting aren't the same, Anna," I muttered, focusing on my poker face. She'd already flitted off, willfully ignoring my obvious discomfort.

Matt gave me a lecherous look. *What* was Anna thinking?

"I'm sure we can find common ground," he oozed. *Ugh*, spare me. My law firm job didn't even use my degree, it was merely the entrance fee for employment.

"So, you live in Boston?" Matt hummed.

No, I live in KissMyAssia, on the corner of Never Lane and NotAChance Road.

With effort, I swallowed the instinctual response. I aimed for forcibly polite, given this was Anna's party. All I wanted was to slip upstairs and nap in my own bed. Realizing this, I decided on my course of action.

"I do live in Boston, and I'm so happy there," I gushed. "I wouldn't move for anything. It's such a wonderful place. A shame it's so *very far* from here."

Hint, hint, nudge, nudge, suspicious wink. I'd hoped reminding Matt I was geographically undesirable would cool his advances, but he upped the ante.

"It sounds great. I'll have to visit sometime. Who knows, maybe I can stay with you." More ogling ensured.

The acrid wash of his cologne assaulted me as he stepped closer. He murmured the next comment low, eyes darting as though he knew he stepped out of bounds.

"So, you've got to be a TikTok accountant, right?" he asked with a leer. "You've got the body for it. That's hot."

He brushed a hand up my side, but I slapped it away.

Nope, hard limit. Cue the banjo chase music. I excused myself and ran for the sanctuary of my room.

Chapter Three

The ancient papasan chair in my bedroom called to me, with its fading cushion and ragged quilt. Curling up with my new book-friend Poppy, I sunk in and angled a hand over my lids to block out the rays breaking through the blinds.

Why did Anna interject herself so fully into my personal life? Did I give off an aura of pitifully-single-and-lonely?

No, it must be her. No one else tried to thrust me into relationships with men who were obviously off.

Then again, I can be pretty . . . blunt. Perhaps everyone else was afraid of me. I needed Anna to be afraid of me. What would scare little Strawberry Shortcake?

As I plotted my response to Anna's meddling, a blast from the past barreled into the room. Before I could even look up, a tornado of hair-sprayed blonde locks and purple crocodile boots yanked me from the chair for a tight hug.

"Hey, girl!" squealed Patricia Baxter. "Your momma said you were up here."

Trish was one of my closest friends in high school, although we'd lost touch over the years. A young Robert Downey, Jr. look-a-like followed on her scaled heels.

"Trish! I can't believe you're here!" I held her in front of me. "You look amazing. What are you up to?"

We'd always teased Trish for her southern proclivities, but goading today's outfit would be too easy and, therefore, not worthwhile. She plucked a dusty trophy off a shelf.

"Nothin' as exciting as powderpuff junior year, that's for sure! After that game, we were legends. Le–gends."

When Trish convinced me to do powderpuff football, she assured me it was all fun and games. More likely, she wanted to tease me for all eternity. Still, we teamed up to take down the quarterback, fittingly named Earl, triggering an endzone dance and "Goodbye Earl" sing-a-long for the history books.

"Jex, I'd like you to meet Tom, my fiancé." Trish motioned to RDJ-junior with a broad smile, her face softening as she turned to him.

"Thomas Connell, nice to meet you."

"Please tell me you're here to save me from this party," I pleaded with her.

"Sorry, lady. Just dropping off a gift, but you should come out tomorrow. A bunch of us are going to Kicks."

Kicks was a half country, half Top-40 club on the edge of the county. To draw as large a crowd as possible, the DJs alternated between honky-tonk and pop or hip-hop. We'd come to appreciate the under-twenty-one nights, and even learned a little line dancing.

Actually, I was terrible at line dancing, but I could flail in the right directions to the beat of the music.

"You know what, I'm in," I told her. A little fun would do me good.

* * *

The sun began to set as I joined the crowd of people in the living room grouped around a ribbon-laden Matterhorn of presents. An empty chair waited between Anna and Matt. My sister let slip another grin. Give me strength; the bonds of sisterhood are only so strong.

I took the appointed place as the unwrapping commenced. The group *oohed* and *aahed* over toys and crib sheets. Anna received a full complement of baby clothes, and someone even made a four-tiered diaper "cake" with rattle topper. It all made me rather tired.

That, and fending off Matt's not-so-subtle attempts to rest a hand on my thigh.

Gift-opening complete, I stepped outside to get a breath of fresh air. The effort to continue to look pleased was taxing. I'd need a full can of WD-40 to un-smile. With any luck, the crisp night could reinvigorate me for whatever remained.

How much more was there to a baby shower? If only there was a countdown timer, like on New Year's Eve.

My parent's backyard sat against a man-made lake and housed a screened pool. They'd lined the screen's frame and the patio furniture with about a hundred tea candles in mason jars, the effect casting a flickering glow.

I stood there, watching the blending of light, my arms wrapped around myself as I cleared my mind. The smell of cut grass and chlorine made for a distracting combination. Birthdays in the summer. Pool parties, slip and slides, and ice cream on the lawn. Food fights and cake caught in the filter. Fragments of my past mingled with the present. It hadn't been so bad living here as a child.

"Not going to make a run for it, are you?" Ryan's rich voice startled me. He must have come to stand beside me while I burrowed into memories.

"I will push you into this pool if you tell me they need me," I replied. He laughed and shook his head.

Ryan stood beside me as he had before—hands in pockets, body relaxed without a care in the world. The position and fitted button-down displayed how broad his shoulders were and the strength in his arms. Even odds I needed to wipe my drool off this gorgeous dress.

Still, I gave him a mirthless smile.

"You're not here to vouch for Matt, are you? I don't think I'm up for it," I said, and waved him away.

His eyes widened and a chuckle played at his lips, apparently taken aback by my frankness.

"No, just checking on you."

His charming half-smile gave me palpitations, and I did my damnedest to keep from hyperventilating. My shoulders tightened, the nervous energy fluttering in my system.

"And why do I need checking on?" I countered.

You're free to save me any day, Ryan.

"Matt was concerned you wouldn't sit closer to him. He wanted to come out here personally, but I convinced him not to over-saturate himself."

"*Closer*?! The man moved his chair nearer every time I inched away!"

"Yeah, I noticed that," he said with a snicker. "He isn't that bad of a guy once you get past the leering and innuendo. At least he didn't do *the wink*. It's his signature move."

"Is a finger gun involved?" I asked with my own laugh. He chuckled but shifted closer himself.

"One of these days, I'm going to kill Anna for all this. It's like she doesn't know the meaning of the word *no*."

"She's happy. She wants you to be happy."

Ryan set a full smile on me, and I thought I might faint. My body may as well be laid to sizzle on the blacktop in the mid-day sun. A full blush heated my checks. He seemed to respond to it, so engrossed in watching me redden.

We stood a few minutes in silence, watching the flames dance in the jars while the wind brushed the trees.

Laughter meandered from the house, but we were alone on the patio. He was only inches away, the faint scent of his cologne or aftershave drifting in my direction. The woodsy aroma, like the forest after a heavy rain, mingled well with the candle wax and burning wicks.

I wondered what it would be like to smell it up close, and drifted into thoughts of watching him spray it on while he dressed.

No.

I'd been on my own for a while, but was I so deprived I'd lust after someone obviously out of my league? Sure, I am beautiful and desirable and all the clichés the mascara ads say, but I'm also a realist, and Ryan was . . . *wow.*

He also lived in another state and had a modelesque girlfriend. I'd learned this lesson already. I could hear it now from Anna, especially on the heels of my last dalliance.

Besides, singlehood provided the breadth of freedom I'd always longed for. No one criticized how I spent my time. No one interfered with how I lived my life.

At least, that's what I'd always told myself.

Standing with Ryan made me think of all the things I wasn't getting with that freedom, even my activities with the fun electrician that were non-existent since. Perhaps that was the problem. "Good vibes" only carry you so far.

I quickly pushed those thoughts away. No matter my view on my relationship status, Ryan was not going to change it. I didn't know anything about him. Hell, I didn't even know how he knew Anna.

"We should get inside," he said. "They'll be finishing up, and I'm sure your mom will want help cleaning."

Well, shit. The tangent into my dating life—or lack thereof—burned through my time with him. It probably made me seem tense and distant, the easy banter from before another fading memory.

I guess I was tense and distant.

Nice, Jex. Great first impression.

*   *   *

Come Saturday morning, my mother and sister busily scrubbed and disinfected every surface in the house. Anna's nesting phase had come early, and predictably my mother encouraged it.

I slept in late, hoping to avoid most of cleaning duty.

"You want me to scrub the *inside* of the fireplace?" I whined when I emerged from my room.

My parents used the fireplace once every ten years. They lived in Florida, where life was sustained by air conditioning. Going without A/C would be like Vegas sans gambling or flyers for escorts.

"It's a safety hazard," she reasoned.

"*It's a safety hazard*," I parroted back.

I even threw in a few f-bombs to convince her to back off, but she must have caught onto my game because she doubled down on chores. Chick was lucky I loved her.

By the time the sun set, I itched to get out of the house. I dressed in my best outfit, which wasn't much considering I hadn't packed for it. The ratty jeans returned, but I switched to my new heels and dug a black, zippered tank top from the depths of my closet. Curls refreshed, gel wing, and a lip stain, and I was ready to go.

I looked good . . . I looked acceptable . . . I looked in desperate need of tanning thanks to too much time in Boston's winter gloom. *Sigh.*

At Kicks, I made it past security as a Lil Nas X song I didn't know blasted the room. The thunder of the bass rumbled in my chest and made it hard to breathe.

Sweat and alcohol spiced the air, and my feet stuck to the floor. If these shoes got destroyed, I would rain down fire.

Trish and Tom were with a big group at the end of a long, sealed-oak bar. They introduced me around, and we requested a throw-back from our high-school days and made fools of ourselves on the dance floor. When a slow number came on, we refilled our glasses and planted a flag on one of the leaning rails at the perimeter.

"So, isn't your birthday coming up?" Trish asked. Tom wrapped his arms around his soon-to-be wife. We rocked to the music in the stuffy heat of the dance floor.

"Yeah, in July. That's some memory you have."

"Nah, mine's the week before."

"You're about to hit twenty-five?" Tom asked.

"Apparently, the week after Trish."

"Sweet," he replied. "Did you know the brain doesn't fully develop until around the age of twenty-five?"

"Uh, cool." I caught Trish giving him a fierce look. Twenty-five didn't seem like a big deal, but everyone's different.

The dance floor sweltered in the mass of partiers. Excusing myself, I slipped through to find the bathrooms down a hallway at the back. People loitered in the narrow corridor, including the indisputably sexiest guy in this bar—maybe even the state.

Tall-Dark-And-Handsome leaned casually to one side, his knee bent so his foot rested against the wall. The white sleeveless tank and faded jeans fit to a muscular frame that displayed an obvious preference for working with his hands. Intricately patterned tattoos snaked up his arms and disappeared into the shirt.

His full mouth quirked into a mischievous grin as he caught me assessing him. He combed a hand through chocolate-brown hair, clearly posturing to show off a toned upper body.

This guy was the living embodiment of a red flag, which only made him more enticing. Still, the last thing I needed right now was a bad boy.

I avoided eye contact as I passed and hurried into the women's bathroom. Wiping cold water on my neck and wrists, I drew a few long breaths to calm the sensation of warmth that couldn't only be from alcohol.

For the second time this weekend, anxiety forced me to assess if the warmth was similar to the surreal heat that powered the altercation with the drunk. I couldn't live like this. Why didn't my family live somewhere moderate?

And, because I was a coward, I fussed with my phone for a solid ten minutes to outlast bad-choices guy.

Of course, I wasn't so lucky. There he stood, breathing all the air in the hallway. As I walked by, he planted a foot on the opposite wall to block my exit.

Stopping short, I took a deep breath to prepare for an awful pickup line, the kind only effective when you look that damn good. He might be scramble-your-brains hot, but the liquid courage in my veins throttled me through.

"If you're about to ask if it hurt when I fell from heaven, you'd be better off staying posed against the wall," I snipped, and waved him away.

Straightening, his imposing height towered over me. His gaze washed down my body, that grin spreading to a wolfish smile. He dropped his chin as if to say *come, little Jex, let me devour you.*

Oh, yeah. T-r-o-u-b-l-e.

Sliding sideways, I attempted to pass, but Mr. No-Boundaries grabbed my ass as I stepped by—yup, whole-hand, like he owned it, boldly palmed my backside so unapologetically you'd think he'd grabbed *himself.*

As I spun to smack that chiseled jaw, he yanked me against him. His arms captured me in place as he leaned back and forced me to sandwich him against the wall. Wrestling me close, he snickered as I squirmed in his arms.

With the way we were positioned, anyone looking would think *I* jumped *him.*

"I'm not sure if you got the message, but I rejected you," I noted.

He shook his head, that smile playing at his lips.

"What about—there must be something wrong with my eyes," he replied, his voice a mellow timbre, "because I can't take them off you."

"*That's* your pickup line? It's barely a step above, 'I lost my number, can I have yours.'"

He laughed, though. The exchange seemed to spur him on, since he pulled me tighter.

A flare of heat sparked from his touch as he brushed my hair away from my face. I'd never known it was possible to be both metaphorically *and* physically that hot.

"Harsh. Maybe you're so gorgeous I forgot my line."

Rolling my eyes, I patted his chest and my hands stayed there of their own accord.

"You were better off quietly looking pretty."

He tucked a hand into my back pocket, the other lifting my chin so that I met his deep brown eyes. Warm fingers pulled my face closer, the scent of cinnamon and smoke filling my head with regret-later ideas.

"We could be pretty together," he murmured against my lips. "I'll bet you're exquisite bent over the bathroom sink."

Tucked into his body heat, with my hands against the firmness of his chest, did delicious things to my traitorous lower half. I was already warm and relaxed, both from the alcohol and the sweltering dance floor. For a moment—one tiny, half-beat of a moment—the image he suggested flitted through my head. His eyes were half-lidded, the desire clear.

Shit, he was serious. It wasn't bravado.

Nope. So, so many red flags. Time to jump ship.

"Stop. The charisma is too much," I deadpanned. "How will I resist the ooze of such sex appeal? Bathroom trysts are my *favorite.*" I leaned heavily on the sarcastic tone.

"We could go to my place," he suggested. "Take our time. You deserve to be savored."

Rolling my eyes, I twirled and rolled myself out of his arms. The move was surprisingly stable, given my heels and the lemon drop shots Trish had insisted on.

"Don't go," he teased. "I thought we meant something?"

"We'll always have Paris," I called over my shoulder, and escaped into the crowd to find Trish and Tom.

Putting Tall-Dark-And-Handsy out of my mind, the two Ts and I spent a while talking and dancing before a few familiar faces joined us. Ryan, Kim, and a new guy I didn't recognize wove their way over to us.

They must have been pre-gaming, because Kim swayed on her stilettos. I tried to introduce them, but they knew the group. The newcomer presented his hand to me.

"Thurgood," he offered, and I couldn't help but groan on his behalf. "I'm named after Marshall. My mother was a fan of history."

He wasn't much taller than I was, with tawny skin and a bulldog frame that radiated with energy. He'd buzzed his hair in a fade, but what caught my attention the most was his smile—his high cheekbones accentuated the cheer in his expression. It was easy to see why he'd be friends with Ryan; they both smiled easily.

"At least your name's unique. You have no idea how many Jessicas there are in the world."

"You're Jessica?" He scrutinized me through now-cautious eyes.

"Yeah, but call me Jex. Jessica is too painful to bear."

I feigned dramatics, but he fell lost in his thoughts. Ryan clapped a hand on his shoulder and gave a good shake.

"Don't mind him, every so often his brain floods and we have to restart him," Ryan joked. He beamed that thousand-watt smile and my own brain hiccupped.

"He goes by Pinch, so I guess you could say he understands something about nicknames."

"Do I want to know why they call you Pinch?" I asked.

"Gotta buy me dinner first," Pinch said with a laugh.

Midnight flashed by as we rotated between the dance floor, the bar, and a wooden deck on one side that hung over a patch of tall grass.

Several wooden picnic tables were set in two lines. The deck was half-empty, the club already starting to clear out. I'd switched to water, since Drunken Jex was far less appealing than Sober Jex, and was surprised when Pinch brought a refill for my glass.

"I can't tell if you're sweet or smooth," I admitted.

"Can't I be both?"

"Smooth it is," I replied to laughs and ribbing from the group. He held out a hand to ask me to dance, and I obliged.

Line dancing was basically supersonic sign language, with your feet, to music. Pinch was quite good; perhaps I'd only needed a solid partner. He attempted to teach me an obnoxiously complex set of steps to "Sin Wagon" as Ryan merged into the mob on the dance floor.

"Mind if I cut in?" he asked, an amused expression on his handsome face.

"Oh, yes!" I burst out. "Save me from advanced mode. I'm sorry, Pinch, it's making me dizzy just watching you."

As Ryan took my hand, the DJ flipped to a remix of "7 Rings" by Ariana Grande. The song had a smoky quality to it that didn't lend well to anything other than grinding close. We stared at each other awkwardly.

"Just dance with me," he said, as he pulled me to him.

Chapter Four

Ryan

This was a bad idea.

I shouldn't have asked Jex to dance, not with everyone so focused on her and with Kim puking in the bathroom.

The gentlemanly thing to do was return to my ex, but I stopped putting up with Kim's shit months ago. Almost six months, actually. She had her friends in there to help. I only agreed to bring her tonight to make sure she didn't do something stupid.

Had it been that long? I needed to ask Kim to move out of my apartment, but hadn't found the heart to do it. Every week I told myself to give her one more, since she had nowhere else to go.

I'd only gone to get Kim a water from the bar, but there Jex and Pinch were, struggling through some ridiculous dance. I could tell she'd both befuddled and entranced Pinch immediately, and I couldn't even blame him.

I knew how he felt.

Her beautiful face might be screwed up in agitated concentration, but she took the steps pretty well. Her hair bounced as she flipped it this way and that, and all I could think of was threading my fingers into it while she danced with me.

Jex had been stand-offish, but my guess was it had more to do with Kim than anything else. My ex had no right to be territorial, but I hadn't had the chance to set it straight with Jex—if I even should.

Things all around were . . . complicated. The whole shit show made me tense, and I could tell Jex noticed.

There on the dance floor, her hands rested on my shoulders and mine on her hips, but there was enough space between us to fit another person entirely.

I was screwing this up, massively. I'd think I'm doing fine talking to her, but then she gets adorably nervous and blushes and the blood in my brain rushes right to my dick. If I could just relax, at least she wouldn't think I was a damn idiot.

The bass reverberated through us as the mass of people swayed in unison. Jex scanned everything in the room other than me, anxiously flitting from person to person until she couldn't avoid looking at me without being dismissive.

Our eyes locked, those gorgeous hazel-blues displaying frazzled desire. Her hands gripped my shoulders tighter as she breathed in a few heavy breaths. An involuntary smile spread across my face at her reaction, and I enjoyed watching her cheeks pink-up as her gaze dropped to my mouth.

Interesting, the smile did it for her.

It was impossible not to draw nearer as the thrall of the song tethered us together. Our bodies close, my hands circled around her and lured her tighter against me. Her arms folded against my chest, her fingers tapping absently in time to the song and ticking at my excited nerves.

Electric static sparked. The beat drowned out everything else, focusing us onto each other as though we were alone on the floor despite the constant brush of others.

Soft skin and gentle curves seeded indecent thoughts of carrying her off somewhere more private. She peered at me through long lashes, her mouth only inches from mine. I wanted to breathe her in, to reciprocate the need churning in her gaze.

"It's only dancing," I murmured, but it felt more like a reminder to myself than a comment to her.

My body competed with my brain, the urge to use the moment as an excuse for recklessness nearly suffocating all logic. It was too much, entirely too much. I spun her around to avoid doing anything I'd regret.

Well, I wouldn't regret it, but I didn't feel like dealing with the disaster that would unfold for either of us.

Turning only escalated the problem.

The track chanted about desire as I folded myself around the curvy ass and thighs haunting my thoughts for the last day. The beat carried us away as we matched the slow and deep rhythm.

Carefully combing her hair out of the way, I rested my cheek against her head and inhaled her scent. The skin on her neck pebbled, and I knew without seeing her face how much it affected her. After all, her ragged breathing matched mine.

My hand spread across her stomach, gripping her side to cinch her closer and leading her through the dance. It made her ass grind against my pounding hard-on, but she leaned into it and threaded her fingers into mine.

I did *not* need the encouragement.

Nuzzling her shoulder with my chin, my eyes closed to focus on her touch, her honey-sweet scent, and the friction between us.

To think about what it would be like to be like this, with her, on our own.

To have my hands on her body.

My mouth on her skin.

She sighed against me, the dance escalating my need for her. This was such a bad idea. Or a good bad idea, depending on which half of me won.

The song transitioned, and the spell broke painfully. We lingered a moment longer, both relishing the residual energy of the dance.

Jex turned to me, our eyes locking in a silent conversation. It reminded me of everything else going on in the world, and our little bubble burst.

My mouth formed a hard line, and I rubbed the back of my neck. She pinched her lips together, then gave a heavy sigh, as if to say, *That's okay, Ry. We don't need to address it.*

Shaking her head, she pivoted and led us to the deck and away from the now-suffocating dance floor.

Yep, totally screwing it up.

* * *

Jex

Ryan and I sat at an empty table on the patio and made small talk, the respectful distance restored.

I'd enjoyed dancing with him. A lot. Too much. Probably wasn't a good idea, but I blamed Ariana Grande.

It was calming to be out of the din of the heavy base mixed with twang. Tom and Trish joined the reprieve, and we spent a while talking about nothing in particular.

The guys were arguing about last week's Panthers' game when Trish scooted closer to me.

"So, enjoy dancing?" she asked, her face like the cat that caught the canary.

"I don't remember Kicks being this fun in high school."

"Or this hot. Like really, really hot," she replied, fanning herself. I grinned, my eyebrows waggling at her.

Should I have danced with Ryan? Probably not. Would I do it again? *Absofuckinglutely.*

Kim emerged under the supportive arm of another of the group. Vomit crusted her cheek and shaky fingers combed through the mess of snarled knots in her hair.

Ryan stood to give her his seat, but no one else offered any help. I slid my water toward her. Her glare was so caustic it could probably peel paint from the wall.

An uncomfortable silence settled as everyone shifted awkwardly in their chairs. I was sure everyone stopped breathing entirely, myself included. If it weren't for the music, you could have heard a pin drop.

As if sent from on high, Pinch returned from the bar. He beckoned me to my feet and grabbed Trish as he passed. Tom followed us inside as we all ignored the last several minutes.

It neared one in the morning when a string of profanities spilled out of the edge of the club. Kim sloshed a drink around in her hand while Ryan tried to snatch it from her. She took long swallows from it when she wasn't waving it in his face. The motion made her top sag in a way that was nearly R-rated.

"Don' you toush me, I'm not a child and I will drink as I damn well pleash," she spluttered.

"Let's talk about this outside," he pled.

"I'm not going anywhere with you."

Ryan noticed the attention in the room had come to rest on them. He grabbed her arm and lurched them both out into the parking lot, glass and all. By the time the door slammed shut, people had already returned to their own drama.

"Kim's got a small drinking problem," Trish whispered.

"Small?" Tom countered. "The woman's a lush, Trish. Don't sugar-coat it, it is what it is. She's a raging bitch even when she's sober. No wonder Ryan broke it off."

Trish bristled at his brusque tone, but my ears zeroed in on the last part of his statement.

They weren't dating. *Exes.* I carefully folded away my glee; wouldn't do to be openly elated at this moment. Still, the possessive dynamic between them confused me.

"If she can't handle her alcohol, why do they go out?"

"Oh, that's all Kim. Ryan's tried to get her to stay home, even stay home and drink, but she won't do it. She goes out without him; slips away when he isn't paying attention."

Trish's mouth fell at the corners, and I guessed she'd tried to help as well. It seemed Kim's circle of friends had dwindled severely. The teensiest, tiniest bit of pity and remorse bubbled up in my mind.

"Has she tried to get help?"

"Rehab, the works, nothin' takes," Trish said. "They even had an intervention. I can't for the life of me figure out why Ryan's still cleaning up her messes. She's done some pretty horrible things."

Trish seemed to realize how personal the conversation was and moved on to more neutral ground.

"So, how long are you in town for?" she asked.

"Only the weekend. I go home Monday morning."

Anna scheduled an early flight so I would still be able to fit in a half-day of work. Dealing with the early morning airport run was about as enjoyable as non-anesthetic surgery, but it was part of the deal. Regrettably, Trader Joe's wouldn't just *give* me the food.

"Well, we should do something before you go back. What are you up to tomorrow . . . er, today?"

It seemed Kim may not be the only one short on friends, since Trish gazed at me like she hoped I'd propose a sleepover with jammies and popcorn.

"Nothing, I'm all yours."

She beamed, and we planned our Sunday together.

As I left the bar, I searched the crowd to see what Tall-Dark-And-Handsy got up to, but he was nowhere to be seen. I didn't crawl into bed until after two.

* * *

I lay awake, unable to sleep, unable to drift away. I'd lost count of the number of times the air cycled on and off. Even Norah Jones couldn't calm me, and the woman's supremely reliable.

None of it worked. I felt restless, but couldn't pin down the source of my irritation. The hot, claustrophobic cocoon of cotton sheets wrapped around me, restrictive instead of comforting.

Getting out of bed, I spent a while picking through my room and collecting careful piles of things to keep, things to toss, and things to donate. Tiring of that, I trudged into the kitchen to find something to eat. I wasn't particularly hungry, but there was no wrong time for night cheese.

My mother's car keys sat lonely on the kitchen counter.

Perfect.

Susan Kantor drove a cherry-red Mustang convertible. The car was out of character for my usually demure mother, who never cruised with the top down. I'm decently sure she's unaware of how to "cruise" at all. Likewise, she never cranked the sound above the volume of elevator music.

I, however, quickly flipped the latch and powered down the collapsible roof. After plugging my phone into the jack, I waited for the subdivision to fade behind me before blaring the music.

Never underestimate the restorative value of a power ballad. Headed for the highway, I sang into the peaceful expanse of night sky.

Deserted road stretched into welcoming darkness, and the power from the engine fueled my euphoria as I throttled forward onto I-95. Cool wind played with my skin, sending my nerve-endings dancing as my hair whipped around my face.

My mother wouldn't like that I took the car for a joyride. My father would have a conniption if I even asked. But, Lord, I needed this so much more than I realized. I'd left my problems and stressors in my father's garage and could finally breathe again.

Dawn yawned on the horizon, with flares of pink and yellow seeping into the sky. By the time the gas gauge flashed a warning, I realized I had been driving for more than an hour. As I headed home, I stopped at a gas station to fill the tank to at least the level it was when I first set out.

Maybe Mom would never find out about my little excursion? The chance of that was slim to none; mother dearest wasn't the one to worry about.

Early morning humidity stuck to my skin as I slowly roasted in the Florida weather. Those pinpricks of heat rose drastically as I pulled up to the pumps.

My fingertips and toes tingled and a heaviness rest in my chest. Initially, I paid little attention to it, deciding it had to do with the early hour and the rush of driving the 'Stang.

Or maybe it was seeing the bird's nest on my head in the windshield reflection, which could certainly make anyone's blood boil with embarrassment. I really should have worn a hat.

The scrawny attendant checked out the window from behind his bullet-proof partition. When I waved a twenty in his direction so he'd turn on the gas, he winked at me through the window.

Ugh, what's with people?

After pumping the right amount of gas, I went into the store to pay the attendant, and disappeared through a back hallway to find the bathroom and fuss with my hair.

That faint heat escalated to a steady thrum. As I pushed open the door to the parking lot, buzzing energy ran lightly through my limbs. I panicked, again remembering the burn that built in my system when the drunk attacked.

What could be threatening in an empty parking lot?

When I made the turn around the pumps, I discovered the reason for the warning. A man with three-day stubble leaned against the convertible. He lit a cigarette as I approached, and I stopped instinctively. As he lifted his arm, the butt of a gun peeked out under his grease-stained jean jacket. The jacket alone was a red flag—the only guys who wore them around here were guaranteed bad news.

"This yours?" he asked, blowing smoke from the drag on his cig. He nodded at the convertible and took a few steps toward me.

His actions fanned the flames, the heat no longer a whisper. I paced a step backward, gauging whether I'd make it into the store before he caught up. My brain shuffled through the options, mentally calculating the chances of success between trying to hide in the store or leaving altogether.

"No," I said shortly, and attempted to maneuver around him. The top was still down. I could easily throw my purse inside and speed off.

He stepped in front of me, blocking the way.

"If it's not your car, then you shouldn't drive it. Why don't you stick around until your owner gets here?"

The fire flared and breathing became difficult. My instincts blared a resonating siren, and I twisted to see two other men to my back and side. They surrounded me, blocking all exits. One had handcuffs! What was with people lately? Did I give off injured-little-bird signals?

"Take whatever you want." My purse landed at the smoker's feet. "I don't care, just leave me the fuck alone."

I'd said it with gusto, trying to emit *back-off* energy. He said nothing and left the purse where it lay. He barely even glanced at it. His eyes fixed on me as though I were the only thing in existence. Shit, I should have watched that trafficking documentary.

The inferno raged under my skin, and my mind began to tilt yet again before finding center. The calm settled in, heat sloshing in my limbs. The world fell away until nothing remained but the fifteen feet around me. It took less time to reorient than before, but the movements were no more deliberate.

The man to my side had been inching his way closer, boxing me to the pump. I sensed his shift and whirled to face the threat. He leapt—*leapt*—at me, catching my arm.

My hand slipped through his fingers as I effortlessly slid to the side. His force sent him flying past me as he lost his balance and sprawled onto the asphalt. Dude was a remarkably inept kidnapper.

The second man came at me, the handcuffs open in his swinging hand. He grabbed my wrist and brought the handcuff up, but my hands were faster. My fingers swooped around the arm holding mine. The restraint clicked into place as he locked it on his own wrist.

When he realized what I'd done, he yanked his hand away and I allowed him to toss me around with him.

We danced in tandem toward the pump. Anticipating our next steps, my hand smoothly twined under the thick u-shaped road stop. It took less than a second to clasp the open bracelet around his free hand on the other side.

Trapped, attached to the post, the man's eyes blackened with anger. He kicked at me, vulgarities streaming, but I easily avoided his limited reach. My skin still burned, but the thrill of besting them both thrummed through my system.

Fuck, yeah! Chuck Norris, eat your heart out.

By that time, my first attacker had recovered. He seemed unaffected by the scrapes bloodying his skin. He faced me from the other side of the parking lot where he'd landed earlier but didn't approach again. He must have been left behind a few grades at abductor's academy.

With his face contorted in concentration, he wrenched an arm backward as though he drew on a longbow.

The breeze came slowly at first—merely a whisper raising goosebumps on my neck—but it quickly escalated. Wind rushed past, flicking my already-wild hair as he wrenched at the atmosphere with all his strength.

I planted my feet and braced myself to avoid being swept away, but the choice was as much about fear as strategy.

Each drag of wind grew more forceful, each matched with a sudden blaze that stoked the fire in my veins. A dry-tinder wildfire burned through my body, but this new sensation smoldered. Thicker, hardier.

My heart pounded like the beats of helicopter blades reverberating across the earth. I froze in place, having no idea why I stood there instead of hiding.

He reached his limit and released his hold with a malevolent sneer.

Air screamed toward me, whistling and wailing like a hurricane. The signs in the parking lot whipped madly and the trees around the lot thrashed in every direction. One of the gas station windows cracked from the pressure. An alarm went off in the distance.

Dirt and gravel from the lot scoured the skin from my face and arms. Hot, heavy air shoved against my body, but my position never budged or buffeted. I simply stood my ground, wide-eyed with panicked breaths, as my mind fought to reconcile what happened with reality.

Distaste plain on his face, my attacker upped the ante. Inhaling deeply, he brought his hands to his chest and spun them around a basketball-sized sphere.

It was almost comical, until he focused his energy and thrust his hands and arms forcefully forward . . .

. . . at *me*.

A shock wave of air hurtled in my direction, demolishing everything in its V-shaped path. The force dug a scooped depression in the pavement and uprooted two more road barriers on its mission to kill me.

And yet, my body still stood there, a deer in headlights, watching death charge toward me.

Holy shit.

My skin hummed and tingled, the pinpricks painful like a limb finally regaining blood flow. The atmosphere around me curved and arched. Hazy flickers of orange-red fragments materialized at the ends of my reach, licking and roiling in a hellish bubble. It flexed automatically as I gasped and prepared for impact. Bracing for what I assumed would be very painful, I put my arms over my face in a pathetic attempt to save myself.

The shock wave smashed into the bubble with a deafening ***crack***, thundering into the distance. I'd expected to be thrown by the blast, but it burst into a million particles. The remnants powdered my arms and body harmlessly.

I inhaled, and the bubble contracted and shrank into my skin as easily as if I had commanded it.

The retraction provoked a sudden surge of burning power. The heat in my veins overflowed, unaccustomed to the barrage of sensations. The inferno consumed my body, and filled every molecule with exothermic energy.

Panicked and screaming, I mimicked his motions, trying to dispel the blaze threatening to reduce me to ash. My arms came level with my heart, as his had done a moment ago, and I drove the heat to collect between my palms.

The energy sparked and jumped between them, growing with every quick breath. Blood thumped in my ears in time to the beat.

The man, no longer staring dumbfounded, turned to run for cover.

The mass grew heavy. I dropped my arms, too weak to maintain the pressure. The weight caused my body to pivot, the force swinging my arms overhead before my hands released.

Energy flew as a searing burst of hot air. The flux of fire scorched the ground like the pavement on a sweltering summer day, leaving a wave of melting heat in its wake.

The charge slammed into the attacker, propelling him into the air. He landed splayed out on the blacktop, his clothing in singed tatters. Raw and red skin sizzled, his hair completely burned away.

My mind felt strangely calm, even as my lungs ached and my hands and chest throbbed. My only thoughts were to get to safety as he lay there moaning to himself.

There was no time to debate what happened. Instead, I ran to the convertible, scooping up my purse as I went.

As I reached for my door, two little bee stings nipped at my back. A stab of electricity surged through me and warred with the low-roasting coals still under my skin. Muscles seized as I collapsed to the ground, the excruciating pain resonating in a massive, full-body cramp.

Conscious, but barely, Jean Jacket hefted me over his shoulder. With the cig in his mouth, he reeked of nicotine. I tried to think through the murky haze as I heard the trunk *pop*.

He unceremoniously dumped me inside, my cheek cracking against the edge of the trunk opening before he tossed my purse in with me.

My last thoughts were of the stench of cigarette smoke as he slammed the lid shut.

Chapter Five

When I awoke, the nightly To-Do list overhead reminded me to brush my teeth and do twenty crunches. I groaned and covered my face with a pillow, snuggling into the familiar covers of my bed at my parents' house.

I'd had the *weirdest* dream. This guy at a gas station tried to hurricane me to death, and some skeevy dude stole my mother's car. My subconsciousness was a strange place.

Bit by bit, the events of the night trickled into the fogginess of my memory. I needed to lay off the whiskey lemonades.

When I tried to sit, my body ached with the effort, screaming at me to avoid any attempt at movement. Bruises ringed my wrist and arm where I'd been manhandled, and my head thrummed in a constant, dull ache. Nausea crept up my throat and threatened a sandpaper tongue.

So, *not* a dream.

Going momentarily light-headed, I fell onto the bed and lay there for a long while, confused and disoriented.

How had I gotten here?

Jean Jacket dumped me into the trunk. Cigarette smoke still clung to my hair.

My father appeared as I was about to attempt to sit again. Really, I was going to get up. It was happening.

I glared awkwardly at him from the prone position, refusing to so much as shift my head.

"Get dressed, we're going," he said. The stern expression relayed that he was already in assholitis territory, and I hadn't even mouthed-off yet. I could sense the argument coming and curled into a ball. Sandy grit rubbed at my skin in the sheets.

"Where are we going?" I grumbled through the covers. Given my present condition, I didn't feel like going to the bathroom, let alone out of the house.

Scratch that, I *really* needed a shower.

But he'd already withdrawn from the door. No explanation; no further information. I glared at the space he'd occupied and tried to work things out in my head.

Pain proved that I had not dreamed the prior night's events. Maybe I could convince him to drop me at a walk-in clinic? Yeah, I needed a doctor, both for the scrapes and apparent mental instability.

Gingerly getting to my feet, then inching along, I made it to the bathroom. The reflection in the mirror displayed even worse damage than I'd originally thought.

Skin streaked with bits of dirt and gravel. My right arm covered in fine red scratches. A purplish-blue bruise the size and shape of an egg spread over my left cheek, and a yellowing-but-defined hand imprint ringed my wrist where the guy with the cuffs grabbed me. Otherwise, though, I seemed thankfully intact.

Twisting, I found the two neat prong marks that pocked the skin of my lower back, barely to the right of my spine. They were sore, and the muscles around them tender. I winced, certain I'd earned a permanent reminder of the prior night.

I heaved the contents of my stomach into the toilet before twisting the shower handle as hot as it would go. The scalding water soothed the soreness, and the massage from the soap seemed to help. The scratches itched uncomfortably, and I wondered how much Neosporin I could cover myself in without overdosing.

Last night definitely happened. I was lucky to be alive, even if I still had no idea how I'd gotten home.

After dressing and agonizingly diffusing my hair, I limped downstairs to find my father waiting for me at the kitchen table.

"Are you going to tell me where we're going?" I asked.

"No."

"What if I don't want to leave? I'm not in the mood for going anywhere other than to bed."

He ground his teeth as he rolled his eyes. He seemed to have adopted the habit from me, but I was still the all-time champion and returned an exaggerated version. That'll show him.

"You realize you were brought to my door only semi-conscious last night?" Troubled eyes bore through me.

"Does that mean you're going to tell me what happened?" I asked.

"No."

"No, you won't tell me, or no, you don't know?"

"No," he said, and my irritation spiked.

"I'm not going anywhere unless you tell me what happened and where we're going. Someone had to Liam-Neeson me last night."

"I wouldn't bring you somewhere you'd be unsafe."

"I didn't think I'd be unsafe in Mom's car either!"

He sighed, frustrated.

"Listen, kiddo. I don't want to deal with it any more than you do. Neither of us have a choice right now."

I didn't understand his meaning, but his eyes were hard set and his jaw tense. There'd be no changing his mind like this. At least I'd get answers if I went with him.

"Fine," I said tightly, "but we need to stop and get something to eat along the way."

He simply nodded and walked to the garage.

* * *

Silent rage shaded my thoughts.

My father and I barely spoke on the ride to our mysterious destination. I tried to pry information out of him, but he refused to disclose even the tiniest detail.

"Can't you at least tell me who dropped me off?" Frustration tears threatened at the corners of my eyes.

"They'll tell you themselves. I don't want to have anything to do with their kind."

"What do you mean, 'their kind'? Is this some sort of cult? I'm being attacked by a cult?"

His only answer was silence.

"Tell me!" I snapped, my already sore muscles tensing and my throat raw. I'd popped an ibuprofen before leaving, but it hadn't kicked in yet. We'd stopped at a convenience store, but the food only eased the ache in my stomach.

"I wouldn't explain it right anyway," he said. "Can't you ever go along to get along?"

I turned away.

Free will is a muscle that needs exercise, or it can atrophy into lulled compliance.

We didn't speak for the rest of the forty-five-minute drive. He turned onto a dirt road that disappeared into the woods at a dense stand of pepper trees. Branches scraped against the car as it jostled down the ill-maintained road. The only signs were "No Trespassing" warnings lining a high, chain-link fence at an otherwise undefined border.

The thicket gave way to a gravel road with cars parked along one side. After a few bumpy minutes, we entered a clearing full of cars parked in a gravel lot. A single-story, stucco building stretched the length of the entire parking area and disappeared into the tree line on each side. It was so non-descript I could only think to describe it as "beige."

We parked beside an SUV and got out of the car, making our way to the only door. The solid wood had no paneling or peephole, like a misplaced interior door, as if they'd stopped building the adjoining room and decided to leave the entry as-is.

As we approached, the door swung outward and a tall man in jeans and a red-checked shirt emerged. Shaggy, auburn hair was neatly trimmed along with a graying beard. Farmer John here had a mid-life crisis and became a college professor. He was probably in his late fifties, but something in his posture suggested not to underestimate him.

He shook hands with my father and motioned for me to follow him inside without introducing himself. Before we got to the door, I realized my father wasn't following. I turned to find him getting into his car and ran to him before he could speed out of the lot.

"You can't leave me with a cult," I hissed hoarsely. His blank expression provided no answers.

"I'll be back tomorrow," he replied, his face hard and his eyes flat as he glared at our welcoming party.

"*Tomorrow*?!" My voice cracked, my skin chilling in a cold sweat. He wanted me to stay here overnight?

"You'll be fine. You've always been good on your own. You don't need me now." My father said it calmly, but that telltale vein on his neck twinged.

"This isn't a sink-or-swim situation, Dad. Can we please go home?" Desperate, I pled with him, something he would probably see as a sign of weakness not to be indulged.

"I need you to have a little faith in your Old Man for once. I wouldn't leave you here if I thought you'd be in trouble." He grimaced. "Well, you're always in trouble, but you know what I mean."

He threw the gearshift into reverse and spun out of the lot. Apparently, he didn't want to stick around anymore than I did.

Studying my host, I loitered in the parking lot before reluctantly shuffling to stand beside him. He patiently waited, holding the door open for me.

* * *

The entrance split off in three directions. We walked in silence down a windowless corridor to the right.

The central path led to a lush courtyard with real sunlight filtering into the room. I felt the urge to wander in that direction, but little doubt Red here would disapprove of a detour. Besides, getting lost in a cult compound seemed like a bad idea.

After several long hallways and turns, we entered an English study with walls lined by mahogany bookcases filled with thousands of books. At the back, in front of a bank of tinted windows displaying the woods, a large split-driftwood table nearly the width of the room was covered in books and papers. I'd have thought it nice if I hadn't been trying to avoid a panic attack.

People milled around a group of overstuffed armchairs and couches situated at the front. Most of them were strangers, but I was shocked to see Trish and Tom cuddled on a couch. She perked up as I entered the room but didn't rise to greet me, instead only nodding with a contrite smile. I eyed them and tried to place any more faces.

My escort went to a chair to the right of another man with salt-and-pepper hair and a white polo. Red nodded to the seated man as he dropped into the chair beside him. I lingered near the doorway, ready to run if need be.

"Welcome to Haven," white polo told me. The faces of every person in the room swiveled in my direction. No pressure or anything.

"Haven?" I asked, silently memorizing faces to describe them to the police later.

"Yes, this is our home. I'm Peter Nell, I lead the Clara in this region. You've met Henry Olen." He motioned to Red. If he had called it a "compound," I might have fainted right there.

We stared at each other for a long moment. My hands clasped together, twirling the ring on my finger. How far was it to the road from the main door? I should have counted steps or something.

"I'm sorry, Clara?" I asked, but instead of answering, he motioned to the couch beside him.

"Please, sit," Peter instructed. "We have a lot to discuss."

"Oh, I'm not interested in whatever you're selling. I'm happy with my current spiritual choice and don't need any steak knives," I replied, then flinched at the sass. Probably best not to provoke the cult.

Still, Henry's smile slipped out, although he covered it with a hand.

"All facts to the contrary, considering you came to our door," Peter said.

"Not by choice," I muttered.

"Your father is trying to do what's best."

"By leaving me overnight with a cult?" Fear seeped into my words, my mind beginning to whirl again. I concentrated on my breathing to avoid passing out.

"This isn't a cult." His placid voice was undoubtedly meant to be reassuring, but I gave him a dubious look.

"We aren't what you think of as a cult. We are a group of people who have come together to help each other, share our experiences, and try to protect ourselves and the world as best as possible."

He was so casual and assured I almost believed him.

"*The world?* Really?"

They were a psychotic cult. A psychotic cult filled with hero complexes. Fabulous.

"I'm sorry if that sounds dramatic, but it's truer than you know. This is the only Clara in the state."

"What do you mean, Clara?"

"Just how we refer to ourselves."

"And troop and league were taken."

"And troop and league were taken," he replied.

At least he didn't seem perturbed by my attitude. Henry did a better job of hiding his amusement, although the smile still ticked at the corner of his mouth.

"So, what exactly are you saving 'the world' from?" I gave "the world" air quotes.

Peter assessed me for a moment.

"The Kier, mostly, and it's what *we're* saving the world from. You are included."

My breathing stopped entirely, my eyes going wide. They *were* going to brainwash me.

The revelation flipped my stress response to emergency mode, and I felt the slightest tingle of heat in my fingertips. I spun toward the door, but Ryan's broad frame blocked the doorway. His forest-green eyes and easy smile were tight. He stood in my way, catching my arms with his hands. Was *everyone* in this cult?

"Someone had better start explaining what the fuck is going on right now!" I shrieked.

Ryan tightened his grip, but I struggled against him. Real tears fell from my eyes.

"Hey, hey, it's okay," Ryan murmured. My chest began to heat. Although he certainly made me flush, that wasn't it.

"Oh, great," I groaned. My vision blurred as the heat in my chest reverberated in my limbs. In half an instant, Ryan was moaning on the ground and holding his groin while I ran down the hallway as fast as my legs could carry me.

Panicked, I sprinted away from the crazies to make my way back to the road. All the halls looked the same as I skirted around corners. I wasn't entirely sure which way I'd come from and felt a surge of relief when I saw the green room at the split.

Turning to the door on the left, I pushed out into the mid-morning sun. Daylight blinded me as I adjusted to the shock of light. Frantic thoughts fueled the fire, and I made for the break in the roadway.

Gravel shifted under hurried steps, and I fell more than once. Pebbles stuck to my skin and left little craters on my palms and knees.

My breathing heavy, I approached the main dirt road when a guy my age and an older woman stepped out from the trees. He leveled a shotgun and commanded me to stop. I dove behind one of the trucks.

"Don't shoot!" I called out, but there was no response.

I attempted to scoot myself under the belly of a car, but the woman dragged me out. I swung my arms and kicked with my legs, but none of the blows connected.

"Love, we don't want to hurt you," the woman said. "We could let you run out to the road, but it's fifteen miles in either direction to civilization." She had a slight British accent, warbling the word "civilization."

The woman held my face, forcing me to gaze into clear, green eyes. Soft, light brown hair fell in wavy clumps around an oval face. She was probably my mom's age, but barely taller than me.

"Just take a few deep breaths," she soothed.

"Oh, so a taser's not meant to hurt me?" I sobbed, crumbling in the woman's arms.

"That was the Kier, not us," she informed me. "In fact, Eli here is one of the reasons you woke up at home this morning." She nodded at the guy beside her, who still had the gun trained on me.

"Oh, Eli, stop that," the woman scolded. "I told you the shotgun was overkill. She's harmless."

"Doesn't seem harmless to me," he muttered.

Gulping in air, I rubbed at my cheeks and tucked my hair back to get it out of my face. It took several moments for the fit of hysteria to fade.

"You got me out of the trunk?" I sniffed through only slightly panicky, tear-blurred eyes.

"Yep, although right now I'd like to put you back." He'd lowered the double-barrel, but only so it pointed at the ground instead of my head.

Cold, blue eyes stared at me, daring me to run again. High cheekbones framed a long face with buzzed, blond hair. Marks of every shape and size littered his arms, a scar even split one of his eyebrows. He could probably moonlight as a younger, prettier Channing Tatum, if you ignored the scowl and ratty shirt.

He glowered at me with obvious annoyance. Between my pounding head, and the ever-present aches, I had zero reserve for suffering a guy like him, trunk rescue or no.

I tried another lunge away, but the woman used the opportunity to twist both of my arms behind my back. She whispered in my ear.

"Shush, it's alright. If you don't calm down, Eli's going to tranq you. That's a wicked hangover without any of the fun."

"I want to go home. I want to go home *now*," I whimpered. My thoughts became erratic, my lungs barely getting enough air through the panic. A pinch stung my arm.

"You are home," the woman said, just before the world went dark again.

Chapter Six

Eli

What a fucking nightmare.

"That could have gone better," Brit groused, ever making understatements.

Jex had gone limp in her arms, forcing Brit to maneuver the girl into a mostly standing position. She was plenty strong enough; she didn't need my help.

After recapping the tranquilizer syringe, I assessed the helpless form in front of me. Jex's curls bounced with the breeze, the brightness turning the darker brunette locks a fiery shade of red in the overpowering sun. Pale lips parted slightly, but she breathed evenly, so I knew she'd be fine.

That bruise on her cheek had really come in overnight. The menacing purple yellowed at the edges and would probably take at least a week or two to heal.

I was going to slaughter the asshole who did that to her. He wouldn't last three minutes once we find him.

When Peter directed me to tail her, it seemed like busy work. Something to get me out of his way, especially since the others had been part of her little friends' group already.

And yet, I was relegated to sitting on my hands in the van. I'd had to watch her get drunk on the patio at Kicks while guys leered at her like they had a shot. I'd had to post up outside her house all night, but at least Pinch came to keep me company.

When the Kier dropped three guys off at the gas station, we assumed it was coincidence. Nothing more than an unhappy accident.

But then the guy in the jacket parked himself against her car, and we knew. They'd been searching for her.

And they got what was coming, mostly.

It was pretty magnificent watching her gleefully overtake them. They were clearly inept. The Cole was either getting shoddy in his old age or they'd severely underestimated her. Despite obviously being scared, she still found the backbone to defend herself. A spark was there, she just needed someone to wrestle more out of her.

Peter'd instructed us, expressly, not to intervene. I had to watch from the van, unable to stop it, while that asshole hid like a coward behind a gas pump and snuck out to shock her. We were ready to murder him right there when he let her head bounce off the trunk.

Dead-man-fucking-walking. On second thought, I'd make it slow. We needed information anyway.

He'd shoved his buddies into the Mustang and skidded out of the parking lot. We only followed, per the order, but knew we needed to take her back when it was clear they headed for the Kier's base of operations, at the Farm.

After chasing them for miles, we managed to run them into an embankment. The guy Jex burned was out of commission, but the other two didn't hesitate to get out guns and blades. The idiot in the jacket even tried to tase me without reloading the cell. Pathetic.

We'd waited too long, though, and the Kier started streaming out of the field. Barely had enough time to jump in the empty Mustang and peel off.

The Kier were always striking at us, trying to weaken our support structure. What they wanted with Jex—enough to send Delaney, of all people—I didn't know. She was an anomaly who hadn't been raised in a Clara; she wouldn't know anything.

From what I could tell, Jex was spoiled and sheltered from reality. Probably had everything handed to her, with that body and face hand-picked for raunchy dreams. Probably skated by on batted eyelashes and breathy pleas.

Peter was going to ask me to train her; he was always scheming like that. Guess I couldn't blame him, given I was the best there.

Even as undisciplined as she was, I could mold her into something valuable. She was strong, if soft, but she needed to put in the effort. Given the shitty attitude, I suspected I'd need to be strict to keep her on track.

It'd be pointless, though, if she couldn't get her shit together. Twice now, she'd let her guard down and allowed someone else to have total control over her. That's not a luxury we could afford. And she had totally lost it when we'd been very patient with her.

Well, Brit had. She can go ahead and think I'm an asshole.

Jex was wild. Wilder than I'd expected. As wild as those curls and that mouth of hers.

Shit, I liked her soft.

Might be fun to tame her, though.

"You tranq'd her, you carry her," Brit said as she shoved Jex's dead weight into my arms. The girl's body warmed my skin.

Well, fuck.

I hoisted her over a shoulder and lugged her inside.

What an absolute fucking nightmare.

* * *

Jex

For the second time that day, I woke up unsure of where I was. From the odor of old books and leather, I guessed I was in the library, sprawled on the couch while elephants tromped their way across my forehead.

"Why am I here?" I whined to no one in particular.

"Because you're *special*," scoffed the guy from before. Eli, was it? He no longer had the shotgun, but his voice still dripped with venom. He stood in the doorway, blocking my escape route. I gave him the facial equivalent of the middle finger.

"You panicked, and we brought you inside." The British woman held a cloth to my head. "Come on, sit up, got to get the blood flowing," she beckoned as she propped me against the back of the couch.

Almost everyone had filtered out of the library, but Peter and Henry remained undisturbed in their chairs.

"You mean Eli here drugged me," I retorted, but only Eli seemed to think it was funny. She grimaced.

"I'm Brit, by the way. Short for Brittania. Unoriginal, yes, I know. Mum and Dad were not the most creative."

"Brit, what am I doing here?" I asked again, adding wide eyes and a little pout to the request.

"You're about to turn twenty-five years old, which makes things unstable for your abilities. It will get better after your birthday, what we call the Acceptance. And it seems the Kier know about you, so we need to be extra careful."

"I'm sorry, 'the Kier' are the bad guys?"

"Yes. The Kier attacked you. They do enjoy their chaos, and have for thousands of years. It's part of why we oppose them."

I searched my memory for cults that had been around for a thousand years. The Masons? Knights Templar? *Oooooooh*, the Illuminati. That sounded fun; I wouldn't mind joining the Illuminati.

"The Kier believe the world would be better served with them in charge," Peter clarified. "They want to control the region, and care nothing for those they hurt."

"The Kier is filled with evil dictator-types?" I asked.

This cult was convinced that a group of mad, power-hungry people were trying to get to me. I should never have answered Anna's phone call.

"Not exclusively, but that's the idea. The Kier in our area have been jockeying for years to expand their illegal operations and amass more power, but they're reckless, greedy, and cause destruction wherever they go.

"Displays like this morning at the gas station exemplify why we need to keep them in check. They destroyed the area and could have killed you, or the attendant, or themselves—and did it with little thought for the broader consequences. Actually, Ryan, would you please ask Trish to bring Vaz in?"

I hadn't even noticed Ryan sitting at the table. The far end of the table. My paranoia and anger set off at the reminder he was here. Was that why he kept seeking me out? I replayed each of our interactions, reassessing them.

But, on his way out of the room, Ryan crouched in front of me on the sofa. He put a hand to my battered cheek and turned my chin so he could see the bruising better. His thumb brushed the vicious mark with a tight-lipped frown. It was oddly intimate, but just as swiftly he retracted his hand and walked to the exit.

Eli leaned against the doorjamb. He forced Ryan to wait before sliding sideways to let him pass.

Geez, that Eli guy's a real asshole.

"I don't get it. If they're so powerful, why do they want to kill me?" I asked.

"They didn't want to kill you, they wanted to take you," Eli huffed, but Peter gave him a glare that told him to *knock it off.*

"They may have thought you had useful information. The Kier have been escalating their attacks on us recently, even taking some of our Guards and holding them hostage. You are decidedly Clara, given your lineage. I understand from Trish you exhibit very few of the characteristics we consider Kier."

The real implications of his statement hung unsaid in an awkward pause.

"But at least some," I confirmed.

"Not all."

They thought I could be evil?

Yeah, I had no interest in staying here any longer.

"This has been fun and all, but I'd like to go home now," I sighed.

"You can't leave. It isn't safe," Peter informed me.

"Oh, from the evil Kier, that's right," I snapped.

"You must learn to control your abilities, or the consequences could be dire. We aren't sure what the Kier want, but you will stay at Haven until we can find something permanent. Your rental car has been returned—"

"This is absurd. I live in Boston. My life is there. I have a job, an apartment, and a cat."

I had no intention of abandoning my wonderfully placid life for a cult.

"Not anymore," he replied. "Your apartment is being packed. A sub-lessor moves in next week. Your cat is being flown down personally. She even gets her own seat on the plane."

My face must have been bright red with anger, because every inch of my skin heated.

"And my job? I can't walk out on them."

"Your boss understands. In fact, you work for him because of us."

My brain lurched over the revelation.

"What does *that* mean?" I asked.

"He's what we call a Guard—someone from the public world who assists us but doesn't have abilities. They simply believe in our mission to protect the community."

I seriously doubted my boring, dim-witted boss with chronic back problems and angina was fit to *guard* anyone.

"So, I only worked there because you think I'm part of some hokey cult?"

"It isn't a cult, and your inclusion is no longer an open question. Your actions at the gas station confirmed what we suspected." His deadpan expression couldn't keep the bile from rising in my throat.

"Will you tell me what happened?" I asked him. Brit held my hand, and it actually felt kind of nice.

"When we learned you were in town, I asked Eli and Pinch to watch over you. They subdued your attackers and brought you back to your parent's house so you'd wake up somewhere familiar."

"Riding to your rescue, princess," Eli cut in. Glaring at me, his face formed in a wicked grin. I calculated how good my aim would be at this distance.

"Trish suggested if you woke in your room here you might be less than cooperative," Peter added.

"I don't have a room here."

"And it seems it was all for naught," he chuckled. Brit stroked my hair reassuringly.

Peter's statement finally sunk in—Pinch, too. Everyone was in this cult, but they'd hidden it from me for days. Years? Trish and I were close in high school. It stung that she kept it from me.

"What about before the trunk, the fighting and the wind and the . . . the fire? What was that?" I asked.

"A select few have exceptional talents, what we refer to as an enhanced essence. It is part of who you are, a part of your DNA. You are able to access it in a way most people cannot. Think of it as an assembly line—most people operate at about twenty percent capacity, but some of your bodily systems run between eighty and ninety."

Trish entered the room. A small hawk gripped her arm, its talons digging dangerously deep into the leather glove. The bird's beautiful gold-and-brown feathers blended seamlessly together in a fray of color.

"Trish, good. We were explaining essences to Jex. Why don't you give a demonstration?"

Trish only smiled. She sat in one of the empty chairs and closed her eyes. Her face serene, she breathed deep as her body relaxed and her face slackened.

The hawk took flight, circling the large room before beating shimmering wings to land on the carpet in front of the couch. It perched there, examining me, tilting its head to the side.

"Trish, kindly make a few trips around the room again," Peter asked.

The bird vaulted into the air, circling the room, before landing on the arm of the sofa.

Peter explained, "Trish can transfer some of her essence to an animal. It allows her to control its movements and communicate with it. She prefers the hawk, but also has a Florida panther and—"

"You keep an endangered Florida panther here?"

The place was a zoo, and then there were the animals.

"I assure you, she's very happy with us," Peter said.

The bird watched the exchange intently.

What in the wizarding world of holy shit was this? A few moments passed as I scrutinized the hawk for any sign of my friend. Or a joke. It had to be a well-planned trick.

"Trish is really in there?" I asked, tweaking my face in an incredulous expression.

No one in my family had ever mentioned this before, and I knew damn well I hadn't just been zoned out at the time. I thought about my father's statement on the ride over—*they'll tell you for themselves; I don't want to have anything to do with their kind.*

Maybe it was recessive? I should have paid more attention in bio. I decided it'd be the first thing I asked my dad about when he returned tomorrow.

"Invite her to demonstrate," Peter suggested, interrupting my mental tangent. The wild hawk was completely calm, as tame as a house cat, with no sign of aggression.

"Ok, erm . . . hop on one leg," I requested. It felt utterly ridiculous. I was talking to a bird like a person. Still, the little hawk lifted a talon and began to hop back and forth.

"Can you hold your wings out?"

The hawk unfolded its wingspan. It held the pose faithfully, like the tail of a quarter.

I let a few profanities fly that would drain all the blood from my mother's face. The bird turned its back and lifted its tail to show white, downy feathers.

Alrighty, so that's Trish, then.

It skipped over the arms of the chairs to where Trish's perfectly still body remained seated. It reattached itself to the glove and, in another instant, Trish was up and running.

"That's amazing," I whispered.

"Thanks," said Trish, "it's not what you can do, but it's good at parties." Frowning, my eyebrows furrowed.

"But I can't do anything. Last night was the first time anything like that has ever happened to me."

Well, except for the drunk. I reflected on the burn in my muscles, how the scorching fire in my chest consumed me and took control. The contrary, cool ache after.

Trish looked to Peter for approval.

"We'll let what she knows sink in before going any further," he replied, turning to me. "Your situation is unique. We'd believed your abilities failed to meaningfully manifest until this morning."

His words left me mildly annoyed. I thought I was taking it pretty well, all things considered. I hadn't even tried to escape in the last twenty minutes. See, I could play nice with the cult that believes in superheroes and magic.

"Eli, why don't you show her to the Practice Room. I've cleared it for the rest of the afternoon," Peter added.

Eli seemed happily smug at the suggestion. A little too happy for comfort.

"What's in the Practice Room?" I asked.

"Self-defense training. Eli is one of our best."

Ah. Eli relished the idea of tormenting me. Day One and I already had an enemy, who could beat me up, with the blessing of the boss. I had to find an out.

"I think maybe I should settle into my new room first," I suggested.

"Thought you didn't have a room," Eli muttered.

"No, it will be fine," Peter said. "Channeling your essence is very taxing, and the best way to learn to harness and control it is with physical exercise. Here, we train in self-defense, both for its usefulness for that purpose and out in the field. You are already quite far behind. The Practice Room is your best option. I'll see to it you aren't disturbed."

Peter's statement sounded suspiciously close to a dismissal, but I let it go. He seemed like a good ally to have, and I didn't hate him. Yet.

"Fine," I sighed, "show me the Practice Room."

"Let's go," Eli replied, then left without so much as a glance to confirm I followed.

Chapter Seven

Eli's commanding stance consumed the blue square of low-pile carpet that ate up most of the massive, windowless space of the Practice Room. Steel-blue eyes watched me carefully, his sweats and moth-eaten Fratelli's shirt feigning an apathetic attitude, but I saw right through it. His tall frame was rigid, obviously tense and strictly controlled.

Apparently my presence was offensive, and he planned to do the maximum necessary to make clear how little patience he had to give. You know, like earlier, when he drugged me.

Once Trish got past her profuse apologies for keeping me in the dark, she explained that she didn't know I might be a fellow cult member until Friday. Apparently, not everyone is born with the woo-woo, and even then it might be so weak it couldn't manifest. It was assumed I was an almost-dud until I *threw a fireball.*

We wasted a ton of time trying to find workout gear to avoid this precise moment. A towel rack and water cooler guarded the door, so I took a cup to delay crossing into the white box that marked the boundary of the mat.

That white square outlined the room about five feet from the wall. It looked benign, but I assumed it was the graphical equivalent of the ropes to a boxing ring. A cage with invisible bars, that white line.

Racks of poles in varying sizes, plastic rifles, bamboo swords, and various other plastic weapon reproductions lined the wall between the two entrance doors at each end of the room. There were even foam and wooden nunchucks. Some B-movie bullshit right here.

The floor had a strange give under my feet, as though it would bend under my weight. I bounced a little, testing it out. My pulse jumped with its own anxious energy under the weight of Eli's cautious gaze. When I raised my head to ask, he answered before I could get the words out.

"It's suspended on a spring set. Not enough to give you a boost, but makes it easier on the body to fall," he explained.

My stomach churned, but I strode into the square without flinching. *Pause for applause*, I made it without fainting.

I watched Eli, nerves buzzing, both from uncertainty about what happens next and the way he studied me.

"Heard you kneed Ryan in the crotch," he said, grinning, but embarrassment plucked at my cheeks.

"I didn't mean to. Actually, I did, but it wasn't something I tried to do. Although I guess I tried to, since I did . . . " This was going to be harder to explain than I thought. "I don't try to hurt anyone, it just happens."

"I don't know what you mean," he replied.

I switched my ring from finger to finger, but those hard eyes scrutinized the anxious tick harshly. He raised an eyebrow as if to tell me to *try to keep it together.* I forced my arms to my sides, but it didn't resolve the frenetic nerves.

"I've never had to fight anyone for real before. I took a self-defense seminar a few years ago, but I don't have a frame of reference for any of this."

"Then, how did you overpower those guys at the gas station?" he asked.

"You mean, while you and Pinch skulked in the background and had a good laugh as I was battered and bruised?"

I cringed. That came out a bit harsher than intended, but the stun gun bites still ached despite the painkillers. My hand instinctively moved to rub at the marks. Jerking back, not wanting to incur another Eli-branded death glare, I froze and settled for awkwardly putting my hands on my hips.

Smooth, Jex.

Eli did a mediocre job of hiding his amusement.

"There was no skulking. You heard Peter—we were ordered not to get involved unless there was no other option. Shouldn't you be grateful we stepped in at all?"

It was tempting to poke at his ego, to test how far I could push that self-importance. It would be easier to pick a fight than have a real fight and it would burn through some of the time.

But something told me I'd be seeing a lot of the Practice Room and its innocuous white border. Best to get the character-building over with.

"I don't *do* anything," I said, my hands waving in the air. "It automatically happens. I get attacked and my chest burns and I react. I don't like hurting people, even if they are drunks who want to kill me or—"

"You killed a drunk?" Brilliant blue eyes went wide, the hue taking on an impossibly lighter shade.

"I didn't kill him. I only sort of . . . hospitalized him." His expression relayed how absurd that was. Fantastic, even the crazies thought I was crazy.

"He had a knife and slashed up my back," I added.

"He did *what?* Let me see."

Eli rushed over, his long legs eating up the space between us in only a few quick strides. I pivoted so he could see, but he stopped so close that the nape of my neck prickled. He tugged at my shirt and bra straps to expose the fine tear. Sucking in a breath, I tensed as his warm fingers grazed my shoulder blades. We both froze.

"You can't do that if I'm going to train you," he murmured at my back, the tone low.

"Do what?"

"Shy away when I touch you. You need to react rationally and instinctively, and not based on the fear of touching, or being touched, by your opponent."

"Noted," I replied. He might be brusque and irritating, but at least he'd seemed genuinely concerned about the injury.

Already in my personal space, Eli stood far closer than necessary. Two fingers brushed down my neck, then across the length of my shoulder and back. His hand left a warm trail that raised goosebumps as he prodded at the skin around the healing scar. It was unexpectedly soft, which only urged my nerves closer to the edge of a conniption.

My face warmed, and I glanced over my shoulder at him. Those baby blues searched my reaction, completely ignoring the reason he'd given to touch me. A gentle warmth in my chest pulsed in time with his breaths.

Lord, I needed to get laid. Preferably with someone other than this asshole.

He broke the contact, glancing away as if he'd agreed that *this* was a bad idea.

"Tell me again how you attacked those guys last night," he asked, returning to business. Frustration swelled at the inability to adequately explain myself. I faced him again.

"I don't know. I get this hot sensation and my body constricts and I"—searching for the right word, my hands flicked forward—"go. I've never tried to do it on cue before. Hell, I spend a lot of time worrying it will happen."

"What do you mean, hot sensation?"

"Like when you're afraid, only it's heat instead of nervous energy."

If he tried to tell me he never got afraid I might still smack him, burn or no burn.

"You sense a threat, and the essence reacts," he said. That sounded about right, so I nodded.

"Why don't we start with a few exercises and see if we can trigger it," he suggested.

"Sure, I can do that."

He held his hand out to me, palm up. I reached forward to give him my own. When our fingers connected, he palmed my wrist to brush his other hand over the circle of yellowing bruises.

I'd glanced up at Eli, trying to read his expression, but he suddenly yanked my hand forward at an obtuse angle and twisted. Pain surged up my wrist and arm as I felt myself falling, flipping forward to land flat on my back. My head bounced against the mat as white and black splotches danced across the ceiling. He wasn't in view, but I could hear him laughing.

"Number one," he announced derisively, "your opponent intends to harm you. You don't give an inch, you take it."

"Any other sage words?"

"Never allow your milk to sour," Eli said. He grinned like a fool. Now he wanted to make jokes. Everyone's a comedian.

"Gee, thanks."

He presented his hand again, but I only glared at it from the floor as if it were a snake ready to strike.

"Are you going to help me up, or is this another ploy?"

"Try me and find out."

I figured I'd be better off getting up on my own, although my wrist already throbbed from the last few minutes. And this morning. I rubbed at it before catching myself yet again. Losing the bad habit was going to be a challenge.

Back on my feet, Eli watched me expectantly.

"What?" I snapped at him.

"I have an idea, but I don't think you'll like it."

I tensed, about to ask him what the idea was, when he leapt at me in two long strides. Startled, I lurched away before tripping on my own feet and falling backward on my ass. He halted when I fell, nearly diving over me.

"Your idea was to trip me?"

"I thought maybe you needed to see the threat for it to work."

"Oh." Exactly what every girl wants, a guy with a mission to trigger her.

"The drunk . . . where were you when he came after you with the knife?" He removed a plastic dagger from the racks.

"Outside my apartment, in an alley. He kind of snuck up and grabbed me."

Eli stood behind me and gripped my shoulders as I struggled through recreating the attack. Imitating what happened was useless. I felt no flare and couldn't even clearly remember what had happened. After all, I'd spent nearly a week desperately trying to forget. He perpetually muttered under his breath as we worked through it.

We went back and forth for the next hour, with Eli trying to find a way to make me feel threatened as he delighted in tossing me around on the mats. I hit the floor countless times, although he never once found it himself.

My spaghetti strap popped and frizz haloed my face. My head already throbbed, and Eli's "training method" wasn't making it any better.

He'd swept his leg out in a circle, taking me out at the ankles and sending me tumbling to the mat. As I fell, he grabbed an arm and twisted to drop me onto my stomach. My cheeked throbbed every time he did that. You'd almost think he enjoyed watching me wince in pain.

Normally, he'd let me up after I hit the mat—not this time. Nope, instead, he straddled my back with his legs locked around my hips. He leaned forward to rest his elbows on both sides of my head, his body against mine to pin me to the floor.

And then he refused to move. Guy had some serious superiority issues.

Eli demanded that I buck him off but, after more than a minute, I still couldn't get free. Every time I'd rock him even the slightest to the side, somehow he'd clamp down with his knees or feet and I'd flop back to center.

Sweat soaked my scalp and dripped down my neck and shoulders. The heat from his body only intensified my ire.

"Get the fuck off me," I snarled.

"Make me." He laughed, and wrenched my ponytail to the side. "You should get rid of this, you know," he chuckled into my ear. "It can be used against you. It could be dangerous."

Oh, hell no. My curls were a part of my identity. He may as well have told the Pope not to wear his pointy hat, or Tom Selleck to shave his mustache.

"Admit it—you're just some lost, little girl barely able to rub two brain cells together or we'd have been done and moved on by now."

Eli tugged a little harder, wresting my head back, and I fought the involuntary spark low in my gut. The last thing I needed was for this guy to figure out I enjoyed a bit of manhandling.

I rolled my eyes at him, but he yanked me to my feet solely so he could send me careening against a wall.

Both panting in frustration, his face tightened with vexed annoyance. Sweat covered us both. My muscles ached and my neck and shoulders were so tense they practically popped every time I moved. I actually did want to kick his ass and was sure he felt the same.

"This isn't working," he told me.

"Thank you, Captain Obvious."

"You don't need to make snide little comments. I'm trying to help you."

"Really? 'Cause it seems like you're just trying to prove how much better you are than I am."

"I am better than you."

"And yet you're still trying to prove it!"

We glared at each other for a moment before he reached for me. I caught the shift in his weight before he advanced and felt the heat come to life.

It was slight, small compared to how it had been before, but it was there. I embraced the energy, letting it soak into my limbs and coaxing the bonfire to build.

I ducked under his arms as he sprang at me, and whirled in time to plant a swift kick to his back that sent him rolling away from me. *Ha!*

Eli rebounded, his face red with teeth bared. He lunged again, his balled fist hurtling straight for the purple target on my cheek.

Catching him at the wrist, I dodged and allowed his momentum to carry him onward as I matched his forward movement. After two parallel steps, I brought the fist down under him, the forward energy rerouting so that he sailed over headlong.

Eli used his arms to strike the ground before he landed, cushioning the fall as he thudded to the mat. Giddy, I stepped aside and cackled.

But as quickly as it flared, the heat settled and sloughed away. I tried to stoke the flames. It was hard to do with Eli lying on the ground, even as I nimbly hopped from one foot to the other.

"Heat's fading. Better get up, pretty boy," I told him. He swung around to examine my movements.

"It worked, then?" he asked casually, kicking up to his own feet. He was completely unscathed and didn't even look winded. The anger was gone.

"What worked?"

"My attack. I figured it would only be effective if you got worked up enough, emotionally. Fear, anger."

He straightened his shirt, all evidence of my only achievement of the day smoothly erased with a few tugs.

"Let me get this straight, asshole—you spent the last hour giving me mat burns so that you could argue with me enough to get the essence to flare?"

"All warfare is based on deception," he answered.

"That supposed to be rule two?" I asked.

"No, that's Sun Tzu."

I sighed.

Fucking Eli.

* * *

I'd expected to spend the rest of the day as it had begun—with Eli overpowering me and finding yet another way to make me bruise, bleed, or breathless.

Instead, he taught me basics. We went over stances and blocks, and he even demonstrated a few forms. For a guy barely this side of psychopath, he actually became quite patient when he thought I focused. By dinner, the information overload flooded my brain and my stomach grumbled in protest.

With a little time for the initial shock and anger to wear off, I recognized they wouldn't simply let me go—and maybe I shouldn't be so quick to leave. The Kier *had* tried to kidnap me. At least one of them tried to kill me. It seemed relatively safe . . . *safer* here.

Plus, Trish's demonstration couldn't be ignored, nor could my own display of firepower. If nothing else, I'd learn what I could and then escape. They seemed very focused on my birthday. Perhaps after I could control my essence they'd let me go.

"My" room was a simple rectangle with an attached bathroom and closet. The white linens and a cream bedspread were comfortable and soft, the bed flanked on each side by heavily tinted, floor-to-ceiling windows displaying the courtyard foliage. Little doubt my calico would love slipping in and out of the little latched awning windows at the bottom. A small, cream couch and wooden desk rounded out the furniture in the room. The paint was—you guessed it—beige. Very asylum-chic.

Trish and I also found some spare toiletries when we were rooting around earlier for workout gear, so at least I could shower and wear clean clothes. Still, I longed for my fuzzy bathrobe and socks, which I supposed were being shoved into boxes and flown cross-country.

After managing a shower, and the maximum recommended dosage of ibuprofen, I went hunting for food.

The kitchen was at the end of a long corridor, near the front of the building. White wainscoting lined the walls of the simple dining room with—surprise—beige walls. Cafeteria-style tables and benches filled the room.

Henry, Brit, Peter, and another woman were already seated and eating in silence at a large table long enough for a dozen people. The double doors leading to the kitchen were propped open, and chicken and rice seasoned the air. I made a plate and found a seat.

"Where's Pinch?" I asked.

"He's more of a night owl, so he patrols now," Peter answered.

"Is he an owl?" I asked, only half joking.

"No," he smirked.

"He doesn't eat dinner with you?" I resisted the urge to use *us*.

"No, he prefers to take his meals in private."

The silver-gray hair of the older woman sitting at the head of the table was braided and twisted tightly into a bun, not a single wisp or fly away in sight. The crisp, white button-down could probably cut paper, but she tempered it with lustrous pearl studs. She returned my glance but said nothing.

Peter caught my examination and tilted his head in the woman's direction.

"This is Aster."

Aster continued to cut her chicken with a severe expression, the knife moving with a surgeon's precision. A bird's-head cane leaned against her chair, the length an intricate filigree in mahogany.

"Nice to meet you," I prompted, hoping for something but getting nothing.

"Aster is a Valen," Brit told me, but Peter glared at her. "What? She'd find out soon enough anyway."

"You know I'm going to ask," I said. Peter sent Brit an unhappy expression.

"A person with an essence like yours is known as an Amory. Your abilities are based in your nervous, respiratory, and circulatory systems. Basically, an evolutionary enhancement that produces your unique skills. There are also those we refer to as Valens, with enhanced musculoskeletal and adrenal systems. Both groups are hardier overall, though."

"So, Valens can't do what Amories do? It's largely physical?"

"A Valen's essence does not manifest in the way an Amory's does, but it is no less capable. Valens are much stronger and faster; they heal quicker. Every Amory and Valen are paired to protect each other," Peter explained.

"They act as a bodyguard?"

"A Valen does not protect their Amory blindly. They must work together—two poles, each with their own strengths and weaknesses. He is there to balance you, Jex. Someone to rely on and trust. It is a different kind of relationship. Traditionally, the Valen and Amory are life partners."

"I'll essentially be dating my Valen."

Great, an insta-boyfriend. For people who claimed not to be a cult, they certainly had no issue assuming control over all of my decisions.

"It's not required, but only a coupling by Valen and Amory can produce children with enough talent for their abilities to manifest."

"So Trish and Tom . . ."

"Yes, Tom is Trish's Valen. In fact, Brit is Henry's Valen." He motioned to the two at the table. Brit smiled wide. A female Valen! Mother nature looked at society and gave a big ol' middle finger to the patriarchy.

"And you two are together?" I asked, wagging a finger at them.

"A true Pair, married twenty-seven years," she beamed. Henry squeezed her hand.

I thought back to my father's reaction to leaving me here and wondered why my parents chose not to live with the Clara. Yet another question for my interrogation log.

The group resumed eating, the metal of the silverware clicking against plates in the silence. Peter seemed to be on a roll with info sharing, so I pressed my luck with another inquiry.

"Trish mentioned she can't . . . do . . . fire," I said. It still felt screwy as hell to talk about this.

"Everyone is a little different. The universe is dependent on balance, so each Amory has two elements to oppose each other. We call them Dualities. There are varying degrees of each, but most will fall into one of five categories. Trish's is known as serobestia, for plants and animals."

Serobestia. I let the word roll around in my mind, trying to commit it to memory.

"Does that mean she can control plants?"

"Half of the Duality is an aggressor, more literal than your latent, secondary ability. In Trish's case, she has an uncanny regenerative ability. She could not only heal quickly but, in time, replace entire limbs."

"And you are . . ."

After I'd asked, I realized it might be a very personal question, like asking him if he wore boxers or briefs. He didn't hesitate, though.

"Orisalvus. Similar to sight and sound."

"And I would be . . ."

"Ignisunda. Fire and water." I reflected on the instances of my Duality triggering, and each began with a lingering heat. Plus, you know, the *fireball* I'd launched across the parking lot.

"Then water must be my secondary, because I haven't tried to drown anyone yet." Maybe. I hoped.

"It isn't that extreme, Jex. The primary talent is almost exclusively offensive and the secondary defensive. Yin and yang, a little of one in the other, but no more. It's more likely that the water in you will manifest in a less obvious way. With more tangible Dualities, it's typically an effect on how your body reacts."

Except that I'd made a fucking fire force field that incinerated everything that crossed it.

"My water half will make me harder to kidnap?" I asked, and he chuckled.

"Likely more to do with dexterity. As you approach the Acceptance, you will probably find you are more agile than you used to be, and will have an easier time escaping attacks than others."

I kind of liked that. I didn't relish the idea I'd have to rely on someone else, a Valen, to keep me safe. It was satisfying to know I might not have to.

"I'll be harder to catch. That's good, considering they've already tried to abduct me once."

Brit smiled at that.

"So, how are Valens and Amories paired? Are there applications and interviews?"

"Your Valen is predetermined. Most Pairs are raised together to make the bond stronger and easier to form, but that is not always the case, and he is the only Valen you will ever have."

My heart dropped into my stomach. I was going to be stuck with a complete stranger? I'd have to trust someone I didn't know with my life.

"When do I meet him?" I asked, hoping for an exceedingly, exceptionally long time from now.

Peter looked to Brit, the corners of his eyes tightening.

"You already have," he answered, "it's Eli."

Chapter Eight

Motherfucking Eli.

My mind tilted again, only this time not from magical nonsense. I felt dizzy, as though the room were not only spinning, but twisting, turning, and doing one-eighties.

"What do you mean, *it's Eli*?" My tone mirrored Anna's screechy voice, but I had trouble reining it in.

"Eli is your Valen. Your situation is unique," Peter explained.

"And I didn't know him *why*?"

The entire table of people suddenly found their food plates very interesting.

"It's complicated, a story for another day."

"That's all you can say? *It's complicated?*"

Hold on, deep breaths. Screaming at Peter wouldn't convince him to share.

"I'm sure Trish told you that she and Tom were family friends. Henry and Brit were neighbors. My own Valen was someone I thought a cousin until we were old enough to understand. Suffice it to say, Eli would have moved to Boston and integrated into your life. I believe your boss had a job available. The Northeast Clara expected him. It would have been quite seamless. The attack in the parking lot forced us to speed the timetable, which is unfortunate but such is life."

Great, they'd found me a husband to manipulate me into a marriage. No wonder the guy seemed to hate me.

This was so much worse than a cult.

Staring off in stunned silence, my mind struggled to reconcile this new information with every past interaction. Eli? Cruel, egocentric, bossy Eli?

The idea that he'd be able to charm his way into a relationship of any kind with me was laughable.

Another thought hit me.

"I'm expected to *couple* with Eli?" I said his name with such acidity that Brit reached for my hand.

I couldn't even look in Peter's direction. He would have known this before sending Eli to beat the stuffing out of me. *Eli* would have known this before beating the stuffing out of me. Before letting Jean Jacket drop me into the trunk. Before drugging me!

"It is not something you are required to do. No one is going to force you into anything. Of course, we strongly suggest you at least give it a try. Our population has declined in the last century."

Give it a . . .

His tone was nonchalant, as if he'd suggested I try out a new hair color or join a yoga class. This stranger asked me to both screw and bear children with a man I barely knew or liked.

Oh, hey, Jex, nice to meet you. By the way, you're a freak of nature and we're going to use you as a broodmare with some asshole who hates you.

My sight lost focus as my lungs struggled to expand and contract with any regularity. The distaste must have been obvious, because Brit tried to smooth over the news.

"Take a few deep breaths, lovey," she murmured into my ear. "Let's not get ahead of ourselves. We know Eli can be stubborn, but he's quite sweet once you get to know him. And you may find that, over time, you feel something more for him."

Whoa, whoa, whoa. This could *not* be happening.

"The first time I met him, he held a shotgun to my head and had a hard time lowering it," I retorted. "He doesn't seem to be any more thrilled than I am."

"Eli understands this is difficult for both of you. He has the fortune of being more prepared, but you are in similar situations," Peter's even voice said. It took all of my strength to cap the fury festering in my chest.

Couple with Eli. My appetite gone, I stumbled out of my chair. Fuck that, fuck these people.

"I think I'm just going to go to my room."

"We understand," Peter replied, but as I made it to the hall I heard him ground out, "Well done, Brit."

*   *   *

The ceiling of "my" new room stared back as my mind worked through dinner's revelations. A new headache piled onto the already sore muscles that seemed impervious to painkillers. My ring passed furiously between my hands. *Ring finger, twist, toss, pointer finger, twist, toss . . .*

My only salvation seemed to be breaking down the situation into its pieces; otherwise, I was going to start shredding shit.

I debated whether I could truly leave the Clara right now. I needed control over my Duality, that much was clear. I had no way of gaining that outside of Haven. Plus, they were protecting me from literal evil, so escaping felt pretty foolish.

Staying meant being chained to Eli. On the upside, Eli could run circles around most opponents. *Fight* circles around most opponents? He could kick some serious ass.

Although he'd taken liberties when throwing me around the room, he'd been careful to prevent any real injuries, despite full contact.

And, yes, fine, he's nice to look at.

But, on the other hand, Eli's an egotistical, unapologetic asshole. He hated me, his energy unsettling and prickly. He was arrogant and enjoyed humiliating me entirely too much. Plus, he failed to laugh at my jokes. Minus fifty points.

What I needed was a good cry, a tub of ice cream, and a few hours of true crime documentaries to clear my head. The emotional breakdown stalked in the back of my mind, threatening the control I'd so carefully constructed and reinforced since my father first loaded me into the car.

I tried to call Anna, but her cell went straight to voicemail. Weird.

Brit and Trish knocked while I planned which things in my room I could afford to smash against a wall. They folded themselves into opposite sides of the couch by the door, and Brit patted the space between them.

"We wanted to make sure you settled," she said softly. "With everything. Not only Eli, but all of it. It's a lot to absorb at one time."

I wasn't sure how to respond. On the one hand, I thought I had been taking the information overload in stride. On the other, I'd had a minor meltdown in the dining room.

"Was it like this for you? And Henry, I mean."

"Henry and I were close friends. We even dated in junior high, before anyone explained the relationship to us. We were a little awkward at first, but we sorted it out."

"And you didn't resent it, having a husband picked for you?"

Trish reached out a hand and held mine.

"You don't have to run off with the guy, but try to get to know him. Don't want him? Don't take him," she said.

"Many cultures have arranged marriages," Brit noted.

"Pairings are fated from birth," Trish added. "They're decided by—"

"No, Trish. Peter's orders."

"Peter can shove off, she should know this."

Brit sighed dramatically and continued for her. "Pairings are determined by the compatibility of your essences, and to ensure that biologically the ability can pass. It isn't so unguided; there's even a higher instance of true Pairs in our region. Tom and Trish are in love. Henry and I are quite happy together, even after all this time."

None of that sounded like an answer, but I let it slide until I could interrogate Trish in private. What if I wanted a wife, or didn't want a husband at all? The whole thing sounded pretty archaic.

"Can I be honest?" I asked. I took a breath, unsure if I wanted to divulge this information.

"Of course." Brit smoothed my hair with a kind smile, but her posture was stiff.

"A part of me would prefer to hitchhike to my parents. In the rain. With an ax murderer in the car."

Trish's hand tightened in mine.

"Jex, we explained to you why you need to stay—"

"Not because of Eli, specifically, but I don't want to have anything to do with *any* of it. I think I'd be happier if I sorted out my Duality and went home. I'd rather live my life as if I never knew anything about it."

My life pre-Duality may have been predictable and boring at times, but I'd been happy. Ish.

"Except that would be the problem," she warned me. "You can't. You *do* know, and your essence will manifest fully around your birthday. Training is primarily to teach your body control and to condition you for what comes. The Acceptance is . . . much more than a marker of time.

"The Kier will also see you as a piece on the board. You must understand this is not something you can run from. Your Duality is a part of who you are."

The impending birthday began to look more like a death sentence. It sort of was a death sentence. Once capable, they'd send me out into danger—with Eli, of all people—to risk my life for some abstract concept of the common good.

"I'm never going to have a normal life, am I?"

The weight of those words sat on my chest, even though I barely said them aloud. They bulldozed over and buried me whole.

I'd never be normal. This was my life now, provided I could survive the next three months to my birthday. Acceptance. *Whatever.*

Perhaps if I could learn to control my Duality, proved to Peter I could be stable on my own, then they'd let me go my own way? Eli certainly wouldn't mind.

Brit put her hand over Trish's and mine.

"Normal is relative; it's based on the world as you know it. The people out there, the ones who go about their lives completely ignorant? They're the abnormal ones. In here, you fit right in. Why would you run from that?"

The silence stretched for a few minutes before they stood to leave.

"We are here, you know, and everyone else. You are not alone and have people who care for you."

Her kind tone seemed intended to comfort, but I couldn't help but feel so very alone.

* * *

Later that night, after my frayed nerves settled, I decided to explore in the courtyard. I rolled off the bed, tired feet protesting but complying, and struggled into my leggings and sneakers.

It only took a few twists along the indistinguishable hallways before I was completely lost. The lack of differentiating features was becoming a problem. I needed breadcrumbs, or string, or maybe those neon flags they use to mark trees.

After entirely too many wrong turns, I realized the place was basically a giant U-shaped building—residences on the left, communal spaces and entrance at the bottom, utility rooms like the Practice Room and library on the right, with the atrium in the middle.

Most of the doors I came to were locked, and the ones that weren't were inconsequential. Along the way, I discovered a supply closet, three other empty bedrooms, and a sitting room with two Louis XVI-style couches and nothing else.

After yet another turn down a corridor, I discovered a door leading to the outside. It had a thick square of glass centered at head-height with the same strange tint I'd noticed on the windows in the library and my room.

Twisting the deadbolt, I jerked open the door to check the viewing port from both sides. However, when I examined the outside, the door appeared as a single, solid piece of wood. The area where the window should be felt cold to the touch. The Clara had devised a way to see their visitors without being seen themselves.

The forest abutting the building tempted me to wander into the woods, but I decided against it. I didn't know the area yet, and it would be difficult for them to find me in the dark if I got lost—if they even realized I'd gone missing.

Still, the enticing sight of the woods gave me pause. I'd camped regularly since childhood, so the woods were a special bliss. The wide seclusion was calming, secreted among the trees surrounded by everything and nothing at once. Jumbled rows of trunks would fill the space while still leaving enough room to breathe. I could see for miles, and yet the forest was all that looked back. I'd pinned leaves, instead of stars, to the ceilings of blanket forts.

My contemplation broke when a beefy guy in black-on-black combat gear ambled down the path toward my door. I pulled the door mostly shut, curious. The guy was on his cellphone and hadn't seen me hide my unsanctioned exit. Not exactly a win for spatial awareness on his part. He paced in the clearing near the door as he finished his call.

"No, I'll bring it to you," he told the person on the other end. "It's fine. No one will figure it out. Yes, I'm sure. I'll drop the bag off tomorrow."

Uber-mann *mhmmm*'d a few more times, but I wasn't going to risk discovery. Closing the door, I replaced the bolt softly and decided to work my way back to my new room. I came to an open door along the ecru expanse and peered inside.

Peter relaxed into his chair in the library. His hand held a book, but he scrutinized me instead of reading it. I never saw the flicker of eyelids as I entered, which meant he was already watching the door when I approached. That's not creepy *at all.*

Well, Peter did say his Duality meant sight and sound. That trick probably came in quite handy.

He didn't greet me, only watched for a few more moments before returning to his page. I meandered along the bookshelves, running a hand over the bindings. They were worn, the leather and heavy paper cracked and torn, the smell of dry pages in the air.

These were not simply display pieces. Each had been read and re-read repeatedly before and while finding its home in this room.

There seemed to be no discernible order to the stacks. I turned to ask Peter, but he was immersed in whatever he studied. Written in an unidentifiable language, I couldn't even read the inscription on the cover. He'd propped the spine on one hand and flipped the page, using only the thumb from that same hand.

How could they expect me to believe they weren't a cult when everyone acted so bizarre?

Wandering around the room, I approached the bank of windows to stare out into the forest. Static trees showed no movement, not even from the wind.

My hand brushed the smooth top of the meeting table. The edges were rough, left raw by the carpenter and sealed in shellac, but still beautiful in its natural form.

Papers and books spread across the surface—blueprints, schematics, reports, and photos. An inscription had been burned into the center:

Avast, the greater ships that sail
an' moor 'fore the morrow's storm,
For in the cove that shelters both,
keeps crew and king forlorn.

Whilst sound against the evil din
that thrashed about beyond,
The ships that held treasures tell'd
not added to their songs.

The bay that 'twas the gentle arms
of mother's loving grace,
Prevented those from gaining forth
in life's unending race.

It seemed à propos to inscribe prose about risk in a place where they planned it. My fingers traced the markings before I headed through the door and out into the hallway. I never said a word to Peter, and he returned the favor.

My bearings straight, I followed the corridor to the T-junction I remembered from when I'd first entered the building. The main doorway also had a disguised window. It must have been how Henry knew we'd parked without the help of a visible peephole.

Taking a right at the "T," what I thought of as a courtyard was a large indoor atrium. Overhead, a sophisticated array of windows enclosed the space, some with winding handles. The glass allowed the sun to shine through during the day, although now only stars glinted in the distance.

The lush area flourished with plant life. Wide paver and dirt walkways snaked through the foliage, the air fragrant with sweet decay. I roamed along the paths, stopping to admire the variety of flowers and fruits.

A low bridge hung over a koi pond with large orange-and-white fish, and I wandered over to the neighboring sitting area.

Settling into a wide, A-frame swing chair, I stretched out and tilted my head to watch the stars shift as I swayed. It was so easy to let go of focus and lose myself in the back-and-forth motion.

"Gonna make yourself sick like that," Pinch cautioned.

Startled, I sat up so quickly I nearly fell off the seat entirely. My heart raced, but he only laughed at my clumsiness.

"Help you with something?" I snapped. What's with these people sneaking up on me?

"Meh, I'm bored. Not much out there tonight."

He plopped onto the seat beside me, leaning nonchalantly with an arm on the backrest. I wasn't in the mood for talking to anyone, but I didn't feel like asking him to leave either.

"What exactly does one do on patrol, anyway?" I inquired

I'd been a safety guard in elementary school, but it hadn't meant roaming the woods at night. Pinch didn't seem like the yellow reflective belt kind of guy.

"It's not really a patrol, I just like to walk. The woods help me think."

"Does that mean you're having as much difficulty adjusting to this as I am?"

He didn't look much older than me. Granted, I'd gotten the short stick when it came to being informed of everyone's little secret early in life.

"Oh, I'd say I'm adapting. Not that any of us have a choice." His amiable laugh returned.

"It is pretty bleak, huh?"

"But at least you get to light shit on fire," he consoled.

"I do get to light shit on fire. And what is it you get to do?"

I'd asked him with humor in my voice, but he wasn't laughing anymore.

"I'm . . . complicated," he flustered. "Sorry, I've never gotten used to sharing this kind of thing."

I kicked myself. I'd known this was a personal question, but disregarded the instinct when Peter answered without flinching. Not that I should be surprised by that either; it seemed like it would take a lot to faze him.

"No, I'm sorry. I didn't mean to pry."

"It's okay. I suppose I'm just not as comfortable as the others." His face slackened, his eyes unfocused as he tapped his fingers on the swing.

"Brit says we're the normal ones, that people who are clueless are the ones with issues."

"Wow, she really laid it on thick, huh?" he chuckled.

"She did give me the 'things will work out for the best' speech."

"Did it register?"

I rolled the question around in my mind.

"Potentially."

We rocked quietly until sleep dragged at my eyelids.

"Does everyone live here?" I asked.

"Most have their own homes. There are more than fifty Clara in the area around Orlando alone, not including Guards. Way too many to house everyone, and it's typically not safe to keep everyone in one place like that long-term."

"And you have the room next to mine. You can point me in the right direction?"

No use getting lost when you had a knowledgeable source handy.

"Sure. I, uh, snore pretty loudly. That's why they put me at the end." He winced, but it wasn't very convincing.

"Does that mean I have approval to smother you in your sleep?"

"If you want to sneak into my bed, I'm not going to complain." He wiggled his eyebrows at me, but I smacked him with the back of my hand.

"Like I need my love life more complex." I laughed.

"Yeah, what's up with that?" he asked. "Did he finally tell Kim to get out?"

It took a moment to realize he referred to Ryan, and not Eli.

"I was thinking about Eli. Nothing is going on between me and Ryan."

His expression announced disbelief, but he let it pass.

Pinch didn't try to regulate his emotions like everyone else here—what you saw was what you got. It was refreshing.

"Having trouble coming to terms with Eli as your Valen?"

"I'm not comfortable with the idea of anyone being forced on me. It feels like I'm being assigned a husband, and I don't even know I want a husband."

Fine, that wasn't entirely true. It had at least a little to do with the person and not the position, but it seemed a bit too forthcoming to air that concern to Pinch. He squinted at me.

"Is it because you'd rather have a wife, or—"

"Oh, no. Well, that's not what I mean. He's so . . . him." Pinch snickered at that.

"Eli's a good friend, so I suppose I'm biased, but he's a pretty solid guy."

Dizziness set in again and hugged my knees to my chest.

"In the end, I guess it doesn't matter," I sighed. "It's not a requirement, so I shouldn't let it get to me."

"Requirement or not, the Pairs end up together the vast majority of the time. Remember, you'll be working closely with him, trusting him entirely, while you depend on each other to survive. You'll be put in life-

or-death situations, and some of that emotion and adrenaline will boil over. It's only a matter of time."

Great, I'm going to be brainwashed after all.

"Not to mention all the issues if you try to see someone else," Pinch continued. "Having someone else that close can be a big strain on outside relationships. Even if he's the least jealous guy in the world, any boyfriend, fiancé, or husband will have animosity toward Eli based on the bond that forms between Valen and Amory. And then there's the fact that—"

"Okay, okay, I get it. Life's hard enough."

I mulled over the possibility of a future with Eli. Still, I flinched at having so little choice in the matter. Pinch seemed to notice my discomfort, and I tried to backpedal.

"I guess he can't be all bad," I hedged.

Crap, that's not helping.

"I mean, he seems fine."

Even worse, Jex . . .

"I think I'm still a bit overwhelmed. Once things calm down, I'm sure I'll feel better about all of it."

Now I'd told Eli's self-professed "good friend" how shitty I felt about the match.

"Besides," I laughed nervously, "Ryan's still tangled up with Kim. I mean, not that Ryan and I have even . . . Even if he were, I might have still chosen Eli . . . that is, if either of them were even the slightest bit interested . . ."

I babbled along, my mouth spewing the run-on nonsense without restraint.

"Regardless, it could be that Eli is the better choice. Honestly, the whole thing is a giant distraction from figuring out my Duality, which is the priority."

Cutting myself off, I bit my bottom lip to keep from railing on. Pinch looked at me like I had four heads.

I should've gotten paid for digging that hole.

"Sorry, I've been having trouble expressing myself lately," I admitted. I didn't think my little speech had convinced him of anything good, but nothing could be done about it now.

"What happens, happens," he reflected. It might not be Sun Tzu, but it was no less enigmatic.

"Is everyone around here so cryptic?"

I didn't expect an honest answer, but he gave me one.

"Only as it relates to you. Today, you found out that reality is completely different from the world you understood. You're taking it well so far, but everyone's expecting you to implode at some point."

"Nice, y'all think I'll lose it." The crazies were worried about me again.

"We worry giving you too much at once might make things harder than they need to be. Life is difficult enough without adding anything else to the mix. 'One step at a time,' according to Peter."

"Does that mean it gets worse from here?"

I couldn't imagine it being any more convoluted than it already was.

"There is a lot in the world that most people don't know about or choose to ignore."

Chapter Nine

"Caffeine. Someone get me caffeine," I groaned. I awoke in my new room with a monster headache and shaky muscles.

I staggered my way to the kitchen. I was not a morning person by any definition, and it felt entirely too early for any sane person to be moving around.

"Mor-ning," Brit cheered.

Brit, it seemed, was not afflicted by mornings. She sat on a barstool at the island reading the paper. I grunted an incoherent response while searching the fridge and cabinets for a Dr. Pepper. Or five.

Some smoke cigarettes. Some drink alcohol. My bad habit was soda. I'd even tried to quit once, but it only made the cravings worse. I was fairly proud of my current two-a-day status. I hadn't had any since the prior morning, and the withdrawal leeched at my energy reserves. Instantaneous emotional relief rewarded my efforts when I found some in the pantry.

"Fizzy drinks for breakfast?" Brit mused. I made a face and nodded at Brit's mug.

"I prefer my caffeine carbonated," I replied.

"Breakfast was an hour ago. There're leftover pancakes in the fridge," she said. I nuked a plate of them in the microwave.

"Where is everyone?" I asked. I hadn't seen a single person on my admittedly dazed jaunt to the kitchen.

"They went into town. One of the Guards didn't report to work this morning. Should be back any minute."

By the time I emptied and washed my plate, we heard cars pulling into the lot and went to wait in the library.

"I'm telling you something's wrong," Eli bellowed to Peter as they passed the threshold. "It isn't like Jack to be a no-show."

"I understand, but unless we know for certain, we can't risk sending someone to the Farm," Peter replied.

"What's happened?" Brit asked.

"Jack never reported to the garage. No response at the apartment either. I sent Maxon to get the key from Lita."

As if on cue, Peter's cell rang. He lifted it to his ear, muttering a few *mmhmm*s, before telling the person on the other end to return to Haven.

"The place is trashed, and not just from a fight. Whoever came for Jack was also looking for something," he informed the group. They'd been armed like G.I. Joe on steroids. Eli even wore a sword sheath strapped around his torso.

"What could they think a Guard would have?" Ryan asked, unclipping his holster. "Do we even know it was the Kier? There are several other groups—"

Eli cut Ryan off.

"Immediately after the attack on Jex? It's obvious the Kier are behind it. I don't know how they found Jack's home, or Jex for that matter, but we have to organize a rescue."

They argued for at least fifteen minutes before another pair entered the library. I assumed this was Lita and Maxon.

Lita channeled a Latiné Lara Croft—khaki shorts and a black tank top stretched over tanned skin. Her dark hair formed a thick braid.

Uber-mahn Maxon, on the other hand, was the same bulky guy I'd eavesdropped on my very first day. He wore the same black-on-black outfit and buzz cut. They were probably in their late thirties.

"We can't go charging into the Farm without verification." Peter's serious tone invited no argument.

"We have verification," Lita told him, and handed him a business card with a single letter in the center, a "C."

"It was the Cole himself," Eli said.

"It could be a set-up," Ryan commented. "They could be waiting for us to rush in. We don't even know where they went."

But, in a matter of minutes, another call came through. Peter *mhmm*'d and *yup*'d, then instructed the caller to return to his post.

"The lookout said two vans passed the Farm gates at four this morning. Never saw who was in them. We need to proceed cautiously. If the Cole left a calling card, he wants us to know.

"Ryan is right. This could be a distraction. If we all go after the Farm, it would split us up and allow them to attack here or any number of other targets. We don't know what they're looking for. Until we do, we're blind.

"For now, assume they're keeping Jack in the pens near the fields until we know more."

Peter continued barking out orders.

"Eli, Weapons Room. You know the basics of the layout, so put it together for eight. Henry, pull the plans from the DOJ and see if we can access the feeds. Brit, help him if he runs into any trouble with the firewalls. Ryan, call Roger and Emily. Tell them to come in."

The room rushed with activity as people moved about. They cleared the table of the previous night's research and new documents were added. Henry and Brit brought in a large blueprint and spread it across the center of the chaos, but it was quickly surrounded by a mass of new notes.

The group huddled around the ancient table as they planned and debated the best course of action. Brit scribbled so fast the paper kept tearing.

I sat quietly on the couch, watching the action with wide eyes, until Peter remembered I was there.

"Ryan, please escort Jex to her room. Her boxes just arrived and she could probably use help." He addressed me directly. "You may as well unpack. I don't know when we'll be able to find you someplace else to stay."

Peter shifted to the table and continued debating logistics with the group. I guessed I'd been dismissed again.

Ryan led me to a wide, wooden deck running the length of the back of the building. The atrium's leaves pressed against the glass of a row of black-framed, folding doors spanned half the length at center. Stacked boxes waited by the door on the other side.

"Kinda pathetic," I mumbled to myself. My entire life fit into less than twenty measly boxes.

Cringing at my melt-able makeup in the Florida heat, I suggested we move everything inside the hallway first and, after that was done, began carrying everything to my new room.

I'd opened the bedroom door and started stacking boxes in a corner when I noticed the carrier resting on the sofa.

"Georgia!" I squealed, running over. The shriek surprised Ryan, who dropped his box and searched the room with stress on his face.

"Georgia?" he asked.

"My cat," I said. The calico sprung out of the carrier and rubbed against my legs until I picked her up to cradle her like a newborn. I brought the cat to sniff at Ryan.

"You screamed over a cat?" He gave me grief, all the while scratched behind Georgia's ears.

"There was no scream. It was more of an excited . . . exclamation."

"An excited exclamation?" His brows raised as he grinned at me.

"Yes. That's my story and I'm sticking to it. See, she likes you."

The feline nuzzled her chin against his hand as he rubbed under her neck. *Don't blame you, baby girl.*

"I think you just adopted a cat, Ry."

"I didn't expect to be a parent so soon. How will we work out visitation?"

"You're welcome to spend your free time here. You know, if Kim doesn't mind."

He grunted.

"Kim's lucky she still has my roof over her head."

I knew this, but hearing it straight from him went a long way in resolving my discomfort around it.

"I thought you two were *a thing*."

"It's complicated, but not *a thing*, no."

He leveled that patented Ryan smile at me, his eyes studying me as my face flamed. My gaze slid to the floor, embarrassed. I can't be fawning over the guy all the time.

Grimacing, I put the cat down. She slinked away to investigate the windows.

Ryan insisted I switch to unloading the contents as he hauled the rest of the boxes down the hallway. It should have set me on edge, to be "unpacking" here, but having Ryan with me made it kind of nice. Normal, even. Settling.

The sofa near the door became my command center, giving Ryan the opportunity to brush by as he worked. He'd bump my hip or pat my shoulder when he passed, even once slinging an arm around me to ask why I had a pair of long-handled kitchen tongs. When I explained they'd become my new favorite multipurpose tool, he laughed so loud Georgia darted under the bed.

The teasing touches pricked at excited nerves, his playful smile sparking a warmth in my gut.

All the boxes safely tucked into my room, he promised to come by later and returned to the library to help with planning.

Unpacking my belongings felt like a mixed blessing. On the one hand, it was an immense relief having my comforts. I longed to shower with my own, non-travel-sized shampoo and conditioner, to curl into my fuzzy bathrobe and dress in clean pajamas. But on the other side of the internal debate, I knew it would make it that much harder to leave this place.

Could I leave it all behind? Probably. Maybe. Not that I had a place to go other than my parents' house.

The last box awaited when Eli came to the door.

"Peter wants us to work on your utter lack of self-defense skills," he muttered. Apparently, he didn't like giving me lessons any more than I liked getting them.

"And how long will I be defending myself this time?" I asked him.

"Peter commanded, 'as long as it takes.'"

Ah. Peter decided to leave Eli out of the rescue, probably because of me.

"Are you going to act like this the whole time? I'd like to know if I should pop some aspirin now."

He glared at me, fuming. I noticed my suitcase and four more boxes piled in the hallway.

"What's with those?" I motioned to the stack.

"They were by the front door. I passed them on the way and figured they were yours."

Carrying them inside—with no help from Eli—I opened a flap. Picture frames sat on top, followed by my school yearbooks and favorite novels. I smiled, wiping cardboard dust from the box off the frame's glass. My high-school best friend beamed up at me, an arm around a younger Jex. I remembered taking the picture before our senior formal, one of the happiest memories I had. I felt grateful to have the frame, but didn't understand how it ended up here.

Unease wiggled into my mind. My father must have dropped these off, but why hadn't he come in? Wouldn't he at least say hello?

Clothes, hats, shoes, and spare hair products filled the second box. I didn't keep much at my parents' house, just enough to get by during a visit.

My parents must have packed all of my stuff, but I didn't understand why. It didn't need that much space, and I'd already pared it down substantially in an earlier bout of insomnia.

Cold, electric nerves coiled in my chest.

The third box was even more confusing. It was filled with family pictures of me. Baby's First Album. School photos. A cardboard tube with my bat mitzvah portrait, along with my confirmation tallit. Stuffed at the bottom was my favorite teddy bear. I hadn't seen him in years.

The boxes held the contents of my room at my parents' house. It was everything of mine they had. Everything of *me* they had. Even my bed sheets were wrapped around an old porcelain doll, a gift from my grandmother and the last thing she'd given me before she was gone.

Realization wrest back the curtain. They'd purged me from their home and quietly deposited my entire life on Peter's doorstep.

Like my father did yesterday.

There was no note, no call, no message. Not so much as a word of acknowledgment.

I called my parents' house, but the antiquated machine clicked on. Anna's number and both my parents' cell numbers chimed a message that *the caller could not be reached*, without even ringing. I thought about yesterday, when I'd tried to call Anna and it went straight to voicemail.

They must have blocked my number.

My thoughts spiraled. Why would they block my number? How was I supposed to check in? Tears threatened.

They were leaving me there, discarded without a second thought, like the boxes.

My mind replayed the image of my father's face, filled with disgust, when he dropped me off to Henry. How he didn't even say goodbye at first. How he spun out of the parking lot without glancing back.

I don't want anything to do with their kind.

Was this . . . disownment? Were they *mourning* me?

My heart split in two, the space where my family lived crumbling and cracking. At some point I'd started crying, the tears irritating the scratches on my face and neck.

If I went to my father's house, would he throw me out? Pretend I wasn't there?

I tried calling again, but still *the caller cannot be reached.*

My father could be . . . my father *was* stubborn and single-minded, but I always knew he loved me. He could be an arrogant despot, but I'd never questioned the base emotion that he did it because he cared.

Fathers love their daughters.

Right?

I wondered what my mother said to him as he dumped my belongings into a box. Did she fight for me? Did she cry? Or did she help collect the keepsakes?

No, this was my father's doing. My mother has always been weak, in both personality and vivacity. She'd gone along with whatever my father wanted, and trusted in him to be the leader. The Alpha. The Man-of-the-House. No, this had my father written all over it. He made this decision.

Even Anna, for all her assertiveness, still obeyed my father's commands. She'd even let my call go to voicemail yesterday, before blocking my number today.

My thoughts went in circles as I tried to rationalize his actions.

Again, *the caller could not be reached.*

No, he intended to make a clean break. The message was clear—you're no longer welcome. We don't want reminders of you.

Hot tears tracked jagged paths down my face. I wiped them away, my face already sticky and raw.

Eli leaned against the doorframe, trying awfully hard not to escalate things. He fidgeted with the hem of his shirt and refused to look at me. If he tried to be nice to me, I would scream.

I caught my reflection in the window and understood. A mess of red splotches painted across a face with eyes almost swollen shut. The collar of my shirt was soaked, as were my shoulders and the ends of my sleeves. I pulled it off, the wet suddenly acid burning my skin. I didn't care Eli was there. It didn't matter.

Salt pricked my tongue as I licked raw lips. The tension in my neck and shoulders ached as I hunched over my things.

My things.

Not my parents.' Not the Kantors.' Mine.

It was just me, alone.

I went to the bathroom to splash cold water on my face, then sat on the bed. How does someone act when they've been so thoroughly ejected from their family's life?

My legs folded against my chest, and I stretched the discarded shirt over them. I wiped my face on cloth-covered knees. Eli came over to slide me under the covers. He sat on the side of the bed, his hand resting on my shoulder.

"Tell me what happened?"

I could tell him. The question was, did I want to?

"It's everything I have, from my parents' house," I explained.

He still didn't seem to understand.

"When my dad dropped me off yesterday, he said he'd be back today. This morning, I find out he's packed everything I own, everything they have of me, and left it on the doorstep. He may as well have written, 'and don't come back' on one of the boxes."

He looked speechless, unable to form the appropriate response. What do you say to someone who's been disowned?

The sobbing became an uncontrolled avalanche as I burrowed into the bed.

Eli went to the bathroom and returned with a wet washcloth. He gently wiped my face, then folded it and laid it on my neck to keep me cool. His eyes were dull, his mouth drooping at the corners. He looked sad, for me, which almost made it worse.

He refreshed the washcloth twice but mostly just sat cross-legged at the end of the bed, quietly thinking with a hand on my blanket-covered ankles. I dropped in and out of an exhaustion-induced sleep.

"I think I'll leave you to it for a while," he finally said, his mouth set in a firm line. He seemed angry now, but for the first time since I'd met him, he wasn't angry *at me*.

"I'd appreciate that," I replied, struggling to drag in a few long inhales through my stuffed-up nose.

I thought of calling my parents again, of trying to talk some sense into them. I desperately wanted to hear my mother's voice, but knew I couldn't.

If I could even get her on the phone, what would I say?

Hi, Mom, why are you abandoning me?

Instead, I spent the rest of the day in my room, in my bed, staring at the wall and replaying every memory of my family.

Around lunch, Brit knocked on the door, but didn't disturb me after confirming I still breathed. She left a sandwich plate on her way out, which I barely glanced at. Ryan also came in around four but, like Brit, he only checked in before silently exiting.

A few hours later, I flipped the shower to its coldest setting and stepped in. The freezing water cramped my muscles and made me shake violently, but I needed the wake up. It soothed my swollen skin. I reached for the soap, but my hand found the water control instead.

Twisting the knob to "off," I slumped to the tile floor, my legs folding to my chest like a Pavlovian response to the tears.

My thoughts flipped between absolute despair, and absolute rage, and absolute nothing. Pain deafened all other emotions, so there was no in between.

I cried into naked knees for a long time before Trish found me. She took the bathrobe from the hook and put it over my shivering body.

I barely moved—not when she came in, not when she covered me, and not when she sat on the wet surface to wrap an arm around me.

"If you needed help, you should have asked," she murmured to me gently.

Trish did her best to haul me up, carry me to the couch, and get my clothes so I could dress. Retrieving a brush from the counter, she pulled it through my snarled hair. Georgia cuddled into a catnap beside me, purring softly.

Brushes and semi-dry curly hair don't mix, but the slight pain provided a desperately needed distraction. As she ran it through my hair and braided it, she spoke.

"The summer before junior high, I overheard my parents arguing about a girl at school. The girl's parents had died, and the family who adopted her didn't want to have anything to do with Dualities or the Clara. The girl had to be enrolled in my school because of redistricting. They debated moving, out of respect for Peter and Henry.

"I didn't connect the dots that it was you until Peter asked me to check in on you at Anna's party."

Adopted. I grappled with the information.

My real parents died.

No, Danny and Susan Kantor were my real parents, even if they weren't biologically. Even if they no longer wanted to be. Even if they thought to return me like some ill-fitting gift.

Hair duty complete, Trish stroked Georgia and frowned. I stared at the blank space opposite the couch.

"I wish I knew what to say," she murmured. "I suppose I can only remind you that you're not alone. You're stuck with me for life, girlie, so learn to deal with it."

Trish smiled at me, but I could only nod a thank you. She tucked Georgia into her lap. Her face went slack with the same expression I'd seen in the library the day before.

Georgia padded across the couch toward me. She pushed her nose at my hand and nipped my finger. When I didn't react, the cat bound into my lap and nuzzled my stomach. She stood on her hind legs and put her paws on my chest so I was face-to-face with the feline. I peered at my own empty gaze reflected in her glassy eyes.

"I'm sorry, Trish, I'm not up for talking right now," I told her. "I'd rather just sit with the two of you, for a bit?"

Trish let Georgia go, but the cat remained cuddled on my lap. I petted her absently as Trish held my hand. Her calm presence soothed the ache fractionally, but it wasn't enough.

She led me to the bed and wrapped the comforters tightly around me, tucking them in and creating a cocoon.

My mom used to do that when I was little. Then she'd say that if I got enough rest, I'd become a beautiful butterfly.

I sobbed quietly into the pillow, then had to flip it over.

Trish left at some point; I don't really remember. It all blurred together after that.

At some point in the middle of the night, I moved my parents' boxes into the closet. I didn't want to see them, to be reminded. Crawling into bed, I ignored the second plate of food Ryan left. All the ice melted in the glass of soda and the condensation formed a thick ring of sweat.

I slept, my dreams flooded with images of what used to be my family. I dreamed of meeting Anna's first boyfriend. He'd accidentally called our mother "sir" and forgot to cut the tags off his new polo.

I dreamed about the day I graduated from college, stopping at the end of the row so Mom could snap her own photos.

I dreamed of my grandparents. I'd lost all but one grandmother, but I always thought of them together during the holidays. Would I ever be welcome in her home again? Did disownment extend to her as well? The idea of never seeing Grammie's smiling face made me wake in a cold sweat.

I tossed and turned before finally falling still from sheer exhaustion.

* * *

I didn't get out of bed for more than the bathroom until early on the morning of the fifth day.

When I did, however, I did it with flair.

My family and all that grief moved into a locked room in my mind. I added deadbolts and door chains and nailed boards to keep it shut—then, did it again for the next door, and the next, until I'd finally put enough of a barrier between every-day me and that room.

Only simmering fury remained, which funneled into iron resolve. If my family wanted to be rid of me, so be it. I'd lived my life by limiting their company for the last several years, and I could do it again.

I didn't need them.

I promised myself I wouldn't allow their small-minded cruelty to impact me any longer.

The reprieve from training was the only victory I could count. My aches had largely healed; only the bruise on my cheek remained as a grotesque shade of yellowed chartreuse. I gave it one, maybe two more days, tops to fade completely away.

Strolling into the kitchen, I found several people eating breakfast at the dining tables. Loading a plate of French toast, I poured a Dr. Pepper and joined them.

Time to smile and do a little song-and-dance.

"Morning!" I said brightly, with too much enthusiasm.

The expressions returned were a mix of confusion, pity, and genuine worry.

"What's on the agenda for the day?" I asked Peter, adding some pep in the words. *Nothing to see here, certainly not an empty husk propped-up by rage, carbohydrates, and false cheer.* He searched my face for a long time before responding.

"If you're up to it, you can try some training."

Eli sat at the opposite end of the table, refusing to make eye contact. It was kind of wonderful having him wary of me; might even make a day on the mats tolerable. I filed "hysterical crying" away in my back pocket for a rainy day.

"We're going to be gone for a while this morning. You'll be okay alone?" Peter added.

"I won't be alone—Eli's with me." I showed a toothy grin. Maybe I should ratchet it back a bit, because I could practically hear the brains whirring around me. Peter only nodded.

The rest of breakfast continued in silence, and I hummed quietly to myself. Everyone watched my movements and face slyly, which only made it harder to keep up the positivity.

They all anticipated another crying spell, another breakdown, but I'd finished wallowing. No, the time for that had passed. I was in full-fledged wrath, channeling it all into forced joy.

I'd finished changing for my torture in the Practice Room when Brit and Ryan came into my room.

"Are you sure you're alright?" Ryan asked carefully.

"Oh, yeah. I'm fine. It's way easier to ignore the trauma. You should try it sometime."

"We can stay behind if you need us."

"I don't see why, unless you intend to kick Eli's ass when he does something callous."

"You know what he means, honey," Brit soothed. "We are more than happy to sit with you if that will make things better."

"And leave Peter and the rest short-handed? No, go save the world, or whatever you're doing. I'm fine, everything's fine. I even got bacon for breakfast. It's a nice thought, but you should go."

They meant well, but continuing to treat me with kid gloves was going to drive me insane. I'd already switched to game mode, ready to deal with Eli's insanity.

Ryan turned to Brit and asked her to give him a minute. She slipped out the door without another word.

He stood close, his hands flexing at his sides. I think he wanted to hug me, but didn't know how to manage it without being awkward.

"You know this is ridiculous, right?" he asked.

Irritation piqued. I knew he didn't expect a response to the hypothetical question, but I answered anyway.

"What's ridiculous is that you think I'm going to wilt and fall apart the second you leave. I'm not that dependent on you, Ryan. I don't need you to survive."

"I know you don't *need* me, but on Monday, you—"

"Five days ago, I found out that my entire family abandoned me, probably because I'm here. My father apparently has no love for this place or Peter or anyone else connected with it. They discarded me the minute I stepped through that door. How can you fault me for reacting the way I did? Honestly, I spent five days too many languishing in things I cannot change."

My temper rose—an old friend's embrace at a time when I needed it. Blood flew through my veins. Who the hell did he think he was? He thought I *needed* him? That I couldn't make it through one day without him around? We barely knew each other.

"That's not what I meant. We don't want you to be in so much pain. Seeing you like that was"—he searched for the right word—"difficult. It was difficult. For all of us."

He surrendered and enclosed me into a tight hug.

"What I need right now is for you to go with Peter," I insisted. "Come back with all your limbs and most of your blood, and then we can discuss how much I do or don't need you."

I could see in his eyes that he didn't know how to take that. Guilt at being so brusque poked its head out, but it had to be said. Ryan gave a tight-lipped smile.

"We should be back in a few hours."

He kissed my good cheek, and I felt the blush flood my face. Well, that ruined any tough girl image I'd been able to build.

"Try to stay safe, okay?" I asked him.

"Yes, ma'am," he replied, lighting up one of those charming smiles. He tipped an imaginary hat and disappeared out the door. Such a dork. He made it impossible not to like him.

Chapter Ten

Georgia stared at her automatic feeder like she could Jedi-mind-trick it to drop a few scraps. I watched from the sofa, waiting to see if it would work.

Peter'd instructed me to find Eli so we could begin today's round of assault and battery. I was procrastinating and knew it, not excited at the idea of having to face him. He'd been more stunned by my outpouring of grief than I was. My emotions still felt very raw, but it wouldn't get better sitting on the couch.

I even called Trish, but she informed me that Peter had ordered her both not to overwhelm me with more information and also not to enable my avoidance of the Practice Room.

Begrudgingly, I wound my way to the Practice Room and, miracle of miracles, didn't get lost. I might actually learn the layout of the building.

Eli stretched at the center of the mat, that same imposing quality inhaling all the air in the room. He faced away from the door, his long arms extended over his head with hands together. Biceps and shoulders flexed as he went through the motion, stretching up before bending at the waist and reaching to the side. The movements were strangely beautiful. I watched him for a full minute before it occurred to me he had no idea I'd entered the room.

Seizing the opportunity to sneak up on someone else for a change, I tiptoed my way toward the middle of the mat. Stalking slow and quiet as I crept forward, I visualized the terrified look on his face. His mouth would hang open in horror, with eyes wide in shock. My chest subtly warmed at the thought, and I shook out my fingers to loosen the joints. If I had a mustache to twirl, I'd be all set.

My fingers reached out to tap him on the shoulder, but he spun and swiftly brought an arm around. I felt myself tumbling back before I'd even registered what happened.

That familiar contempt edged his amused expression as he hulked over me, locking me onto the mat. His hand cupped behind my neck to brace my fall, but he released it so that I'd thump to the ground. One of my arms was caught beneath my own body, and my legs were trapped under his.

"You're late," he scolded.

"I got lost?" I squeaked. He didn't seem convinced.

"Next time, leave earlier."

He still held me down, pins and needles pricking at my extremities from blood loss and the awkward position. Menthol and spiced aftershave invaded the space between us.

"Too soon for ninja sneakiness?"

"Think so?" he chastised, his mouth twisting into that too-familiar smug grin. He finally relented, helping me up. "I'll show you what you did wrong."

We spent an hour going through the proper techniques for walking.

Yes, *walking*.

He taught me to spread my weight over each foot, to walk on only the balls of my feet, and to run in that position. How pressing all of my toes into the floor would steady my balance. How to stack my body like building blocks and contract my core muscles to maintain my center. About avoiding the joints in the floor, the weak points, and placing soundless steps.

I thought my feet might fall off and my abs were so sore it hurt to breathe. He seemed intent on teaching me all this sneakiness technique, and for once I actually had the teensiest bit of fun doing it despite my instructor.

We took a water break, and my legs cramped and rebelled at any movement. When I complained, he introduced me to the torture device known as a foam roller.

At exactly ten minutes, though, he returned to basic defense. He taught me to roll out of falls and counter throws, how to cushion a fall with my arms. He even made me practice falling backward on the wooden floorboards stretching the far side of the room. He demonstrated more stances to build on the work from Sunday, but I had no easier time than before.

The maneuvers made my stomach twist and my temples throb. He seemed to recognize my frustration and suggested we switch to sparring. I knew little about actual fighting, other than what I'd seen on TV and in movies. The foreboding feeling was hard to ignore, but I knew he wasn't going to let me out of it so easily.

"You can't rely exclusively on your instincts and emotions. Get a feel for integrating your training with your essence," he informed me.

"Except I don't know what to do. I've only barely started and you want to jump to intermediate?"

"Give it a shot. Offense or defense, doesn't matter, whichever feels right in the moment. The dojo is the best place to learn since I'm not actively trying to hurt you."

"That's debatable," I muttered.

"Better now than out there. See if you can get your essence to flare on command."

"Thank you. Why didn't I think of that? While I'm at it, I'll find Jimmy Hoffa and the complete set of Amber Room panels."

What I wouldn't give to be back with Georgia and her food bowl.

"You need to learn to use everything at your disposal," he told me. "Go for sensitive areas—knees, eyes, throat. In close-combat, there are no rules."

I approached him cautiously, but he grabbed my shirt by the shoulders with both hands and jerked me toward him. I managed to escape his grip, but in the process went stumbling away. My feet caught, and I took a dive to the floor before tumbling out of it in one of my now well-practiced roll-outs.

Before I could regain a fully standing position, though, he twined his arms with my own and locked them behind me.

Practically carrying me, he thrust us both forward and shoved me face-first into the red mats hung along the wall. Sweat smeared across the surface of the pad as the weave chafed at my good cheek. I tried to maneuver my arms free, but he jammed his hips hard against my ass to wedge me to the wall.

"Going to have to do better than that, buttercup," he chided, his breath hot on my ear.

Sweat had already soaked through my shirt and made my skin slick. Twisting, I rolled my shoulders and slipped free of the bad angle—a move I never would have even tried without my newfound dexterity. Shoving my hands down, I caught him by surprise and pivoted to swing an elbow at his head.

The euphoria of success died swiftly. Eli dodged the blow with a hair's clearance and snatched my wrist as it passed to slam it into the mat above my head.

I might not be eating the mat anymore, but facing him meant a front-row seat to Eli's amused expressions. His eyes skimmed down my frame as I struggled in his grasp.

I thrust my free palm into that infuriating face, arching his head and neck backward, but he was too tall and kept me pinioned against the wall. Prying my hand loose, he twined his fingers with mine and slammed my other hand over my head so that it joined its match.

Eli gazed at me, a laugh playing on his lips. Sweat dripped from his neck as his body tucked in close, his hips grinding hard against mine with both of my arms fixed over my head.

"Try this time," he teased.

The vise-like grip locked my arms overhead. I twisted my shoulders, but couldn't budge him even an inch. In all my jostling, he crossed my wrists together so that he could restrain both with one large hand.

His free arm hung loosely at his side, taunting me with how little I challenged him. When several minutes passed without progress, he used that damn hand to snap the spandex waistband on my leggings.

I refused to reward him with a wince.

Asshole.

With his hips locked against mine, I could tell exactly how much he enjoyed the grapple. This would be a lot more fun if he weren't such an arrogant jerk.

"Pin," I said.

"Can't tap out in real life, princess."

He rested his forehead against mine, displaying how much confidence he had that I couldn't dislodge him. The scent of sweat and mint mingled as we breathed at each other for a moment and I worked out an escape plan.

I struggled against his hold, throwing my weight around and even head-butting him once, but each time I hit the mat in the same position I'd started in. My head ached from knocking into the wall, even with the added padding. He clasped my wrists so tightly I thought new bruises might form.

"You're hurting me. Get off."

"I'm not releasing. You need to think about those mounts I taught you."

Snort, *mounts*. It was never not funny.

His face inches from mine, that wrath simmered in his eyes. The taut muscles in his shoulders and arms flexed as he anticipated and countered each move.

Think, *think*, *think*. Eli had more experience, more expertise. His own Duality—making him stronger, faster, and probably with better reflexes—ensured only an infinitesimal chance of success, which was undoubtedly the point. *Ugh, that ego on him.* So certain he could best me. It's a wonder that giant head fit through the . . .

"I'm going to give you one more chance to let me out before it starts for real," I warned him. "Don't go crying to Brit when that happens."

"It was supposed to be 'for real' the minute you stepped in the box."

I pursed my lips. Fine, we can play it that way.

I shifted to the left and, as he swung us in the opposite direction, I used his momentum to free my knee and bring it up as hard as I could to his family jewels.

My knee connected, and I was rewarded with the most satisfying grunt. He staggered away, his curses echoing loud against the walls. Bro-points to him for not falling on the floor.

Men could be so dense. I didn't even need my essence for the move. It's not like he hadn't known I'd done it before.

"I tried to warn you," I reminded him, rubbing at my arms. He didn't seem to be listening, but I continued anyway. "Only doing what you told me, using everything at my disposal."

He directed more obscenities at the ground.

Eli took the loss about as well as could be expected and decided extreme conditioning was the best punishment. He sat back, barking out counts like a drill sergeant. I did hurricane drills, mountain climbers, and laps around the room until I was dizzy. He made me do sets of exercises in quick succession in a rotation. Punches, lunges, push-ups, crunches, punches, lunges, push-ups, crunches.

The workout went on into late afternoon, breaking only for ten minutes while we inhaled some sandwiches for lunch and I chugged about five gallons of water. I was on the verge of passing out. Or throwing up. Or both.

He called for another break and I moaned.

"I . . . cannot do anymore," I whined, as I collapsed onto a stack of folded gymnastics mats. Sweat pooled on the surface beneath me. *Yuck.*

"When you think you've hit your limit is the perfect time to train. You need to learn to tolerate being exhausted and functional at the same time."

"The only function I can perform right now is breathing, and even that is a challenge."

It would take a lot more than a little pep talk to get me to move. The distant sound of cars tearing into the lot saved me.

Peter and Henry carried a limp figure on a make-shift stretcher through the main door, while Brit and two others hauled in packs.

Maxon also hobbled toward the door, Lita under one arm and Ryan the other.

They carried the stretcher down the hallway and disappeared into a locked room outfitted as an infirmary. They hoisted the figure onto one of four cots filling one side. Brit and Lita rummaged through the cabinets for medical supplies on the opposite side.

Peeking over Eli's shoulder, I found a girl with a white-blond pixie haircut only a shade darker than his. Blue eyes blinked, unfocused. Eli ran past to sit beside her, glaring daggers at Peter.

"Jack's fine," Peter told him. "Only a few scrapes. Nothing to worry about. We only want her in here as a precaution. They were using sleep deprivation, and we don't want her to pass out until we rule out a concussion."

Lita wheeled a machine over to the cot and shooed everyone away.

"That's Jack? Jack isn't a guy?" I asked, surprised.

"Dud wishes she were," Maxon snickered from the hallway, but Brit smacked the back of his head.

"Jacqueline," Eli told me. "They hate her because she can destroy them all, despite her size."

He was uncharacteristically protective, and things clicked in my mind.

"Jack's your sister, isn't she?" I asked. I didn't need it, but he nodded a confirmation.

*   *   *

Eli

They hauled Jack's pale, slight frame to the infirmary. Disoriented, her head swiveled as she babbled in long, run-on sentences about the concrete stall where they'd confined her.

The story of her escape was nothing short of miraculous, but I'd expect nothing less out of her. The Kier stashed her in an old barn in the middle of nowhere with a few bottles of water and a bucket to piss in. Between interrogations, music blasted at deafening levels to keep her from falling asleep.

Five days with only desperate, short bursts of sleep and water to drink left her delirious and easily confused.

Lita cinched rubber tubing around her arm before wiping the area with an alcohol swab and inserting an IV needle. She snapped on a fluids bag and hung it on a hook on the wall.

"You can't sleep yet, sweetheart," Brit cooed at her, cupping her face with a hand. "They need to check you for a concussion and then you can pass out. Just a little longer, I promise. It will be okay."

Jack's eyes rolled back, unfocused, the paper pillowcase crinkling as she rocked her head. She was one of the strongest people I knew. Seeing her reduced to chattering nonsense was a shock.

When Jack first went missing, Peter cut me out of the investigation of her disappearance and rescue. I thought it might be because my lazy little Pair was so pathetically behind. I hated that he did it, but couldn't even really blame him. Jex would get us both killed the second we stepped out the door if she couldn't quit whining and force her body and mind to exert even a minor amount of control.

Still, after Jex had that meltdown, there wasn't much for me to do all week but twiddle my thumbs. She'd taken her parents' actions pretty hard. Peter tried to push me into spending time with her, rationalizing that

I'd be able to help her through it, but using dead parents to bond wasn't how I operated.

No, instead, Peter assigned Ryan to the rescue and gave him authority to select his team.

I didn't give a flying fuck about Ryan's ability or rank as Captain of the Guards. Sure, he was good with firearms, but that wouldn't mean shit facing down someone who could implode your eardrums or suck the air from your lungs with barely more than a thought.

From what I could get out of Henry, the Cole sent Delaney to question Jack during her captivity. She palmed one of her guard's cellphones during an early morning interrogation session. She waited until they'd thrown her into the horse stall before texting Henry and pinging her GPS location.

The Kier guarding her must have discovered her five-finger party trick, because they ran like the cowards they were. Jack sweltered, alone, locked in an overheated barn for hours before Ryan's team assembled and got her out.

Fuck Ryan and all his preaching about patience and preparation. Patience could have gotten her killed once they turned the fans off in the barn. He should have known she'd be severely dehydrated and in rough shape already. The heat could have killed her on its own.

Peter should cut his rank for this. He even let someone get hurt. Sure, Maxon sprained his ankle acting like a dumbass, but he was still under Ryan's oversight.

Besides, Ryan's recent behavior made it clear he didn't deserve his standing.

If you'd asked a few weeks ago, I'd probably say he was a reliable soldier. Logical. Focused. We weren't friends, but we got along because he wasn't plainly offensive either.

Now, though, the guy had totally lost his mind. He ran after Jex like some love-sick puppy, obsessing over her and touching her constantly. He had no issue pawing at my Pair like he had any right to her.

The guy needed to take care of his own house before chasing after mine. That live-in girlfriend of his was a walking nightmare, had been since her brother died.

Come to think of it, Ryan had been staying here since Monday, so who knew where he stood. He'd be sorely mistaken if he thought he could swoop in and switch out my Pair for his girlfriend. No fucking way would I let that happen. The Pairs were chosen for a reason, and Jex didn't need some pointless distraction from her training.

Lita monitored Jack and Maxon in the infirmary while the rest of us moved back to the library to discuss the mission and outcome.

Mr. Charisma himself dumped the contents of a backpack onto the table. They'd collected everything they could find at the barn for information—empty wrappers and tins, balled-up and shredded paper, a few pens, and the dead burner phone Jack used to send out the SOS. Henry matched the burner to a plug and started charging it. Much like Ryan's leadership skills, it all looked like a heap of worthless trash.

Picking through the pile, the results were mostly useless. The tins and wrappers told us nothing other than one guy's preference for Skoal chewing tobacco.

Still, I picked up a ripped piece of paper with numbers on it. Most of the digits had been torn off, but "7-58" was clearly visible.

"Here," I called out. The group's attention snapped to the scrap in my hand.

"Anyone have any clue what it means?" Henry asked.

"Could be anything," Brit answered. "Could be a phone number, GPS coordinates. Hell, it might just be a passcode to someone's gym locker."

Jack had been kidnapped, tortured, and left to rot in a concrete oven, and we had nothing to show for it but three numbers and a dead burner phone that was probably wiped clean.

I wouldn't let that be the end of it. Couldn't. Jack deserved better, and the Kier had been pinching guards left and right the last few weeks. They searched for something—something they thought we had or knew about.

So, while the others were distracted by Ryan's trash heap, I surreptitiously turned on the burner and forwarded the GPS ping to my phone.

"I can cross-reference these numbers with our databases," I offered to Peter. "Maybe something in the catalog will hit. I'll see if Pinch is open to do some hacking, although I'll need to get him supplies."

Peter'd totally bought into Ryan's bullshit, because he looked to the Guard's Captain for an approval.

"That would be appreciated, thank you," Ryan answered. Fuck you very much, both of you.

I slipped out the door to draft Pinch for a side quest. Sure, we'd poke around in the electronic files of the county, state, and otherwise, but first I wanted to stop by the barn and figure out what Ryan missed.

*   *   *

Jex

Eli spent the rest of the afternoon off distracted by whatever was going on with Jack.

My dream of another reprieve from training evaporated when Peter directed me to run the reservoir.

Run the *what*? The entire thing?

The expansive, man-made reservoir looked like a lake. It sat about a quarter mile north of Haven's building, apparently still on Clara land. There was a boathouse at the shore, and a thirty-foot dock stretched into the middle of the water, with guardrails along one side and at the end.

I made the trek around the lake and limped to the porch. "Running" would have been a generous description, but "A" for effort, right?

Stepping onto the back deck's platform, I sprawled out on the boards and pulled off my shoes and socks to let the open-air wash over my feet. Cracks in the wood caught my clothes and hair, but I didn't care. I lay there, the sun beating down on me, while I tried to reanimate my limbs.

A courageous palmetto bug flitted a little too closely, but I didn't have the energy to swat it away. I named him Wes and planned our evening lying on the deck together.

A cold glass of Dr. Pepper was the sole reason I could find to get back up. My second for the day was far past due. It was like a mirage in my mind, and I used the image to will myself toward the side door.

I reached for the handle when Henry came out of the atrium's slider.

"Going somewhere?" he asked.

"Kitchen," my throat scratched out.

"Meet me back here in five."

My spirit flew away like cash in a casino. More? There was more? At this rate, I'd be unconscious by dinner. If I made it to dinner.

"Can't I have a little break first? I'm exhausted."

"It's not that kind of practice. We're going to work on controlling your Duality."

He settled himself onto the bench of one of the picnic tables dotting the wooden deck along the length of the building.

After chugging my sugary caffeine shot, I hobbled to Henry's table and hoisted myself onto the surface. Open question whether I'd be able to stick the dismount, but it was still easier than trying to maneuver into the attached bench.

While waiting patiently for him to finish with his phone, I attempted to force blood to my limbs and muscles. As long as little moving was required, I figured I could swing it.

"To command your essence," he began, "you need to use your focus and determination to force the element to respond. Clearly, you have access to your Duality. You should be capable of calling it at will."

"How exactly am I supposed to do that? It only works when I'm threatened. Or maybe angry. I don't really understand it all yet. Besides, I thought it would work itself out on its own after my birthday."

"You will gain full use of your essence around your birthday, but not control or competence. You still need to train your mind and body to channel it—not only to protect yourself, but so that you can do good over harm. Control is a major difference separating us from the Kier, and we don't want to hurt people."

"Why you? Why not Peter?"

That probably sounded like I didn't want his help. The truth was, though, that Henry'd barely said a word to me since I'd first arrived. By contrast, Peter'd been purposefully patient with explanations.

"Peter is busy, and he wouldn't be the one to teach you in any event. He isn't ignisunda."

"But you are?" I asked, but he only nodded at me.

"What do I do first?"

"First, you meditate."

His response made me grunt. *Meditate.* As if thinking of nothing could suddenly snap my concentration into place. At least no moving was required.

"That's easy enough," I replied with false bravado. Sitting cross-legged on the tabletop, I placed my hands on my knees and began to chant ooom-sahs.

"This is serious, Jex. You must master your mind. Training with Eli will give you the physical strength necessary to channel your elements and teach you some discipline and control, but you need to have mental focus as well. The best way to learn is through meditation."

The table shifted slightly as he joined me on the top. The late afternoon daylight filtered through his dark auburn hair, turning it a brilliant shade of orange-red. He took my closest hand, laying my palm flat against his with our elbows resting on our knees.

Shrugging at him, I sighed and closed my eyes again.

"Concentrate on your breathing and clear your mind of anything it comes across."

Staring at the back of my eyelids, I tried my best to do as he instructed. I saw blackness and fought to keep the mental images from forming. They crept in around the edges, trying to elbow their way in.

Henry tried to walk me through some visualization exercises, but I couldn't concentrate. Despite my best attempts, recent events muscled their way into my thoughts. I'd been running mostly on distractions to avoid thinking too much about, well, *everything.* Keeping my mind from wandering seemed a feat all on its own.

He repeatedly admonished me for fidgeting, and required that I remain connected to him on the tabletop, which only exacerbated my anxiety. He insisted I sit perfectly still, chiding me repeatedly about my inability to execute the task—which, of course, only made it worse.

After about half an hour of this insanity, he suggested I count my breaths in slow succession. Inhale for four, exhale for eight.

In for four, and out for eight.

After a few minutes, my heart rate finally slowed, and my breathing steadied. Henry's voice offered direction.

"Picture yourself at the gas station. It's before sunrise and the air is warm. Three men are threatening you and you're terrified."

I breathed in for a count of four and formed the image of the gas station that night. The vibrant memory played in my mental movie reel. Three men surrounded me after I'd rounded the pump. I could almost smell the gasoline and dust from the parking lot.

"You are attacked by one, but he misses you."

I exhaled for a count of eight, recalling the agile dodge, the feel of his body brushing by mine, and the triumph at successfully escaping his charge.

"You are attacked by a second man and handcuff him to a pole. He's unable to get to you."

I breathed in for one . . . two . . . three . . . four, visualizing the red-black anger in his face as he futilely kicked in my direction.

"You see the first man at the edge of the lot."

His shaggy-dark hair appeared in my mind, his palms red from the fall. A tingle of heat tickled the pads of my fingers and the skin where our hands touched.

Six . . . seven . . . eight . . .

"He hoists the air, towing it with his essence, and then releases it in your direction."

Heat crept up my arm, twisting around my elbow and stopping in my shoulder. It should be painful, it was before, but the burn had become familiar and mostly amounted to discomfort.

Another count of four . . .

"He gathers his essence and sends a shock wave."

My hand melded to Henry's as if they'd physically melted together. The heat chased across my shoulders and my chest constricted. I gasped at the burn, my muscles tensing under the stress, but his hand pressed firmer against mine. I forcefully exhaled.

Eight . . .

"You sense the shock wave approaching. The pressure sucks at the air along its path."

Fire hissed in my chest as it spread to my remaining limbs. My skin boiled and my brain became a flurry of lit timber, each breath fanning the flames. The discomfort ratcheted up to an intense, buzzing irritation. I struggled to separate the heat from true pain as I wrestled with the torrent.

I breathed in a ragged four-count, the inferno in my system so strong I might as well be strapped to a pyre soaked with gasoline.

"Jex, open your eyes."

An oval of flames surrounded us, formed perfectly and completely solid. No fragments this time, but real flames snapping and rippling madly. The bubble obscured our view of the rest of the deck. I checked for holes or gaps.

My mind searched the surface, trying to reconcile the fact I had created another fire bubble. On purpose. I *controlled* a fire bubble, for the most part.

Me, a person who barely managed to make cookies without smoking up the kitchen.

"Why isn't the table burning?" I murmured, trying to keep my focus and avoid any accidental arson.

"I don't know. There are some things you'll have to figure out on your own."

Shifting my focus, I attempted to thin the field so we could see out. The telltale waves of exhaust distorted my vision as I watched the fire bubble wash the air with heat.

The fireball had burned the attacker in the parking lot, so I knew it could scorch, yet the only heat I felt now zipped around in my bloodstream. I struggled to keep the sphere steady but couldn't keep the broad smile from my face.

"That's enough for the time being," Henry said. "Return to your breathing."

"Be one with the bubble," I joked.

"Concentrate, Jex," he snapped. "Letting the bubble go could be dangerous if you don't properly expel the energy. Focus on siphoning it away, bit by bit."

Resuming my counts, I visualized releasing each tendril of flame into the sky. The heat faded, and so did the bubble, evaporating into the air. I watched it slowly wick away as the burn in my chest receded. When I broke our hold, the trapped energy dissipated, and my palm felt frozen in the sweltering climate.

We worked for another half an hour, this time with Henry talking me through visualizing my power as a physical thing I could control with my hands or words. He tried to keep me focused, but I was exhausted and still adjusting to the idea I could make fire appear from nothing.

It was also impossible to control my excitement at the successful bubble, which made concentration even more of a problem. He seemed frustrated. Annoyed, really. I'm sure acting like a kid who'd scored the golden ticket wasn't a great way to endear me to him, but I couldn't help it.

Henry left to check on Jack, and I returned to my original napping plan. Along the way, though, I saw Eli in the atrium's sitting area. He swayed in the hammock, his hands behind his head while gazing up at the atrium windows in the fading afternoon light.

At first, I thought I should pass by, but my instincts told me not to leave him alone. He needed someone to talk to, to vent, about Jack. He glanced my way as I approached and rolled his eyes.

Nice to see you, too, asshole.

He angrily fiddled with the fraying hem of his shirt. It's no wonder he dressed like he was always on his way to the gym; it was a miracle any of his shirts survived at all.

Tempting the fates, I opted for the hammock beside his. I tried to get into it gingerly, pushing it to the side and swinging in to sit, but the hammock flipped and I tumbled out the back. Tailbone struck concrete, and I groaned in pain, but Eli only laughed at me. It seemed to be his favorite pastime.

"Glad my pain amuses you." I sighed.

"Me too."

"We already know you're sadistic. I suppose I shouldn't be surprised."

Surrendering for the swing, I tried to keep most of my weight off my bruised behind while still catering to the cramps and aches from a day of entirely too much activity and not enough junk food.

Eli only watched from his relaxed position in the hammock, a smile etched at his lips. Every time I shifted uncomfortably, it grew a little wider. My taskmaster had dimples, which I hadn't noticed before. Probably because he rarely smiled.

"Everyone survive?" I asked him.

"Maxon has a mildly sprained ankle and two broken fingers, but he'll make do with a splint and walking cast. Jack will be fine. She's sleeping it off. No major damage."

"At least they made it back in one piece."

"No thanks to Ryan and his band of idiots." He said it with so much contempt I shuttered.

"Did something go wrong? Is that why Maxon is hurt?"

"No. Maxon was showing off and kicked a rotten door. Idiot fell into the room and rolled his ankle." He wasn't even looking at me anymore, choosing instead to stare into the trees.

"Then why, exactly, is Ryan at fault?"

"You were there the other day. He didn't want to go after Jack. Not even try. If we'd done what he wanted, we'd be collecting pieces of her from the morgue."

Ah, Ryan had offended him by not immediately jumping on the bandwagon to go guns blazing into an unknown situation.

"Ryan was trying to keep everyone safe," I reminded him. "He never said they weren't going after Jack, he only wanted more confirmation."

"Confirmation we would never have gotten," he sneered. "She was already at their safe house by the time we knew she was gone. Did he seriously think the Kier would ransom her? They intended to torture her for information and then kill her. Henry's been bargaining with them for weeks to prevent more losses."

He alternated between wringing his hands and fraying the hem.

"Caution and inaction are not the same. Would you have insisted on a rescue if it had been anyone else?"

"Can't you see past your sad, little crush?" he snapped. "Caution only gets you boredom, self-loathing, and mediocrity."

"And maybe not being killed," I muttered.

"No, princess. Caution is why people settle into their average lives with their average two-point-four kids and average jobs. They get so consumed by never losing anything that they refuse to try for something more. Anyone happy with average is pathetic."

Except I had been happy with average. I had the average job and life. It wasn't so bad. I even wanted it back.

"I don't think you get to say anything about it. When was the last time you were that way?" I asked.

"I've never been ordinary. It's not what life has designed for me. Even if that wasn't the case, I'd never allow myself to be so useless in life."

"Useless," I repeated. Tears pricked at the corners of my eyes. "You really think that people who want nothing more than a normal life are useless?"

"The worst kind. People who want average don't deserve it. They strive for nothing and should get nothing. A waste of space." He spat the words, as if he'd swallowed rotten food.

Standing, I struggled to find a response. I had to get away; I refused to let him see me cry over what he'd said. I turned to leave.

"Wait, Jex . . ." he called, but I swiftly marched away from the pavilion, past the pathways through the trees, out of the atrium, and through the first door I came to.

Once I'd composed myself, I came face-to-face with a wall of gleaming blades.

Chapter Eleven

Lights clicked on. Covering every inch of the opposing wall were swords, knives, daggers, and axes of every kind. Some blades were small, only two or three inches long, but a set of polearms rested in a rack to one side along with several other pointy-looking spears, a case for hunting bows, and even a two-man battering ram. At the end of the wall, in the far corner, a door stood open beside a viewing window.

The square, matte-gray ceramic tiles were spotless, not a speck of dust in sight, and the caustic burn of bleach and ammonia burned my nostrils.

The far-right wall displayed gun racks and safes stacked from floor to ceiling, all organized to allow the assortment to fit neatly on the wall.

Behind me, on the wall with the door, shelves stood in even rows filled with boxes of ammunition, belts and holsters, safety glasses and earplugs, and even bullet-proof vests. Surplus practice dummies and mats were stacked in the corner.

Approaching the viewing window, I discovered a second, smaller room with acoustic-foam walls and wooden floors. Dividers created the lanes of a firing range. A pad of paper dummies hung on the wall by the entrance next to the glass.

Taking a wild guess, I assumed I had found the Weapons Room.

I felt strangely drawn to the wall of sharp metal. It was intimidating, all that destruction on display, but *so shiny*.

I removed one of the smaller knives, holding it away at first. The six-inch blade's intricately carved wooden handle felt good in my fingers.

"Tanto," Eli said. I jumped, not expecting him. He leaned against the doorway, arms crossed, watching my reaction with a frown.

My brow furrowed, and he nodded to the knife in my hand.

"It's called a tanto, basically a dagger."

The last thing I wanted or needed right now was an Eli-branded lesson. Rolling my eyes, I replaced the dagger in favor of the next weapon in the line. It was bigger, the edge more than a foot long and slightly curved. I lifted it from the pegs.

"Wakizashi," he provided.

Unsheathing the sword, the blade felt different from the dagger. It had more heft. Yes, it was longer than the first, but it seemed that there was more than extra weight. It was more substantial. I rolled it around in my hand, finding its center of balance. They had recently cleaned it, because the edge shone in the harsh lighting.

"You don't want to go straight for the long swords?" Eli asked. "That's where all the new Guards head when they see the wall."

None of the other weapons seemed interesting, so I went for a second short sword.

"Actually, the one you want is the katana when you already have a wakizashi." Eli pointed to one of the much-longer swords higher on the wall. "You'd combine the wakizashi and katana, not two wakizashi."

Good ol' know-it-all Eli, back to aggravate me.

"I don't want a longer sword. I'm not even sure if I can handle these. Can't I keep the wagazaki?"

"Wakizashi," he corrected.

I frowned.

"Start with something else or try one at a time. Really, you should go back to empty hand. Weaponry is an advanced skill; most don't use real blades until they've trained extensively."

He watched me, as if willing me to replace the swords in their pegs on the wall. He probably only cared what Peter'd say if he brought me back cut to ribbons.

Mustering my confidence, I settled my hands onto the woven, criss-cross pattern of each pommel. My fingers wrapped instinctively around them, the top two fingers holding the grip with the rest settling comfortably. My essence burbled and faded, but a nudge in the back of my mind told me I'd know what to do.

I allowed my right arm to swing, and Eli rushed forward. I wasn't expecting his advance, and the flame in my chest suddenly surged. I knew he meant me no harm—probably—but somewhere in my subconscious, my essence didn't care for his intervention.

Heat reverberated in my system. My legs miraculously fell into a fighting crouch, the swords brandished before me and halting his charge.

He stopped short, putting his hands out in a stick-up, "don't stab me" pose, and dissected my movements for a long moment before relenting.

"Look, there's only so much saving I can do here," he told me. "I can't be your knight in shining armor if you chop your own arm off."

"I'd rather save myself anyway," I retorted, flipping one of the weapons around with my wrist.

"Just keep it away from your head, and be careful, hey?" he cautioned.

Be careful? How was I supposed to do that?

You know what, *enough*. Everyone assumed I was so helpless. I mean, yes, my Duality was unpredictable at best, and the fighting seemed more on instinct than intention at this point, but he acted like I'd hack off a finger simply holding the blades. It pushed me over the edge, and resolve settled in my gut.

"How would I defend with these?" I asked.

"You wouldn't. You need to swap one for a katana."

My eyes rolled at his single-minded response.

"I told you I don't want that. I'm more comfortable like this. What do I do?"

He stepped forward, but my excited essence buzzed in my veins. The heat gave me confidence, and I had a sudden idea.

"Go stand behind the wall," I told him, "I want to try—"

"That's not a good idea," he cut me off. "I told you, it takes a lot of hard work and practice to get to a place where you are comfortable holding sharpened steel. Put it down. I promise we'll come back to it later."

The obvious lie rankled. Eli had no intention of ever letting me back into this room, or at least not for several more years of daily torture. He probably contemplated snapping the key off in the lock on our way out as a precaution. That controlling air drove me up the wall. My hands tightened on the grip.

"Your funeral," I scoffed.

My body still ached from a long day of training. I exhaled, trying to concentrate. Maybe I should take Eli's advice and try later?

No, if he had anything to say about it, the chance of a later would be non-existent. I'd be damned if I let him keep me from at least trying to use the swords.

Aside from the paltry hour with Henry to walk me through it, I hadn't been able to consciously will the essence to act. Maybe Eli sulking in the corner would help trigger it.

One hand felt like enough for the time being, so I spent a few minutes getting comfortable with the blade by stabbing and slashing at the air. My wrist loosened, not releasing the grip but creating a range of motion.

It felt nice to have something in my hand that could do real damage. No mind-numbing meditation to leash my essence first. No eons of training just to tap someone on the shoulder. A sword could be deadly from day one.

It was empowering.

Autopilot took over. My wrist allowed the blade to swing freely, the bottom half of my hand letting the pommel go so it could revolve unhindered. The sensation startled me, and I lost my grip. The knife clinked to the floor only inches from my toes, and I quickly stooped to pick it up.

Eli was visibly tense, his face a pained expression of worry and anger. I could tell he wanted to run over and rip the waka-whatevers from my hands, but he seemed to anticipate that it would only trigger my fighter's response. To him, it must be like watching a car go off a cliff—tragic, but nothing you can do about it. *Sucks for him.*

I tried the swipe again, this time allowing my muscles to move as they wanted. The edge made a full circle, my arm never actually moving and instead relying on the flexibility in my wrist.

The sword swiveled in my hand, balanced lightly on the edge of the webbing between thumb and forefinger, in control but appearing to be flying of its own accord. It made perfect, vertical arcs around my hand. I tried it with the other hand a few times before attempting a coordinated effort.

Moving the swords in unison made it click. My muscles willed the blades into their fluid motion, forming neat circles. Centripetal force sped the motion. I marveled at how easily I controlled them, alternating between holding the grips firmly and letting them swing loose on the edge of my hand. I crossed them in front of my body so they'd pass within a hair of each other without touching.

My feet moved on their own, a step back, then forward, and I settled into the movement. I took more steps and executed complex weaves combined with intermittent stops while the blades circled to my sides, crossed, swung to one side and then the other. They curved over my head and snaked into a disjointed X behind my back as I turned. I even loosened my hold on the hilt, letting the pommel slide over my hand to hold the grip downward and executing another rotation before resetting the hold.

I gracefully danced and spun, the swords whistling as they whipped through the air. They felt like extensions of my body, the movement as effortless as breathing. It felt *right*, as though I had been born with them in my hands. The combined exhilaration and comfort left me purring.

I found myself moving faster, my momentum increasing the pace. The knives continued to fly, and I panicked, trying to think of how to stop without hurting myself.

Forcing myself to calm, I slowed, allowing the force to turn me about. My eyes sighted a rubber practice dummy in the first moment, and in the next, the weapons sailed through the air. The blades thrust into the dummy's chest with a *thwack*, sunk in a good four inches with the pommels wobbling back and forth.

Eli blanched. He ran to the dummy to confiscate the blades and held them close, as if to save *them* from *me*.

"I think that's enough with weapons for the day. Let's go back to the Practice Room," he told me.

My chest still heaving from the exertion, I groaned. *More* exercise? Wasn't six hours enough?

He waited until I got near the doorway to approach the struts in the wall and replace the swords. As we walked out, I passed by Peter and Brit, who'd stopped to watch my little display. They exchanged a glance, but didn't share their thoughts with us.

Eli walked me through new forms for the rest of the afternoon, jarred by my voodoo magic with the practice dummy. He seemed pensive, his instruction more rote and his reprimands with fewer barbs.

The fight had put us both off, in different ways. The rollercoaster of a day never recovered.

I couldn't seem to get my bearings, to make my essence act again, or even keep myself on the defensive long enough to have a real chance at trying it. My stomach churned and my body *hurt*. I longed for a hot shower.

When we finished, he walked me to my room. It was late. The hall lights cast an unnatural yellow glow against the beige walls. We never spoke, only walked in silence while I followed his lead.

When we reached my door, he paused. Maybe he was tired; at least I wasn't the only one feeling worn.

"Thanks. They can probably smell me two states over. I need a shower like a fish needs water," I joked.

Yeah, not a joke. I could smell *myself*. Not a good sign.

"Imagine how I've felt struggling through your presence all day," he chided. He rubbed the back of his neck. He seemed almost . . . nervous?

"You're one to talk. They'll have to clean the mats with a mop thanks to you."

His mouth turned up at the corner, and I thought he might smile at an intentional funny.

Instead, he lifted my chin with those long fingers. There was barely time to register his intention before he leaned forward and pressed a light kiss to my lips. It was soft, only lasting a few seconds.

"Thank you," he murmured, before disappearing down the hall.

The kiss surprised me. I knew *that* was expected, but Eli didn't seem the least bit interested in me. Well, not for more than being pressed against me on the mats, at least. The effort he took to antagonize me seemed so contrary to that gentle kiss.

Perhaps he thought he'd "give it a try," to see what it was like? It wasn't bad, just . . . surreal. Unexpected.

And what was he thankful for? All I'd succeeded in doing this afternoon was angering, frustrating, and scaring him.

Confused, I rerouted to the kitchen to grab a sandwich, then went into my room to soak in the best shower of my life.

*   *   *

Ryan

Four hours of sleep was all I could manage. My room at Haven was still too strange, even though exhaustion dragged at my body and knew I should be dead to the world. I couldn't force my brain to stop, to relax enough to allow me to drift off.

Resigned, I tugged on my gray sweats and sat at the desk to continue working. Peter wanted to construct a new building connected to the existing tunnels under Haven and the lake. The Kier escalated their attacks recently, and we simply didn't have the space to house everyone in an emergency. Not for a longer time frame, anyway.

Captaining the Guards might sound critical, but all too often it meant bureaucratic nonsense and enough paper to drown in. It was one of the reasons I was taking business classes; I'd been totally unprepared for this part of the job.

Hunched over the desk, I combed my fingers through my hair and tried to force the scope of the project to work within the budget allotted.

"That will pull out your hair," Jex's voice came from the doorway. As I glanced up at her, she bit her lip as if to prevent herself from saying anything else.

She'd tied her hair up in a loose ponytail, her sexy figure on display in the leggings and tank top. She'd gotten tanner in the past days, her skin now a subtle golden-pink tint.

"You care if I lose my hair?" I asked, amused. That telltale blush spread across her face, and she blinked. Her fingers toyed with the ring on her finger. I smiled, knowing I could make her nervous even from across the room.

"Don't *you* care if you lose your hair?" she asked, like it wasn't awkward at all.

"I suppose I do," I replied with a chuckle. I scrutinized her, resting my head on my fist and waiting to see what else she might say.

"What are you working on?" she asked. I spun the computer so she could see the spreadsheet on the screen.

"Peter wants to make an addition to Haven, an out-building. He asked me to put a budget together."

"An out-building?"

"He wants to build an emergency bunker. We have something similar already, but it's out-of-date, and . . . I don't know why I'm telling you this, it's not remotely interesting."

I shook my head at my own awkwardness.

"Hey, I've got a random accounting degree, remember? I probably know Excel better than you do." She laughed. "I could help, might mean you get home faster."

"I've been staying here for the last week. It's easier this way. Kim doesn't have anywhere else to go."

"Oh?" she asked, the glee written all over her face. It was sweet, the way she dutifully tried to hide it. If she kept looking at me like that, I'd drag her into the room and slam the door shut.

She had this way of making me trip over my own words. I carefully thought through my response.

"Kim hasn't been herself in a very long time. We ended it months ago, but I couldn't stomach turning her out. After a while, it sort of lingered, and I didn't know how to extract myself. I realized recently that the situation did neither of us favors."

I tapped a few keys and slapped the laptop closed.

"I'm sorry, Ryan," she told me.

Her hands smoothed the front of her pants, even though they were leggings that couldn't wrinkle. The nervous ticks made it so easy to read her reactions.

When I first met Jex, I'd worried my interest was only a rebound. The situation with Kim had been bad for a while. Between her habits with the booze, and the lying, and the cheating, I'd stuck around a lot longer than any guy with a modicum of self-respect should.

Breaking it off with her granted the most immense relief. And then guilt over the relief. Relationships can be a real mind-fuck.

I probably shouldn't be looking for something new with Jex. Her tie to Eli could be a problem—but not insurmountable. I'd make do for the right girl. From everything I'd seen, she was more than worth the extra complexity. Wouldn't hurt to test the waters, see how it felt.

"Aren't you supposed to be asleep?" I asked her, sprawling in my chair. I scratched the back of my neck to show off my bicep. Girls love that shit.

"Tried and failed," she answered, her eyes glued to the flex in my arm. "It feels like I mainlined coffee all day."

I sauntered over to stand in front of her, her eyes watching every step with focused attention.

"You admitting you failed at something? You must not be from around here." I grinned.

"No one humble at Haven, huh?"

"It can be a bit much. Everyone takes the mission very seriously, not that I can blame them."

I planted a hand on the doorjamb and leaned over her, tilting my head to the side to sweep my eyes over her curves. Damn, she looked good in leggings. Her ass would fit perfectly in my hand.

"Come on," I said and held out a palm.

I really just wanted to touch her, but she took one look at my hand and cringed. Fucking Eli and his Machiavellian bullshit. She grimaced, as if reading my thoughts and agreeing.

"Eli can be a real ass sometimes," I told her.

"Sometimes?" she replied with a laugh, but she took a leap of faith and put her hand in mine.

I led her down winding hallways until we came to one of the exterior doors.

"Where are we going?" she asked.

"You'll see."

Stepping into the night air, I guided her over the planks of the deck, across the grass, and toward a path that wormed its way through the trees.

The forest was alive, even at this time of night, the cicadas singing and fireflies buzzing and flitting on and off in the dark.

We cleared the trees near the dock that stretched into the middle of the reservoir. The edges of the platform and handrails were lined with little, white lights.

Jex and I crossed the dock, the nearly full moon reflecting light from the green-blue water to dance across the wood. It filtered through the slats, and reminded me of the night I met her at Anna's shower. It'd been barely two weeks, but felt a million years ago.

Still, Jex's face relaxed, a small smile playing at her lips. She held my hand tighter, and the serene expression grew until joy radiated from her. Her reaction to the setting was a reward all its own.

Out at the end, only the sound of water lapping against the deck broke past the dead-silent night. We leaned together against the railing, watching the darkness. The opposite shore and trees were visible, but the world beyond only a black void. I breathed deep in the crisp air, comforted by the solitude.

"It's so peaceful," she told me.

"I thought you'd like it. Been meaning to bring you out here. It reminds me of the night we met."

She beamed, bumping her shoulder against mine.

"I'll have to irritate you more often," she replied.

"You're the least irritating person here. Granted, you are funny, and beautiful in the moonlight."

I tucked a few flyaways behind her ear, my hand lingering a moment longer than necessary as our eyes met. Shifting, she leaned to face me from the corner of the railing, practically begging me to pin her in.

"Why, Ryan, are you flirting with me?"

"Do you want me to flirt with you?"

"Oh, no." She poked a finger at me. "If you can't admit to coming onto me, you definitely won't be coming into me."

I threw my head back and laughed, not bothering to withhold the shock.

Jex's lack of filter was one of the things I liked most about her. More often than not, she'd say what we'd all been thinking anyway—she's just the only one brave or bold enough to voice it.

We talked for a while about everything and nothing, our feet toying with the other's and finding reasons to leave touches on each other's skin.

I told her about my family, about moving to Florida when I was fifteen, about college and my business major.

Jex talked about her old job and living in Boston. I asked gently about her family, but she shut down. Her face tightened, the corners of her mouth dropping in a frown. Well, that was a massive fail.

Looking out at the trees, I tried to give her some space to sort out her feelings. As I glanced away, though, she tapped on the scar at the crook of my neck.

"Battle wound?" she prompted.

"It was a long time ago," I sighed. "I could make up some outrageous story, but it was barely a bar fight. Guy came at me with a knife, and I didn't dodge fast enough."

The shimmering light skimmed across her face as she absently traced the line. Nervous energy danced in my system from her touch. She sucked in her bottom lip, hooded eyes carefully examining my neck. I moved my arm to brace against the opposing post and cornered her at the bend of the dock railing.

Gazing down at her, I watched her struggle to figure an easy way out. Her breathing sped, her face flushed, and her pupils widened as she stared up at me. My heart pounded faster with every second until I thought it would burst out of my chest and skip across the surface of the water.

There's always a moment, when you're with someone and the attraction pulls you together. You stand close, breathing hard, the anticipation a blend of agony and excitement as your brain and heart war.

She wanted me to kiss her. I knew it as certainly as if she'd said it aloud. We'd been flirting for the better part of half an hour and were all alone out on the dock on this gorgeous night.

Should I kiss her? Probably not. Things with Eli were messy enough, and Kim still slept in my apartment.

Still, those alluring blue-green eyes and that wild hair muddled logic and desire.

She averted her gaze, searching for anything else that might distract her. It fascinated me, watching her gaze flit from place to place while that fierce wit sorted through her thoughts.

"You seem lost, little Firefly," I observed.

"No, I know exactly where I am."

"And where's that?" I countered.

"Fantasyland."

I smiled, and our eyes held. Leaning in closer, my body pressed against hers. My own breathing flustered as I slipped an arm around her waist. Her lips parted, setting off a chain reaction that flooded my veins with a mix of adrenaline and arousal.

Light played over the face so that when she licked her lips they shone. I tilted her face up to examine the barely there bruise still on her cheek.

"I'd like to murder the asshole who did that to you," I commented.

"The back of the line is that-a-way." She laughed nervously.

Anxious warmth settled in my chest. I held her close, my forehead resting against hers and enjoying her proximity and the anticipation that came with it.

My skin prickled as I brushed my nose against hers. Her mouth was relaxed and only an inch from mine, her breath soft on my lips as nervous energy danced in my bones.

My mouth tentatively skimmed against hers, when someone came stomping through the trees.

Pinch exited the tree line and walked toward the dock. Jex and I froze, then jumped apart immediately. I guess neither of us was ready for the judgment patrol.

"Nice night, eh?" Pinch called, his voice carrying from the shore.

We both glared at him so intensely it might actually strike him down. He returned a grin.

"Probably should get inside. There's much worse out there than me," he warned.

"Gee, thanks," Jex grumbled sarcastically, but I was the only one who heard it. I chuckled.

Jex followed me into the compound, our fingers laced with our thumbs playing. We stopped at the door to my temporary room. She brushed her hand across her mouth, as if still thinking of our almost kiss.

"So . . ." she said.

"So . . ." I replied. We each gave tense laughs. Awkwardness restored. *Thanks, Pinch.*

"It was nice of you to bring me out," she said, and I nodded.

She stood there for a few heartbeats longer, her eyes pleading with me to try again. The bubble out on the deck had burst, though. Pinch acted as a reminder of just how complicated things would be if we took the next step.

Jex pivoted to return to her room, while I planned a searing-cold shower. She combed her fingers through her hair and forced out a hard exhale.

Watching her walk away broke me a little.

I wanted her. Had wanted her since the moment I met her. I realized she was more important to me than anything someone might say about it.

"Screw it," I muttered and snatched her hand. Wrapping my arms around her in half a second, I drew her close and threw caution out the window.

Chapter Twelve

Jex

Ryan held me captive in his arms.

Finally!

His mouth found mine, and we devoured each other like we could only breathe in air from the other's lungs.

This was nothing like Eli. Eli's kiss was feather-light, hesitant and unsure. Ryan kissed me as if it were the last thing he would ever do.

A torrent of desire flashed across my skin. It was so dense and real I could taste it in the air. I could tell he felt it too, his body responding to my reaction. I skimmed my hands up his shoulders, around his neck, and let one play in his thick hair.

We stood in the hall, forgetting everything else, for what felt like an eternity that wasn't nearly long enough. He braced me against the door, his legs driving us together and his hips grinding against mine. Hands skimmed under my shirt, one arm around my waist and then up my back and playing with the band of my bra strap.

It ached wherever he touched me. Stars formed behind my lids, lost in the heady and intimate feel of his embrace.

Still, thoughts of Eli snuck in under the haze of lust. In the back of my mind, I thought about everything Brit told me about him. And Eli *really* didn't like Ryan.

Actually, what I wanted was pressed against my hip *and* stomach, but that was beside the point.

Reminders of the calamity with Eli reasserted logic, and it made me hesitate.

Could I do this to Eli?

No, I wasn't doing anything to Eli.

Was I?

I needed time to work through it.

My mind warred with itself while Ryan continued to barrage me with sensations. He moved his mouth to my neck and ear, his hands kneading the muscles along my spine.

I began to think I might not stop, to pull away, when my hand found the doorknob. I twisted it and we both fell backward into his borrowed room.

Ryan could have caught himself, except that he tried to save me as well, and I dragged him down with me. We lay there laughing on the floor before sanity returned. He held out a hand as if to help me up, but silly me still hadn't learned this lesson yet.

Ryan hauled me flush against him on the floor as he kissed me fiercely. His hands returned to their exploration, and I let out a frustrated sigh.

"Ryan, we shouldn't—"

"Never thought I'd see the day I'd have to fight with Eli for a woman," he muttered, releasing a heavy sigh.

"It's complicated."

"Evergreen statement," he said. "Look, I know the deal with him. No strings. Let's just have a little fun, Firefly. Are you okay with something more casual?"

Reading his expression through the needy haze proved challenging. I'd wanted him from the very second we'd met. It wasn't remotely exclusive with Eli; we weren't even dating. Eli was well aware there was something between Ryan and me.

Thinking about it more, it pissed me off all over again. Who was Eli or anyone else to say who I *coupled* with?

My eyes drifted down his strong frame, the gray sweats hanging dangerously low on his hips. The thinning white tee left little to the imagination from this close. I deserved an award for the gargantuan effort not to run my hands up those defined abs until tonight.

"I'd be interested in that," I replied, before I could stop myself.

"You should know I'm not going to be casual with anyone else, so you know where I stand." His face was serious.

"Way to bring down the mood, buzzkill." I laughed, but he chose that moment to stroke his hand between my legs. I groaned, tendrils of pleasure spreading from his touch.

We continued making out on the floor like hormonal teenagers, with him massaging my center through my leggings. I shifted on top of him, playing with the band of his sweats as I ground against his thick shaft. His hands gripped my ass, urging me to buck against him all the more.

Ryan flipped us over and I giggled. *Did I just giggle?* Yes. Yes, I did. What was he doing to me?

He lay between my legs, feathering kisses down my body and wrestling his shirt off one-handed. His shoulders were as defined as I'd imagined them, his body practically perfect and demanding that I lick each scar and mark. The devastating sensation of his skin on mine lit every nerve in my body.

He tried to push a hand under my leggings, but they were too tight, so he sat back and peeled them and my soaked underwear off altogether. He stared up at me from my feet like he was starving for me.

"Go sit in the chair," he instructed, his voice low and thick with need.

The bed was pushed into the corner, but a large, upholstered armchair sat beside it in the middle of the far wall. I took a seat carefully, not wanting to, *ahem*, get anything on the surface. The last thing I wanted to do was explain to Peter why Ryan's chair needed to be cleaned.

Ryan snatched at my knees so that my butt perched on the edge of the chair. Peering up at me from the floor, he spread my legs and grazed his hands along the inside of my thighs. My face burned a little in embarrassment, but his wicked grin beamed as he took in the sight of all of me on display for him.

Leaning his body between my legs, his lips continued to toy with mine as one of his hands met my core. His thumb found its target, the pad circling and playing with my clit. I sighed into his mouth as we continued playing our tongues at each other.

Heat built in my pussy and my breathing went erratic. He pushed in two thick digits, finger-fucking me slowly while his thumb worked. I moaned, his hands driving me steadily toward the edge.

Ryan smiled against my lips, then left a trail of kisses down my body. I moaned when his tongue found my slit, and I gripped the armrests so hard my fingers cramped.

My body thrummed along to the tune he played. That tongue did magical things, first making slow circles before licking straight up the center of my core and tonguing my entrance around his fingers. Oh, he was *so* good at this.

"Oh, *fuck me*," I moaned too loudly, lost in lust-fueled euphoria. I felt his smile.

"That's the plan," he paused to tell me. "I don't know if I'll be able to hold back much longer if you keep making those sounds."

For another long minute, he watched me strain and writhe from his hand alone and sucked my arousal obscenely from his lips.

Movement caught my eye, and I realized that we'd been too carried away and forgot to close the door. It probably wouldn't have been that big of a problem, given the time of night and that this was one of the last rooms in the row.

But when I looked up, I found Eli standing in the hall, watching Ryan bring me to the point of ecstasy. He froze, his face blank and his body stiff.

Ryan sensed me tense and turned to see what pulled my attention. He peered at Eli lurking in the hallway, but only shrugged before slinging my knee over one of the arms of the chair and returning to his task. He was giving Eli a better view, either to tell me he had no intention of stopping or to tell Eli to up his game. Or both, I guess.

Eli crossed his arms at me, but I was too far gone in the feel of Ryan's fingers and mouth.

Knowing Eli watched made it all the more erotic. On the one hand, I hated him and hated the expectation weighing on us. But a little part of me, a little heathen part of me, wouldn't have minded his inclusion. The thought of him grappling with me a lot more naked than normal flashed unbidden.

Ryan pinched my thigh to bring me back into the moment. My spine arched as his fingers curled inside of me. My eyes rolled as I hissed out in pleasure. He increased pressure and speed, playing my body like an instrument he'd mastered.

My orgasm had been steadily building, my hips urging him on. I breathed hard, my body writhing as I focused on the feel of Ryan's attention and his body braced between my legs.

He'd started stroking himself with his free hand, and I could sense his breathing kicking into higher gear. My hands wound through his hair, both playing with it and gripping the strands so that they directed his face. He let out his own groan in pleasure.

Through nearly closed eyes, I could see Eli still watching. He'd moved to lean against the doorjamb, his head tilted to the side with his arms crossed tightly over his chest. I expected him to be angry, but he looked . . . mesmerized. His eyes were transfixed on my face. He even sucked in a breath when Ryan made me gasp.

Ryan's lips and tongue plied my clit with attention as his fingers plunged in and out. The sensation overwhelmed me. The anticipation of being with Ryan after wanting him for so long, and the need for a release from the coiled tension, all built to a crescendo.

I was on the cusp, riding the edge of an orgasmic high, when Ryan made a completely unexpected move and pushed a finger into my ass.

I sucked in a sharp gasp. *Whoa.*

My back bowed, and a soft moan escaped me. His finger *there* hurt for a moment, then morphed into a pressure barely this side of uncomfortable. The intrusion felt more foreign than painful, both wrong and deliciously right all at once. He worked that finger in time with the rest, the added sensation almost overwhelming.

The assault on my senses was too much, too intense. The building tension finally crashed with his haymaker and I came *hard.*

The orgasm picked me up and threw me over the cliff with a force I was sixty percent certain would render me comatose. My grip on his hair tightened, the nails on my other hand digging deep into the arm of the chair. Every inch of my body contracted, the electric shock of pleasure lingering in my hands and face even as it settled.

Ryan continued licking and fingering me through it. I sighed out his name, using as much focus as I could muster to avoid waking the whole county. That seemed to have done it for him, and I heard him groan his own release.

Holy fuck, that was a top ten orgasm if there ever was one. Maybe even top five. I couldn't even fathom having it consistently. I'd never leave the room.

Here lies Jex, dead because she refused to do anything but come on Ryan's face.

The man of the hour beamed at me with a satisfied smile, tickling soft kisses along the inside of my thighs.

The orgasm faded into a lovely relaxation, still occasionally pulsing, but his fingers continued to play with my hypersensitive zones. He grinned sheepishly.

"So, ah, we probably should have talked about this before, but I got a little carried away, and I'm worried this is your first—"

"Yup, very first," I informed him.

"But you seem to—"

"Oh, yeah. Ten out of ten, would recommend. In fact, I'd be disappointed if you didn't do it again."

"Sorry, next time I get a wild idea, I'll talk to you about it first. No going rogue."

"Next time, huh?" I giggled again as he moved up to kiss me, still fingering me, and I didn't even mind it. It was a completely different kind of good than I was used to.

The kiss deepened, and I kind of liked that I could taste my release on him.

Eli cleared his throat.

Well, shit. I'd forgotten about him in my hazy, post-orgasm floating.

"Let's go," he grunted from the hallway. I glared at him with as much ESP as I could muster to make him leave.

"And what, pray tell, makes you think you get any say in what we're doing?" I asked tightly.

"We have training at six. If you don't go to your room immediately, I'm going to ride your ass a lot harder than Ryan just did."

Hmmm. The turn of phrase had the opposite effect of what he intended. I could plainly see that he'd enjoyed the show fine based on the sizeable bulge in his pants.

Dickhead, literal and figurative.

Sigh, fine. I gave Ryan a lingering kiss before standing up to collect my clothes.

"To be continued," I murmured in his ear.

"Sweet dreams," he said through one of those throw-your-panties smiles.

"All of you," I replied, making sure Eli would hear it.

I wasn't about to let Eli get all angsty and impatient as I squeezed into the leggings. My room wasn't far, so I balled everything up and strode out into the hall in my bra with my naked ass bare to the wind.

Eli followed. I could practically feel the daggers as he stared angrily at me. As I walked into my room, he smacked my ass with a hard *slap* of his hand that made me yelp.

"Sleep well, buttercup. You're going to need it," he called through my closed door.

* * *

The next morning, my shoes were laced, my baggies were tied tight, and my hair was wrapped in a half-looped pony. I'd gone the extra mile of wrapping a bandana around my hairline to keep the sweat from my eyes. I might even be learning what to expect.

Jack and Eli were practicing forms on the back deck. Their skin glistened in the bright sun. The motions were smooth and strong, power radiating from the movement. They acted in perfect unison, a well-practiced routine they had obviously performed together a thousand times. Their faces were mirrors of relaxed harmony. They seemed so content.

I watched through the glass doors, not wanting to disturb them. I didn't have the heart to break it up, especially not when it meant more time dealing with last night's fallout *and* the room-from-hell.

Deciding that my morning was free, I didn't know what to do with myself. I'd already had the first ration of artificial happiness and carbohydrates. I was amped up for more suffering and didn't want to go to my room. Even the idea of lounging in the swing chair made me antsy. I searched for something productive to do.

Wooden benches flanked the atrium's sliders, and I folded myself into one. I sat sideways, intent on practicing my mental control. That would make Henry proud.

At the end of the last practice session, Henry suggested using my hands to visualize my essence as a tangible thing. I cleared my mind and began to control my breathing, my right-hand palm up while I willed a fireball into existence.

Not even a spark flickered to life.

After a sold ten minutes of this, my hand cramped and my patience wore thin.

Changing tactics, I recalled the night at the gas station. Walking myself through it like Henry had, my body started to heat. The process was slow, and arduous, and frustrating, but eventually I managed to bring up the faintest ring. A fine sheen of sweat covered my body as I worked at it for the next half hour.

It's just another part of you, like an unused muscle, Henry'd said. *You're connecting to a limb that hasn't fully matured.*

For all Henry's gruff manner, he could be patient with my failures, if unyielding and occasionally patronizing. He reminded me a little of my Dad.

I quickly shoved that thought into its mental room before someone passed by and figured out I was still just three depressed toddlers in a trench coat.

Forming the bubble was all well and good, but my essence seemed to default to the protective measure when I needed it, regardless of my control. The real work was in offensive skills.

I pictured Eli on our first day in the Practice Room, how he'd tried to recreate the fight with the drunk.

Replaying the alley altercation, I imagined how it might have gone if I'd used literal fire power.

My hand ached from stretching it taut, but no flames appeared.

Eli could be such an ass, but I'd admit I felt a little guilty about the night before.

Not about Ryan; never about Ryan.

But my relationship with Eli was a delicate balance. If Pairs were for life, how could I possibly reject that? Even if Eli could be, well, Eli.

I wanted them both. There was no getting around it.

I knew myself well enough to say it would be impossible not to fall in love with Ryan. Not because of the explosive orgasm, although that was a major plus. Ryan's chivalrous nature made me feel so safe and wanted. I loved it when he took care of me. He made the harsh reality of the world fade and let me be at peace.

The whole situation pissed me off, frankly. Gripping the bench, my mind railed at the idiocy of the system I'd been thrust into. The futility of my anger was its own frustration.

Exhaling deeply and closing my eyes, I forced myself to concentrate on the task at hand.

I envisioned the drunk in the alley.

I felt the knife at my neck.

Smelled the stink of his breath.

Tasted blood as I bit into my cheek.

My body began to heat, finding that ember deep in my chest and coaxing it to life.

Straining to keep my breathing even, I twisted my hands over my heart and attempted to transfer the flames between them.

I thought of cold fingers grabbing my shoulders.

Of my feet shuffling over the ground.

And then I rewrote history.

I imagined that when he grabbed me, my skin heated so that it burned his hands.

Because the more I thought about it, he wasn't merely kidnapping me.

The flare of energy emitting from my hands grew.

I imagined building my fireball and hurling it in his direction.

Because the more I thought about it, he wanted to move me to a location where he could control the outcome.

The energy between my palms blistered hotter, my already-primed anger cheering it along.

I imagined finding that spark of life in him, the one that kept him warm and alive, and snuffing it out. I imagined stealing it for myself.

Because the more I thought about it, I knew he'd meant to kill me and make me disappear.

The exercise carved my focus down to the dense ball of fire between my palms. I lost sight of the source of heat, assuming that the well in my chest would supply it.

I failed to notice the first threads of cold weaving into that supply.

Cool, foreign strands slithered out and collected in the sphere, the contrast stark despite how the energy interlaced and blended with my own.

Shit, what had I done?

Chapter Thirteen

Cool threads melded into the fireball. I gasped, my breathing hard and palms sweaty. I smashed the fireball to the pavers, thinking it would burst harmlessly without flammable material. Instead, it lit the brush at the edge of the pathway on fire.

This area of the atrium was lush, so there shouldn't be any dry kindling. It was part of the reason I'd chosen this particular bench.

Leaping for the fire extinguisher, I rushed back and smothered the flames before they spread too far.

Just a tiny, itty-bitty, minute amount of property damage about ten-feet deep in a semi-circle around the bench. No one would notice, right?

The residual chill lingered even after my body came fully under control.

So much for mental discipline.

Shaking out my hands, I settled in to take another shot at it—really, I would—when Georgia trotted past. She moved with purpose, but I called her name and she looped around in my direction.

"Georgie-baby, what are you doing out here?" I cooed. I could have sworn I'd closed the bedroom door. I didn't want my feline friend to become a nuisance, given I was regularly a nuisance myself.

The cat only purred, nudging my crossed legs. She sat primly for a moment, holding my attention, before turning to walk away. After a few steps, she glanced back at me and jerked a summoning head shake.

"What is it, girl? Is Timmy in the well?" I gasped dramatically, my hand on my chest with exaggerated wide eyes.

The cat swiveled to glare pointedly at me as if to say *kiss my furry butt.* I'd figured Trish was in there and had my confirmation.

My whiskered friend took off, forcing me to chase after her. She sprinted through the winding pathways of the atrium, and we played our own weird game of cat-and-mouse as Trish-Georgia evaded my attempts to catch her. It was actually kind of fun.

I lost sight of her once as she ducked through the fronds of a set of large Queen Anne palms, but managed to pick up the trail after briefly battling with the foliage. She took a left at the "T" by the front door and headed toward the library.

As we approached, she slowed her pace to walk more casually. We stopped behind the wall before the open doorway. Henry and Peter's muted voices sounded from within. Georgia prowled into the room, her tail up.

"We shouldn't push her, Peter. She's still young." Henry's voice was assertive but not demanding. I could tell he tread lightly, trying not to step on Peter's toes. "What Jack's been through is difficult enough."

"We are only asking her to elaborate on the interrogations and give a better description of who took her," Peter replied. "Other than the calling card and Delaney's involvement, she's disclosed almost nothing. It's imperative we learn which of the Cole's people attacked so we can respond accordingly."

"And if it's worse than we thought?"

"We need information and she is the only way we can get it. It's bigger than her. She can't claim memory loss to avoid having to deal with it. I understand being abducted is distressing, but we can't protect her without knowing what to protect from," Peter rationalized.

Henry raised his voice, the anger clear in his tone. "She is traumatized enough. She's blocking the memories. Recalling the details asks her to relive it."

"And we should endanger others to shelter her from her own experiences? This could make her character stronger. We both know she isn't terribly resilient. It's not her fault; we baby her. All of us, not just Eli. Perhaps if she were to suffer her life, it would harden her."

"Is that what it's come to? Harm her to help her?" The tension overflowed from the room and swept into the hallway.

"We will do what we must," Peter's stern tone replied. "As the Nell of the Southeast, I have the authority to issue directives. It's not your decision to make."

"Then I want to be the one to question her. It will be easier, coming from me."

"Fine," Peter acquiesced. "Ask Pinch to assist if need be. Eli mentioned Tai Chi at the back. I'm sure he will want to be involved as well, but remind him what we discussed earlier."

He paused a moment before continuing.

"It would probably be easier if I am not there. It'll let him curse me openly instead of trying to hide it."

The room fell silent. Henry must have exited through the side door. We'd approached from the opposite side of the easiest path to the deck. I paused, waiting for Georgia to slip out the door.

"You can come in now, Jex," Peter called to me.

Shit. Ninja-sneakiness failure yet again.

I turned the corner, head hung and aiming for penitent. Peter motioned to an open couch beside him. He sat in his favored spot, rubbing behind Georgia-Trish's ears. Was that a little weird? It felt a little weird.

"Was it that obvious?" I stared at the carpet, afraid to meet his eye. My shoe dug little grooves into the weave.

"No, I don't think Henry was aware. You can blame Trish. She hasn't quite perfected being a house cat.

She'll need to practice more if she expects to play at spymaster with Georgia."

My calico huffed at him.

"Are we in trouble?" I asked.

"It was a personal conversation. I'm not sure all involved would appreciate the intrusion."

Henry didn't come across as a very prideful person, but Peter seemed to think his censure would embarrass him. I chewed on my bottom lip.

"Will there be a punishment?"

"No, I think that would be counterproductive. Remember, eavesdroppers rarely hear well of themselves."

He would know, given his Duality.

Excusing us, I followed Georgia-Trish out into the hallway. We wandered aimlessly for about half an hour, with a stopover to the pantry for kitty treats. Without more direction, I surprised myself and entered the Practice Room of my own free will. Perhaps masochism was a side effect of my enhanced essence.

Needing to burn-off excess energy, I struggled to free one of the heavy, standing kick bags from the corner. Leveraging against the wall, I finally managed to budge it half a foot before shoving it over. After awkwardly walk-dragging it out, I heaved it to a standing position.

Off to a great start.

Mimicking Eli's demonstration from the day before, I went through as many kicking techniques as I could remember. I progressed to punches when he came through the door. He seemed as shocked to find me practicing as I was to end-up in this room.

"You need to get changed," he said. I frowned. My perfect outfit wasn't going to get any use?

He tilted the bag on its edge to roll it against the wall with almost no effort at all.

"Where are we going?"

"A contact got us a lead on one of your attackers. He's in a hospital outside Kissimmee."

"The burns were that serious?" I cringed. Even if he was *evil*, or whatever, it still chafed that I'd hurt someone that badly.

"No, not him. The one you handcuffed. We still haven't located either the wind-wielder or the guy who put you in the trunk."

"Then how did he end up in the hospital?"

Handcuffs couldn't have done that much damage.

"He stupidly tried to take a knife to Pinch after we car-jacked them. It did not work out well for him. We've been checking the hospitals, figuring he'd need real medical attention. Transfusions, surgery. Pinch is effective."

"You want to go to the hospital and question him?"

"No, I want to *escort* him from the hospital, bring him to a safe house, and then *question* him."

Something about the way he'd said "escort" and "question" raised the hair on my neck.

"And why am I involved?"

"Because Pinch is dead to the world at the moment, and you're the only other person who was there that night and can identify him. Plus, Peter seems to think it will help if we do something as a team, and that you need experience, and that he's incapacitated so it should be low risk, and a lot of other reasons I don't feel like discussing." He gave a dismissive hand gesture. "Ask him if you want to know."

Hurrah. I was wrong earlier. They weren't going to wait until I was ready to send me into harm's way; they're doing it immediately. It'd be nice if there was more of a ramp-up to the felonies.

"Do I get a choice?" I muttered.

"No."

"Don't suppose I could talk you into bringing someone else with us?"

We needed a buffer. This was a disaster waiting to happen.

"It's one hospitalized guy. I think we can handle it."

* * *

Eli

Our target recuperated in a crowded building surrounded by employees, visitors, and the occasional police officer.

We stared at the hospital directory map in the lobby. Jex suggested we buy a floral arrangement at the gift shop so that we looked like we belonged. It was actually a smart suggestion.

I wasn't expecting her to take much of an active role in this job. She was still skittish about employing her training and Duality, not to mention flighty, careless. . .

I let out a breath. Jex's training, really all of our time together, had been a steep learning curve for us both. She might vacillate between cursing me as a "hard-ass" and a "tight-ass," but she still made progress, so I called it a win. It shocked the hell out of me when I found her practicing on her own.

"He'd be out of post-operative care by now," I noted, shifting the ugly green vase filled with daisies to my other hand.

Removing my phone from my pocket, I checked the time. Hospitals had cameras and guards; we needed to limit how long we stay here. Jex eyed my old Nokia phone with a frown.

"You get that thing at an antique store?" she chided.

"It's unhackable. Intensive care is on four."

"Only because no one knows how to use it anymore. Post-critical care is on seven."

"You didn't see the wounds; Pinch did not hold back. He's lucky he survived."

Pinch was pissed the fuck off over what they'd done to you. Admittedly, we'd all gotten protective of her, not just Pinch and Ryan.

"You only stay in the ICU until you're stable. Pinch and Stabby McKnifeWounds got into it, what, a week ago? Maybe more? He'd be improving by now."

Again with that attitude. Normally, I liked my women a bit bratty. Jex took it to a whole new level, but I couldn't do a thing about it right now. I'd purposefully limited the social part of our relationship.

Jex needed to focus on controlling her Duality, and on acclimating her body to accept her power come the Acceptance at her birthday. It could kill her if she didn't adequately prepare.

"We should ask someone," I suggested.

"Yes, I'm sure that conversation won't raise any suspicions. *Excuse me, where can we find the man with the handcuff bruises and stab wounds? We need to steal him for a bit.*"

Another deep breath. It's like she purposefully goaded me, just to see how far she could push my control. Somewhere out there, the fates had a fan-fucking-tastic time laughing at our pairing.

Our bickering was starting to attract attention when Jex's eyes narrowed and focused on the help desk.

A teenage, fragile-looking receptionist manned the hospital's information desk. She drew little scribbles on one of those monthly calendars that doubled as a desk blotter and chewed on the temple tip on her glasses.

Rushing at her at full steam, Jex wailed incoherently and collapsed onto the raised countertop. Her arms flailed about, howls of pain and agony ringing against the echoing hallways.

"Where is he? Where is he?" she moaned as she beat her head with her hands.

It took a second for the surprise to wear off, but I attempted my best shell-shocked expression and stuttered my way through the phrases, "knife attack," "emergency room," and "last week."

Face pale, the receptionist furiously tapped at the keyboard.

"Sam Jones?" she asked. "Take the elevator to the seventh floor and it's on the wing to the right."

Wrenching Jex away from the desk, I practically carried her to the elevator while she keened and went limp in my arms. We continued the charade until the doors closed safely.

Smart. Very smart. A bit impulsive and attention-getting, but it did the job.

"That was easier than expected," I noted.

"Speak for yourself. I'll be red enough to look like a tourist out of SPF for at least ten minutes."

She combed her hair with her fingers, fanning her face to alleviate some of the redness. At least she wasn't flushed with anger at me for once.

On the seventh floor, we hustled away from the nurses' station to a room at the end of the hall. There were remarkably few people on the floor, and we slipped into the room unhindered.

"Sam Jones" was asleep in his bed. Machines buzzed and chirped at regular intervals. The little blue and yellow flowers on his white hospital gown contrasted starkly with his growing beard. I left the flower vase on the cabinet of Jones' roommate.

"Ugh, hospital stink," Jex muttered.

We began shutting the machines down, one at a time. Starting with those monitoring vital signs, we first found the buttons to mute alarms, then carefully unplugged or flipped power switches. I expected a nurse to fly through the door from some unknown silent alarm, but no one interrupted us.

We wanted "Jones," or whatever his name was, as compliant as possible for the trip out. We saved the morphine drip for last. Jex had done pretty well until now, but she cringed at the prospect of cutting off his painkiller. She hesitated, staring at the line, so I switched it off for her and removed it myself.

With a glance at the septuagenarian asleep on the other side of the curtain, she rolled over a collapsible wheelchair. I hauled Jones off the bed and dumped him in it. She moved his banana bag to a hook on the side and shoved the plastic bag with his personal effects into the pouch on the backrest.

"Now what?" she asked. I cracked the door, but nurses patrolled the corridor. They'd know Jones shouldn't be out of bed.

"Once we leave the floor, he's any other patient." Jex whispered.

"What do you suggest?"

"I'll call the elevator. When it arrives, you wheel him down while I hold the doors. We get to the first floor and out the front like we're going for a walk."

Nodding, I stood behind the wheelchair.

The door creaked as she peeked out. No one was in the hallway, but this was by far the most dangerous part of the escape plan. Jones' nurses would recognize him, but not us.

Jex breathed deep for a moment, calming herself, and casually walked out the door and down the corridor. She hit the down-arrow button on the elevator panel and furiously twirled that ring on her finger. I'd tried to break her of the nervous habit, but she refused to relent. The ring had become worse than a safety blanket to her.

A nurse checked in on patients at the other end of the wing. She'd just entered a room when the elevator doors slid open. I schooled my face into a blank mask and anxiously anticipated her signal.

Now or never.

Jex waved me out, and I swung the door to Jones' room open.

Pushing the wheelchair into the hallway, I forced a nonchalant pace for the trek to the elevator bank. The wheels squeaked slightly on the tile. Seconds ticked by with excruciating sluggishness.

To Jex's credit, she did not break into tears. She dutifully guarded the doors, preventing them from closing on us.

As I finally wheeled into the elevator car, I glanced one last time into the hallway. No one ran after us, but the nurse left the room at the end. She shuffled her way toward the nurse's station on the other side of the elevator bank. Her path crossed right in front of our escape route.

Jex pressed the "Door Close" button like an over-excited five-year-old. The doors inched together as the nurse walked by.

The nurse glanced over her shoulder, not paying attention. Eyes flitted across us in the elevator car, then did a double-take as her face went stark white. She glanced at Jones—her patient, near unconscious in a wheelchair—then at Jex, and locked eyes with me for barely a second as the doors shut.

"Fuckity dicksticks," Jex cursed. That was a new one.

It was too late for the nurse to stop the elevator, but she'd definitely figured out that something was wrong.

Jex's hand paused over the panel after pressing the ground-floor button. Her eyes zoomed in every direction as she worked out a plan, then hit the button for three.

Her gaze roved over my frame for a moment. As she eyed me, she drew her long curls into a looped ponytail.

Stripping off her shirt, she stood in front of me in a revealing maroon bra and jeans. Wide, expectant eyes peered at me.

My gaze instantly went to her tits, and how the lace wrapped perfectly around them. It took a gargantuan effort to push away thoughts of everything I was dying to do to her.

I'd mostly avoided allowing our relationship to dip into more physical territory. Adding sex meant yet another distraction. She needed to focus on her own body, not mine. Pushing her to succeed had become my singular focus.

Mostly. One little slip, one kiss, which I'd thought might help me gain clarity and assure myself I was doing the right thing.

It made it worse.

Walking in on Jex and Ryan should have turned me off entirely. I'd been livid when I found them. I kiss her, then she's screwing around with *him*?

I had a long, hard think after that, debating whether I even wanted to see this through. There were platonic Pairs, although I'd never heard of a platonic true Pair.

Except, I definitely didn't want that. If I wasn't careful, I might lose her to him.

I'd planned to wait to pursue her until after the Acceptance passed. Now, though . . .

Watching her come, hearing her moan his name . . . it made me hard just thinking about it. I'd never thought myself a voyeur, but I couldn't get the image out of my mind. I imagined her with that same expression of ecstasy, only it was my name she praised.

"Well, take your shirt off," she said, snapping me out of my thousandth fantasy.

"Now isn't the time for that."

"No, perv, we hide in plain sight." She removed the bag of Jones' clothes and thrust them at me. "We're switching shirts. They're searching for a curly-haired woman in a blue v-neck and a man in a white t-shirt. We're going to give them a woman in a t-shirt with a bun and a man in whatever Jones wore when he checked in last week."

Shit, I'd completely zoned out, all because she stood in front of me shirtless. For all I criticized her about keeping it together under pressure, there I was allowing her to be my blind spot.

After throwing on my shirt and knotting it at the waist, Jex rolled her jeans up to her knees.

Jones had been wearing a black muscle shirt and plaid button-down. At least the bloodstains were barely noticeable, even if my abs showed through the knife slits. I wore the cover-up loose and unbuttoned to keep blood from flaking off on it.

Jex found it extra funny to stick her fingers through the slits and poke my stomach when I wasn't looking. The woman was going to drive me insane.

When the elevator doors slid open for the third floor, she motioned for me to wheel Jones out. My eyebrows drew together as I frowned.

"Why here?" I asked.

"The nurse knows. We can't go out the first floor anymore. We have to go down the stairs at the back, or maybe find a freight elevator."

We weren't able to find the freight elevator, and as the time ticked-down the paranoia became unbearable. We needed to get out of the hospital; the longer we spent wandering around, the more likely we'd be caught.

Frustrated, we found the most isolated stairwell possible and carefully, step by step, rolled him down to the first floor.

We finally located an exit leading to the loading dock. The ramp would make it easy to get Jones to ground level. Several men loitered on the other side of the bay, though, apparently on a smoke break.

The trip down the stairs hadn't been kind to Jones's wounds, which seeped crimson through the thin hospital gown.

Thankfully, I'd parked the car on the side of the building nearest the exit door. Jex's eyes shifted between Jones's lifeless form and the group of guys.

"Move the car, Eli. Get as close to the loading bay as you can and stuff him in the back seat."

"What about those guys?"

"I'll take care of the guys."

"How are you going to manage that?"

She looked at me, incredulous, but I shook my head and shrugged at her.

"You're well aware I have boobs, Eli. I plan to Erin Brockovich them."

"You're going to *what*?"

Scooting her jeans low, she rolled up the shirt and tied the knot as high and tight as she could make it without leaning into public nudity. The bra showed under my threadbare shirt, the outline and design peeping through. She ran her teeth over her lips and pulled her hair out of the bun and tossed it around a bit.

Fuck me, it took her barely ten seconds to become the center of every male fantasy.

"Well?" she asked again.

I stared at her, speechless.

When I didn't respond, she huffed an annoyed breath and burst the door open. The grand entrance immediately drew the attention of our group of obstacles, and she strutted over to them. I watched from a crack in the door, shaking my head at her antics.

"Excuse me! I said, *EXCUSE ME*!" she called.

They stopped talking entirely to ogle as she sashayed over. She even added a hitch to the sway of her hips, accentuating the hourglass figure. Couldn't even blame them. With that wild hair and smooth skin on display, she looked like Aphrodite come to life.

She positioned herself away from the door hiding Jones. Clever girl.

"Hey, baby, can I be your future ex-husband?" one of the guys asked. Yeah, that was original.

I sprinted out, down the ramp, and around the corner.

"I'm sooooooo lost," she responded, stretching out the "so," making it three words instead of one.

But then I'd turned the corner and couldn't hear anything else.

Idling, I maneuvered the car around the building and stopped by the ramp.

Jex had twisted the upper half of her body, pointing to the opposing side of the building. It made her back arch, and the shirt lifted another half-inch. Each one of the guys watched her with rapt attention.

"What's your name, sweetheart?" a burly guy in a janitor's uniform inquired.

"Call me Jessie," she purred.

I would never let her hear the end of this.

As I rolled the wheelchair down the ramp, Jones' leg fell out of the stirrup and I had to stop to fix it.

Jex's breath hitched at the hiccup, but the guys carried on, undoubtedly misinterpreting her response.

"I'll show ya' the way personal if ya' like," the guy offered. His southern accent slurred the words together while he talked to and leered at her breasts.

"Oh, I don't know. I'm here with my boyfriend, but somehow I wandered off."

She giggled—Jex fucking *giggled* at the guy.

"He can get *real* jealous." She pouted. "I'd love for you to point me in the right direction."

The group pivoted toward the door I'd come from—as I hefted Jones into the car at that exact moment.

"No!" she squeaked, and searched for words. "I came from over there and no luck! There are too many hallways. I get turned around a lot."

She flipped her hair and tugged at the shirt collar. No one noticed the guy with crazy eyes shoving a bleeding man into a car.

With Jones loaded into the backseat of the car, I stowed the wheelchair out of sight in the stairwell. Throwing the passenger-side door open, I gestured at the vehicle.

"Oh, silly me, there he is," she said to the captivated crowd. "Better get going!"

She sprinted to our waiting car and practically dove through the open door. I peeled out of the lot and nearly T-boned a car getting into traffic.

Once we made it to the intersection, I pulled the bloody shirts off and grimaced. *Disgusting.*

Jex had done well. Very well. We made it out of the hospital with only a nominal amount of interference.

I had to admit I was impressed. Perhaps I'd underestimated her?

No, she could still be lazy and careless . . . but when she set her mind to something, the world would bend for her.

"That was kind of amazing," I admitted.

"What's amazing is that men will fall for anything when boobs are involved." She cackled.

"No, I mean the whole thing. The receptionist, changing clothes, those guys. It was brilliant."

"That sounded dangerously like a compliment."

"I think we'll live, *Jessie*."

She grimaced.

"I will burn your ass to ash if you ever call me that again."

Chapter Fourteen

Jex

An abandoned gas station off the turnpike served as the safe house. It stank of stale hot dogs and congealed slushie mix, thanks to the boarded-up windows. Red bands tied the nozzles to the pumps and the sign announcing prices read, "O t of Servi e."

We carried Jones in through the back door and heaved him onto a table. In the refurbished storage room, clean, white drywall met clean, gray linoleum. Eli retrieved his phone and made a call.

We set to work, handcuffing Jones to the steel table at his wrists and ankles. After resituating the drip on a stand, Eli started cataloging wounds and treatments. I checked the injuries, not really knowing what to look for, but it appeared a few of the stitches had torn. Eli made another note on his chart.

"Do we try and fix him or is Peter sending someone?" I asked.

"We wait. Lita is a doctor, she'll know what to do."

I cleaned the cuts with alcohol and checked Jones for any other damage. He was practically unconscious, so it made it easy to manipulate his limbs in the search. We worked quickly while I called out injuries and Eli made notes. He lined up instruments for Lita's use.

Lita, Maxon, and Ryan arrived about an hour later. The sun shone a bright triangle of light through the door into the dim room.

The three of them gaped visibly when they saw us. Eli and I looked at each other, and realized we were both still in costume. Eli's bare chest greeted our guests, and I still sported the full whoregalia. Embarrassed, I ran to the bathroom, grabbing the bag we'd stuffed our clothes into on the elevator.

With the v-neck reinstalled and my hair tied up tastefully, I stepped into the storage room and threw the bag to Eli.

"I kind of liked it better before," Ryan whispered as he leaned in behind me. I gave his arm a good smack.

Lita frowned over Jones' stitches. Muttering under her breath, she used a hook-like needle to sew the wounds shut. Maxon and Eli were seated at a card table they'd set-up during my retreat to the bathroom.

"He's going to be out for a while," Lita told us.

"What's a while?" Eli asked.

"Couple of hours at the least. We should take shifts watching him."

"I'll take the first shift," Maxon offered. "You two look beat. Head back to Haven."

Exhaustion sapped the last of the energy reserves in my weak muscles. There had been too many days without real sleep on top of the adrenaline crash. Eli rubbed his face and neck, too.

"Come on," Ryan said. "I'll drive you. Peter gave you my car anyway. I only came to get it back."

"We got blood on your seats," I admitted, wincing.

Ryan being Ryan, he only shrugged and said he could get it out. I absently wondered how many times you had to spill blood on your upholstery before you knew offhand how to remove it.

We shuffled out to the car. Ryan piled me into the front passenger seat beside him, got in, and placed a possessive hand on my thigh.

Eli looked like he might try to wedge into the seat with me just to spite him. Fatigue won, and he tucked into the backseat to nap for the ride home.

* * *

A glass of Dr. Pepper fizzed happily on the kitchen counter. I perched on a barstool, the caffeine from my earlier glass already zipping through my system. I might be violating my restriction with the third glass, but I rationalized that the count reset when you've slept for eight hours.

It was late, well after dinner, but Lita stood in the kitchen scooping the soft middle out of a football-shaped bun that looked like it had been soaked in something spicy. She stuffed ingredients in the middle and popped it into the microwave.

"Chorizo and beans?" I asked her.

She began mind-willing the microwave plate to turn and dismissively refused to look away.

"It's a pambazo." She placed a heavy emphasis on the "ba," and I realized she had the slightest accent.

"Is Jones going to live?"

I'd been awake for all of half an hour, so she was the first person I'd run into. It was entirely possible he no longer breathed.

"Yes," she answered in a short, crisp tone. I got the distinct feeling she didn't want to talk to me. Still, I gave her an "and?" hand wave.

The microwave beeped, and she removed the plate before turning to eat at the counter.

"We will know more later. Pinch is particularly good at getting information," she answered.

Thinking of what Pinch would probably do to get the information was a bridge I didn't want to cross right then.

"What happens to him now?"

"They pick him up tomorrow morning for custody. He'll be tried and probably jailed."

Tried and jailed? The concept of a penal system never crossed my mind.

"You put them in prison?" I asked.

She heaved a sigh and forcefully tore at the sandwich with her fingers.

"The DOJ have a specialized facility," she answered. "It's somewhere in Kansas."

"Not Area 51?" I grinned.

Lita barely even looked at me. The Arctic wasn't as cold as her shoulder. Can't win over everyone, I suppose. I took a long drag on my soda.

"So, what do you think? Will he give up his buddies?" I prompted.

"You'll have to ask Peter. I don't know he wants others to have that information."

The subtext read, *I don't know he wants* you *to have that information.*

"I think I'll do that," I told her, and ventured with my liquid energy to find him.

I had a strong hunch Peter would be in the library. It seemed like the unofficial war room. Or maybe it was the official war room.

In any event, I was dead on. He and Henry poured over more stacks of paper on the conference table. Neither of them spoke, instead passing the pages between them. I cleared my throat as I walked in.

"Jex, to what do we owe the pleasure?" Peter asked.

"Just curious whether we were able to learn anything by our foray into the world of kidnapping. It was nice being the abductor for a change."

"Yes, Eli has already provided a report. Highly creative with the receptionist." They both smiled wide in an expression worryingly close to pride. It made me uneasy, especially since most strong expressions were foreign on the normally unreadable Peter.

"I've recently learned that a hysterically crying woman makes people uncomfortable," I replied.

Henry's smile slipped. His poker face wasn't nearly as good as Peter's, but he'd get there.

"It would seem so," Peter said. "Mr. Jones has confessed to taking part in your attack, not that we needed him to."

"And he's going to be arrested."

I wanted to make sure Lita hadn't been feeding me a line. She'd been unwilling to talk to me, and I didn't know her well enough to detect subtle lies. Peter wouldn't bend the truth. He might choose his words carefully, but he would be honest.

He surprised me by confirming it.

"You work with the DOJ?" I squeaked.

"Technically, we *are* the DOJ. They integrated us into the Department in the '40s. Who do you think owns this house and the land it sits on, who funds the operation?"

"Everyone here is some kind of special agent? *Brit* is black ops?"

The laughable image of Brit fighting off four guys using only their bare hands skimmed across my mind.

"Brit is quite adept, you may want to rethink your assumptions. She is a Valen after all," Peter noted.

"We still operate independently; they only lend us support. Although, it would be fun to have an action figure," Henry said with a snicker.

My mind shuffled through my memories, readjusting what I'd thought in the moment.

"If you're—if *we're* the DOJ, then how did Pinch get Jones to talk?"

Peter seemed to sense the underlying question. I had assumed something very unfortunate and painful prompted Jones' sudden disclosure.

"He was not harmed in the interrogation. Thanks to Lita, he's probably in better shape than he was at the hospital. Pinch is quite persuasive without the use of force. We are not the Kier, and I am not the Cole."

I took that to mean Pinch had scared him into talking, which didn't seem legal either, but it wasn't worth arguing over.

"He has provided us some insight into why they tried to take you. He also divulged the names of his fellow Kier. We are searching for them now."

I didn't think it was worth parsing the fact they actually had taken me, either.

"There was a specific reason? They're the bad guys. You'd think kidnapping the good guys was in the job description."

"You've caught the attention of a man named Arthur Cole, and his second-in-command, Frank Delaney. They lead the Kier's Southeastern sect."

"He's 'the Cole' or his last name is Cole?"

"Both. When named to lead a region, we take the title as a name for continuity and as a rite of passage. Nell is both my name and title."

"Did Jones say what the Cole-Cole wants?"

"They believe your talents would be better suited to the Kier's way of life. My guess is they were hoping to indoctrinate you into their beliefs."

"I don't understand. I thought my lineage is with the Clara. If that's the case, I can't be one of them?"

"The Cole is exceptionally good at manipulating people. He may believe you can be convinced or deceived to follow him."

More brainwashing. What's with this place?

"He thinks he can con me into becoming evil?"

That made little sense. I couldn't understand how someone would be able to influence me to steal, kidnap, or kill.

Granted, I'd already both stolen and kidnapped, if for the greater good.

"You are somewhat of a special circumstance. It's not something you should worry about. You are where you should be and will remain."

He'd said it with such conviction that I almost believed it, too. Almost. I needed to know why the Cole was so eager to convert me. If I could negate it on my own, he might leave me be.

"But why does he want me, in particular? I'm not trained or useful. Ignisunda isn't even that uncommon or powerful."

Henry'd let slip during our training that ignisunda was middling in its importance in the hierarchy of Dualities.

"You are not within the normal parameters in many ways, and your Duality is one of them. You seem to have a much deeper power reserve than we'd expect, despite the lack of training. Until you came to us, we'd believed you had very little use of any ability. I suspect you will continue to develop and may even be able to manifest your water in some tangible way. We will know for sure after your birthday in July."

Birthday. Right. Every time I successfully blocked that black spot out of my mind, someone had to remind me.

"There's something I don't understand. If I'm supposed to be tied to my Valen, why isn't Eli in danger?"

"The Kier may believe that, given how new your bond is, they can break it easily and connect you to someone they approve of. They tend to discard partners they feel are inferior."

Fantastic, another insta-boyfriend, only this time he'd be an egomaniac . . . or, *more* of an egomaniac.

"Did Jones explain why they took Jack?" I inquired.

"No, although he may not have been a party to it. The Cole likes to compartmentalize his operations. He likely has multiple facets of one scheme running concurrently."

"So, we have no idea what he's after other than that he wants an Amory protégé."

My statement made Henry frown.

"It's only a matter of time, and not something to concern yourself with. As I've said, you are safe and secure. This is your home. No one is going to force you to do anything you don't want to do."

Except spend eighty hours a week in the Practice Room with a maniac who took pleasure in tormenting me.

"There is one thing," Henry said. He removed a book from the table. It was old and worn, the brown binding creased and ripped.

"Aster dropped this off for you earlier. You need to read it, cover-to-cover," he instructed. "No exclusions."

Hefting the tome in my hand, I turned it over to inspect it. There was no writing on the cover, no title page, nothing to give it a name.

"What is it?"

"Think of it as a guidebook for Dualities."

"Will it tell me how to handle my Valen?" I muttered. Henry ignored the sass.

"It is more of our history, and an explanation of the true world. Please be careful with it, copies are rare. It's not something we like to keep written," he explained.

I enjoyed a good book, but reading an encyclopedia cover-to-cover seemed a bit much.

"Do I have a time frame for this assignment?"

"It's not an assignment. You should want to do it. You must know and understand this information."

He gave me a serious face. I hugged the book to my chest while backing out of the room, but successfully suppressed the urge to salute.

* * *

Figuring I should finish my homework sooner rather than later, I looped around to the swing chair in the center of the atrium. There were a lot of people loitering, though, and the chair and hammock were occupied. Peter must have called everyone in after Jones started talking.

My bedroom still felt a little claustrophobic, so I headed to the back deck instead. The picnic tables were busy, too, but a full moon lit the sky. Whether I made any reading progress or not, I really couldn't sit inside any longer.

Doja Cat's "Boss Bitch" blasted through my earbuds for motivation as I wound through the trees toward the reservoir, hoping there might be something closer to the shore. I relied on Doja so much to keep me moving that she and I were basically best friends.

Mosquitoes raged in the heat, but at least nearer the shore it was tolerable. I walked along the water, spying a set of loungers and a small table on a platform about a hundred yards from the dock. Little, white lights lined the edge, like the dock, and a set of four torches planted at each corner reeked of Citronella even from here.

A figure lay on one of the loungers, but the space was plenty big enough to share. Plus, there was a table, and the book Henry'd given me was hefty, so whoever used the lounger would just have to suffer my presence.

Stepping up onto the deck, I found the watertight box of matches and lit each lantern. Eli's cold eyes and severe expression faced into the moon as though he absorbed its beams or some ridiculous shit like that.

Maybe he did absorb moonbeams. Who knew?

Picking the less-dirty of the two benches, I plopped the book down and flipped it open. Between the moonlight and the torches, it wasn't half-bad for reading after all.

Eli did his best to pretend I hadn't stepped onto the platform. His brow wrinkled as the hand under his neck massaged at taut muscles. He was tense, but Eli's constant state was tension.

That oddly patterned tattoo peeked out from the cut-off sleeves and fraying fabric of a band shirt for some group I'd never heard of.

Refocusing on my homework, most of the subjects in the book were unrecognizable—a lot of it was in Latin, and it kept using names like nouns. Who was Moira? Why was Abram protecting her? I stopped at the chapter titled, "Essence Inverses," and struggled my way through the text. It all sounded like gibberish, frankly.

The solitary buzz of the cicadas grated on my already frayed nerves. And, all the while, Eli laid there as though I didn't exist. I skimmed the pages, but didn't absorb much, instead watching his chest rise and fall evenly from the corner of my eye.

Finally, I snapped.

"Can I ask a question?"

"Don't see a way I can stop you," he replied. He refused to tilt his head to look at me as he spoke.

"Thanks, I love a warm welcome."

"It's Florida, isn't it hot enough for you, sweetheart?"

I fiddled with the book pages.

"What do you know about inverses?" I asked.

"What do you want to know?" he returned.

"How does it work?"

"That's rather advanced for you, don't you think?"

"How would I know if it's advanced if none of it makes any sense at all?"

"Fair enough. What makes you ask?"

"Aster left this book for me, but it's confusing and it would be easier to have someone explain it to me."

Eli rolled his eyes, sighing heavily.

"Do your own work, princess. I'm not here to give you shortcuts." He closed his eyes entirely.

Huffing, I adjusted my position and tried to force myself to read.

The feat proved impossible. His comment stung. I'd been working really hard, both for myself and to prove to them I could handle my Duality. I'd thought he recognized the effort after we "retrieved" Jones.

Still, I know I can be . . . a lot. But I shouldn't be a lot to my Pair. *To him.*

Eli sat only ten feet away in absolute silence, acting as my own personalized distraction. Here was a man I was supposed to spend the rest of my life with. Hell, I was supposed to . . . what was the word Peter'd used? They expected me to *couple* with Eli. Lord, have mercy on us both.

The agonizing hush pulled the strain between us taut. We fumed together, saying nothing in an anxious quiet. I feigned reading the book and fiddled with my ring. He scowled at the trees, over the lake, up at the sky.

Tree frogs joined the cicadas' harmony, having a livelier conversation than Eli and I had ever had. We had nothing to talk about; I barely knew him.

"So, how much older are you than Jack?" I asked. I put a pleasant resonance in the question, hoping to undo some of the mutual irritation.

"Five years."

"When was your birthday?"

"February, but I'm a year older than you."

"And how do you feel about all of this?"

His fingers tapped the wooden chair beside his head. He finally turned his face in my direction, but his eyes narrowed.

"I'm fine, Dr. Phil, and you?"

"I'm sorry, I don't have a frame of reference. I was hoping you could share." My face pleaded for a real answer. He huffed a breath and surprised me by providing a genuine response.

"About Jack's kidnapping, the Dualities, or having *you* around for the rest of my life?" he grumbled.

Yep, that pretty much summed it up. I shrugged.

"All of the above?"

The true weight of the situation seemed to register, and a trace of the chill faded.

"Bad. Good. Too soon to tell."

"I still charge for the hour if you only talk for five minutes," I quipped.

He grunted, the harsh staccato of his fingers against the wood returning with a vengeance.

"Does that mean you have more questions? I wanted a few moments of peace."

Frustration tweaked my ire. The man was so antisocial, so impossibly withdrawn. Some people constructed stone walls; his were titanium reinforced.

"Excuse me for trying to get acquainted," I grumbled. "We hardly know each other. How are we supposed to work together if we can't stand a single conversation?"

He sat forward in the lounger, planting his feet on the deck boards to face me square.

"Maybe if you weren't so annoying, I wouldn't mind talking to you," he snapped with a tilt of his head.

My temper rode high, the slightest bubble of heat stoking my anger. I slammed the book closed.

"Maybe if you weren't such an ass, I'd be less annoying."

"Who's more likely in the wrong—me, minding my own business, or you, intruding on my time when you had no business being here?"

"You are such a child. I came out here to read." I jumped from the bench to loom above him. "Are you so self-centered you thought I came here for *you*?"

He vaulted to his own feet, using his size to hulk over me and mirroring my disdain.

"*Were* you reading? Or were avoiding your responsibilities by asking inane questions?"

"I'm sorry, I forgot you don't know what a book looks like. When was the last time you attempted something more advanced than a diagnosing-psychopathy checklist?"

We stalked around each other like rams preparing to charge.

"At least I have redeeming qualities," he sneered. "You surrender the second anything gets too difficult. Forgive me for not wanting to talk to a woman who spends ninety percent of her time whining."

It took all of my willpower not to hurl the book at his head. My words dripped with acidic scorn.

"And what redeeming qualities might those be, hmmm? It's certainly not *good humor* or a *charming wit*."

"You 'bout done?" He threw his hands in the air. "Fuck, you're insufferable."

"Better obnoxious and fun than cold and quiet."

"You think I'm cold? Hardly. You just don't get me hot."

"Ha! *You* might not get hot, but your dick sure loves pinning me to the mat."

"If it's my dick you want, you should have said that in the first place. Just know I'll still want you to *actually follow through*."

My furor burst, and I slapped him so hard it knocked him off balance. My ring scratched a fine tear across his cheek. Blood smeared on his nose.

He glowered down at me, his chest heaving, emotion roiling in penetrating, deep-blue eyes. He wiped the blood from his face and looked at it under the moonlight. His intense gaze narrowed on me.

I knew I should do something. Help him, run for my life, something. Instead, I stood there, stunned, looking at him and at my hand.

When he surged toward me, I expected pain, but he grabbed my neck and crashed his mouth against mine.

Firm lips demanded I surrender to the kiss. It was reckless and impulsive, as though the cork finally popped and he simply couldn't keep it contained anymore.

My insides curled at his familiar, musky aftershave. I was so drawn to the heady scent that even tasting mint on his tongue left me edgy and breathless.

The remaining heat in my system rushed from the connection, flooding my face, down my neck, and raging to the tips of my fingers and toes.

The kiss was sudden and unexpected, and in that moment, I couldn't think about anything else.

Desire crowded my synapses, and I was surprised to find I kissed him just as hungrily. My hands found his chest, but I used them to urge him closer instead of pushing him away.

His forceful attack overtook any hesitation. He was completely in control, and I didn't feel the slightest compulsion to fight it.

The ground wavered as my body drowned in heat. He wove his hand into my hair and tugged, using the leverage to bend me against him. It brought lovely images of him wrapping his hands in my hair in more serious contexts.

I slipped my hands under his shirt and across the bare skin of his back. Sinewy muscles were taut beneath the thin fabric, and my body screamed to tear that stupid rag off of him.

An all-consuming need demanded that he touch me, taste me. I didn't even care that blood from his cheek smeared on my face. I wrapped my arms around him, his body accepting the pressure and molding itself to mine.

The compulsion was so strong I worried I'd strip down and beg him to fuck me then and there.

What is happening right now? This is insane.

Leaning back, I broke the connection.

That pleasant warmth radiated wherever we connected. His heart pounded, matching my own.

Sanity returned as the flicker of passion ebbed. His hand still held my face, keeping me close as he braced me tightly against him.

"Be with me," he breathed. "Just the once. We have to try. I won't . . . I'm trying not to pressure you about it, but . . . please."

I gazed up at him, those beautiful eyes pleading with me, his puffy lips still red.

He'd said *please*. All the angst had dropped. His anxious gaze searched mine for answers.

But this . . . whatever . . . alarmed me. Terrified me. My body, my essence, responded to him. Strongly. Almost uncontrollably. I had no idea what *trying* with him would look like, or what it meant.

I took a quick step back, away from him.

He opened his mouth to say something, but I cut him off.

"Don't you ever do that again."

My voice cracked, spoiling the show of strength I'd hoped for. I spun, grabbed the book, and ran for my room.

*   *   *

In the morning, I immediately sought out Jack to convince her to spar with me. She was my same height and build, and Eli said she could kick some serious ass. Of all the people I could train with, she was probably the one person he'd approve of.

Was it cowardly to make her a buffer between her brother and I? Probably.

Would I do it anyway? *Absofuckinglutely.*

When I found her, though, she and Maxon were putting coffee into to-go cups.

"Peter is sending me to therapy," she lamented.

"What's wrong with therapy?"

"They took me. I'm back. What's there to talk about?"

I may not be a psychiatrist, but I was pretty sure that it wasn't the way to go about it. Not that I should talk.

"You nearly died. Is he all that wrong?"

"I didn't die. I need to go back to life as usual and everything will sort itself out. If you like it so much, you take the appointment for me."

"Me?"

"Yeah."

The idea of talking to anyone, about anything that had transpired in my life the last several weeks, immediately overwhelmed me.

"No."

"Exactly."

Jack looked so much like her brother—almost exactly the same hair, same chin and high cheekbones, same intense eyes. A miniature Eli, but a few years younger and female. Frankly, if Eli's personality flaws extended to her, she probably needed therapy more than most.

"Fine, I'll go with you."

She whirled on me, blue eyes wide and her mouth slightly open. At least I could get the drop on *her*, even if her brother was inscrutable.

"Excuse you, you'll *what*?" she said.

"I'll go to the appointment with you. Not in, of course, but maybe I'll make one of my own."

"Would Eli approve of that?" Maxon's voice called from the kitchen. He'd stacked pancakes and bacon into a triple-decker sandwich and folded a paper towel around the whole thing.

"Eli can suck my ass."

Jack snickered.

"She definitely goes now," Jack announced.

Half an hour later, we pulled up in front of a little stucco building, the white and brown sign the sole indicator of its occupants.

Maxon and I dropped Jack at the door, then went to the greasy spoon across the street to cool our heels for fifty minutes. We commandeered one of the window booths and ordered a second breakfast.

Mostly we made small talk, just passing the time. He seemed like a nice enough guy, but your standard townie. Grew up in the area. Went to UF. Liked the gym, the Gators, and fishing.

That is, until he admitted he'd been trying to get Lita to go out with him.

"You have been *what* with *who*?" I teased. "Have you met Lita? Pretty sure she doesn't like *anyone*."

"She's particular. I'm wearing her down."

"Please tell me you aren't repeatedly asking her. No means no, my man, even if it's only a date."

"She hasn't technically said 'no,' yet. When I asked her a few weeks ago, she didn't respond at all and walked away."

He looked so hopeful. It was kind of adorable. Here's this big, brute of a guy nervous about a girl.

"So, then what have you been doing?"

"Buying her lunch, running errands for her. I cleaned her car last week."

"You cleaned her . . . she's got you bad. What does she say when you do something nice for her?"

"She smiled once."

Oh, it was too funny.

"Only the once?"

He winced. Could probably be nicer about this, but the poor guy needed to be put out of his misery.

I'd opened my mouth for more commentary when he got a call. He excused himself and went outside to take it.

I played with my phone for a while, but the deluge of notifications quickly overwhelmed me. I hadn't checked social media much since, you know, magical Armageddon.

As I turned to check out the window for Maxon—who still paced the parking lot, phone to his ear with a stern expression—a familiar face stared back from a counter stool.

Tall-Dark-and-Handsy, the walking red flag from the bathroom hallway at Kicks, watched me intently as he sipped a coffee.

Dark jeans. Black, fitted shirt. Cocky disregard for social boundaries. He looked even better in the daylight than he had through the haze of modest intoxication.

Lord, help me. I had enough complicated on my plate already. Yet, again, this guy was the last thing I needed.

When he got up from his seat, I speed-dialed Trish.

"Hey, miss thang, Eli's been look—"

"Talk my ear off."

"What?"

"Talk to me about anything. Don't stop until I tell you so."

"Erm, okay. So I've been thinking about redecorating the spare bedroom."

Handsy rounded the row of tables and stood beside my booth.

"Uh-huh."

I smiled, nodded slightly at him, then pointed to the phone.

"I've been thinking yellow stripes, but you never know what guys like. Tom isn't into interior design at all . . ."

Cocking his head to the side with an amused grin, Handsy slouched in the booth seat across from me. His coffee-wielding arm landed on the table and he stretched the other across the padded backrest.

The mug clunked onto the surface. Long fingers rotated it as he studied me, the bottom scraping against the surface, but all his attention was on me.

". . . but it's really hard to choose. Gray is so drab."

"You need to go with your gut, hon," I replied, watching those deft fingers manipulate the cup. My face warmed as nervous heat simmered in my gut.

Trish continued gabbing.

He picked up a sugar packet, dropped it to the table, and used his fingertips to skim it across the surface in arcs. All the while, those hickory-brown eyes focused on my reaction, mischief shading the slight smirk on his face.

". . . not to worry about it, we have money in the budget, especially if we do the work ourselves."

Our eyes met, the intensity in his gaze fermenting the bubbles of heat in my chest.

"You have to see it every day. May as well be pretty."

"That's what I said! So . . ."

Handsy abandoned the sugar packet, tapping the table twice and raising an eyebrow.

I pointed at the phone and mouthed "on a call" in as exaggerated a fashion as possible.

His eyes never left me, not even for a moment. His jaw flexed as his fingers rubbed firmly against his palm. The tension in his gaze and his grip caused little, thrilling tendrils to snake under my skin. I didn't know an annoyed wrist flex could be sexy, but there we were.

Desperate to break the connection, I twisted to look out the window and saw Maxon making his way into the diner.

When I turned back, the booth was empty.

* * *

Jack came out of the appointment a mess.

Yeah, no therapy for me.

Her beet-red face was swollen, her body hunched over in exhaustion. She refused to talk about it, but I was fine with that as long as she'd talked to her counselor.

I sat in the back with her for the return trip—me in the center seat, my arm around her as she meticulously folded and unfolded her tissue. About halfway to Haven, she fell asleep with her head on my shoulder.

She seemed so young. So brittle. She put off this "can handle anything attitude," but it was all a front. Somehow, it made me like her a little more.

And she reminded me of Anna. The thought alone slashed at my heart. I wished I could talk to Anna, just for a little while. To find out about the baby. To ask about Mom.

Somehow, helping Jack layered steel in my spine. I couldn't change the things that happened, only my reaction to them.

As I stepped onto the back deck of the main building, Eli emerged from the doors with Pinch at his side.

For one flicker of a moment, his face fell in regret when his eyes met mine. A half second later, though, his expression returned to the normal mix of annoyance and frustration.

Oh, good, the night before had never happened.

"About time you showed up. Where were you?" he asked, his tone short. The insult formed in my brain and I opened my mouth to tell him exactly where he could go, when he cut me off.

"Never mind. We found another one—the guy you burned. Goes by Grayam. We need to go—"

"Kidnap and interrogate him?" I interrupted, glaring at them both.

"Whatever, princess," he grunted. "Time to go."

He reached for my arm to force me into motion, but I slipped out of his reach. My water was handy, no pun intended.

"You've got Pinch, you don't need me. I'm staying," I informed him.

"Not your call. Or mine, unfortunately. Talk to Peter, he insists you come. It should be straightforward, since he was in rough shape the last time we saw him. Besides, you're the best chance for countering this guy if he decides to use his Duality to attack."

"It's probably a trap," I noted.

"Oh, it's definitely a trap."

I exhaled a deep sigh. "Fine. Let's go set it off and see what happens."

Chapter Fifteen

Grayam holed-up in a rat-trap motel not far from Alligator Alley. We drove through the cracking porte-cochere, and parked in the lot inside the elbow of the two-story, L-shaped building. Four different shades of paint cracked and peeled off the exposed walls and exterior stairs. I wanted a tetanus booster and flu shot just for looking at the place.

"Which room is he in?" I asked.

Eli shrugged. "Your guess is as good as mine."

Grimy, faded burgundy curtains kept light and prying eyes from the windows. Several guests left them open, so we could eliminate those immediately. Three remained on the ground floor, and a fourth on the second story.

We crept closer to peek into windows, climbing the metal-and-concrete stairs to check the top-most room first.

Threatening spring rain smoothed the humidity into a brisk fog. Even though the curtains were shut, the first questionable occupant had opened the window to let the cool air flow through the room. Dr. Oz gabbed about whole-system purity on the TV inside.

"Not this one," I whispered. Eli and Pinch exchanged a glance, and I rolled my eyes at their doubt.

"Guys can't like Dr. Oz?" Pinch asked.

"Guys don't usually carry birth control."

The curtain had been cut too short, and the cool breeze flapped the fabric inward to expose the contents of a table. A purse had fallen sideways, splaying the contents onto the surface. A tampon, a tube of lipstick, an eyeliner pen, and a familiar rectangular packet spread across the exposed edge.

"Oh," he said. *Yeah, oh.*

We quietly descended the stairs and moved to the next closest room. Sounds from within came through the wall so clearly it may as well not exist at all. A man and woman argued loudly and profanely, the woman bawling and shrieking about pornography. Strike number two.

The third room was at the bend in the L-shaped building. We snuck toward it, but a door at the far end of the opposing arm swung open. A man who could've stunt-doubled for Jabba the Hut flipped off the lights as he exited, his closed curtain going dark. Not behind door number four.

Only one window remained. Low light peeked around the edges of the grubby drape. No sound escaped the room, although Pinch whispered that someone was inside.

Eli and Pinch exchanged looks in yet another silent conversation. I shrugged a, *What do we do now?* to the guys, adding my own silent demand that they include me in their deliberation.

Pinch returned a smile eerily similar to Anna's toothy grin. He skirted along the wall to stand at the door, then kicked the sole of his steel-toed work boot into the space above the knob. The door splintered inward, followed by its assailant and his cohort.

Grayam's weak form lay face-down on the crisp, white linens of one of two ratty, full-sized beds. The back of his body had been wrapped in thin gauze and exhibited a spectrum of angry-red blisters. White, frothy sores emitted a sickly sweet stink.

He'd been asleep, but now his eyes were wide as he reached for a cell phone on the nightstand. Pinch flashed to his side, snatching the phone from his hand and pocketing it. Grayam cursed at us all, muttering empty threats and angry obscenities.

The Kier's prognosis was not encouraging. Grayam was disoriented, his breathing rapid as his eyes darted between us. Most of his skin felt clammy and cold, but his forehead and neck burned hot. Every shift of his body made him moan in pain. It made me wonder why Jones got a hospital, while he'd been dumped here with an obvious infection.

The boys each grabbed the injured man by an arm and heaved him through the door. They struggled, straining under his weight. It didn't make sense why they had so much trouble—he wasn't that big of a guy, and both Pinch and Eli were plenty strong. I closed the door, hoping no one would notice and report a problem.

A slight breeze picked up and circulated the misty air. It flicked my hair, cooling the nape of my neck.

The boys got halfway to the car before they had to drop him. Grayam fell to the ground. His stiff body cratered the pavement while his harshly whispered promises of our deaths carried on.

"What's the hold up?" I asked.

They panted, trying to catch a breath.

The breeze built, shifting leaves and trash in the parking lot.

"You try carrying him," Eli snarled. "He weighs a ton."

I rolled my eyes at him, but then connected Grayam's primary—wind—with what I had assumed would be the opposite. Earth.

Our argument allowed Grayam to roll over on his back. His face contorted in pain, even though his muttering barely broke its rhythm.

We noticed too late that Grayam's hand had been making a circular motion, working up to a large rotation as he gathered energy in the damaged limb.

The breeze built swiftly now, and the gusts escalated at a panic-inducing rate.

Chilled air engulfed us in a thunderous squall. Trash and abandoned car parts from the road circled and twisted in the tornado.

The powerful currents knocked the three of us back while my burn victim lay completely unharmed in the eye of the storm.

Pressure in the air shoved at my body and eardrums, the atmosphere heavy from the sudden mass of wind.

My fire bubble popped to life in an instant. It anchored me in place and protected me from the worst of the storm, its formation now second nature thanks to practice and fear-induced need.

Still, my muscles strained as I struggled to concentrate on calling something, anything, that might subdue Grayam.

Eli beckoned to me, yelling to take cover. He'd been thrown back to the building and hugged one of the stairway supports for dear life. A large gash split his arm, probably from a flying piece of debris. Pinch huddled behind a car that vibrated menacingly like it might flip backward, but he still motioned for me to join him.

They were both useless in this fight anyway. Neither could withstand Grayam's wind damage, and I'd already done it once before. It was me or nothing.

Shifting my focus to the prone man, I wrenched a foot from the ground and let it clop down in front of me—then again, and again, slowly making my way to his position. Grayam wasn't a physical threat in his condition; if I could just get to him, I could knock him unconscious.

Electric fear buzzed under my skin, but this time I had my bubble and a plan. Concentrating hard, I used my new favorite trick and shoved all that fear into a little corner in my mind, then shut the door to that entire room, then meticulously barred that door with as many safeguards as possible. I could cry later. Hell, I could cry then if it didn't hinder me, but I had hero shit to do.

Then, as suddenly as it began, the wind died.

The heavy atmosphere sank into deadly silence, the weight of it still beating at my eardrums.

Dirt and rubble formed a wide circle spiraling around Grayam, the picture a grotesque arrangement more like something from *American Horror Story* than a rural motel.

The boys and I walked tentatively toward the lifeless body. The wind-wielder didn't move, not even his chest. Pinch leaned over him.

"He's dead," he told us matter-of-factly. "Talk about a bluff. All that bluster and he dies on us."

I gave him a sour expression.

"Now what do we do?" I asked for the millionth time that day.

"We bring him to Haven. Peter will know what to do," Eli answered.

"You want to hide a dead guy in the car?" I stammered.

"You don't have to sit next to him," he replied coolly, as though I was the one out-of-line. "We'll put him in the trunk."

So, into the trunk Grayam went.

*   *   *

Eli

It's not every day you had a corpse in the trunk. Jex sat in the front passenger seat beside me, as far away as she could get from the trunk. She constantly twisted to glare at the back seat like Grayam would pop out from the pass-through in the armrest.

The adrenaline in my system began to fade. My insides shook, not that I could let it affect me now. I knew Jex well enough to recognize she'd need a quiet space to disintegrate and soon. The quicker we got to Haven the better.

Even though she rejected me.

My Pair rejected me.

Don't you ever do that again.

The initial shock was the worst of it. It caught me off guard after she'd reacted so strongly.

Her demand stung; I'd take a thousand new slices on my skin to avoid even one more like that replaying in my head.

She hadn't meant it, though.

Her eyes had been wide, shining and near tears. Her body trembled. She was petrified.

Not horrified. Not angry.

Anxious panic.

Motherfuckingdamnit, I should just talk to her about Pairs. Her response was *not* a bad thing. Damn Peter and his own anxiety about overwhelming her.

And now she's got me using her absurd curses.

My arm burned, the shrapnel injury likely adding yet another scar to the ever-growing collection. At least it was on my left arm. Getting the glyphs re-etched hurt like a bitch.

I'd called Henry to let them know to expect our impromptu processional. Pinch quietly fiddled with Grayam's cell phone the whole ride, only a few feet from someone rotting away.

My lead foot set Jex even more on edge. She repeatedly reminded me "not to commit crimes while committing a crime." She resorted to staring at her shoes. I didn't think she realized she reached over to hold my hand. She never acknowledged it, but the warmth placated at least a bit of the stress.

When the wind kicked up, it'd taken all of my will not to gather her up and cart her away. The deafening scream of my instinct to protect her sounded louder than the squall.

I couldn't though. Even if I could resist the wind surge, Jex would probably skip toward the danger if she knew I wanted her away from it. Ever the independent contrarian.

I couldn't even acknowledge it after the fact, no matter how much I needed to assure myself she was okay.

Don't you ever do that again.

I'd need to acclimate her to the way her essence responded. Give her more time to adjust. She'd come around, I just needed to find the right moment.

When we returned to Haven, Henry instructed everyone to reconvene in the late afternoon out on the deck.

He also insisted Jex get something to eat and then work on channeling her Duality. She tried to tempt me into the Practice Room, but I reminded her that we follow even the orders we don't like.

I knew she'd ignore it anyway and needed the time to be alone. Ryan had new Guards in, which meant he'd be in the gun range teaching muzzle discipline and not available as her distraction.

I left her to it, patched my arm, and found Jack so we could work on some of her bo forms. She'd been trying to get better with staffs in general, but baby sis had never been great at taking corrections. It irked her not being on the same footing as me.

From one aggravating woman to the next, I supposed.

*   *   *

Jex

The waning sun dissolved into a dreary, overcast sky as the hours lagged. Musky humidity stuck to my skin, the earlier threat of a downpour maturing into periodic drizzles that infused the air with the cloying scent of rain.

After getting home, Henry demanded I work on my focus, so of course I avoided it like the plague. My brain already hurt. It had been a weird couple of days.

Eli was no use. Ryan was busy. So, I lounged in my favorite swing chair and knocked a few more chapters off my newest book instead.

Henry found me in the atrium, so we walked out to the meeting point together. Brit waited for us at the picnic tables along with a woman with rich umber skin who looked to be about her age. Large hazel eyes anchored a pretty, oval face. She smiled throughout their conversation.

They were joined by a bald, stocky man shaped more like an amorphous mass of muscle than a person. His large head met his bulbous shoulders and body as if there were no neck in between.

"Do I know them?" I whispered to Henry.

It might have only been a few weeks, and admittedly half that had been spent languishing in my room, but I could still recognize most of the Clara by sight now. The presence of a new pair left me doubly suspicious given the timing.

"You can meet them later. They're only visiting," he answered. He didn't seem the least bit worried about the appearance of two new faces. As he said it, they nodded to him and disappeared into the atrium.

Peter joined us, still toying with Grayam's cell phone with about as much luck as Pinch. He repeatedly pushed the power button. You'd think the iPhone infected them all with memory erasure for anything other than Apple products.

"Mind if I give it a shot?" I offered. I stood beside him and held out a hand.

He handed me the device, so I worked the buttons and tried to soft-reset the phone. It never flickered or responded to my commands.

"Eli, keys?" I asked him, and he tossed me the ring from his pocket.

I used the teeth of a smaller key to pry off the back cover. The battery had exploded and leaked metallic-smelling fluid into the cavity. The substance crystallized, leaving a fine white powder crushed to the edges. There didn't seem to be any permanent damage, though.

The battery fell to the picnic table with a relieved *thunk*, like it had been waiting all evening for someone to free it. I stripped off a cotton sock and mopped up some of the sweat from Brit's water bottle. The thick material worked against the contacts, rubbing away any leftover grit. Now came the hard part.

"I need one more thing," I told Eli. "Can I please have your cell phone?"

I tried to give my luddite Valen a sweet and reassuring smile. His expression told me I'd failed miserably. Freddy Kruger was more trustworthy, apparently.

Eli looked from me, to Peter, to Henry, searching for someone to save him.

"What are you going to do with it?" he inquired warily.

"You'll get the phone back. I only need to use it for a minute," I told him, my attitude blasé.

At least I'd hoped I could give it back. I didn't know why the battery exploded the first time, but wasn't about to share that concern with him. I needed the juice, and both were old Nokia burner-types.

Eli reluctantly handed me the phone, in slow motion, obviously hoping someone who outranked me would stop the exchange. And yet *I* was the drama queen.

The battery fit snugly into its new home, easily sliding into the slot and connecting with the contacts. I turned the phone over and pressed the power button.

The screen lit up and made a welcoming three-tone chime. The banner read, "Live Life To The Fullest." Even evil needed encouragement.

Scrolling through the phone directory, I started forwarding contacts to Eli's number. He couldn't access it until the battery was back in its rightful place, but we would be ready when the information came through. I did the same for the pictures and videos before moving on to text messages.

Apparently, the Kier were big on texting. I'm sure that was a great selling point. *For the minion on the go. Now with voice distorter!*

I flipped through the messages, but most were innocuous. A text exchange dated around the same time Jack had been kidnapped asked, "Have you found the location?" The response confirmed, "at Carrington." Screen-shotting the entire conversation, I forwarded it to Eli's number before showing it to Peter.

"First," I began, "ya'll need to leave Haven every once in a while for non-world-saving activities. Second, it looks like Grayam was in the search team when they took Jack," I told them, then switched to the internet browser.

"We already knew that," Eli grumbled. "They trashed her place trying to find it. Can I have my phone back now?"

"No." I glared at him. "They knew it wasn't at her place. Whatever they want is at Carrington. Where's Carrington?" I'd lived or visited here my whole life, but knew of no towns, counties, or areas by that name.

No one responded to my question, so I stopped reading the webpage entries to ask again.

Peter and Henry communed silently, their faces serious. These people and their ominous exchanges.

"You're doing that thing again. The one where you don't tell me everything," I commented.

My train of thought went off the tracks as I gaped at the last webpage accessed—a GPS locator service. Grayam must have armed it to send an alert beacon the next time the phone activated.

Spitting an obscenity, I flipped the phone over and fumbled for the battery. Plucking the sim card from the slot, I ran to dunk the empty shell into one of the rain barrels as a precaution.

"We have a problem," I informed them. "They know where Grayam's phone is."

* * *

"What? How is that possible?" Henry asked, panic leaking into his words.

"The phone had a GPS alert on it. When we turned it on, it sent a signal to a pre-selected number with our coordinates. Do the Kier know the location of Haven?"

"Yes," he answered carefully.

"So, they know where we are, that Grayam's phone is here, and that Grayam is MIA?"

Yet again, no one answered my question. Instead, they all sprang into motion.

Henry had his own phone out, calling people to Haven and requesting reports from those monitoring the Farm and other Kier outposts. Eli and Brit flung themselves through the open glass doors, presumably toward the Weapons Room. Peter left so quickly I wasn't even sure which direction he'd gone.

As everyone flew into action, I stood awkwardly on the deck, unsure of what to do. I decided to wait for Henry to finish making his calls. The more I stayed out of the way, the better.

To pass the time, I replaced my sock and reassembled Eli's phone to snoop in it, but he only ever used it for texting and calls with Peter or Henry. There weren't even any contacts. How did someone survive like that in the modern world? My phone was my lifeblood.

When Henry finished his call, he asked me, "How confident are you about defending an attack?"

Honesty was the best policy here.

"Not very, but once the essence kicks in I'll be fine. I want to help."

He assessed me, determining if I would be an asset or liability. The final prognosis wasn't good.

"Stay here, Jex. The only way onto the property by car is through the main entrance. Our scout near the Farm says they're arming SUVs, which means they're going to charge over and probably instigate a fight in the parking lot. Do not—I repeat, *do not*—come to the front of the property. They'll rush in, but you'll be safe here."

This Henry was different. The short, crisp statements echoed the stress in his voice. He tried to convince me we were relatively safe out here, but his tone betrayed his words. Contagious anxiety spread through his demeanor.

"If anyone comes back, raise an alarm. They won't try on foot—it's too far of a trek on short notice. If you see someone you don't recognize, anyone at all, text me and run to the reservoir. Hide in the boathouse. There's a hatch behind the second jet ski. Don't come out unless it's me. *Only me.* Do you understand?"

His taut face broadcast his fear as he issued the directive, his eyes flat-black in the growing darkness. I nodded, too anxious to speak.

He made me repeat the direction anyway.

Henry returned to his calls, so I shrank to the picnic table. Whipping out my phone, I wielded it like a weapon, ready at any moment to send out the alert.

I wanted to hide *under* the table, but didn't think it would reassure Henry I could handle this.

He left me hunched over, barely glancing back as he careened over the main path of the atrium.

Rain dripped in a light patter. The looming thunder clouds drained away all the light until the sky was a chaotic blend of gray-black. Canister lights on the walls at the ends of the deck struggled to compete with the impending storm, casting a pallid yellow against the glass doors that dissipated quickly on the wooden expanse of the deck.

People shouted from the front lot. Peter's voice projected through the air, commanding Guards to move cars into place while Pairs set-up a defensive line. I kept checking my phone, both to keep track of time but also to shine a light in the area.

After more than an hour, the shouts died and abandoned me to my thoughts. I'd paced around the table so much it probably wore a track in the deck boards. I'd taken my ring off entirely, twisting it between my fingertips, trying to get the stingy light to flash off of it.

Unable to move, both from fear and Henry's direction, I sat completely alone in the threatening gloom. It was restrictive, like a big straight-jacket of the unknown.

Three more hours passed like that. What was taking so long? The battery on my phone ticked down to eleven percent before I consigned myself to the murky darkness of the rainy night. It would probably be better for my night vision anyway, right?

Sounds crept from the shadows of the trees and ricocheted in my thoughts.

Small animals rummaged through the bushes.

Mosquitoes and flies buzzed around the lights and nipped at my exposed skin.

A slow, steady, meandering movement rustled the underbrush.

The woods were not as deserted as they seemed.

My breathing all but came to a standstill. I gripped my phone so hard the buttons on the side left little indentations on my palm.

I tried to tell myself that it was paranoia making me antsy. There's no boogie man, no monster in the closet.

It was all a figment of my imagination.

Nothing goes bump in the night.

It's all.

In my.

Mind.

SMASH!

Sound bursting through the silence startled me so bad I jumped and shoved my knees into the wood of the table. A vehicle plowed into the gates at the front of the building. Metal dragged along in tinny screams.

Shots rang out, an uneven volley that echoed into the sky and chased the distance. The cracks reverberated in the air as destruction met large, immovable targets. Some bounced off large, metallic objects, while others skipped and plowed into the dense thud of concrete and stucco.

An explosion shook the ground and left me breathless with fear. A hawk circled the building, its caw echoing in the night sky. A high-pitched, keening whine pounded against my skull, but then died as quickly as it began.

The extremes overwhelmed—from quiet to cacophony. I squeezed my eyes shut and tried to block it out. The burn in my system rose to the threat, aiming to roast my heart and lungs.

Attempting to dissipate some of the energy, I visualized hands wrapped around that ball of fire in my ribs, squashing it and forcing it to heel. Once the discomfort receded, I spread the heat evenly through my body to avoid searing my chest more.

I was finally learning to control it.

I hugged my battered knees to my chest, gripping my legs tightly until the blood drained from my fingers.

An eternity passed before the noise died again, but the heat in my chest refused to subside. I had no idea if the return to calm was good or bad.

The burn escalated, fear rocketing through me.

No, not fear. Instinct.

I primed my essence, sensing the threat.

I didn't even have time to open my eyes when the heat flared in my veins, setting off my fight-or-flight response.

My body stretched flat to the picnic bench and rolled under the table.

The sword whistled by in a horizontal arc before swinging vertically and sinking into the seat. It cleaved almost clean through the two-by-fours, the metal glinting underneath in the meager deck light. I'd been sitting there only a few seconds before.

Blood already coated the edge of the blade.

Scrambling out of the end, I ran toward the path to the reservoir. My phone slipped from my fingers, forgotten on the lawn in front of the deck. I made it to the woods. The oaks and box elders stood as silent pillars in the twilight.

Moonlight filtered through the clouds. Shadowed, low-hanging branches and fronds whipped at my face and body. At a certain point, I lost sight of the path. I slid on the wet ground, disoriented and terrified.

Keep running. Find the boathouse.

Ragged breathing made my lungs ache in protest, but I continued to sprint to safety. I pleaded with lady luck that I hadn't gotten turned around to run straight into my attacker's arms.

Was this how I died? In the woods, running for my life?

In the movies, it was so easy for the heroine. A little training montage, some exciting music, and suddenly she's breaking open sparring bags and kicking the villain's ass.

That wasn't real life. Real life can kill you and there's no second chance. I could die here. Even if I survived, my life could irrevocably change.

Don't go getting existential now, Jex. Focus.

Get to the boathouse. Everything will be fine if you get to the fucking boathouse.

Heat sung in my skin and torched my muscles. My steps stirred the leaves and scrub, the noise heavy against the ghostly frame of the trees. There was no hope of being quiet; it was far more important to be quick. I heard nothing of my pursuer, who was either too silent or drowned out by my own thrashing.

I tried not to look back.

If you look back, what's chasing you will be real. And it will catch up.

Eli'd taught me better, but I couldn't help it. Curiosity killed the cat.

The figure was right on my tail. The tall woman's porcelain face glowed in the faint moonlight. She was completely bald with a wicked pattern etched into her scalp. I did a double-take, slowing me down enough that she seized my shirt and jerked my torso to the side.

The move spun me out of control until I slammed into the trunk of a large tree. The breath knocked from my chest, and I doubled over trying to recover.

My pause allowed her to strike, though, and I only scarcely noticed her wind-up. She thrust a short dagger at my gut. My feet side-stepped as the blade whispered past my ribs. I felt the barest kiss of wind as it opened a long slice in my shirt when I dodged away.

I thought they wanted to kidnap me, not kill me!

Adrenaline throttled me past the light contact. Twisting, I used her forward momentum against her, grabbing and thrusting the daggered hand upward while shoving her shoulder back. A well-placed foot was enough to cause her to lose her balance, her feet slipping out from underneath her on the muddied grass.

She loosened her grip on the dagger as she fell backward, probably from surprise. I couldn't say I blamed her—I was surprised as hell, too.

Her slim arm slid through mine and my fingers tightened to catch the guard of the weapon. It was lighter than I'd imagined, and I carefully rotated the dagger to the proper grip. At least, it felt like the proper grip.

Stepping away a few paces, I took my stance and watched her regain her feet as the burn consumed my body.

She wasn't down for the count, and it was clear I couldn't run from her. She'd catch me. She'd already caught me. I could only hope that my essence was strong enough to get me through the next few minutes.

The woman shuffled to her feet. Dirt and debris caught on her clothes as frantic, assessing eyes shot from me to the knife and back again. Electric-silver channels snaked up her arms and over her body, pulsing underneath her clothes.

An evil smile found her lips as she reached an arm overhead and withdrew a long sword from a sheath on her back. The wide, T-shaped pommel and hilt supported a blade at least three feet long, the edge widening toward the end and terminating in a deadly point.

My brain whirled, dizzy with fear at the almost certain death and dismemberment sliding with a *snick* out of its sheath. The dagger felt tiny and inadequate.

She shuffled around in the brush and tried to corner me against a set of two closely spaced trunks. My breathing slowed, heat exhaling in each breath. I rotated the smaller blade with my wrist and waited for the calm. Dodging and shuffling, I waited for the world to stop, to fixate, to settle.

My attacker, however, was not so patient. She moved lithely, slashing at me in quick jabs and wide swipes. The edge whistled as it cut the air.

She thrust the sword forward, trying to gore my torso, when the essence finally flared. I flowed sideways again and barely avoided the thrust as her momentum carried her forward. I used her moment of shock to swing my inside hand across. The butt of my weapon smashed into her face. Her nose crunched and blood sprayed across her face in the vague light.

She staggered backward, wiping her mouth with her empty hand before she spat on the ground.

All of my senses whittled the world down to this one interaction. The swaying trees in the distance blurred, leaving only her and our little clearing, with no distraction.

The scent of her blood mingled with the earthiness of the dirt on my face, the sweat on her skin so rich it coated my tongue, my throat clogging with flecks from the trees and the grass and the underbrush.

My eyes focused only on her, and the rest of the inanimate world fell away. I could almost taste her anger, my fear sour in my throat.

I should have been happy I'd wounded her, but knew this was bad. I needed to incapacitate her enough to stop the attack. I realized I wouldn't last the night if I failed to seriously injure her.

I might have to kill her.

She attacked with a new intensity, and I did my best to maneuver away from the striking weapon. The right course of action was to get closer and remove the advantage of a longer weapon, but I still couldn't bring my head to merge with my actions.

I ran scared—just a little, lost girl, ducking behind trees while she whacked away at them. Eli would be supremely disappointed.

What I needed was fire power to even the playing field, but nothing came. That part of my talent was inaccessible, locked away behind a door with a bolt. I panicked at the idea my essence could fade before the fight finished.

Numbness settled in my fingers and toes. I was tiring, my muscles aching. If I didn't find a way to take her down soon, she'd wear me out until I was helpless.

In the background of our grunts and heavy breathing, I registered the sound of growling. A large animal prowled around us, its snarling rumble interrupted by intermittent hissing.

The woman and I were playing ring-around-the-rosewoods when the golden-brown fur of a Florida panther sprang from the shadows. Feline eyes shifted in a flash of control—a single shutter of the lens giving the barest hint of recognition. *Human.*

It lunged at the woman with claws extended, catching her with its open maw working into her shoulder. A cry ripped from her lips as she collapsed under the weight of the animal. It gnawed at her neck as her eyes widened in shock and pain.

My heel caught on a root as I backed away, and I sprawled onto the ground. Crawling through the wet leaves, I scrambled into the root system of a large tree. The darkness spared me the explicit image of a woman being eaten alive.

My chest ached, my lungs burning from the frantic run and subsequent attack. My heart prattled so fast it made me worry I was having a literal heart attack. I clutched at my ears and tried to hum to myself, but nothing could staunch the fear at the sound of the scuffle in the clearing.

The screams faded away, the remaining sounds of gruesome ripping with intermittent pops and tearing.

Then, the violence stopped.

It took several minutes for the adrenaline in my veins to fade, my body left shaking with fatigue. I might have had a front-row seat to a lot of violence lately, but it paled in comparison to watching a woman be eaten alive.

The panther disappeared by the time I gathered enough courage to peek back. The ragged remains rested in the clearing. I avoided seeing any more than necessary to stagger toward Haven.

After finally finding the path, I almost collided with Henry as he headed in the opposite direction. I forgot I still held the knife and came within inches of friendly fire.

"You were supposed to go to the boathouse," he scolded. Shaky, I glanced back in the direction of the clearing where the stand-off took place.

"I got lost again."

Something in my tone must have worried him, because the reprimand never came.

Instead, he motioned toward Haven and whatever destruction awaited us there.

Chapter Sixteen

Haven's parking lot was awash in light, even at one in the morning. Lita directed the triage effort while Peter and Henry reorganized the group.

My earlier trick with the cell phone designated me the electronics expert, and Ryan and I were delegated to the attacking vehicles and the devices they carried.

It was suddenly very, very cold as the night's chill settled deep in my marrow. I threw on a heavy jacket. My face couldn't seem to find an expression other than neutral.

Two large SUVs had rammed through the chain-metal gate. They'd stopped haphazardly at the far end. Several of our cars were arranged against the building to create staggered barriers. Another two of the Kier's vehicles had retreated from the melee, and were long gone by the time I joined the clean-up crew.

Dust from oversized tires spinning out in the gravel still powdered the sky, the grit mixed with gunpowder to make the atmosphere thick and stuffy. It smelled like the air had been set ablaze, peppered with the metallic traces of blood. My stomach rolled as the scent stuck to my nose and tongue.

Swiss-cheese SUVs were riddled with varying sized holes and craters. I floated around the area, my mind not connecting with the chaos. Somewhere in my brain, the thoughts of pain and exhaustion isolated themselves until I could be alone and break down in private.

Compartmentalization was quickly becoming my third superpower.

There were no bodies, but defined depressions were scattered around the lot, mostly near the new vehicles. Feet had shifted the ground and made wavelike formations beside wide dents the size of fully grown humans. Blood and fragments of other organic material circled the areas where death stood watch.

They emptied the pockets of the bodies before moving them, leaving small piles of life amid ruin.

Eli had been asked to secure the Kier's weaponry, but I still caught him poking his head back out the door every so often to look for me. It's not like I'd evaporate into thin air. What could he possibly think I'd fuck up so badly I needed monitoring?

Ryan and I picked through the bits in search of anything useful. A scrap of paper. Wallets with nothing but a few bills. A pot of chewing tobacco. Cell phones. We shoved everything into a duffel bag Ryan carried over his shoulder.

After finishing the gruesome scavenger hunt, we plugged a piece of equipment under the dashboards of the cars to download the vehicle computer records.

It was all so clinical and detached.

The library was packed with people and activity, so Ryan dumped the contents of the duffel onto the kitchen counter. I started giggling to myself, hysteria causing momentary mental instability.

"What?" he asked.

"Everything and the kitchen sink," I snickered. *I crack myself up.*

Ryan gave me the appropriate response—a worried expression.

We separated the loot into piles. Electronics here, location items there, information in the middle. The work felt like it dragged for hours. I sifted through a pile of pens with the logos of companies and hotels on them. One announced it was "Stolen from Printopia." Ryan picked through receipts and bits of paper. We set aside anything useful, although we threw nothing away.

The adrenaline fully drained from my system about halfway through the duffel bag. Loss wore on me, and my shoulders hunched as my lids began to sag.

My skin was clammy and I leaned into Ryan reflexively. I rested against his body, my cheek to his chest, while I sunk into the realization of how many people had died.

We worked at the piles with tired hands. Ryan braced an arm around my shoulders and slid me closer.

His familiar scent drew me into the comforting embrace, and I nuzzled against his neck. His jaw rested on my head, his fingers drawing circles on my arm. I forgot myself for a minute and let it feel good being near someone who cared.

"Any progress?" Eli's clipped tone jabbed at the headache forming behind my eyes. He watched with an intense quiet, his eyes flat with a hint of fire burning in the background. *Surprise, surprise*, Eli's annoyed.

Shifting away from Ryan, I tried my best to clear the frog from my throat.

"Was anyone hurt?" I asked.

"A few were injured, no one mortally. Two Guards are missing but we'll find them. We were better prepared, and a strong defense always defeats a half-assed offense."

The words provided an immediate sense of relief. My earlier melancholy faded a little, replaced by that bone-deep exhaustion and chill. I felt the tilt, not realizing I had started to lean against Ryan again. He replaced his arm on my waist and gathered me nearer. Eli's expression slid into a scowl.

Fuck Eli.

"What happens now?" I muttered. I was too tired and Ryan too comfortable to care about how Eli took it.

"Peter instituted a lockdown. No one goes in or out without his say-so. He's called a meeting to discuss what happens next."

Ryan sighed and said, "I guess we'd better get to it." He made a show of kneading my back a bit longer.

Eli glared menacingly at Ryan and tilted his chin, looking down his nose. It wasn't hard to do, since we both slumped on stools, but the intention was obvious.

"They need anyone who isn't essential to bring supplies up from the bunker," Eli responded. "That means all Guards, even you. You should be able to track Lita down on your own. Jex and I will go to the library."

Eli turned his focus back to me, a smile playing on his lips. He offered his arm and asked, "Shall we?"

My eyeroll aggravated the wicked headache. Ryan's body tensed beside me. I could feel him silently pacing his breathing and trying to remain calm.

It's flattering to have men fight over you, but not if you're dead on your feet and recovering from a near-death experience. It just didn't seem important.

I stood but didn't accept Eli's arm. It wouldn't do to encourage their impromptu pissing match. This didn't have to be a competition; I wasn't seriously dating either of them.

Annoyed, I staggered my way to the library. Neither one of them had any business trying to claim me for themselves. Goading each other wouldn't endear me to one or the other.

People filled the library, most of whom I didn't know other than a name and a face. I sat in the remaining empty couch spot.

It was a little satisfying to relegate Eli to standing, until he perched on the arm of the sofa, leaning against the back of it with those long arms. It forced me to rest against him if I wanted to slouch into the couch. Which I did. I wanted to lay back and pass right out. Bastard.

Trish sat beside me, completely comfortable, and took my hand. She gave a small smile but never made eye contact. I tried to thank her, to tell her the panther saved my life and that I owed her, but we were surrounded by other people. Gushing at her seemed like a bad idea. I could be grateful later; I needed all my energy to keep my eyes open.

Peter paced in front of his abandoned chair. The entire room fell silent, their eyes trained on him.

"We were assaulted on our own land," he declared, his tone gruff. "Retribution will be addressed. The Kier will strike again, this time with more concerted intent, after failing so spectacularly. We can no longer stay here long-term. We need to move to preserve our privacy and safety."

The room broke into frantic whispers.

"Will we have to move our homes?" asked a small woman with a high voice.

"Not immediately. The attack occurred here and we haven't seen any other breaches. We have already started the process of finding a new location, but it will require time. The Clara have inhabited Haven for more than a decade. I know it will be difficult, but preserving our lives and livelihood is paramount. It outweighs any love we may have for this place. It's only a building and land. We can find a new home."

"What time frame are we looking at?" asked a tall man with shockingly white hair. His arms and legs were crossed and his jaw clenched.

"We will probably need several months to complete the process. As quickly as we can, everyone will be temporarily moved into the emergency bunker. It's underground and defensible, if out-of-date. As upgrades are completed, we will start with those living outside of Haven.

"There have been other strikes recently, but even this half-assed rescue attempt is an escalation. Everyone must be on high alert.

"In the meantime, no one is to go in or out of the gate without my express authority. You are free to leave, but you might not be allowed back onto the property. The entrance is our biggest weak point, one which I'm sure the Kier will use to the fullest. It's imperative we limit our risk. That's all."

The meeting ended and people trickled out. Henry called me aside and waited until the room cleared of everyone except us and Eli.

"What happened in the woods?" he asked.

"I was nearly decapitated multiple times."

Henry wanted to rehash this now? There should be plenty of time to discuss later, after gorging on high-fat comfort food and a long night's rest.

"We know you were attacked, but who neutralized the Kier?" *Neutralized.* I liked that. A nice, little euphemism for "mauled."

I considered his question. You'd think the answer perfectly obvious, given the damage to the corpse.

"Have you found the body?" I replied.

"Yes, but the marks look like a panther."

"Your point would be?" He'd better get to the point *tout de suite.*

"Trish worked reconnaissance as her hawk at the front of the property during the attack. The panther's pen was open. Do you know who piloted it?"

A thread of fear wound its way into my tangled gut.

"No, I assumed it was her. Isn't xenophobia–"

"Serobestia," Eli cut in. I gave him the best glare I could manage.

"Isn't *serobestia* the most common? Who else here can do what she does?"

"It is quite common but manifests differently in each case. Trish can't inhabit every animal and the panther has been unpredictable for others. She's the only one allowed to navigate it."

My pulse already beat too hard in my veins. It shouldn't matter when I came down to it—the panther saved me and not my attacker.

Still, paranoia clouded my already hazy thoughts. The woman attacked from the other side of the property, away from the Kier.

She came straight for me.

The panther, too. I could've easily become its victim.

I also debated telling them my essence faltered entirely in the woods. As it was, they already knew I had to be rescued by an unknown savior, and that was after the conversation on the deck when Henry essentially told me to let the grown-ups handle the fighting.

Fair point to them. My essence *had* failed when I needed it most. Self-doubt settled in my chest.

I added "a good cry in the shower" to my pre-unconsciousness To-Do list.

Couldn't let Peter, Henry, or Eli see it though. Between the limited information, and then assigning me to the back deck, they already trusted me in half-measures. I didn't think I could handle even more bubble wrap.

"Then your guess is as good as mine," I answered. "All I cared about was that it attacked the right person. Whodunit wasn't my concern."

Peter frowned and dismissed us, instructing me to work with Ryan on firearms training first thing in the morning. He must have heard that I begged off Ryan's offer earlier in the day.

The fridge and my bed called to me, in that order. Eli, however, blocked my exit.

"We should help them carry up supplies," he told me. My vision blurred, and the room spun momentarily.

"No, *you* should help carry up the supplies. I should go to bed."

Mustering as much strong-and-independent as I had in reserve, I staggered in the door's direction. My strength finally broke as I passed him, and I had to catch myself on his shoulder. He grasped me at the waist and shifted me to the chair.

My jacket fell open, and he inhaled sharply. It was already freezing in the room but I was too tired to wrap it closed again.

"Henry!" Eli shouted, fear seeping into his voice. Henry came running back into the room.

"What's the hold up?" I slurred. "I just need to get to my fluffy, comfy bed, and I'll be fine in eight to ten hours. Preferably ten."

"I'll get Lita," Henry said and rushed off.

I didn't understand all the fuss, and then looked down at my shirt.

That "close miss" with the dagger had been a little too close. Cloth and skin were slashed open. The edges of the angry and puffy slice still bled slightly, adding to the blend of crimson and rusty-brown coating my front. My shirt soaked through with a deep-red stain that flowed down the front of my black leggings. It didn't hurt at all; I hadn't even noticed it.

Shit, that edge was *sharp*.

So, that was what shock felt like. It wasn't so bad. I closed my eyes, the temptation to pass out pulling me under. Eli's face was in mine in an instant, shaking me.

His hand held my cheek, his thumb forcing me to look into frantic eyes.

"No sleep right now. You need to stay awake," he told me. "I'll slap you if I have to but I'd rather not."

Weird, he normally relished that kind of thing. His panicked voice barely pierced the fog.

Eli picked me up and hustled us toward the infirmary. My whole body ached, but I let him maiden-carry me. I could complain about it later.

Lita met us halfway and told him the cots in the med room were full. He headed off in another direction and entered a room I didn't recognize. A bed and sitting area were positioned across from a bathroom.

He gently placed me in the bathtub and moved away to let Lita work. The first thing she did was cut my shirt and pants off.

"Don't get any ideas," I slurred while pointing at Eli, who watched anxiously from the doorway. Lita gave a little smile, and I felt a rush over small victories.

"Go get her a change," she instructed him.

"Nothing skimpy," I added. "I know you're going to get something skimpy and *no*."

She undressed me the rest of the way and used the shower to rinse the blood from the areas below the wound. She prodded at the edge before dumping some iodine on the slash and wiping away the excess.

The needle barely made a dent in my haze as she sewed the gash. It was odd to see the skin handled like repairing a torn pair of pants. She covered it with a bandage.

It only needed eighteen stitches and there was no major damage, only an absurd amount of bleeding after being left too long without care.

The prognosis she provided seemed strong. It didn't require a transfusion, but she inserted an IV of saline and attached it to a banana bag. Two needles at once and I hadn't even cried yet.

Lita wrapped me in a towel and handed me the change of clothes Eli'd brought in. Flannel pants and a tank top, and the heavens did smile upon me.

She left me alone to try, gently, to dress myself. More clothes to be lost to blood stains. I hoped this wasn't a pattern forming or I'd be out of wardrobe before the month ended.

I staggered out of the door, but Eli was there to help me to the bed. He pulled back the cover for me and balanced the saline bag on top of the wooden headboard. I snuggled into the soft sheets, already half-way to asleep.

The two of them exchanged words in hushed tones. I was in and out, only picking up on disjointed pieces of the conversation.

"It's superficial, but she's bled a lot. She needs . . ." Lita murmured.

". . . that will need to be done?" asked Eli.

". . . here for the night."

"It's fine. Thanks, Lita."

"Can I sleep now?" I muttered, readjusting the pillow under my head and shoving another between my knees.

I vaguely recalled someone draping a blanket over me, but it was overshadowed by the pleasant darkness that settled on my mind.

* * *

I gasped awake, sitting straight up so quickly I nearly fell off the bed. The sudden movement pulled at my stitches and painfully dislodged the IV needle and tape. No way was I putting *that* back in on my own.

It took a solid three minutes for my heart rate and breathing to settle. I'd woken up in yet another room I didn't recognize. I wasn't even scared. Honest.

Blackout shades were drawn over the windows, but the split in the fabric exposed a wide palm frond. My room had a similar view and I figured this was one of the bedrooms that lined the atrium. The light beat down on the leaves and reflected softly into the room. Late afternoon, then.

The walls were the predictable beige, but with hunter green and navy plaid the linens. I floundered off the bed and barely maneuvered onto an upholstered ottoman. Huffing to feed my lungs, I hoisted myself to a standing position while pins and needles prickled in my limbs.

I felt weak, so very weak.

An oversized entertainment center consumed the long wall shared by the hallway. Books, picture frames, and trophies lined the shelves. The plaques varied between High Mark, Gold, or First Place. Some were consecutive, but they were all spaced out over the last fifteen or so years. I didn't see a single award below the best. Second place medals didn't get displayed, if there were any.

I had started thinking of it as the "ego wall" when I found the very center. In the middle of the cluster of awards was a five-by-seven photo of a young boy and girl in martial arts uniforms with their parents. The kids raised a trophy as tall as they were, each parent mussing the hair of a child. The photo was all teeth and goofy looks. I took it off the shelf to study it in the dim light from the bathroom.

Eli came into the room. He saw what I was holding and his face instantly lit with anger, his blue eyes shining bright. He snatched the frame from my hand and wiped at a fingerprint I'd left behind. He placed the frame gently back onto the shelf, recentering it with care.

"That your family?" I asked. He looked from the photo to glare at me. His eyes were again held by the cold, calculating expression I was so used to.

"Now that you're up, you should go see Lita. I'm sure she'll want to check your stitches."

He turned his back on me to leave, completely disregarding both my question and my presence.

I hate being ignored when I've asked a question. Growing up, my feelings and wishes were often brushed aside. No one here seemed to care that they did it, too, and especially not Eli. They all guarded when and what they told me, and I had long since tired of the practice.

"It's a simple question," I snapped, my tone sharp. "I suggest you answer it."

I hadn't meant to threaten him but that's what happened.

Eli froze and pivoted to glare fully at me. He must have seen the irritation plain on my face, because the first seed of a smile tilted at the corner of his mouth.

"And what, exactly, will happen if I don't?" He asked, stalking toward me. The smile blossomed into a full-blown grin. "You've gone against me on the mats, you've had your fun picking through my personal life. You've got an idea what I'm capable of, and I know exactly what your limitations are. What threat could you possibly pose to me?"

He laughed at me. Again. *Fuck, he's an ass.* I wanted to summon a fireball and burn him up, to torch that smug backside.

"You don't think much of me, I get it. You can at least show a little courtesy. Answer when I ask you something, even if it's to tell me you don't want to talk about it."

It seemed like every conversation we'd ever had was an argument.

"I don't feel like dealing with you right now," he sighed, and I saw for the first time the weariness in his features. Gray bags ringed his eyes as his shoulders hunched.

"Did you sleep at all last night? What good are you if you pass out?" I retorted.

"I stayed out to help with clean-up, and then in the infirmary, but I got a few hours." He tilted his head toward the bed at the end of the room.

"You slept *here*?" I tried really, really hard not to let the shock show, but that cocky smile returned.

"It's my room, my bed. Does that bother you?"

"Why bring me here instead of my room?"

He hesitated.

"Lita said you needed to be checked every two hours. It was easier to have you here than go to your room to do it."

Mental gears clicked and turned, and my anger ebbed. Eli woke himself up every two hours to check on me, to care for me. He'd helped me when I was broken, and I was being hostile.

I should probably leave, before I made the situation worse. I walked to the door, stopping for a moment beside him.

"I'm sorry. Thank you," I muttered.

A moment passed where our eyes met. I tried to show him gratitude instead of the normal anger, frustration, and irritation. His face softened into an expression I didn't understand. He must really be exhausted.

He led me by the wrist back to the wall of awards, looking at the picture as awkward anticipation charged the space between us.

"Yes, that was my family," he said. "I was twelve. Jack and I won the under-thirteen division for partners sparring. Our parents died six months later."

My chest tightened, the revelation a heavy weight that dragged at my thoughts.

I remembered how he'd sat with me in the aftermath of my father's rejection. He knew not to try to talk through it in those first few moments, instead sitting quietly to keep me company while I grappled with it.

"I'm so sorry," I told him. I'd been apologizing a lot lately.

"Shit happens and then you die," he said shortly. I guess that was one way of putting it. "We moved to Orlando with our aunt and uncle. It was fine. We didn't spend much time with them. Mostly we were here."

I nodded my head like I understood, even though I didn't. All thoughts of my own family had been blocked out to avoid another meltdown. Going down that path would only spur the rage, and we were almost being civil. Try not to ruin a good moment.

"It must have been good to have somewhere to go." I turned toward him and shifted my hand so I was more holding his than being gripped at the wrist. "And Jack? Is she Valen or Amory?"

"Neither."

Shocked, I looked up at him.

"A Duality doesn't always pass, or doesn't meaningfully pass. We call them duds, although don't let Peter or Henry hear you say it. Another reason why there are so few of us."

"Jack is just a Guard?"

"She is not *just* a Guard. She's one of the best fighters we have. She's included in everything we do, and she's never treated like one of the herd."

So much for keeping the peace. Plan A, Don't Make It Worse, was back on.

"I suppose I should go find Lita."

"That's probably a good idea."

I pivoted to the doorway again, but remembered the moment in the woods. He was my Valen; he deserved to know if I had problems calling my essence under pressure.

"One other thing—I tried to summon my essence to protect myself last night and it wouldn't trigger."

Attentive eyes jumped from the photograph straight to me. Inside, my anxiety at discussing what happened clanged against my chest and begged me to stop.

"What do you mean, 'it wouldn't trigger?' You've struggled before with calling it on command."

"This was different. I felt the burn and fought fine, all things considered, but my fire wouldn't form. I couldn't even get a bubble going, even though it was fine earlier in the night."

I'd felt rather good about my control before it disappeared. Talk about anticlimactic.

"This is the woman in the woods?" he asked.

"Yes."

"It can happen sometimes, even after the Acceptance. You're still new at it. Triggers are very unpredictable before you gain control. Your essence might have struggled to respond appropriately if she only used a sword."

"Does that mean if you try to fight someone you might get your ass kicked?" I teased. I tried for playful, but it seemed he was all out of playful at the moment.

"No, I'm more than skilled without the extra help," he sneered. "Don't ever doubt I'll pound Ryan into the ground when I want to. Besides, I'd want you there to watch."

When, not if. I hadn't even considered Ryan in the equation. I rolled my eyes at him and spun back to the door. *Whatever, jackass.*

"You said his name," he spat. "In your sleep. You asked for him."

Well, shit.

He'd bent over backward to make sure I was safe and surviving, and I'd said another man's name. I didn't even know how to respond to that, so I frowned and kept heading for the door.

"You know you're meant to be with me," he said to my back. "The Pairs are intentional design, true Pair or not."

I halted, then cursed myself for failing to make the strong exit by ignoring him. My chin shifted, speaking over my shoulder so I wouldn't have to face him.

"I'm meant to be with someone of my own choosing. Me, not some random person plus-twenty years ago, who knew nothing about either of us.

"Thank you for what you did, but perhaps it's better for both of us if you stop assuming we're soulmates when we can't even stand each other."

If he said anything after that, I didn't hear it.

I left the room in favor of my own and a long, hot shower. Lita could wait. Hell, comfort food could wait. I needed to feel clean. I'd seen too many people get hurt, too many get killed. Somehow, the shower felt like the first step in the right direction.

Chapter Seventeen

Ryan

Peter cornered me during the clean-up and directed me to teach Jex to use a firearm. Ninety percent probability he had some kind of ulterior motive, but who cared? He handed me a sanctioned excuse to spend time with her.

Jex needed to learn to shoot with whatever she felt the most comfortable. Until she could call and control her essence on command, her ability to protect herself was too uncertain.

Her injury shoved my plans to the back burner. We'd spent hours together sorting through the wreckage after the attack, but I assumed she'd tell me if she were hurt.

My heart still thrashed in my chest, remembering how she looked as they rushed her down the hall—her body as limp as a rag doll, with skin so pale the veins spider-webbed under them in faded-red streaks. She slept for three days afterward, only waking when Brit or I cleaned the wound or forced her to down food and meds. Even for days after she moved gingerly.

Jex was lucky, so damn lucky. The shallow slice had already closed up neatly in the last week. She pushed herself too fucking hard.

Peter put her on light duty, which meant she still had to work on her concentration and focus but at least it saved her from combat training.

Eli's lessons seemed to be mostly about throwing her around the PR. Sure, he taught her forms and technique, but if you're grappling with someone at her size, you've already substantially increased your chances of getting injured or killed. He probably just wanted to touch her, the dick.

Jex was . . . a study in unpredictability. She had no filter for speaking her mind and it was funny as hell. She could socialize and bring everyone to tears with laughter, but then hide in her room and resisted coming out except for training.

Jex pretended, poorly, to be completely fine. She still struggled with being here, with what her parents had done, and with the attack. She refused to talk about it, but it weighed on her.

Who could blame her? The strength it takes to keep moving after something like that . . .

When I first found out about Dualities, the world became huge and unknown. It helped to know my family was working with the Clara—we had a clear dividing line and were on the side of Good. It helped me find discipline and reassurance that I had solid people to rely on.

Well, most people.

I didn't know what Eli's problem was. It's not like he hadn't known about her or that this was an eventuality. Maybe he thought kicking her in the ass constantly pushed her to succeed. He liked to plot shit like that.

Granted, he'd always had an attitude, always thought himself above everyone else. Normally he could be civil. His self-importance inflated drastically around her. Even Jack gave him shit for it, and Jack didn't much like Jex either.

More for me, I supposed. Even if Jex couldn't fully be mine, she'd still be my Firefly. She deserved to be protected and cared for. She deserved better than him.

Which was why I asked her to meet me in my room this morning. We should be at the range, but I wanted to make her feel good. To remind her she could be happy here. To let her know she had options. She was so stunning, sometimes I hardly breathed around her. I'd been dying to get her back into my bed.

So, I got little tea candles and mason jars from the pantry and set them up like that night at Anna's party. Shards of light had flickered on her face on the pool deck, that hourglass silhouetted and begging to be touched. I barely found the words to speak to her then, but I'd make up for it.

Now, in the darkness of my room, the candles shone dimly as the flames reflected on the glass and emitted a gentle glow. The balmy scent of burning wicks and melting wax overpowered the room a bit, and I worried I might have gone too far. I fidgeted with their placement, nerves droning in my gut.

I'd wanted Jex from the first moment I laid eyes on her in that dress. It swung around her legs and hugged at her waist until it took all of my control not to cup her ass under the skirt. I still got semi-hard just watching her cheeks pink-up whenever I smiled at her. Still had difficulty controlling my hands around her. If anything, the attraction strengthened the more time we spent together.

With the Bluetooth speakers connected, I selected my favorite "slow mix" playlist. She'd remember dancing at Kicks a million years ago. Jex remembered everything. I even wore the same gray sweats I'd been wearing the last time she was in here.

I had every intention of continuing where we'd left off when Eli interrupted us. I couldn't wait to see what she'd do with those lips and that tongue. The crazy things she'd say and the sounds she'd make with them.

And so I waited.

She pushed open my door as Niall Horan's "Slow Hands" kicked on. *Perfect.*

"Hey, I thought we were . . ."

Her voice trailed off as she took in the setting I'd created for her. At first, her eyes went wide in surprise, then faded and settled into that serene smile I loved to see on her face. The tension she perpetually held in her neck released, and her shoulders dropped forward in relief.

She had on a pair of drawstring baggies and a tank top with a sports bra. She wore some variation of the get-up everywhere now, almost like a uniform. Sometimes with skintight leggings that showed off her curvy legs and ass, sometimes with looser pants like now. She seemed to prefer the bras with weird cut-outs and designs peeking through, which only made it more fun for me.

"I thought we'd stay in," I said, and approached her.

"Oh, you did? And what made you think I'd rather be here instead of shooting stuff?" she said with a grin.

I offered her my signature smile, the one I knew would send her over the edge. Fuck, it was hot watching her breath catch, seeing her respond to such a slight gesture.

With the lock on the door twisted into place, there'd be no interruptions this time.

Seizing the drawstrings hanging at her waist, I twisted them around my hand and used them to yank her against me. She wrapped her arms around my body automatically.

"Now, Firefly," I chuckled, "do you really want to go to the gun range?"

"Do I get to play with your gun either way?" She smirked, and I barked out a laugh. Where did she come up with that shit?

"In all seriousness, a gun isn't a toy. You don't play with it, Jex. Gun safety is important and needs your full commitment."

"And now I'm back to Jex, huh? Don't be such a buzzkill, lawful good."

I shook my head at her, but it only made her smile wider.

Soft, spiral curls cascaded to the middle of her back. I loved playing with her hair. It was the perfect representation of her—wild and beautiful.

"I like this," I said, tugging on a curl.

"I thought most guys like running their fingers through a girl's hair?"

"Most *men* prefer whatever gives the most effective grip."

"Ugh," she groaned, but hugged me tighter. An uncharacteristic giggle escaped my fierce ray of sunshine. I'd climb a mountain fueled by her reactions alone.

We swayed to the music, my arms capturing her in place. Her head rest on my chest with contentment plastered on her face as we drifted. I hummed the words to her, reveling in the feel of holding her close and guided by the gentle harmony.

The world muted to let us have a soothing moment together.

I led us to the bed and spun her back to it. My hands cupped her face, gazing into those intense, bottomless eyes that so easily saw the world for what it was. They reflected the desire she undoubtedly saw in mine, the playful flit of dirty thoughts evident. Damn, I was rock hard just from that look.

As I kissed her, my lips toyed with hers before deepening it to let our tongues weave together. We stood there for a long moment, lost in the taste of each other, both savoring the eagerness and affection.

When I finally broke the kiss, I reached into the nightstand for a condom. Holding it up to her, I gave her a silent ask.

But she sealed her lips shut to keep from spitting out whatever her crazy mind had come up with.

"What—"

"Fun safety," she burst out.

"Again, what—"

"I'd rather do fun safety than gun safety. *Fun* safety has my full commitment."

"I think we need something for your mouth to do that isn't talking."

Jex *hmphed*, but I pushed us both onto the bed, settling myself between her legs. My hands roamed over her body as I explored her mouth with my tongue. She wrestled off my shirt and teased the waistband of my sweats. Eager hands played with the hair below the band.

We lingered on each touch, each breath, drawing out the anticipation. My forehead rest against hers as I tried to fill every fracture in her heart with soft words and gentle nudges. My own heart demanded to care for her, not just to satisfy her now but to safeguard her.

Stripping her shirt off revealed irresistibly smooth skin splashed with freckles. I scraped my teeth down her neck and nibbled at her earlobe as I worked her pants down. She sighed when I tucked my hand into her panties.

Plying into her slit, I thrust first one finger, then a second, in time to the beat of the song. Quiet moans urged me to finger her harder. She was so wet and ready, as she curled her own hands into my hair.

Fuck, I was going to lose it the second I was in her. Had enough, I tried to peel her bra off, but she stopped me with a hand.

"Hang on," she told me, and extracted two short kunai throwing knives from the front straps of the bra, before reaching behind and under the band to relieve a third. When she tossed them onto the nightstand, I almost came right there.

"Should I check for more weapons?" I asked.

"A strip search would be the best option. After all, we take fun safety very seriously here."

Laughing, she squirmed and wiggled off every last stitch of fabric until she lay naked beneath me. It took every ounce of effort not to bite along her full hips and breasts. The stitches from her run-in with a dagger had already dissolved. Aside from the angry line along her side, she barely had a mark on her. So different from all the scars covering my body.

My thumb ran along the wound, nicely closed but still rosy and mottled. She'd undoubtedly start earning her own battle scars soon enough; we all had them.

She looked at me defiantly, daring me to say something about her curves or the injury, but I could only supply a lascivious grin. I wanted to indulge in every inch of her. Later, I'd make her come on my tongue again. For now, I had other plans.

She used her feet to push off my sweats and boxers. I sat back on my knees, stroking myself. My cock was hard as steel, desperate to sink into her warmth, but then she had to bite that sexy-as-fuck bottom lip.

"Keep doing that and I'm going to fuck your mouth," I warned.

Her breathing hitched. She liked it rough, huh. She couldn't be any more perfect if I'd designed her myself. If she wanted to be tossed around, I could do that for her. She was plenty ready for it.

Rolling the condom on, I jerked her toward me by the ankle and wrenched her legs wider. I kissed my way up her body until my mouth reached one of those perfect, tight nipples. She thrashed as my tongue and teeth tasted her while I teased her clit.

Oh yeah, she was primed.

I lined up with her entrance and thrust into her wet pussy with one hard drive. She inhaled sharply and let out the most erotic moan. Her eyes drooped, the hit of pleasure and pain exhaling on parted lips.

Jex was *stunning*. That sly smile and those mischievous eyes flashing in the candlelight. She was so tight I worried she might struggle to take me. I let her adjust to my size, although I needed the moment as much as her.

Our tongues danced together as she hooked her ankles together against my ass. I waited hilt-deep inside her until she tilted her hips and I knew she was ready for more.

I wanted to make it incredible for her. So, I withdrew almost all the way and surged in with another hard thrust.

Fuck, she felt good.

She sucked in another gasp, so vocal. Eyes rolled, her teeth worked at puffy lips, undoubtedly trying to rein in the involuntary noises spilling over them.

Oh, no. This wasn't a moment for restraint, so I drove fully into her again. And again. It became frenzied, and her legs clutched my waist as I fucked her harder.

Hair splayed out, her pupils blew wide and darkened as her breaths escalated to a rapid pant. I settled my arms over her shoulders, using them to leverage into her deeper and rolling my hips to hit every sensitive spot inside and out.

Jex stretched her arms overhead to grip the pillow as I pumped into her, her fingers straining against the fabric. Her eyes closed in pleasure, mouth agape, with her back bowing and presenting those perfect tits. She tightened, her orgasm creeping closer as her moans raged all the way to my balls.

The song flipped to a fifties-sounding melody, and a woman crooned about being a "Freak." Her body relaxed as she snickered, murmuring how she loved this song.

In an instant, Jex rolled us over and straddled me. Maybe she'd picked up some grappling after all.

My Firefly maneuvered over and sank down onto me, then swayed side to side with her head dropped back. Her face radiated with euphoria as it shone in the glimmer of the tea lights. I kneaded her thighs, her ecstasy soaking into my skin.

Unruly hair spilled over her shoulders as she leaned forward to rest her hands on my chest. She rocked more fully to the music, enthralled by the sensation of having me inside her while humming along with the song. Reminding her to focus, I bucked under her, making her giggle again and mutter a *fine, fine.*

Sitting up to face her, I swung my legs off the side of the bed so my dick dug deeper. She rode me in earnest, and the salty sheen on her skin coated my tongue as I devoured her shoulders and breasts.

Gripping that gorgeous ass, I spread my legs to give her more range and encouraged her to go harder. Her arms wrapped around my neck, writhing against me while she ground down on my cock.

The scent of sex on her made my blood boil and my mind race. I was close, too close. I needed to get her there *now*. There'd be time for more later; she wasn't leaving this room until I was satisfied she felt well and truly fucked.

My thumb circled her clit, and she responded with more growling moans. Driving herself onto my shaft, her body quivered as she sighed my name in whispered praise. It took every ounce of willpower I had to let her enjoy this a few minutes longer.

Jex bit that lip again, so I used the hand on her ass to slap it hard. Her pussy momentarily tightened even harder around me, so I did it again. She shook her head and gave me a foxy smile. If this became a battle of wills, I would not win.

"Come for me, Firefly." I whispered in her ear. Lacing my fingers into her hair, I tugged her face even with mine with just enough pressure to prick her scalp.

Our breaths blended as we focused on each other's responses. She rode, and I moved inside and with her, our bodies dancing together in a syncopated rhythm so natural it felt practiced. The tantric connection tied us together like an intense, living thing.

"Come for me," I pleaded. "Come on my cock. Let go, Firefly. Let me watch."

Her face in orgasm was the purest joy, first fragmenting as if in pain, then spreading to rapture as she called out my name once more.

I'd die a lucky man if only I got to hear it again.

I couldn't hold it anymore even if I wanted to, and came hard into her. My balls pumped for several long moments, and she continued to ride me through it.

It was intoxicating. Jex was intoxicating. Her heady scent, the way her skin lit in pinks and reds, the gleam in those sparkling eyes.

We exhaled together; she remained in my lap as we kissed long and thorough. I wrapped my arms around her, cocooning her so close she could probably feel the heavy beat of my heart.

Jex and I rolled around in bed the entire day. We talked a little about Haven and the Clara, but mostly we avoided the topic. She seemed determined not to let her life be about her Duality, which was fine by me. I'd lived my entire life without one. We'd make it work.

The situation might not be perfect, but Jex was perfect *for me.*

Eli was going to learn to share, because no way in hell would I let her go.

She was mine now.

Chapter Eighteen

Jex

Following the attack, Peter didn't just circle the wagons on the Clara—he encased us in iron. The default around here seemed to be to protect first and be proactive later.

More than a week passed since the attack on Haven. Weekends used to be my own haven but, with everyone locked up tight for going on ten days, the stress permeated every interaction.

I'd braved my parents' boxes enough to retrieve the rest of my novels, but even they grew old after a while. Trish and Tom took residence in one of the closer bedrooms but, by the time my daily round of flip-the-floozie finished, I wasn't exactly sociable.

Ryan became my bright spot. Being with him, in any form, soothed my soul. He was the one person here beside Trish who cared for me and watched over me without an ulterior motive.

Still, we didn't have much chance to spend non-bedroom time together. Eli gave no mercy and made no allowances.

I'd thought at first Eli wasn't interested in me. Since our foray into kidnaping, he'd become openly hostile to Ryan, to the point of even scheduling training sessions to cock-block us.

He had been difficult before; now, he was downright infuriating and irritable.

Didn't help that every interaction since that moment on the deck made my essence flare brighter merely by proximity. My body ached for him, the constant need to smother the flames one of my biggest distractions. That first training session with him after had been almost unbearable.

His ask ran through my head in a constant hum.

Be with me.

Not that he seemed equally afflicted.

There was a moment when I'd rolled my ankle during a bad pass. I sprawled on the floor as he crouched at my feet and prodded my ankle. Even after he'd grunted not to be such a baby, he still held my foot as his thumb rubbed over my skin and that infuriating heat slipped up my leg.

His eyes dragged along every inch of my body, his intense gaze rippling with hot desire. I thought for a moment he might dive at me and give in again.

But his control reasserted itself. Major points for respecting my boundaries.

After that, I used his attention and my response to it as part of my mental focus exercises. I shoved that distraction behind yet another mental door, albeit one I could never fully close.

Guilt over the developing bond with Ryan fought with the rational part of my brain, reminding me Eli otherwise would have little interest in me out in the "real world."

Not a great duo, the two of us.

Jack would join the sessions for chunks at a time to teach me different throws and how best to redirect the momentum of a larger opponent. Her demonstrations taught me a lot more than Eli's figure-it-out-yourself methodology. It was surprisingly helpful.

She also didn't have her brother's ire for me, and I guess I didn't hate her so much either. She even made a YouTube playlist of moves from something called aikido, or hapkido, or something like that.

Mostly, I wanted to be alone. In Boston, I'd had my own apartment and life. I could come and go as I pleased. Now, I didn't have a choice. The feeling of suffocation converted to hostility. Best not to subject other people to me carrying that mood around.

I admit it might also have to do with the woman in the woods. One minute she'd been a living, breathing person, and the next she wasn't.

Poof, there goes a life.

It wasn't like Grayam, who'd gone (relatively) quiet into that good night. I'd heard the woman's bones break, her terrified screams. Smelled the scent of blood and body. Seen the mauled ruin of rent flesh. You'd think I'd be desensitized to that kind of thing. I watched serial killer docs, for crying out loud.

I knew, really knew, it was her or me. I understood it, conceptually. She wasn't there to give me a hug or offer life advice.

Yet, I could still see her whenever I closed my eyes. That horrified face, filled with pain, lurked in my consciousness, patiently waiting to jump forward when I least expected it.

I didn't even know her name.

Our second Saturday in quarantine limped by as I hobbled my way into the kitchen. I'd showered, but even that couldn't soothe my aching muscles. Today's training session had been especially brutal, to the point I had personalized footmarks on the mat to reference.

The one benefit of so much work—at the time, it's hard to feel much of anything else. For those hours, I could be peacefully empty of emotion.

Still, Eli noticed my fatigue—both physical and mental—and told me to take a rest afternoon. Haven became suffocating with nothing else to occupy my anxiety.

Outside, the monochrome sky shifted between black to gray, with no light to break through. It was as depressing as full-price Louboutin.

Trish perched on a barstool, alternating between picking at some plain ruffle chips and angrily stabbing a spoon into a pint of chocolate-fudge-brownie ice cream. She was so on edge she vibrated, and I worried for a moment she might be convulsing.

The little flowers embroidered on her button-down matched the navy knee-length skirt perfectly, which she'd paired with camel-colored leather cowboy boots and a wide belt. Stress always exaggerated her countrification.

"You okay?" I asked, ever the wordsmith.

She slammed the spoon onto the countertop and jumped from her seat, surprising the shit out of me so bad I flinched. She paced around the room.

"I'm going nutso sittin' around. We've got to find something to do or I'm going to climb up on the atrium windows for kicks."

"Nutso?"

"Yeah, nutso." She sucked in a breath and straightened her shirt.

"Well, where's Tom?"

"Playing *Call of Duty* in Eli's room. Which is what he's always doing. Cheese and rice, you'd think the thing fed him mother's milk."

"Wow, two colloquialisms in as many minutes, it must really be bad."

Trish glared at me with her best one-eyed stare, which wasn't all that intimidating. We'd work on it later.

"What can I do?"

"I don't know, I don't know, I don't know!" she shrieked in frustration. She rubbed her face, her skin contorted to look eerily like Munch's *The Scream*.

"We could set-up some pranks for when the boys decide to grace us with their presences," I offered.

She stopped pacing around the room, but her face and eyes still strained with frustration. Balled fists pounded the edge of the counter in a machine-gun staccato.

"You know I'm no good at practical jokes. My poker face isn't all that great either." She considered it for a moment. "What if we make something?"

"Make something?" I asked.

"Yeah, like muffins or cupcakes."

"You want me to bake? I'm far better at eating a cupcake than making one. Remember that day in home ec?"

"Excuse me, I believe the proper class title was 'Food Preparation,'" she corrected.

"Either way, I still smell dried oregano when I sneeze sometimes," I said with a laugh.

"Point taken."

"We can't go outside. It'll start pouring any minute and it'll be hella muddy after."

For the last week, the Florida sky had opened up and down-poured between four and five o'clock every day. Trish turned her attention to the drizzle starting to *rat-a-tat* against the window. The rhythm of the soft, small pops would pick up in frequency and intensity any minute.

We both sighed, leaning on the counter and fresh out of ideas. Our mood dropped from frustration to depression in the time it took to acknowledge the murky weather.

"We've got to get out of here before we get all weepy," I told her.

Her returning glance reinforced the opinion. I noticed something out the window and a wicked grin spread across my face. Sure, I may be Clara, but I could still plot from time to time, right?

"Hey, Trish . . ." I said to her.

"Yes, Jex?" she sighed.

"What if we didn't stay here?" I asked.

"You mean like going out to the atrium or something?"

"Farther."

"The boathouse?"

"Farther." My grin fixed into place and felt more natural as time passed. Wickedness became me. Don't hold it against me.

"Jex, we can't leave. Peter's orders—he won't let us back."

"He doesn't have to know. In this weather, he'd never think we'd leave. In fact, we'll tell him we're going down to the boathouse. There's no way anyone would follow us."

"How do you plan on circumventing the fence without notice? The gate's locked."

I glanced out the window and confirmed what I had seen before. Ryan crossed the road in a rain slicker and disappeared into the woods.

"I think I have an in with the gatekeeper," I informed her.

If she had gears, they'd have turned. If she had a light bulb, it would have lit up. She spun and flung herself down the hall toward her room.

"Quietly!" I threw the whisper at her as loudly as I dared. "Meet by the entrance in five minutes."

My room wasn't far from the kitchen, so it didn't take long to gather my purse. A girl's purse is her lifeblood; it's her pockets, bank, beauty kit, and weapon, all in one.

After a change into warmer jeans and grabbing my raincoat, I scrawled out a note about the "boathouse" and tossed it on the kitchen counter. With luck, no one would even notice the note, let alone the unofficial excursion.

I met Trish in the hall, but was unhappily surprised to see Tom striding beside her. I scowled at her.

"Sorry," she whined, "he was in our room. What was I supposed to do?"

More people meant more risk of getting caught. Still, Trish wasn't much for sneaking out, and I couldn't expect her to know such things. She'd changed into a pair of jean shorts and flip-flops.

I also reflected that sneaking out was incredibly childish. But, in the immortal words of Dave Barry, "You can only be young once, but you can always be immature."

"Here's the deal," I whispered to them, "treat this like a mission. Tom, go figure out where everyone else is. Do not tell them what's going on, just pass them by. If you think someone is headed toward the front, try to redirect them. Get the car and pull-up to the gate in ten minutes."

"Trish, go to your room and close the door until Tom retrieves you." I hissed with a pointed look.

She pouted at me, but I wasn't swayed.

"Don't give me that. You went to get your purse and came back with a new party member. It's safer to keep you hidden. Tom will get you when he's done scouting everyone's locations."

"What are you going to do?" she asked.

"Convince the guard to let the inmates out."

* * *

My red-and-white polka dot raincoat was a gift from my friend Hillary in Boston. When she gave it to me, she told me I needed more whimsy in my life. Her word, "whimsy." Not the best for blending into the wilderness, but it was all I had. I scurried into the lightly falling rain toward the area where Ryan disappeared into the trees.

Rain-mist mingled with the lingering heat and clung to the leaves, making them droop. The muggy atmosphere trapped body heat in the plastic cocoon of the raincoat, causing it to stick uncomfortably to my skin. Exactly what you need to convince someone to break the rules—sweatiness. At least it was better than chafing.

Long ago, I'd discovered there were three ways to get people to do what you wanted when it was, *ahem*, questionable—make it a statement (instead of a request), disguise what you're asking, or make them want to bend the rules for you. Assert, adapt, or appeal. Like the three R's, but for treachery. Or politics.

Convincing Ryan—good, sweet, lovable, rule-following Ryan—to let us out would require a lot of eyelash batting and vague statements.

The walk allowed time to form a game plan. I trod carefully among the tree roots, paying close attention to the ground to avoid a fall or twisted ankle. Still, my feet always seemed to find level ground, even when it wasn't level. I realized I hadn't fallen once when I went thrashing through the woods last week. *Huh.*

Ryan strode toward Haven, his head ducked to prevent the wind from blowing rain into his poncho. He beamed when he saw me, his eyes lighting in delight, and my heart clanged a smidge in guilt.

"Firefly, what are you doing out here?" Ryan asked. He held his palm out. I placed my hand in his, brushing my thumb over the side.

"Could you please open the gate? We need to leave."

"Need," not want, and a "please" for good measure.

"Did Peter okay it?"

And now for a tap dance.

"We'll be back in a few hours. It's important." I pursed my lips.

"Is everything okay? Is it one of the Guards? I should make a few calls."

"No, no, it's nothing like that." I pulled him a little closer, tilting my head innocently. "Nothing you need to be too concerned about. It's only me, Trish, and Tom. We'll be back as soon as we can."

Projecting stern-but-unconcerned was a delicate balance I wasn't sure I accomplished. He frowned.

"Only the three of you? Why isn't Eli going? You should have your Valen with you if you're going out on a job."

"No!" I yelped, a little too quick with the rejection. "Eli's been a lot lately. It's been days since the last attack. Things are quiet. The three of us can deal with it on our own. It's only an errand."

"You should have a fourth in case you need to split up."

"It's only a few hours, Ry. No one will notice we're gone."

He scrutinized me, suspicion blooming in his gaze. I probably shouldn't have added that last part.

"And who," he asked, "exactly, is unaware you will be gone?"

Shit, this was going downhill. I bit my lip at him, hoping for a distraction, and added a bit of urgency to my tone.

"We don't have a lot of time, we need to go now. Please open the gate."

Best to end the conversation there. I turned to make my way toward the entrance, forcing him to follow.

"Fine, but I'm going with you," he said.

He strode beside me, easily outpacing my steps. Bringing him was a tempting offer, but another person would only complicate things. Besides, I didn't want him to suffer the consequences when he didn't know it was an illicit outing.

"I don't think that's a good idea. You weren't included in the plan."

Ryan winced. *Fuck a duck*. I'd implied he was excluded from a job by Peter or Henry.

"I think they need you here, is all," I hedged.

"Actually, I was on my way to the house to switch with Wade. I'm free for the rest of the afternoon. I just need to tell Henry I'm going."

"No!" *Settle, Jex, settle.* "If we're going to leave, we need to go now. Immediately. I told you, we're in a hurry."

"You're not leaving without someone to watch your back. Let's go."

We'd arrived at the gate, and Ryan opened the padlock. Tom's SUV, with Trish ducked down in the passenger seat, idled toward us. I hopped into the back seat and told Tom to drive through and wait for Ryan.

Tom and Trish turned. She formed a semi-adequate glare.

"What were you saying about adding party members?" she teased.

"Just drive the car. And stop slouching like that, you look ridiculous."

Ryan slid in beside me and buckled his seatbelt. Tom crept away from the gate ever so slowly. I didn't breathe normally until we made it to the main road. It wasn't until we were cruising down 192 toward Orlando that anyone spoke.

"Okay, Jex. It's your jailbreak, so where to?" Trish asked.

"*Jailbreak*?" Ryan stammered, but we ignored him.

Trish and I exchanged look and simultaneously answered, "Retail therapy!"

Tom glanced at his betrothed. "Retail . . . therapy?"

"Retail therapy," I explained. "Noun. When you pay the money you'd spend on a therapist at the local outlet store. Results are strikingly similar."

Some things could only be cured by the perfect pair of wedge heels. It took effort not to crow with glee. Suggest discounted brand names and I transformed into a twelve-year-old at a One Direction concert. Note to self: rail against consumerism later, after I've used up my card limit.

It was all a very, very bad idea, but when shopping was concerned, I didn't care. Neither did Trish. After more than a week of cabin fever, the outlets sounded heavenly.

"Driver, Prime Outlet, please," Trish cooed to Tom. He grumbled, but didn't voice further objection.

Ryan broke the excitement.

"Wait, why are we going to a mall?"

I waited for someone else to clue him in that this was an unsanctioned mission, that we'd finagled the escape through half-truths. He whirled toward me in his seat, forcing me to face him.

"Jex, why jailbreak?" His mouth down-turned and his brows pinched together. *Fuck all the ducks.* I stared down at my hands, twirling the ring on my finger.

"We aren't . . . exactly . . . on a job," I mumbled. He placed his hand over my fidgeting fingers, squeezing a little harder than necessary. I supposed I deserved a little pain. I'd tricked him into leaving, and he might end up exiled like the rest of us.

"We left without authority? Peter won't let us in. If we turn around now and explain it to him, maybe he'll overlook it," he reasoned.

All three of us immediately bellowed a "NO!" The car swerved as Tom twisted in his seat.

"Look, Ryan," he said calmly, "I know you don't like going against orders, but we had to get out of there. Come on, man, you've been locked up like the rest of us. We're going crazy. No one will even know we're gone. What's a few hours?"

"And I suppose this was your idea?" Ryan asked me.

"I may have been the first to suggest it, but I wasn't twisting arms."

He grunted, staring out the window with his "thinking face." I didn't push him. He could think all he wanted as long as he came to the right conclusion—mine.

"I don't suppose any of you are willing to go back?" he asked.

"The feeling on that is unanimous," Trish replied.

"Then I guess I have no choice."

* * *

We didn't go to the mall, even though stains, scratches, and holes severely diminished my closet selection. Tom suggested paintballing and a Target stop to mollify Ryan.

Yes, I agreed to paintballing. Mind control must have been used.

The rain broke right on cue. By the time we made it to the course a good hour away it had already dissipated. The late afternoon transformed into a beautifully sunny day, with a warm breeze blowing to keep the normal Florida heat at bay.

We'd split into two teams, Tom and Trish against Ryan and me. Trish insisted on wearing extra padding to avoid welts, so she was hopelessly restricted to laying sideways behind a bale of hay.

While the boys chased after each other at the other end of the course, I found Trish and stood over her cackling. I shot her in the butt. She shot me in the shin. It was the highest she could aim. I was proclaimed the victor.

We were both "out," so we stripped off the suits to lie in the sun for the rest of the two-hour window. Thankfully, Trish stowed some suntan lotion in the trunk. I switched out my jeans for a pair of my new running shorts, and we spread out in the damp grass.

We used a cup to turn Trish's phone into a speaker to blast some music. It felt good to be normal again, to have girl talk. Hell, to talk about anything that didn't involve training. I hadn't realized how badly I needed it until we lay there together, baking in the waning sun and humming along to most of BLACKPINK's *The Album*.

The boys came back panting and covered in sweat. I cringed, thinking of all the funk that would fill-up the car for the return trip.

They laid with us for a while, and at some point Tom carried Trish off with a devious look in his eye while she snickered. Ryan might have been gross from paintballing, but somehow it didn't bother me so much.

It felt like a date. A *real* date with Ryan. A double with my best friend. Almost normal.

When we inched toward the entry gate, well into twilight, no one approached the vehicle. Not a single leaf or branch rustled in the wind. No Henry charging out of the building screaming, *AHA!* I was almost disappointed. Just a skosh.

A smiling Ryan quickly let us through the gate before slipping into woods. The entry door stood silent against the fading light. If anyone was behind the peek-a-boo window, I couldn't tell.

Tom put in the key and it turned easily. He led us inside, Trish following closely behind with me bringing up the rear.

"Where ya' been?" Pinch asked.

A series of creatively colorful curses popped out of my mouth, but Pinch only laughed. He leaned against the wall beside the door. We should have been suspicious that it wasn't locked.

"Sweet sassy molasses, do not do that!" Trish shrieked. She gets more adorable the angrier she gets. At least I wasn't the only one surprised.

"Peter would like to see you in the library," he informed us.

Joy. I sensed the verbal lashing coming. Nothing like a good reprimand to get the blood pumping.

Ryan waited for us in the library. Brit stood beside him, her hands on her hips and fury on her face.

Before this, I wouldn't have said Brit *could* be intimidating. Now, she was five-feet-five-inches of indignation. I worried she might gut someone to make a point.

Peter and Henry assumed their appointed chairs, but only Henry openly shared a slice of Brit's outrage. Both of their faces were passive, but Henry's body language betrayed him. He clutched at the ends of the armrests, his knuckles fading white in and out. Peter's arms were crossed stone.

"Where were you this afternoon?" Peter asked.

Henry began passing a pen back and forth, clicking it open and closed.

The tension intensified when no one answered, the stretch of silence a mile long.

Brit, nearly a foot shorter than Ryan, snatched his ear and yanked it down to her height. Barely giving any of us a chance to respond, she shoved him forward, ear-first.

"Paint in his hair," she noted.

Peter scrutinized each of us. Trish and I were both in the shorts and tank tops left over from our afternoon under the sun. Paint splattered my shoes. Trish's legs were a light shade of pink. Both Tom's and Ryan's clothes were wrinkled, still sweaty from scurrying around in those horrible coveralls. Plus, we all reeked like we'd been rolling in a trash heap.

"Given the welts, I'm going to assume paintball," Peter reflected. "When did you leave? Did anyone else see or go with you?"

Tom cleared his throat. "We left when the rain started. No one else was around."

"Is this why you checked in on us this afternoon?" Peter frowned at him. His jaw clenched, barely opening his mouth to growl the question at Tom. Coming from Peter, this was quite a show.

"Yes. It's my fault. It was my idea to leave. They wouldn't have gone if I hadn't convinced them."

Tom, falling on his sword. He went up a few notches on the hero scale. I couldn't let him do it, though.

"He's wrong," I admitted. The room shifted its attention to me. I felt a little like the last chicken in the coop with three foxes.

"By all means, enlighten us," Peter said.

"It's not Tom's fault, it's mine. It was my idea. I wrote the note. I convinced Trish and Tom to leave. I tricked Ryan into going with us. If you are going to blame someone, blame me."

Shouldn't it feel better to confess? I felt like crap.

"Yes, we found the note. It appears to be a page from a pad in your room." Peter gave the barest hint of a smirk.

"From She Who Is Fabulous?" he asked. He held up the pad, the phrase embossed into the top of each page with little, metallic-blue stars.

"I'll tell my sister you approve." It popped out of my mouth before I realized I didn't know if I had a sister anymore.

My heart dropped into oblivion and wrenched my gut with it. It felt like I'd had the wind knocked out of me by a mean kick.

I'd carefully ignored my family . . . what *was* my family, since *it* happened. Here and there, like then, there'd be some reminder and it would send me spiraling. I couldn't afford it right now, though.

The grief must have played on my face, because Henry softened a little. His knuckles returned to their natural coloring.

"Here's what's going to happen," Peter declared. "We don't have time to deal with this right now. You will all be punished later, but suffice it to say it will not be pleasant."

"Peter, it's my fault, not theirs. They don't deserve the punishment. Least of all Ryan."

"They went with you knowing it was wrong. They are as much to blame as you are. Your sacrifice is admirable, but unnecessary. You are all lucky we have a much bigger problem. I need your help with a task and can't have you hindered by a restriction."

"So, is it safe to say we are staying at Haven?" I asked.

"For the time being, you may remain," Peter replied.

Trish took my hand and squeezed. The moment of irony struck me, begging to stay somewhere we were earlier dying to escape from.

"The information I'm about to share cannot leave this room, even to Eli. We suspect someone may be feeding information to the Kier. We aren't sure who it is or what they want, but a cell phone was found earlier this afternoon. It's registered in the name of an alias of Frank Delaney, the Cole's second-in-command."

"Do we have any idea who brought it here?"

"Only one person is unaccounted for this afternoon, now that you have been located. I think I'm safe in assuming you were all together?"

The four of us nodded like eager supplicants.

"Since you're the only ones who we definitively know couldn't have left it behind, I'm asking you to assist in the investigation.

"As of now, Maxon is the only one we can't track during the relevant period. You might also recall we found a shredded piece of paper with numbers written on them during Jack's rescue—these numbers match Maxon's phone number.

"I need you to uncover where Maxon was this afternoon, why he was unaccounted for, and what might motivate him to do this."

I flashed back to the first time I'd encountered the man, taking a clandestine call in the woods on my first day.

Trish's hand squeezed mine.

"Peter," she took a step forward to stand before him. "Are you sure it's Maxon? It doesn't seem like him."

"I know this is difficult. I've known Maxon since he was a child and would never have thought him capable of it. Now that we've accounted for the four of you," his eyes shifted to me, "he's the only remaining option. The phone was found in the Weapons Room around six. Jack was there at four-thirty and swears it wasn't in the room. What other conclusion is there to draw?"

"She could be mistaken," Trish argued. "I'm sure there's a good explanation. Ask him where he was. I know he'll have a good answer."

"We can't risk letting Maxon know we are aware. It would compromise him and he might try to run. We'll never find out what the Cole wants or how he intends to get it if it isn't handled carefully."

"You know Maxon," she pled. "We all know him. We have to give him the benefit of the doubt." The dull throb of desperation in her voice betrayed her.

"Enough," Henry thundered. "Peter has made his decision. He gave you orders. Given your propensity to disregard those orders, let me make it clear that you will not be offered another chance. You don't deserve the one you're getting."

"I think they get the idea, Henry," Peter said and turned back to our sorry lineup of absconders. "I expect results from you, now go."

Chapter Nineteen

Trish refused to accept that Maxon was the traitor. She argued for him vehemently every time we discussed it.

I don't think she realized how much it affected Tom to hear it. With each passing conversation, he became more and more distressed. The emotion might change—it fluctuated between anger to outright despair—but it was no less obvious each time.

We resolved to each keep tabs on him throughout the day and maintain a record of his comings and goings. It seemed kind of pointless, short of catching him in the act, but what did I know about investigations?

The evening delivered more bad news. Three more Guards disappeared. They'd been scheduled to leave the Thursday prior for a weekend cruise, but never returned. A search of their homes found them undisturbed, luggage empty and stored away, toiletries in bathrooms, food rotting in fridges and pantries.

Whatever had happened to them, the Guards disappeared before they packed for vacation.

Mid-morning the next day, Ryan and I stood in the gun range at the end of the Weapons Room. Eli had to take Jack to another sanctioned doctor's appointment, leaving the time free for gunmanship.

Ever since the attack, we'd been sneaking off to Ryan's room for alone time instead of learning to shoot. Peter had to have known, but it seemed he was willing to let it slide.

Until this morning, that is, when he told us with absolute seriousness to *stop screwing around and do our duty*.

Given the number of missing members of my cult-away-from-home, I couldn't say I disagreed either. Even if learning gun safety wasn't nearly as fun.

Fun safety. *Snort.*

"Have you ever fired a gun?" Ryan asked.

He handed me a pair of safety glasses and ear protectors more suitable for airport runways than houses in rural Florida.

"No. I don't like guns."

Never had, truth be told. I had friends who hunted, but they could never convince me to go with them. I didn't like the idea of being trusted with a loaded lethal weapon when others were in the vicinity. Peter seemed confident that it wouldn't be an issue, what with my secondary Duality, but I felt a lot less certain.

"It's about awareness and practice," Ryan said. "Everything will be fine as long as you know the rules and remain vigilant."

The gun rested in a leather holster on the small table protruding from one of the alley dividers. A box of ammunition sat beside it. I expected the gun to shine, to glint evilly under the overhead lights, but it was more dull than reflective.

The gun appeared entirely too large for a newbie. Aggressively large, like it might kill me for looking at it wrong.

In junior high, one of my classmates, Garrett, accidentally shot himself. He'd failed to keep the gun properly cleaned, and it fired while he pretended to draw it like in old western movies. Yes, the idiot had been playing around with a loaded gun, something else he'd neglected to think about.

When we visited Garrett in the hospital, he'd shown me the x-rays of his shattered foot. He tried to play it off by getting me to write my number on his cast, but even Mr. Tough Guy couldn't pretend all the time. His face would droop when he thought no one watched. His brow would sweat, even when he smiled. Every motion, even laughing, caused pain to flash across his normally affable face before he composed himself and gave the appropriate reaction.

Garrett remained hospitalized for nearly two months and had to work hard after that to recover. He still limped slightly, especially when he tried to run. I wasn't excited by the prospect it could happen to me.

"I think I've changed my mind," I said. Definitely didn't want to end up like Garrett.

"What are you afraid of?" Ryan asked.

"You know, the whole *getting shot* thing. Not on my bucket list. In fact, it's on my un-bucket list."

"The gun is empty. I'll show you how to handle it, get you used to holding it and, if you're comfortable, I'll teach you how to load it."

The thought of being around a loaded gun—*that* loaded gun—scared the shit out of me. The room spun a little before I remembered I was supposed to inhale after I exhaled.

"Take a breath," he soothed. He placed his hand at the small of my back and led me toward the alley. "Just stand there for a minute. You don't have to touch it."

Just stand there, I could do that. Standing I could handle. You don't have to touch it, just stand there.

That's what he said.

See, I'm fine.

I had the standing under control when he reached over to remove the gun from its holster. I saw him move for it, albeit slowly, and used the opportunity to spin and run for the door.

"I should do some bag work until Eli gets back," I called, dodging out of his reach.

Ryan darted in front of me. The gun was blessedly not in his hands, which he'd put on each of my arms to force me to face him. He blocked my exit yet again. It was impossible to run away from the man.

"You'd rather go back to Eli than spend an afternoon with me?"

I watched his mouth as he flashed that cocky half-smile, the one that said, *I'd rather be doing unspeakable things to you.*

The blush hit my cheeks before I could calm myself down. I met his eyes, more to prove I wasn't embarrassed than anything else.

Ryan caught me with those deep-green eyes, and I fell into them, sinking into a lush, green abyss of thoughts most people don't utter aloud. It made the slight blush rush forward full-force. Seeing him gaze at me like that made me want to strip naked and demand he bend me over the partition.

One would think that all the sex might temper his appeal, but it seemed not. I felt so hot for Ryan you could've fried an egg on my forehead. My sex drive had been insane for the last several weeks, what with all the testosterone flying around.

His head tilted slightly, his arms closing around me like he could see straight into my mind. He chewed on his bottom lip and gave a low laugh. The sound buzzed through me and left me panting.

"Didn't think so," he murmured.

The fear from before faded to ghosts whispering the memory. He drew me closer, his hands fitting perfectly around my ass. I buried my face in his chest, inhaling that scent of soil and forest.

He leaned down, his lips settling on mine gently at first. We kissed softly, but I bowed into it and ran my hands under his shirt and up his chest. How he walked around all day without women demanding to touch him was a complete mystery.

Our kiss continued to heat, his mouth opening to taste mine. Ryan slid a hand into the back of my pants to cup my bare ass. He grinned into the kiss when one of my hands toyed with the button on his jeans. He was already hard, so I grazed a hand up the front of his crotch. His breathing hitched incrementally.

Flipping open the button and dipping a hand past the waistband, I continued stroking my hand up and down against the ever-hardening shaft in his pants.

We rapidly spiraled past PG-13 in public. Ryan cupped my breast and swept a calloused thumb underneath the fabric of my bra to tease my nipple. I moaned into his mouth.

"Go back to my room?" I asked. "I'm not promising you'll get lucky, but I'm not *not* promising you'll get lucky."

I grinned up at him, his cock in my hand, his gaze filled with a deep desire that only added to the excitement. We put ourselves back together and turned to leave.

"Have you told Eli, yet?" he asked over his shoulder.

"I think Eli is aware something is going on."

His question was odd. They had both done their share of posturing.

"No, have you told him you made a decision."

I pulled at his hand to look at him.

"What do you mean?" I asked.

"That you picked me; you're mine. He lost. If you haven't told him yet, I should be there in case he doesn't take it well."

He lost. He phrased it like some kind of contest, and he wanted to be there to claim his victory and lord over Eli's defeat. I said the only neutral thing I could think of.

"I haven't decided anything, Ryan."

"That's ridiculous. We both know you'd rather be with me than him. You have to tell him, if for no other reason than to get him to back off."

He was right, of course. Completely right. Ryan was caring and thoughtful. Loving, even. Eli had a hard time being civil at all. Ryan wanted me for me, not because they commanded him to it. In fact, Ryan had probably been told not to want me. The obvious choice was Ryan.

Still, I wasn't quite ready to let go. Eli was my Valen, the only one I'd ever have, and we'd be tied together the rest of our lives.

There were little moments, barely iotas of time, where something Eli did or said teased at a possible reality. I thought about that night on the deck. I didn't regret what I'd said, not specifically, but Eli'd changed since then. I had changed.

It wasn't as simple as concluding I liked Ryan more.

"It's more complicated than that and you know it," I replied sharply.

"I know it's a delicate situation, which is why I've been trying to stay casual, but dragging it out isn't doing him any favors. This is more than a fling. I thought after the last week and our escape, you'd come to realize it."

"Ryan, you only left with us because you insisted. Nothing more. I didn't plan for it to work out that way."

Angry heat simmered behind my words.

"Maybe you didn't realize that's what you were doing, but you knew you could get me to go along. You knew *why* you could get me to do it. I'll bet if it had been anyone else, you wouldn't have even tried."

Yet again, he wasn't wrong. I probably couldn't have convinced anyone else to let us out, least of all Eli.

"So you snuck out with us. So what? What happened to no strings?"

"You left Eli behind and ran away with me. We circled each other for weeks, and now we're spending every spare moment together. It's been good and you know it. It means something to me. I know it does to you, too."

Charming Ryan rapidly declined into Pushy Ryan, and not in a fun way.

"I wasn't running *away* from Eli or *with* you. I needed to get out for a little while, and you happened to be along for the ride."

"We both know that I'm the better man. What's the problem?"

He said it with such an air of arrogance, and it wasn't the least bit attractive. His whole attitude pissed me off.

My temper, an edge in my mind that never dulled, reared up ready and eager to be of use. I shoved away from him.

"I haven't made any decisions."

"What . . . Firefly, come on. You know that you have. You know what you want, and it's not him."

Irritation bubbled over the brim, each insistence pushing me further into rejecting him.

Everyone kept making decisions for me.

My parents.

Peter and Henry.

Eli.

Now Ryan, too.

Irritation converted to fury. Who the fuck did he think he was?

"I say who I do or do not want, Ryan. Not you."

"I'm not telling you what to do, you've already chosen."

"No," I growled, "I haven't."

He took a step toward me, but I matched the distance in my retreat.

Anger flared, talons of heat gripping my limbs as I balled my hands into fists.

"Jex, please. Maybe I don't need to be there. I care about you. Let's talk about this."

"No," I snapped, and then did a supremely immature thing. I stomped my foot, pounding my fists in the air at my side.

The movement should have been calming, but it had the opposite effect. I belatedly realized that the heat building in my chest wasn't only anger—it was my essence, powering to life from strong emotions.

When I slammed my hands down, the heat in my system dropped off with no warning. It left my body and reappeared behind Ryan. The door, target dummies and all, caught on fire, a sudden blaze of wood and paper.

Ryan cursed and sprang for the fire extinguisher. With all the artillery in the next room, the entire building could explode.

As I panicked, I staggered backward and tripped over a bar stool against the wall. I crawled into the far corner of the room, struggling to regain control. My hands grasped my head as I pressed my nose between my knees.

I wanted it to stop. Wanted the flames to stop, wanted the essence to stop, wanted the world to stop.

I wanted everything to be still, and calm, and peaceful.

And it was.

For one spotless moment, the world stopped for me.

I could feel it, the pressure in the air as everything ceased.

Life stood stagnant while I took a breath.

The second my reprieve lifted, however, the world came crashing forward.

With my next inhale, the fire returned, retracting the inferno into my body.

My heart raced, my lungs barely expanding enough to get in oxygen. I shrieked as the heat plowed into me and pummeled my senses. It felt like being burned alive, my skin searing and sizzling, even though I knew it wasn't doing any physical damage.

My muscles were so tense I trembled. My thoughts raced as I tried to protect myself, and Ryan, and the whole damn building of people.

I had to do something with all the energy but had no clue what. I had to get out of that room and away from the munitions. Away from Ryan.

Leaping from my spot in the corner, I dashed through the now foam-covered doorway. I sprinted past the shelves, through the exit, out the wide double doors of the atrium, and over the deck.

The wood planks barely touched my feet as I escaped into the wilderness. I streaked through the woods, past the reservoir, met the border fence, and vaulted over it without faltering.

I ran and never stopped. I ran and I ran and I ran. My legs ached, but the heat soothed and encouraged me to fly forward.

My body consumed that fire. My muscles were the lick of the flames, my blood replaced by the heat of the blaze. I felt no effort, no strain, nothing. Not the ground under my feet, not the trees as they passed. Just the burn pulsing in time with my heartbeat.

I ran for miles, forever, the distance eaten up by a fluster of fury. It felt good. Really good, the exhilaration and freedom like taking a first breath after sitting at the bottom of the pool.

For the first time since landing on the tarmac at Orlando International Airport, I felt fully in my element, both wild and totally in control.

* * *

The fervor receded slightly, logic returning as I recognized I'd gone much too far from Haven. I needed to head back, or I would lose the trail and have to sleep in the brush, all because I couldn't keep it together.

Making the turn, I raced toward home.

It wasn't difficult to find my way back. I'd left the evidence of my passing in singe marks on the trees and the ground. The branches hadn't hit me because they disintegrated before I reached them.

I'd literally blazed a trail.

The burst faltered by the time I hit the border fence. I made it over without a problem, but it was downhill from there.

The boathouse was only a few paces away when I collapsed. I wanted to soak in the reservoir, to calm my stinging limbs in the cool water.

Crawling toward it, I could hear the approach of footsteps.

"Not a good idea," Henry said. He crouched over me, and I strained to turn my head upward despite the blinding sun. The second he touched me, he jerked his hand away as if he'd grabbed a hot iron.

"We discussed expelling the excess heat safely. You seemed to do much better than this before."

"It wasn't exactly planned," I wheezed.

"Yes, we know," Peter's voice said. "We were watching from the window."

"You were watching from the window?" I screeched. The panic rose again. "How *much* were you watching from the window? Why the fuck didn't you help me?"

"You ran away before we could do anything. Did you think we'd let a novice of your Duality near all of that ammunition?"

I didn't want to hear any more. I rolled in the direction of the water.

"You'll hurt yourself if you do that," Henry reminded me. "You need to cool slowly. Try the breathing exercises, it will help."

Breathing exercises? The man was certifiably insane. When you're on fire, you put it out. You don't calm it down with happy thoughts. Henry cut into my mental tirade.

"I can assure you that getting into the water will do serious damage. The sudden temperature change would very likely cause the protection you have against the heat to break and burn you for real, especially against its balancing element."

My arms flopped backward to lie half-back, half-twisted to stare up into the sun. Several minutes passed while I struggled to regain control of my lungs. Peter looked down over me, an amorphous shadow in the sun's glare.

"We were working nearby and heard you arguing. If anything happened before that, we weren't party to it," he said. The relief washed its own coolness. At least it was slightly less embarrassing.

My breathing finally slowed, the energy sifting off in small shakes. The heat dwindled until only the sun kept me warm. It was cool, too cold, and my body shivered to adjust.

"How do you feel?" Peter asked.

"Like I jumped into an ice-cold pool after spending three days in a sauna."

"I understand that will fade."

I shifted my head enough to see that we were alone. "Where'd Henry go?"

"To get you something to drink. You had an extreme reaction, even for someone new. Your lips are a rather worrying shade of blue. Henry wouldn't admit it, but I think you scared him."

"Major Payne is scared of me? My head might explode."

"I do like your sense of humor, Jex," Peter chuckled. "It's very extreme. Reminds me to be less serious."

"I do what I can, m'lord."

Peter crouched down to sit beside me in the sand.

"Did you know you could project your fire, as opposed to having to direct it?" he asked.

"I'm still secretly hoping to wake up in my bed in Boston. So, no, I didn't know that was possible."

We sat together as silent statutes in the sand. I closed my eyes to the sun, letting it burn black holes in my eyelids.

My breathing returned to normal, now uncomfortable in the restricted position. I turned to lie fully on the sand, knees bent, and hands clasped over my forehead. The sun slowly brought my body temperature back to normalcy.

Never thought I'd be thankful for the boiling Florida sun.

"My Valen was Lillian," Peter offered. He said it so quietly I thought for a moment I imagined it.

I turned my head, but an ache throbbed at the back of my neck. Getting up would be very unpleasant.

"Who is Lillian?" I asked.

"Was. Lillian *was* my Valen." I would have nodded if I could be sure it wouldn't hurt.

"Do you want to tell me what happened?" I asked. He laughed at that in a stiff, one-syllable sound.

"No, I would prefer not to discuss it, but it might be helpful to you."

Carefully, so carefully, I sat forward and crossed my legs. I never spoke, only let him fill the silence.

"We weren't much older than you and Eli. We'd known each other from childhood but had only been officially paired for a year. I was a very . . . how to politely describe it? I was obstinate." He smiled wryly. "My father used to tell me I had serious horse's-ass power. He led the Northwest Clara from Helena."

He gazed out at the water with a blank expression. His words had been slow and deliberate, as if he carefully chose the right way to say what he meant. Peter wasn't one to babble, and this was a lot of personal information from him all at once.

"Will you tell me about her?" I lightly prodded. He sighed heavily, the weight seeming to physically pull at his shoulders.

"She was as stubborn as I was. Am. She'd say I'm still a horse's ass," he grunted. "She had hair so blond it was white. Would say the sun bleached it in the summer so she'd blend better in the winter.

Competitive. Impulsive. Cynical. Your sense of humor reminds me of her. She used to say extreme things, but she would do it to get a reaction. I think you do it because it's what came to mind and you're too reckless to control yourself."

Thanks, I think . . .

"We didn't always get along. We were too alike, too convinced of our own rightness. It made working as a team problematic. She would want to approach a situation from one way and I another and we wouldn't compromise. It was not ideal for us or the Clara.

"Long before Lillian and I were formally paired, I fell in love with my high-school girlfriend. She was the most empathetic, loving woman I'd ever met, so much the opposite of Lillian. Not weak, just easy-going and agreeable. I've always wondered if that was the reason I loved her, because she wouldn't argue."

"You used the past tense again," I pointed out. His eyes grew darker, his once wistful face now hard and flat.

"Julie. Julie was killed. Officially, it was a car accident, but that wasn't it. Most Coles won't allow an open war with the Clara, but the Kier in our region hated the Clara and never hesitated to eliminate any target they could find.

"After her death, we moved the whole family here, to Orlando. That was more than thirty years ago, but that's not why I wanted to talk to you. I wanted you to know about Lillian because I get the sense you are going through something similar. I don't like to discuss it, but it may help you accept your life here and why things are the way they are."

He'd turned to look at me, those hard eyes burning holes in me, daring me to dispute it. I said nothing.

"The week of our wedding—"

"You married your sweetheart?" I asked.

"Yes, Julie and I were married. We were both twenty-six at the time. We were a little old for it, truth be told. Most of our classmates were long since married. People our age didn't date for years and years, but we did.

"The Clara received information that the Kier were staging a gun buy at the U.S.-Canada border the day before the wedding. Everyone still planned on attending, but they agreed that any action would have concluded long before the service. I couldn't go, of course. It was the day before my wedding. What was I supposed to do?

"My father set down strict directives about Pairs, and the primary rule was that you did not move alone. Any mission required both Valen and Amory, no exceptions. Lillian knew she couldn't go to the gun buy without me, as it was against orders. She was furious."

"She went anyway?" I guessed.

"She went anyway. Without the whole group, in fact. Pop wanted to allow the buy to occur and take each group separately as they left. She disagreed, said it would give them the opportunity to escape with the weapons.

"She set off explosives and destroyed the cache, but not before at least three gunners emptied all of their ammo into her. They tore her apart until she was barely recognizable. I was at my bachelor party, completely oblivious to what was happening."

I didn't quite know what to say to that, so I didn't say anything.

"The point I'm trying to make here, Jex, is that you need to have perspective. I'm not going to give you advice on your relationships, but I want you to remember there is more to your Pair than romance. Your Duality is part of who you are, the way you are, and who you are meant to be. You can't ignore it or wish it away any more than you can fight being human. Choosing Ryan because he's normal is a poor way to go about it."

"It's not about that," I told him, but stopped to think over how to word it properly. Look at me, learning from Peter.

"It's Eli. He's arrogant and rude. It feels like we hate each other, or that we're starting to hate each other. Now and then a moment shines through and I think, 'Well, that was kind of enjoyable,' but then it's instantly retracted by the next thing he does or says. He's not nice, and I don't want him picking on me anymore."

"Jex, you know why little boys pull on little girls' pigtails?"

"That's not it. He's too solitary. You can't push me at him and tell him to deal with it. He wouldn't have anything to do with me if we weren't paired. I'm fairly certain if Ryan wasn't interested he'd ignore me regardless. And I have no interest in being a trophy in some macho pissing match between them."

It all sort of tumbled out, but it was the truth. Eli wouldn't even want to be in the same room with me otherwise.

"You don't know that would be the case," Peter added.

"Yes, I think I do. I think Eli was happier before I came along, and now I'm an inconvenience making his life more difficult. Everything else is him putting up with me, or attempting because we're supposed to be paired, or some other reason that has nothing to do with who I am as a person. Now, he's got this *princess* he's shackled to who doesn't fight and can't control her essence. To him, I'm weak and I make him weak."

He didn't respond to my sudden realization. He never tried to dispute it, either; only sat beside me, buried in his thoughts. The more I dwelled on it, the more it felt right.

"Whether he likes it or not, this is the situation you are in," Peter noted. "It's no different from when we first brought you here. Some things are simply outside of our control. My father used to tell me, 'It is what it is.' I won't harp on it more, only suggest giving it a genuine effort. I loved Julie with my whole heart, but you have a chance I never took and wish I had."

We sat quietly for a while. The crash leveled, and I picked at the melted rubber on the soles of my shoes.

"Avoid running again, if you could?" he asked. "It's not safe outside the gates and we haven't found a new location yet. The bunkers still need to be updated, but we're going to bring as many people in as we can. Until we have a new home, we're under lock and key."

I nodded, and he helped me up.

"And, Jex," he added, "you aren't weak. It's quite the opposite—you're too strong. You don't know how to deal with it, but neither does your Valen."

He faced me toward the arched opening seared in the tree line.

"If you were weak, control would be easy. You wouldn't scorch a path fifteen miles in each direction, and all before you reach a full lid. You're simply not disciplined enough. It's good you joined us when you did. I wouldn't want to see what would happen in the next months without some guidance."

"I'm sure that was meant as comforting, but it was more on the line of scary."

Peter chuckled. "Take it as you will."

Chapter Twenty

"Updating the bunker" was leader-speak for daisy-chaining boxes and supplies until my hands were raw. An entire week quietly passed.

The bunker wasn't nearly as dull as the word implies. The enormous underground space began below the main building and stretched in every direction. The rabbit warren of interconnected rooms and tunnels sunk two more levels and extended all the way to the reservoir.

The poured concrete walls had an unfamiliar texture, like waves or grooves in fan-shaped patterns. Some of the lower rooms had slanted floors with drains. The passageways were musty and yet more beige, but the living spaces were bearable, though antiquated.

Peter warned it would take at least a week or two to get everything ready, so other than those obligations life drifted along in an anxiety-riddled normal.

The Kier never attacked again, which almost seemed cruel at that point. What were they planning?

Eli continued kicking my ass every day.

I avoided the gun range, and Ryan. It hurt, but I needed a little space from him. And he needed a little space from me.

The only upside was plenty of pent-up agitation and a shocking ability to channel it into my work on the mats. My essence focus improved drastically. I could create the bubble with no effort, fireballs with nominal concentration, and even shot a fire arrow twice. It only caused a minor amount of property damage. Never managed to project my fire again, though.

Even Eli seemed pleased with my success. I'd topped him twice today, although he immediately threw me off. He took it as a sign I'd progressed, and we moved from predominantly defensive tactics to both offensive and defensive moves.

It was late at night after a long day on the mats. We both reeked and sweat sucked our shirts against our bodies. We walked together toward our rooms along the same hallway, but at opposite ends of the building. As he opened his door, Eli held onto my hand so I'd stop.

"You want to come inside?" he asked.

He hung his hands on the doorframe above him, displaying muscular arms and making his shirt ride up so his boxers showed above his basketball shorts. His eyes bore into me, a sly smirk on his face.

"For what?" I stammered out.

"For sex."

I stood there, shocked.

"We're both disgusting right now."

"Nothing wrong with dirty sex."

"What makes you think I'd even be interested in sleeping with you?"

"It's been days since you and Ryan had that fight, you're clearly frustrated as hell, and you about cut me with how hard your nipples get every time I pin you. Besides, of course you want to sleep with me."

Wow, he really went there. Zero charisma, but points for blunt honesty.

He advanced out of the doorway, his chest bumping into mine to force me to peer up at him. Those steel-blue eyes openly focused on my mouth. My heart stuttered when the tip of his tongue darted out to lick at his lips, making clear his opinion of what he saw.

I . . . didn't know how to process the suggestion. This new approach came completely out of nowhere. Had he been biding his time?

Welp, time to woman-up. Couldn't let him think I was desperate for the D.

"No, thanks. I think I'll get something to eat."

"Great, I'm starving. Only one thing I'd like to eat, though," he cracked.

"You did not seriously say that. For both our sakes, I'm going to ignore it."

A smile played at his lips.

"No, you won't."

He picked something off my shoulder, then tugged at the hem of my tank strap to straighten it. The light touch sent a frisson of heat shooting over my skin.

"Are you coming in, or are you chicken shit?"

I'd begrudgingly admit he was attractive. He leered at me with that gorgeous mouth, even if it spewed the most disturbing things. I'd also admit to a fantasy or two where he was a whole lot less of an asshole and a whole lot more naked.

And he was my Pair.

Things with Ryan were off kilter, but not over. Granted, Ryan knew full well we weren't exclusive; the fight last week established that explicitly.

I didn't know what to do. Couldn't someone just tell me how to react?

Eli gripped my chin firmly, running his thumb along the edge. My essence flared to life, his fingers like a brand on my skin.

"Do I need to give you a countdown?" he threatened, cutting off my deliberation. "Those two brain cells having a hard time under—why does your face look like that?"

"I'm visualizing kicking you in the balls and using the recovery time to escape."

"First, why does it always have to be the balls?"

His thumb dragged along my bottom lip.

"And second," he continued, "there would be no point to hiding because I would find you. Easily. Can't run from me, princess."

The stark shift from distant, cool Eli jarred my perception. I'd thought he only wanted me because of Ryan.

Now, though, his fixated eyes shone like I was a finely controlled obsession. Eli looked at me with the intense focus of a hunter tracking its prey.

I tried to pull from his grasp and failed.

"Balls are soft, sensitive parts that are often left unguarded," I muttered. "Any woman worth her salt knows to go for the balls first."

"You want to go for my soft, accessible balls first?"

"Is this a contest for the worst innuendo? You have them in a book somewhere?" I rolled my eyes.

With his grip firm and restricting, he pulled slightly, so that I stepped toward his room. I scowled at him.

"It must be exhausting being a pain in the ass all the time," I told him.

"I could be a pain in *your* ass all the time, you seem into that."

"For fuck's sake, Eli," I exhaled a hard breath. "That was so bad I died a little. What possessed you to think asking for sex was a good idea? We hate each other."

"Hate sex is the best sex."

"Please, you wouldn't know the first thing about how to get me off."

The hand on my chin tightened to near-bruising level.

"Is that so?" he asked. His expression told me I was both naïve and about to be broken of any misconceptions.

He dragged me closer toward his room, his voice dropping low and dangerous.

"I've been very respectful up to now, but that sounds like a direct challenge. You know how I feel about challenges."

The corner of his mouth lifted, and a little spool of worry unraveled in my gut.

Eli led me by the jaw into his room and swung the door shut. He spun me around to stand at the bend in the L-shaped couch, never loosening his hand.

"Take off your leggings," he instructed as he smirked down at me.

"What? No."

His smile widened, like he'd gotten an idea that he knew I wouldn't like.

"I'm not going to do anything you don't ask me to do," he promised. Anticipation tingled under my skin.

The conversation with Peter still fresh in my mind, I considered his proposition. After all, he was the other half of my Pair. It felt like I should try, even if it scared me a little. Or a lot.

I knew I could stop this right now. Pull from his hold, walk out the door. He'd let me go.

Curiosity won the internal argument.

Rolling my eyes at him, I tried to lean over to execute his request. He kept his hold on my face, refusing to let me do anything other than look up at him as I shifted. Control freak, much?

I hooked my thumbs in the waistband and started to pull everything down.

"I said leggings. Leave the panties on." He gazed at my body, his voice rough. *Hmmm. He's excited by what he has in mind.*

I adjusted, and then awkwardly knelt so I could drag the bottoms off with my jaw still in his grip. It was an uncomfortable challenge to work the fitted ankles off without being able to lean over, which was probably the point. Arrogant bastard.

He held my face only an inch or two from the bulge already obvious against his leg.

"Good, now sit on the couch. Put a foot up on each side."

Unease built, but I did as he asked.

The position at the corner of the L-shape put me on full display for him. It was uncomfortable, having to surrender to him like this. All our training sessions, really every interaction, were about attempting to best each other. It felt awkward; not wrong or negative, just strange.

Readjusting a cushion behind me, he finally released the hand on my face. I laid back as he kneeled between my legs.

He spent a long moment watching me, making me squirm as his eyes flared with intensity, writing to memory what I almost certainly intended to be my last willing submission to him.

I glared at him, my message written all over my face as well. *Enjoy it while you can, asshole.*

It only made him smile more.

"If you think I can't please you properly, then show me how it's done," he instructed.

I hesitated barely a second before his order came.

"*Now*, Jex," he commanded sharply.

The aggression in his voice throttled my sex drive into gear. If he wanted to play this game, I was happy to oblige and tease him with what he'd be missing.

Tentatively drawing down the front zipper on the sports bra, I cupped my breast under my shirt. The fabric was still soaked through, so he undoubtedly got a nice show, even covered.

My other hand snaked between my legs. I pushed it under the band of my panties, but he stopped me with another command.

"No, over them. You're going to come into them for me."

I did as he instructed, using my fingers to play with my clit and opening over the cotton, while my other hand massaged my breast and tweaked my nipple. The fabric was rough and added a delicious friction that heightened the experience.

"Push up your shirt," he ordered, the desire heavy in his tone. I obliged so he could watch both of my hands work. The intensity surged, his fascinated gaze unblinking.

He braced his hands under my bent legs, not making contact but bringing him in so close that his body heat lifted goosebumps on my bare legs.

"Let go," he told me. "Do as you like. I want to see what you look like when you're on your own."

Fuck, I wanted to show him. Yes, he was arrogant, and argumentative, and completely impossible to be around half the time—but the fire-hot gaze he leveled made me both want to hide and dive straight at him. Watching his responses and hearing his demands like this was something else altogether.

Eli's face reflected unadulterated lust as my hands moved in tandem. He barely breathed himself, his muscles taut and straining and teeth gnashing his bottom lip. We held eye contact, but he refused to touch me as he promised.

He leaned over, between my legs, and blew against the side of my knee. The cool wash of air tickled my sweat-damp, bare skin.

"What are you doing?"

"I said I wouldn't touch you, not that I wouldn't participate."

He blew on my skin again—this time, whispering a slow line from my knee, down the inside of my thigh, toward my center. The sweat from our exhausting day on the mats amplified the chill's effect. I shivered in response.

"Eli . . ."

"Tell me to stop, and I'll stop."

I didn't.

He alternated between blowing cold air and exhaling warm breaths against the naked skin of my inner thighs.

The contrasting brushes left my skin tingling. The proximity of his mouth tormented me. I wanted him to quit teasing and touch me already.

When he blew on my hand, the one rubbing my clit with abandon, I nearly lost it. My body contracted at the caress of air.

"Eli, please . . ."

"That's closer."

"You want me to ask?"

"I want you to beg."

Huffing, I returned to my own attention. I'd beg when he did, the ass.

He leaned forward, moving the air current up my stomach and over my exposed chest. His soaked shirt sagged, covering my hand and lower belly.

"Your shirt's touching me."

He lifted an eyebrow, then pulled it off and tossed it over his shoulder.

I'd been pressed against Eli's strong, defined body plenty of times in the Practice Room, but he'd never taken off his shirt during training. It was a whole different ballgame to see it up close, to inhale the mint and aftershave and let the arousal bloom instead of tamping it down.

Radiant heat from those damned muscled arms and chest provoked my desire and the inferno in my veins as he hovered over me. His mouth floated over my breasts, only an inch away as he blew and exhaled on my body. My skin tensed instantly, winding me tighter.

When he moved to my neck, his solid frame looming over me, I couldn't take it anymore.

"Eli . . ."

"Yes, Jex?"

I wanted him to touch me, to use those fingers and that mouth that were so close to my exposed body already. Glancing down at him, his straining arms and hooded eyes demanded it as well.

"Please."

He smirked. A warm breath caressed my shoulder, making me shudder.

"Please what?"

"Please touch me."

His face lit in the devious victory.

"More," he demanded.

"*More?*"

"Once more with feeling. Say my name."

The man's insufferable!

But then he blew cold air down the front of my body, the current rolling over my clavicle, across my nipple, and down my stomach. The sensation dove past my skin and activated each nerve and vein it reached.

Fuck it. I couldn't even remember why I hesitated.

"Touch me, Eli. Please touch me. I need—"

Eli's mouth collided with mine, his tongue demanding as he wrenched me against him. His blaze washed over my cool skin. Those flares of heat, the ones that had scared me so much before, flashed to life at our contact.

My body sizzled, but I embraced it this time. I allowed the heat to overtake me.

Tugging him closer, I wrapped both my hands around his neck and jerked him tighter. His mouth moved to my nipple, and I writhed at finally receiving the contact with teeth and tongue I'd longed for.

His hand dipped between us, his fingers finding my drenched slit immediately. Pushing the crotch of my underwear aside, he thrust into me with unrestrained zeal. His thumb rubbed circles over my clit, making me moan his name.

Holy fuck, did he like that.

Eli's eyes sunk to the deepest ocean-blue, his face tight in focus as he absorbed my responses. His hand and his tongue attacked with an unrelenting fervor. I said his name again and again, embracing his reaction to each praise and plea.

My back bowed, and the tension finally broke. I groaned out my release, riding high on the orgasm as the plunge of heat crashed and flushed out to my fingertips and toes.

Eli watched it happen, his gazed riveted by my response as a smug, satisfied grin played at his lips.

A tiny seed of hope sparked in my gut.

Laughing, I released the stress I'd been holding at the forced togetherness and just enjoyed how much he wanted me despite it.

It was an epiphany; I embraced how good it felt to tease him and see exactly how badly he wanted me but held back. It was stupid of us really, hating each other out of spite for the circumstances.

"I'll do it," I told him. "I'll give coupling a try."

His eyes studied me, his calm exterior returning as a wide smile settling on his face.

"Of course, you will," he told me. Before I could smack the arrogance down, he leaned over and licked up the crotch of my ruined underwear. He hooked a finger under the fabric, the tip brushing my sensitive skin as he stripped them off. Freeing them from my legs, he put them to his face and inhaled deeply.

"Fucking pheromones," he muttered, but his expression dared me to object.

"I'm heading to bed," I replied.

"Thought you were hungry?"

"No, I'm surprisingly satisfied and sleepy."

I fully intended to leave him with some wicked blue balls. As I reached down to wrestle my leggings back on—yeah, that was going to be great fun—he tugged on the fabric.

"I've half a mind to make you walk to your room without these again. Ryan's still staying at the end of the hall."

"Don't get all territorial. I said I'd try, not that I'd let you brand me."

He frowned at that, so of course I pushed on the sore spot.

"It doesn't have to be either-or, you know," I purred.

"I doubt Ryan's into threesomes."

I'd meant dating both of them, not "dating" both of them. I hadn't really considered his suggestion for more than my fantasies.

Eli clearly had.

Would Ryan?

He might, with the right incentive. The mere thought of both of them left my breasts tingling. I leaned forward to whisper in Eli's ear.

"You never know until you try."

The excitement in his eyes deepened.

"It was a joke, princess."

"Was it? *Hmmm.*"

He wasn't against it. I could tell it turned him on. That look . . . I think he enjoyed watching Ryan lick me, enjoyed watching me come on his face. Ryan certainly didn't mind him watching since he'd invited it.

"Something to think on." I slapped him playfully on the cheek.

A miracle allowed me to both get the leggings on fairly easily and stand. He still kneeled at the bend in the couch. I rubbed his buzzed head before moving around him.

His hand whipped out to smack my ass as I walked by, and I gasped at the unexpected sting.

"You're not convincing me I'm making the right choice," I scolded, but he only *mhmmm*'d at the obvious lie.

What had I gotten myself into?

Chapter Twenty-One

Two days later, Peter sent Trish, Tom, Eli, and me on a supply run. Some of the Guards were contractors, and they'd given us a list of items to get from a local hardware depot. Lord knows why I went; I'd never bought a screwdriver that didn't involve orange juice. Maybe Eli was secretly a whiz with tools.

Note to self: come up with a joke about Eli's tools. Or nailing. Yeah, go with nailing.

Ceiling-height metal shelves coated in a thick layer of dust filled the large, dingy warehouse serving as a hardware store. The place reeked of burning wood and body odor. The only light came from failing fluorescents hanging from the twenty-foot ceilings and the open, rolling doors at the far end that led to a lumberyard.

The front of the store was basically a hallway with plastic-paneled walls and a long, laminate bar separating the public area from the warehouse. When we'd shown the list to the disheveled guy manning the counter, he motioned us to the back and told us to help ourselves.

. . . which was how we ended up inhaling mites and probably asbestos while sifting through the shelves.

The long shopping list ranged from small items like nails to confusing wood panel sizes, and there was no discernable organizational system to the depot, so we tore the page into four parts and split in different directions.

We'd been separated for all of thirty seconds when Tom rounded the corner and made a beeline in my direction.

"Fancy seeing you here," I laughed.

"Hey, I need your help," he replied.

His hand cupped around his chin and over his mouth like he strained to keep himself from saying something by force.

The seconds ticked by.

"Plan on telling me, or should we play twenty questions?" I quipped.

He'd gone through the trouble of doubling back, but apparently lost his nerve. I wanted to shake him and scream, *spit it out already!* My comment made him laugh, though.

"Trish said you could be forward. You don't mess around, do you?"

"A function of impatience. The sooner you tell me, the sooner I can help."

He took a deep breath, spilling his thoughts out in one long exhale.

"Trish is cheating. She disappears, sometimes for hours at a time. She won't let me see our bank statements, but I know there's less than there should be. When I ask, she only reassures me we aren't in financial trouble. She has to be cheating. It's the only thing I can come up with."

Incredulous, I pressed my lips together to avoid saying something regrettable. Trish was loyal to a fault, and she enjoyed sharing secrets entirely too much to keep one this big from me.

"Are you sure that's the only option? Maybe she's dealing with something personal, or helping someone else and doesn't want people to know?"

That, on the other hand, was very Trish-like. She'd want to lend a hand without sacrificing the other person's pride or reputation.

"Has she been spending time with anyone more than usual?"

"Maxon. He's been driving her into town. She says she's spending time with Lita, but Trish doesn't like Lita. She doesn't even like being in the same room with her."

Fair enough. Lita was about as friendly as a honey badger.

"Maybe Trish is helping him with wooing Lita—"

The train of thought came to a halt. It didn't explain the missing money.

He looked desperate, a man watching the gallows being built outside his cell. It broke my heart a little.

"Maybe she has a gambling problem? That would explain the hours and missing cash."

The idea was as ludicrous as an affair, but if we were going to assume one could happen, then the other was at least as likely.

"I don't know. I don't think she'd have enough time to get all the way out to the Hard Rock. Besides, she's a terrible card player. She can't keep a straight face to save her life," he reminded me.

"Have you tried asking her?"

"I've hinted around, asking her what she'd done that day or calling her while she's out. She always avoids the question and changes the subject. She tells me her phone died, or she didn't hear it, or she turned it off. I can't confront her. What if I'm wrong?"

His eyes watered faintly, and I thought he might cry. He scratched his neck and finger-combed through his hair, mussing the already faux-messy style.

"What do you want me to do?" I asked.

Trish was a friend, my closest friend. I didn't enjoy the idea she'd cheated on her fiancé, but I shouldn't judge her. My love life had been messy enough. Plus, she took priority in the friendship ranks over Tom.

"Keep an eye out for anything suspicious or strange. If you see them together, or if she mentions anything to you . . . I know you're close."

"You want me to spy on her," I replied. The grimace on his face deepened.

"Don't think of it like that. Just tell me if you see anything?"

"And I can't ask her because?"

"If I'm wrong, she'll never forgive me. She'll insist I don't trust her, which will make *her* not trust *me*. It could destroy our relationship."

"But you don't trust her, Tom. If you did, you wouldn't be asking me to poke around."

"Please," he begged, "help me. I need to know."

I nodded, but solid odds I wouldn't be ratting out Trish anytime soon.

"Actually, there's something you can help me with, too," I hedged. "I need a tutor. Someone I can ask stupid questions."

"No such thing as a stupid question, but what, exactly, do you need?" He squinted, his eyes shifting uncomfortably.

"Lord, no! Nothing controversial. I mean about Dualities. Essences, Amory, all of it."

"Sure. Anything in particular that brought it up?"

"Aster gave me this book and it may as well be written in German for all I get out of it. I tried to ask Eli about inverses, but he was predictably assholish."

"Inverses are pretty straightforward." He pushed his glasses higher on the bridge of his nose, activating teacher mode.

"It's a theoretical way of understanding how each Duality interacts with the known world. Like the balance in each Duality and Pair, most extraordinary creatures have an approximately equal opposite in the realm of magic. We consider those opposites inverses.

"Think of a quarter—inverses might be a vertical, right-side-up Washington head and a vertical, upside-down eagle. Contrary inverses have the strongest and most volatile reactions when they combine or contest each other."

The blood drained from my face.

"Sorry, I lost everything you said after *extraordinary creatures*."

"That's okay," he chuckled. "I'll see what I can find for you to review. You know, a few weeks ago, you learned you have the power to wield fire, and it seemed to have fazed you less than your reaction right now."

"No, I lost my shit at that too." I laughed.

"I can imagine it must have been quite the shock. Ask me anything. About the extraordinary. No such thing as a stupid question, I promise."

Tom turned and drifted into the shadowed shelves. He really was quite sweet and well suited to Trish.

After seeing the two of them together, an affair didn't seem possible. Their googly eyes made even the strongest stomach retch. She told me she loved him, although it was obvious from the way she spoke of him. The only reason they weren't married already was to wait for Trish's Acceptance on her twenty-fifth.

Trish was also unreasonably honest. We'd teased her about being a straight-arrow in high school—she didn't drink, smoke, or even copy homework. People change a lot after high school, but the idea of Trish having an affair was absurd. She didn't have it in her.

She also couldn't hold on to secrets if you'd surgically implanted them to her hand. Granted, I supposed she'd kept a few monster-sized secrets from me over the years.

Still, I liked Tom. He seemed like good people. The least I could do was try to convince Trish to end it.

Turning a corner while turning over the possibilities in my mind, I walked straight into a muscled wall in dark jeans and a fitted black shirt. Tattoos twisted up both arms and disappeared into sleeves stretched over broad shoulders. Deep brown eyes appraised me as his dark, wavy hair fell forward over his brow. His lips quirked into that recognizable wolfish grin.

Hello, again, Tall-Dark-And-Handsy. More than a month had passed since he'd cornered me at Kicks. I really needed the buzz of alcohol to deal with Sir Searing-Hot.

We'd crashed into each other, but he didn't step back. If anything, he seemed to lean slightly in. I'd been able to avoid interacting with him at Jack's appointment, but it'd be inescapable now.

"Should watch where you're going, pretty girl," he rumbled. Hovering over me, he scrutinized my reaction through long lashes so contrary to the rest of his rugged features.

Oh, yeah, I was entirely too sober for this.

The blaze in my veins flared to life. It didn't feel like I was in danger. Well, maybe not physical danger. From swords and stuff. This man could obviously destroy me with barely any effort.

Stop thinking about him destroying you.

"Oh, um . . ."

I willed my brain to work. It was impossible to do anything but stare up at him and replay the image of his mouth calling me *pretty*.

Handsy tilted his head to the side as if studying me, that predatory smile threatening in the hazy light.

"Well, I'm sorry, then," I mumbled. *Peak, Jex.*

I tried to side-step him but, like before, he blocked my path.

"Derek. I'm sorry, *Derek*," he added, watching me expectantly.

"I'm sorry, Derek."

"Good girl," he growled, and I forgot to breathe.

What the fuck was going on? My heart pulsed, and the burn egged it on.

Tense, focused eyes followed me as I stepped back, but he matched my stride. I took another. He stalked toward me yet again, the overhead light shifting to splash shadows over the side of his face.

Another long step slammed my back into the metal shelves in the aisle. Dust powdered the air as the bits precariously stacked on the shelves shuddered.

Thumbs parked in his pockets, Derek leaned far too close. Smoke and cinnamon competed with the stuffy plume of particles in the air. It was the oddest combination.

"What are you doing here?" he asked.

"Just trying to get things from this list."

I twisted to retrieve it, but he pushed his own hand into my back pocket to extract the page. The brush of his fingers against my skin provoked a shiver.

"Hmmmmmm . . ." he purred. "Drywall screws are in aisle 5A, toward the front. Concrete is on the back wall by the bay doors. And they don't sell glass panes here, but Patrick's has them and will cut them down for you."

"Thank you, Derek."

Another *hmmmmmm*, thrummed in approval, left my skin tingling. Why did I like that?

"I can show you where they are. I enjoy taking care of beautiful women."

My face may as well be on fire. He handed back the torn page.

"Do you, uh, work here?"

His laugh was as smooth and rich as aged bourbon.

"No, I don't."

"D, we have to go," a red-headed blur said, but then she rounded the corner and disappeared just as fast.

"You have to go, D," I mimicked.

"Until next time, Jex."

He turned and followed the woman away.

Did I give him my name? I couldn't remember.

Chapter Twenty-Two

The final push to get everyone into the bunker had been hectic. It turned out that some doomsday cult built the structure in the 80's before the DOJ seized it in the early aughts.

The *AHA!* I'd shrieked when Henry informed me of that little tidbit probably shook the trees for miles.

They secreted the primary entrance in an out-of-the-way bend in the atrium's maze-like pathways. Emergency exits were hidden in the boathouse and at the edge of the property line on each side. About three miles down the road, thick steel doors guarded the entrance to a broad underground garage added to the complex for military vehicles.

Every piece of equipment and furniture needed to be hauled down the wide, concrete stairs to fill the rooms and accommodate people. Trish and Tom cleaned communal spaces, while Pinch and Eli led the effort to move the weapons into locked cages in the underground armory. Henry and Peter directed the flow of traffic. Everyone else brought boxes down or moved them to their appointed places.

Lita and I shared a bunkroom in our assigned four-bedroom suite. Tom and Trish also shared, as did Eli and Pinch, and Ryan and Maxon. The units connected in a common sitting area and kitchen.

At least I had a bed, but even my own room and all the freedom of Haven had felt claustrophobic. Jamming into the tight underground space would turn barbaric after too long.

The assignment also put Ryan and me in closer proximity by force. We had an awkward conversation, and he apologized, but we needed to clear the air. I asked Ryan to give me time, and that we'd talk about all of it once I'd worked my way through my emotions.

He'd nodded, but his expression nearly tore my heart out.

Eleven of the bunker's suites were already filled, and Peter assigned each a six-hour watch. Half the suite would patrol the property while the other half remained in the house. We had the fortune of drawing the eight p.m. to two a.m. slot, so at least my sleep schedule wouldn't be too afflicted.

Peter wanted to entice the Kier to attack the building. The only entrance to the bunker from there would be difficult to locate in the atrium, and even then the single-entrance created a bottleneck. The building had to look deserted, which meant no light, music, or other indicators of habitation. We even left the gate and doors unlocked.

The only electronics allowed were voice-activated earbuds, which had silent distress codes unique to each set. If something happened, the entire underground would be instantly alerted to the call.

Three days in the bunker were enough to make a week confined at Haven seem like a vacation in St. Thomas.

Our assigned watch duty accentuated the malaise. Trish, Tom, Eli, and I were always on house duty—haunting our former home, in the dark, for hours. Yup, just me and Eli circling the building in anxious silence.

The bunker had a version of the Practice Room, which was mostly identical except with red mats instead of blue. That same white-lined ring still tormented me, and I'd already seen more of it in those three days than I'd care to in a lifetime. Being forced to walk the house in the dark with Eli after spending all day getting tossed around the mats was not an enjoyable experience.

We were in the Practice Room applying forms to practical sparring. And, because consistency was key, I failed hard at it.

"I suck at this," I lamented.

"You need practice."

"You want me to practice sucking?"

"That was so bad it doesn't count," he groused.

We'd fully committed to giving each other the worst innuendos we could think of. It tempered his animosity substantially. I slowly worked my way into his affection, poking and prodding at weak points, getting him to soften around the edges. Probably didn't hurt he thought he'd get lucky.

I sat on the mat during a water break, passing my ring between fingers. Eli leaned over to snatch it from my hands.

"Knock it off," he scolded. "Either wear it or take it off, but stop fidgeting."

"Hey, I like my ring!"

"Why even wear it? It's cheap." He tossed it back at me. I stuck it on my left ring finger.

"I'm married to myself. The sex is phenomenal."

"That was beneath you."

"You should be less critical if you also want to be beneath me."

"Alright, that was pretty good."

Ryan stuck his head into the room.

"Peter wants us to work on your gunmanship," he informed me. Sighing, I shifted to get up, but Eli's glare demanded I stay put.

"We aren't done yet," Eli snapped. "Combat takes precedence over the firing range."

Ryan came to stand beside me.

"Not if a gun could save her life when rolling around on the mats with you can't."

"While I'm sure she learns a lot by loading your gun, combat requires far more skill and practice. I'm not releasing her until we're done for the day."

Snort. Fun safety.

"Fine." Ryan let out an exasperated sigh. "When do you expect to be done?"

"The same time we're up for patrol."

"She hasn't even fired a weapon yet, man."

"And whose fault is that? At least concrete isn't flammable."

"Whoa, whoa, whoa," I called them to a halt. "If you're going to whip out dicks to measure, I expect you to use them too."

Their eyes snapped to me in shocked silence, so of course I took full advantage.

"I get that this"—I waved a hand between the three of us—"is stressful for you both, and I'm sorry about that. But here's the thing—I'm not going to choose either of you over the other. I like you for different reasons, and I'm not married-off to either of you. You can get along until this whatever-it-is comes to a natural end, or you can parachute out now. Which is it?"

The silence continued.

"And since we're on the subject, you should both be aware that I have one, and only one, goal right now—surviving the next few months. Are there pleasant benefits to spending time with each of you? Sure. But you'll learn to get along or we won't be getting it on. Got it?"

Ryan and Eli looked at each other for a long moment. This gambit would either pay off massively or send the whole stack of blocks tumbling. The guys could both reject me, but I suspected their rivalry was more about feeling threatened by the other than something to do with me specifically.

Ryan's smile broke through first.

"Only pleasant?" he asked.

"Let's say I'm averaging. And, no, I won't tell you where you stand. You'll have to assume you need the most improvement and act accordingly."

An evil grin played at my lips. Tense silence waited for Eli's decision.

He huffed an exasperated sigh.

"Fine, she goes to the gun range," Eli told Ryan. "I expect her at the doors at eight o'clock *sharp*."

"I'll let you know the next time I have a gap in my schedule so you can plan for a break," Ryan offered.

"She needs a lot of work on focus and discipline."

"Henry mentioned breathing exercises. That would probably help."

I cleared my throat.

"If you're through planning whatever torture you have in mind, can I please get on with my day?"

"Be at the doors at eight sharp, Jex." Eli shot me a stare hard enough it could wilt leaves.

"Yes, sir, drill sergeant, sir!"

Ryan held out his hand to help me up, but I looked between it and Eli. It wasn't entirely clear how much of this fragile peace between them would apply to training methods.

"Take my hand, Firefly," Ryan rumbled. "I'll take care of you."

Le sigh, I loved it when he called me Firefly.

I let him take my hand, and he pulled me against him. That gorgeous smile shone and warmth prickled my face. I was still pissed at him for the other day, but I'd missed him beyond words.

We must have paused too long, because Eli barked at us to *get the fuck out* so sharply we both jumped and scurried from the room.

* * *

At seven, Ryan called it a day so I could get a shower and some food. He suggested I try a handgun he called an "M&P 9," which I managed to not only hold but also fire without another panic attack.

Despite the conditioning over the last several weeks, my muscles still ached and only a long, hot shower resolved the problem. Even the constant uniform of "athleisurewear" chafed, literally and figuratively. I opted for a ribbed tank top and cotton shorts with a real lace bra, to pretend at normalcy.

Fine, they were Trish's shorts, but she wouldn't miss them. Surely she'd appreciate the dire need for their sacrifice, given how badly my closet had dwindled. My Boston outfits weren't cutting it for my current lifestyle.

At least the fridge was fully stocked and ready for the long haul. I found some turkey and swiss, took two slices of bread from the middle of the loaf—everyone knows the middle is the best—and added a pickle spear for good measure.

Groaning, I hoisted myself up onto the kitchen island. They hadn't gotten around to unwrapping the dining chairs yet. I could sit on the floor, but I might not be able to get up again. Skipping patrol to sleep on the cement tile seemed like a bad idea.

Shifting back on my hands, I crossed my legs while munching on the pickle and sandwich. *Heaven*, it was absolute heaven.

Finding my phone, I started my "favorites" playlist and Camila Cabello crooned about "Havana" while I munched on the pickle.

As if he sensed I was comfortable, Eli strode in through the doorway. *There goes my good mood.*

Spying me, he walked right up, planted a fist on each side of my thighs and leaned over my legs. It caught me totally off guard and allowed him to pluck my sandwich from my hand.

Before I had time to react, he took two massive bites and consumed almost half my dinner.

"Hey, that's my sandwich!" I whined at him.

"My sandwich now."

"Get your own damn sandwich."

"But I want yours."

"You want to eat my sandwich, huh?"

"That was awful."

"It was at least as good as my sandwich! Now give it back!"

I lunged for it, but he used those long arms to stretch it out of my reach while chomping even larger bites. *Ugh, I hate being short.*

My dinner was quickly disappearing, so I did the one thing I could think of to rescue my precious before it vanished down Eli's throat.

I pinched him as tightly as I could. First on his ear, then his side, before volleying the assault on every space of exposed skin.

"Ouch! What the fuck, Jex, knock it off! That hurts!" he howled, but I refused to relent.

"So does an empty stomach. Give. Me. My. Sandwich."

Almost there. Come on, Eli, you know you want . . .

YES! He used the sandwich hand to block my blows, bringing it within snatching distance. I rescued the last few bites from his grasp.

Pushing off him with my foot, I slid backward on the island and out of his sizable wingspan. He reached over me to grab at it, but I dodged each attempt.

Victory was mine! I shoved the whole thing in my mouth. Not the most elegant of moves, but at least I managed to eat something more. Turns out, I'd picked up a few things in the Practice Room after all.

He grabbed my leg and wrenched me toward the edge of the island, my cackling muffled by the mouthful of food.

"You assume I won't still try for it."

"You want me to baby bird you the last of it?" It came out as *mhf mwaa me ah meme murd mu a mwass o id?*

He patiently waited for me to finish and take a long swig of my soda before he replaced his hands on the counter around me.

Peering at me under hooded lids, and framing me in with those powerful arms, his eyes reflected a vicious glint.

"Yes?" I asked.

He sunk a hand into a pocket, then brought out a small, square packet. It plunked down on the surface beside me.

I looked at him, and couldn't help myself.

I burst out laughing.

How was *that* his move? First free moment alone and that was how he played it? His face screwed up, and I could tell he seriously considered whether he'd confused our earlier conversation.

"No, it's not that," I told him, still giddy but putting a hand on his shoulder to keep him from retreating. "It's just funny. That's not how you ask for sex. You can't be so abrupt. *Here's a condom, thunk.*"

His lip twitched.

"Most women enjoy my honesty."

"Most women are probably charmed by your pretty eyes and prettier muscles."

The response popped out without thinking. The last thing Eli's ego needed was stroking. Other things . . .

"Well, how do you want me to ask you for sex?" he asked.

"For starters, you could try a little finesse. I know I agreed, but don't you want me to want it? To want you?"

A thought occurred to me.

"Would you like to play a game?" I purred.

The hunger in his deep-blue eyes hinted his agreement and suggested he'd like to swallow me whole while at it.

"I love a good game."

He scrutinized me, waiting patiently for me to explain.

"Tell me what you want to do to me. If I'm interested, I'll strip an article of clothing off," I suggested.

"Can I touch you during this game?" he asked.

"Let's see how it goes."

The air hung for a moment. His stare burned into me, making me squirm.

"Only if you play as well," he finally answered.

I wagged an eyebrow at him, a little relieved that he saw the fun in this.

He kicked off his boots and unbuttoned his jeans. They loosened and slung fractionally lower. It brought my attention to the band of his boxers stretched against the "V" of his hips. I licked my lips involuntarily, and his eyes snapped to my mouth.

"We haven't even started," I muttered. A flutter of heat grew in my chest and trickled out to my fingertips.

"And yet I've already agreed." I shook my head, but it only made his smile widen. He uttered the next words with a heavy gaze.

"I want . . . for you . . . to go first," he said, the double entendre hanging in the air.

Pausing to collect my thoughts, I worked out how best to approach this. The Clara's pre-ordained Pairs were for life. If he rejected me—or worse, mocked me—it either meant an unfulfilling sex life forever or I'd have to find someone willing to tangle himself into our Pair. Ryan certainly fit the bill when he put the macho shit aside.

Still, I'd already hinted to Eli at the rougher things rattling around in my brain. He'd seemed open to it, might've even liked it. Trying to read his expression, I decided to dip a toe in the water.

"I'd like for you to kiss me, then kiss my neck . . ."

His eyes followed the curve from my jaw to my shoulder, so I pushed a little more.

"Run a hand down my spine and palm my ass. Lick my breasts, and nip at my neck and nipples."

I watched him closely for his response. Either he'd take the hint that I meant more than simple sex or he'd carry on clueless.

Eli's fiery gaze locked onto mine as he peeled off his shirt. My mouth went dry, taking in his chest and shoulders. Much like Ryan, Eli's body was an elaborate tapestry of scars and marks. An elaborate tattoo spread over one side of his chest and shoulder. I wished I could touch him, to examine the intricate details on his skin.

"Do you like being marked?" he murmured it so low I wasn't even sure he said it at first.

Hot, electric desire zinged through my system. He tentatively toyed with my knee, pushing it around with his palm. His blue eyes darkened deeper than I'd ever seen them.

"Sometimes, depending on where. I don't like nosy looks and questions."

"*Sometimes* that's the purpose of leaving the mark," he grumbled. "If I'm marking you somewhere visible, I want others to know. You shouldn't be shy over it. It means you're mine."

That wrath prowled behind his eyes, anxious and ready. I struggled to keep my outward composure despite his heady answer.

"*Mine*, huh? A little presumptuous," I teased, but his mask slipped slightly as his eyes went flat. Backtracking, I shrugged.

"Like I said, sometimes. Maybe it depends on who marks me." I grinned slyly, which he returned in kind.

That delicious heat hummed through my system. Nope, didn't think I'd mind at all if people knew where he'd been. I supposed they expected it.

I brushed my thumb over the fine line on his cheek, the one left behind by my ring that night I'd slapped him on the deck. The line was barely visible, not even noticeable, but I knew it was there. It felt so long ago.

He captured my hand with his and moved my palm to rest on his neck.

Eli scrutinized me, so I waited patiently for his request. I could tell he debated how much to push in his opening salvo of our little war of words. When he opened his mouth, I froze.

"I'd like to lay you on this island, settle your thighs over my shoulders, and eat you until you beg me to fuck you. I want to taste you while you sigh my name. Watch you writhe and grasp the edge of the counter. I'd like to lick and suck while my fingers stretch you so I can take you hard, once I'm satisfied you've had enough."

My breathing shuddered, the heat in my chest surging from the visual. Shit, I was in so much trouble.

"That's an escalation," I replied. He might claim he was only trying to one-up me, but the heaviness of the rise of his chest told a different story.

A knowing nod was his only response. He'd seen my reaction and knew how I felt about his proposal.

I'll admit it surprised me. Eli generally acted more burdened by me than blessed, but his first offer saw me taken care of. Repeatedly.

One foot pushed my shoe off the other, letting it drop to the floor with a *thud*, then did the same for the second. I put socked toes to his bare chest.

"Help a girl out?"

He took my foot in one hand, the other kneading my calf before peeling the ankle sock off. As he removed my second sock in the same manner, he pressed a kiss on the inside of my ankle, then deepened it, giving a little taste of what he could do.

Goosebumps pricking along my skin. This was not what I expected from him at all.

"Your turn," he prompted. I thought a moment, debating the options of what might come next. Thinking on our exchange in his room, how he'd held my chin almost-painfully, I knew exactly what to say to set him off.

"I'd like you to take me right here, on this island, so desperate for me that you can't wait to go somewhere private. I want you to grip my hips until my skin is red, to stretch me tightly around that big, hard cock you've been grinding against me for weeks. For you to turn me over, fist my hair to bow my back, and slap my ass as you take me deep."

I murmured the last part low, letting eagerness slide through my voice.

"Fuck me hard like I like it, until you can't hold back."

His eyes flared, his body shifting toward me before he caught himself. It was so satisfying. He swiftly reached for his fly.

"Nu uh, socks first," I reminded him.

I bit my lip to tease him, letting it pop free before pursing my lips to blow him a kiss. The game was too much fun. I wasn't ready for it to end yet.

Eli gripped my knees, thumbs digging in to spread my legs so he could lean against the countertop between them. He bent over to pull off his socks.

He pivoted as he straightened, inhaling deeply while running his face up the full length of my body. A hungry growl rumbled in his throat before he placed a chaste kiss at the crook of my neck, teasing me with my initial request. My nipples peaked, and I knew he saw them through the thin fabric. Why had I opted for lace?

A satisfied hum vibrated in his chest. Fisted hands on taut arms landed on either side of me, putting himself almost exactly back into the position he'd assumed when we started this game. Granted, now he stood between my legs, leaning close, with his scent and words looming around me.

Hot energy pricking at my face and chest. Eli dragged the stubble on his chin along my shoulder. It grated against my overly sensitive skin, deliciously irritating it and causing an involuntary shiver. He lowered his voice to give his next request in my ear, the scent of mint still lingering.

"I'd like to fuck you from behind on our knees, with your legs spread. One of my hands would toy with your clit, the other gripping your neck for leverage while I slam into you. I'd love to thrust against the contours of a plug in your ass. I'd have all that wild hair sticking to the sweat on my neck as your pussy strangles me through each orgasm. I want to clean my cum off your legs when we're done. I'd like to leave handprints on your inner thighs, so that every time you cross your legs you remember what I did to you. And nothing would thrill me more than to make Ryan watch while it happens."

I might have momentarily passed out. Could you get a concussion from mental whiplash?

"You've put thought into this," I whispered.

His only response was a hot, heavy *hmmm* that lit my nerves like fireworks on the Fourth of July.

"Only watching?"

"At that point, and let's not pretend you aren't interested in it either." He smirked. "No matter who else you're with, you'll always be *mine*. I'll chase you to the ends of the Earth if I have to."

My skin itched with heat at that, the anticipation demanding immediate action.

"How is it you're better at this game when I have more on," I muttered.

Eli barely retreated enough to allow me to free myself of my tank. He openly leered at the swell of my breasts wrapped in the perfect purplish-gray lace.

He ran his thumb under the scalloped edge of the bra. That thumb traveled under the strap, his nail dragging against my skin.

The tension between us thick, his fingers massaged into the muscles of my shoulder and up the line of my neck. He brought his knuckle under my chin, luring my face closer to his.

"Then bring your A-game," he murmured against my lips.

With the challenge issued, there were so many directions I could go in. I thought to scare him a little, to give him a fantasy that I'd never uttered to anyone and certainly not tried. Something that my brain screamed was wrong and yet . . . oh, did I ever want to do it with him, especially after all our time on the mats.

Eli was so tightly controlled, so pushy, with all that fury seething at the surface. I wanted to see if he could be reckless.

I leaned my forehead against his and let my fingers dance along his clavicle. I scrutinized the shading and design of his tattoo, tracing the outline, as I spoke my next words.

"I want you to tell me to *run*. To chase me," I breathed. "To catch me. To fight me, force me. To tear off my clothes, cut them off, or just shove them aside. I want you to hold me down while you fuck me in any way you like, if you can manage it. I'd like to be conquered, for you to earn the right to use me as you see fit."

I glanced back in time to see unblinking lust rage through him. Watched his nostrils flare. I could feel his heart hammering, or maybe it was mine.

I'd stunned him. It was written all over his face. It stoked the fire in my gut to see him like that. I stilled, waiting for him to voice his reaction.

"Look at you," he finally said. "You want it so badly. Your pupils are blown out like saucers. Have you even inhaled in the last ten seconds?"

I took a deep breath, breaking eye contact. My face flushed as embarrassment burned, the push too far. Too much of my crazy showed. I definitely needed therapy.

But he gripped my chin to bring me back and look at him square.

"What you've asked for takes knowing your partner very well. To have an established trust and a feel for limits. We're not there, but fuck, I'd like to be. I'd love to give that to you, for you to give it to me."

That was a *stellar* answer. I felt myself opening up to him, trusting him a bit more. Some of the ache at the Eli I'd initially met ebbed away.

He placed a soft kiss on my lips. I wanted more and deepened it, skimming my hands over his shoulders and around his neck. He opened his mouth to let our tongues weave together.

The connection spurred a slow-burning brushfire, building steadily and spreading. I could tell he felt it, too.

"This is going to make training with you a lot more interesting," he murmured.

"I can work with someone else." I smirked.

"No fucking way," he rumbled.

I nipped at his bottom lip, not too hard, but a groan tumbled from his throat.

The kiss grew feverish, torching every inch of my body to ash. His long arms wrapped around me, a hand grabbing my ass and roughly wrenching my hips closer to the counter's edge. I writhed against the bulge in his pants. The head of his cock pressed out over that damned band and button as we worked against each other.

"I thought we were playing your little consent game."

"You win, now take off your pants," I demanded.

He laughed, the relaxed sound more of a purr. Horny Eli was so much better than hard-ass Eli. He smiled as we kissed, uninhibited. He seemed . . . content.

"It was the button, wasn't it?"

"The button definitely helped."

Eli set about completing the first task I gave him, his lips flicking their way across my chin and down. Teeth scraped at the bend in my neck, and I froze. My fingers tightened on his shoulders, but I could feel his smile at my uneasiness that he might try to openly mark me.

Fucking Eli.

A small moan escaped as he drew the cup of the bra down, found my nipple, and began to lick at it with his broad tongue. His teeth sunk into my skin, mouth sucking, the bite just painful enough to enhance the pleasure. His mark would be hidden away and our little secret.

My spine bowed into his touch as his growl vibrated in the air. Oh, yes, he absolutely liked what I liked.

It had been an exciting turn of events. I was anxious and so heated and alive for him. I wanted him, wanted him to want me like he clearly did. It was a welcome shift.

He teased the waistband on my shorts, ready to move on to all the ruin he promised, when the sirens went off.

Chapter Twenty-Three

Per emergency protocol, Eli and I mustered in the main hall with the rest of the Clara in residence. I shuffled and side-stepped my way through the crowded room to stand beside Trish.

"Your shirt's inside out and you're all glowy," she whispered to me.

I suppressed a groan. I'd managed to throw on cargoes and boots but hadn't bothered to change otherwise.

"I thought you saw and knew everything that happened around here?"

"Georgia can't get past the steel doors."

"No one will notice if we leave them open a smidge."

"Like I want to walk in on whatever has you all flushed? No, thank you, missy."

"Don't be judgey."

"At least I'm not macking it on someone despite pickle breath."

Pickle breath? I'd only had the one. Subtly licking the back of my hand, I tried to discern if . . . *oh, shit.*

Shit, shit, shiiiiiiiit.

Things just got simpler or way more complicated.

Heightened smell. Sneaking off. Missing cash. Time with *Doctor* Lita Silva. Her defensiveness of Maxon, who'd been driving her into town, and who I'd heard secretly helping someone during that call on my first day here.

Trish was pregnant.

Fuckity dicksticks.

She saw my wide eyes, and somehow she knew I'd connected the dots. Her own eyes pled with me not to say anything.

Later, she told me through best friend ESP.

Fine, I shrugged back. *But there will be a later.*

She only nodded.

Peter and Henry barreled into the room shouting orders. Most of the crowd went to secure the bunker's exits while they assigned the rest to investigate what awaited us upstairs.

Only one beacon sounded an alarm, from a Guard in the western part of the property. The rest of the patrol checked in fine. It might've been an accident, but the Guard had gone silent.

Eli was one of the best fighters they had, and I was shackled to him, which meant that we were assigned to clear and search the building. I should've been happy they finally let me sit at the adults' table, and yet . . .

Ryan begged me to take a gun. His eyes passed between my inside-out shirt, then to Eli, and back. He gentlemanly said nothing, but his jaw flexed slightly as his eye ticked. Weren't men supposed to be the unemotional, non-dramatic ones?

When I wouldn't take the gun, Eli tried to force a sword on me. Both the gun and the sword seemed wildly inappropriate and more likely to hurt me than help me.

Instead, I shoved a jackknife into a boot and snapped a sheathed dagger on my belt. As a "break in case of emergency," I hid a small push dagger in the space where my bra strap met the cup, the side that Eli hadn't taken a bite out of because *ouch*.

Bras had quickly become my favorite place to hide a weapon. It worked for cash and cards, so why not?

Peter assigned Ryan to organize the Guard's cover of the underground garage. At least the post was a relatively safe position. Nearly indestructible steel doors protected the entrance, and backstops lined the area.

Before he set out, Ryan caught me in a tight hug and lingering, heated kiss. He promised we'd spend some quiet time together once the alarm had been sorted. Nothing like a life-or-death scenario to clarify your feelings.

Trish and Tom joined us in searching the compound, given they'd shared our nightly patrol, along with Jack and a few other Guards recognized as solid fighters. Twenty other Pairs melted into the woods as we ascended the stairs into Haven.

Moonlight sifted through the overhead panes of glass in the atrium, casting shadows from the palm fronds and tree branches. Normally, the area buzzed with life, with birds chirruping and leaves rustling underfoot.

Tonight, the uncanny stillness piqued my unease.

Welcome to the atrium, it gets worse every day.

We walked softly through the pathways on quiet feet, even in boots. I reflected on that first week, when Eli'd demanded I sneak soundlessly around the Practice Room. The techniques he'd taught became second nature. At some point, I started doing them as a default.

The night stretched while we circuited through each route. We'd almost cleared the area when our earbuds hummed to life.

Alarms sounded to the south, near the main road and the garage entrance. My eyes widened. Eli and I exchanged a glance, but he shook his head slightly. Nothing could be done now. Even if I wanted to sprint there, it would take several minutes to get to Ryan. Even if I got there in time, what would I do? Sass them to death? Fire and confined spaces did not mix.

My heart ached. We'd searched the atrium for a good while and hadn't seen a single thing out of the ordinary. The place was creepy as hell, but I hadn't felt so much as a twinge of heat in my system. No point searching the building when the action happened far away from us.

Jack rounded the corner.

"Alarm at the garage," she stage-whispered.

"Not our post," Eli replied.

"They need us. We should go."

"No. We follow Peter's order. They can sort it out."

"At least you, then," she urged. "They need fighters. I'll stay with Jex. The building is empty."

"We haven't cleared the building. Stop arguing. Follow the order. If they need us, they'll ping us."

Shadows hid most of Jack's face, but her annoyance clearly showed in her tone. She must really be used to getting her way.

"Then let's split up to search faster. The guy they assigned to me already went to help, and you'd do better than I would on your own. Jex and I will work toward the front and you can come around from the back by the Weapons Room. We'll meet in the middle. The sooner it's clear, the sooner we can report back."

Something felt off. Why were the Kier attacking the garage? Sure, it was the widest entrance into the bunker, and the most accessible from the road, but the doors were five-inch steel. Opening my mouth to voice the concern, Eli cut me off.

"Fine," he rounded on his sister, his face deadly serious. "Move quickly. Play straight, Jack. I'm trusting you not to get her hurt. Anything that happens to her will happen to you, even if she gets so much as a paper cut."

Geez, that was harsh. And a little hot.

Jack only swallowed and agreed.

You would think Eli would give me some measure of a send-off after graphically describing the ways he wanted to violate me. After telling me he'd chase me to the ends of the Earth.

Instead, he nodded tersely at us both and stalked away through the trees. Guy was confusing as hell.

Jack and I wound through the enormous atrium. We passed the koi pond by the porch swings, but even the fish swam noiselessly in their habitat.

Despite the stale air, heat prickled in my scalp. Looming palm fronds distorted my perception, manifesting figures in every gloomy corner. Smaller plants and flowers grazed my legs and left sticky residue on my pants as we walked side-by-side on the narrow path.

A bird flapped in the dark and cawed before settling.

Dark copper flashed in the corner of my eye, but when I turned, nothing was there.

The place was unnerving as fuck.

"Did you know some people think Jack the Ripper was a woman?" Jack whispered to me.

"What?" Not the time to make small talk about *serial killers*, what with the slinking around in the darkness.

"Jack the Ripper. Some people think it was a woman. A midwife, so no one would notice blood on her."

"First, that's random and disturbing. And second, wouldn't surprise me. People are always underestimating the power of women," I replied.

"Too right."

"Do you, ah, have a fascination with your namesake? Should I be concerned we're walking alone in the dark?"

"Oh, no." She laughed softly. "I'd be more worried about what else lurks in the shadows."

"Not as reassuring as intended, Jack."

"Not meant to be reassuring," she sniped.

Okay . . .

Leaves crackled to our left, making me jump.

"Calm down," Jack moaned, "it's probably a snake."

"Again, I say to you, not reassuring."

The prickling of heat slowly amplified as we crossed the courtyard barely dappled in light. The acceleration only added to my anxiety and worsened my skittishness.

Weaving through the maze of paths, we'd only made it halfway to the front of the complex when a sinister figure stepped from behind an overgrown bay laurel bush.

The shape was tall and broad, but I didn't stick around to figure out who it was. I grabbed Jack's arm and sprinted to the "T" by the front door.

Skin crawling with hot energy, the dagger at my hip scraped against my side as I unsheathed it and did my best not to stab myself. Probably shouldn't run with a sharp object, but no way in hell was I getting caught still trying to get it free of my pants.

The figure hunted near-soundlessly behind us with quick steps that only whispered on the pavers. As it chased us through the night, each pad of its feet tugged at the burn sloshing in my system. Cold sweat collected on my neck and dripped down my back and chest.

We turned a corner, but Jack split off onto a side path.

"Keep going, I'll come around behind," she yelled.

"No, Jack!" I called back, but she disappeared into the brush. *Motherfuckingdamnit.*

Heat flowed in my veins like a river of lava, but I fought against the bubble instinctively forming. Creating a ring of fire in the dark would only light me up in a spotlight.

My breathing labored, I took a tight turn and ducked under some low tree limbs. My hunter edged the corner with ease and yanked hard at my braided hair. The grab halted my escape, the force threatening a fall flat on my back. I spun and brought the dagger up in a wild strike.

Essence boiling in my veins, I swung the edge at my pursuer. With the hilt in my fist, blade faced downward, I aimed for the shadowed neck and arms in the gloom. Light flashed off steel as fluid strikes moved over and across the space between us. I switched hands twice as I advanced, trying to confuse him, but he nimbly blocked each attempt with a hand to my forearm.

There was padding on his sleeves, because I connected more than once, but he never faltered. He retreated a few steps, and I heard a snicker from his direction.

That pissed me right off. I'd cut him, but he didn't even have the grace to bleed for me. I'd had him on the retreat. What the fuck was he laughing at?

Anger fed my scorching essence as the assault became frantic. He responded by forcing his own offense, using long legs and arms to press forward and crowd my motions. Panic swelled in my gut as he anticipated each attack. He'd been learning my tactics.

My blade slashed diagonally, but he dodged sideways and knocked the dagger away. The move caused my body to twist. He closed on my exposed back while circling my neck in a chokehold. His other hand trapped my knife-wielding wrist.

Chuckling in my ear, his body draped around mine, he murmured, "You've gotten a lot better. Not good enough yet, though."

The timbre of his voice resonated in my bones. I knew him. I knew that voice.

Seizing the dagger from my grasp, he tossed the weapon into the trees.

Shit, I didn't want to go hand-to-hand with him, even if my essence sang harmonies.

Slipping my shoulder under his arm, I slid sideways out of the chokehold and pushed hard off him, using the momentum to shove him in the other direction while I sprinted for the front door.

Where the hell was Jack?

Barely three steps and he wrenched me back, swinging my body toward the wall. Bracing for impact, I withdrew my Hail Mary from my bra.

As I struck the stucco, he wrapped a large hand around my throat and surged against me, but the controlling position only brought him within my range. My push dagger pressed against his jugular.

Derek gazed at me in the moonlight, a satisfied grin on his handsome face. His strong thigh pinned me to the wall as we both gulped in air.

"Not bad, pretty girl. Tiny little blade, though." He squeezed his fingers slightly. "Could probably strangle you before you did any real damage."

"Give me one solid reason why I shouldn't stab you in the throat first," I spat.

"You've already got me hard, no need to overdo it."

Moving quick, I brought a knee up to nail him in the groin, but he blocked it with his leg.

Dammit, that always works.

"Now, now, play nice," he tsked. Cinnamon and smoke surrounded me as his firm body pressed into mine.

As Derek and I glared at each other, one of the most gorgeous women I'd ever seen skipped from the shadows. Wide, hazel eyes glinted through deep ginger locks. She was petite like me, her all-black cat suit rendered useless by her unbound hair. She carried a large, overstuffed duffel bag.

"If you two are done with foreplay, we should exit. Unless you want to kill a few more?"

A hint of insanity flashed in her eyes.

"No, we have what we came for," he replied. I struggled against his hold, unclear what he intended to do.

"She's impatient, but spunky," Derek told me. "You'll like her. Eventually."

He snatched at the dagger in my hand and disarmed me without so much as flinching, even though it sliced his finger to execute the maneuver.

My dagger disappeared into his back pocket. May he stab himself in the ass the next time he sits.

Sucking at the cut, slightly bleeding fingers played with his bottom lip and brought my attention to his mouth. He chuckled, the low, dangerous sound lighting up my traitorous libido.

"Stop teasing her, Delaney. We only have a few more minutes before they leave us here, and I don't feel like walking back to the Farm through the woods."

"You know damn well they aren't leaving without us. Quit spoiling the fun."

The woman tossed a hank of rope in his direction. He caught it and bound my wrists together before doing the same to my ankles.

Movement over his shoulder caught my attention, and Jack stepped out of the trees.

"No, Jack, run! Get Eli! Call Peter!" I screamed.

But she only shook her head at me.

The woman approached her, silent words exchanged as they made eye contact. Jack nodded. The redhead brought a fist up, wound all the way back, and punched Jack in the face so hard it knocked her clean out of one of her shoes.

Jack lay on the path, out cold, her temple already an angry red.

"That was too easy. Ya'll need to learn to take a hit," the redhead chided.

Then it clicked into place.

"Jack betrayed us."

"Put a tracker on your phone and everything," she said with a snicker.

Derek hoisted me over his shoulder. My friends and the other Guards were still in the building, so I shrieked as loudly as I could.

The woman shoved a minty rag into my mouth. Instantly, my head spun, my limbs weakening. In desperation, I worked my ring off my finger and tossed it at Jack's prone body to hint at what happened.

My last thought before the world faded was how the woman asked whether they should kill "a few *more*."

End of Book One

The Duality Series

Dying To Know What Happens Next?

I'm sorry, and you're welcome.

Duplicity, Book 2, published on April 11, 2022.

Freebies, extra book content, deleted scenes, alternative POVs, and ARCs are available to those who sign up for my newsletter at **www.beccafogg.com**.

Need to talk to someone about that ending? Are your fingers itching to get out the red string?
Join the **Hidden by Fogg** Facebook group.

Also by Becca

Plots, Schemes, and Scandalous Means:
Four worlds collide in this 18+ fantasy romance standalone novel. The Thief is the Queen's sword and shield, protecting her and the Realm from the Queen's enemies. The Rabble is a revolutionary, serving the Duke's desire to overthrow the Crown. When the Thief and the Rabble intersect on equal-opposite missions, the result is an outcome no one anticipated.

Acknowledgments

First, a massive thank you to you, the reader, for making it to the end without lighting your book on fire or deleting it from your library.

Second, this book would not have happened without my husband's support. It took me ten years to finally sit down and finish it, and I could not have done it without him.

Third, this book would not be remotely the condition it's in without Ashley, Rachel, Ira-Rebeca, Susan, Matrice, and Mackenzie from Nice Girl Naughty Edits. Thank you for your work, and your encouragement, thoughtfulness, and patience.

Fourth, a huge thank you to Jess, Hillary, Ally, Chucky, and my Mom and Dad. For being amazingly supportive, and also for respecting my boundaries by not reading this book. I love you all.

Is that enough guilt? I appreciate you beyond words. I'm so glad we have such a trusting and honest relationship. You're like family to me. (I'm mean, *you are*, but that's beside the point.)

And, last but not least, thank you to all my fellow writers in the TikTok and Facebook communities, who have patiently answered my tireless questions.

Glossary

Essence: the inherent power within a person.

Duality: the manifestation of an enhanced essence in those born to a Duality pair.

Valen: a person with enhanced musculoskeletal and adrenal systems. Valens are typically stronger and faster than other humans, with better reflexes and healing abilities.

Amory: a person with enhanced nervous, respiratory, and circulatory systems. Skills fall into one of six categories (in order of frequency):

> **Serobestia**: plants and animals
> **Terraer**: land and air
> **Ignisunda**: fire and water
> **Orisalvus**: sight and sound
> **Menscorpis**: body and mind
> **Moira**: time and space

Duds: a person born to a Duality pair without an enhanced essence, or where the enhancement is slight.

The Acceptance: the point around the twenty-fifth birthday when the body matures enough that the entirety of a person's enhanced essence becomes active.

Pair: a matched Valen and Amory.

True Pair: a matched Valen and Amory where the tie is based upon fate, and not simply compatibility. Similar to a soulmate.

Inverses: equal-opposites among the extraordinary.

Kier: the bad guys.

Clara: the good guys.

Nell: the leader of that region's Clara; also taken as a surname.

Cole: the leader of that region's Kier; also taken as a surname.

Haven: the main compound for the Clara in the Southeast.

The Farm: the main compound for the Kier in the Southeast.

. . . and, of course, more to come.

Oh, you're still here?
And you wanted more?

Eli
That Night on the Deck

There were too many people in the building. The constant hum of conversation and movement in the halls grated on my nerves. I couldn't even relax in my room, since it was at the corner to the main intersection to the residence rows.

Instead, I picked my way through the woods to find the farthest platform from the building. Gnats buzzed, but I needed solitude.

A little calm. A few minutes of muting deprivation to dull the edges of my irritation.

I laid back on the wooden lounger and closed my eyes. The cast of the near-full moon soaked into my face, bleeding through my lids, but at least it was a constant and unwavering presence.

For ten blissful minutes, I was alone with the hum of the cicadas.

The deck shifted as someone stepped up and lit the torches at each corner. Lemony Citronella muddled with the crisp, honied scent of Jex's shampoo, so complex it may as well be perfume.

Great, just what I needed.

Her presence jabbed at the stewing agitation already settled in my gut. Can't a man breath? I massaged at my neck, trying to relieve some of the tension.

Fuck, if this is paired life I'll go insane within the month.

Jex dropped something heavy onto the picnic table, the bench rumbling as she pulled it out to take her seat. Pages flipped.

I worked at ignoring her. If she had a book, perhaps she'd leave me alone.

"Can I ask you a question?"

Of course, she wouldn't leave me alone.

"Don't see a way I can stop you," I replied, refusing to encourage her by acknowledging more than her words.

"Thanks, I love a warm welcome."

"It's Florida, isn't it hot enough for you, sweetheart?"

Book pages rustled. Still with the nervous ticks I couldn't break her of.

"What do you know about inverses?" she asked.

"What do you want to know?"

"How does it work? I don't really get it."

Inverses? Where did that come from? She should go find Pinch. He was better at explaining that shit than I was.

"That's rather advanced for you, don't you think?"

"How would I know if it's advanced if none of it makes any sense at all?"

"Fair enough. What makes you ask?"

"Aster left this book for me, but it's confusing and it would be easier to have someone explain it to me."

Rolling my eyes, I sighed out some of the building frustration. If she was out here with a book about inverses, then Peter probably ordered her to read it fully. She never understood that she couldn't take the easy road for this kind of thing. You'd think the woman thrived on finding loopholes.

"Do your own work, princess. I'm not here to give you short-cuts."

Huffing, she adjusted her position and returned to page-flipping. Her agitated sighs shattered my silent retreat. I refused to acknowledge her, and she continued avoiding working on something that was probably vital to our survival.

Several taut minutes passed while we feigned indifference to each other's presence.

"So, how much older are you than Jack?" she asked brightly.

"Five years."

"When was your birthday?"

"February, but I'm a year older than you."

"And how do you feel about all of this?"

I finally turned to look at her. The book lay open on the table, the section she read from smack in the middle of the multi-inch tome. Of course, she'd start somewhere in the middle instead of at the beginning—reinforcing that, yet again, she wasn't taking this seriously.

"I'm fine, Dr. Phil, and you?" I chided.

"I'm sorry, I don't have a frame of reference. I was hoping you could share."

Moonlight skimmed over her face. Tired eyes pleaded for a real answer, that infuriating mouth tight with unease.

"About Jack's kidnapping, the Dualities, or having you around for the rest of my life?" I grumbled.

She shrugged.

"All of the above?"

She looked overwhelmed, and an idiotic little voice in the back of my head made me feel bad for snapping at her.

"Bad. Good. Too soon to tell."

"I still charge for the hour if you only talk for five minutes," she quipped.

I grunted. How much more of this would she force me to endure?

"Does that mean you have more questions? I wanted a few moments of peace."

The fatigue slid from her face, replaced with an incrementally tightening annoyance.

"Excuse me for trying to get acquainted," she bit out. "We hardly know each other. How are we supposed to work together if we can't stand a single conversation?"

I sat forward in the lounger, planting my feet on the deck boards to face her square. If she wanted my attention, she was about to get it.

"Maybe if you weren't so annoying all of the time I wouldn't mind talking to you," I snapped with a pointed look.

She slammed the book closed, her gorgeous face flushing from that temper I'd become so familiar with.

"Maybe if you weren't such an ass, I'd be less annoying," she replied.

"Who's more likely in the wrong—me, minding my own business, or you, intruding on my time when you had no business being here?"

"You are such a child. I came out here to read." She jumped from the bench to loom above me. "Are you so self-centered you thought I came here for *you*?"

No, I think you stumbled onto my free time and decided it could be used as your distraction.

I vaulted to my feet, hulking over her. "*Were* you reading? Or were avoiding your responsibilities by asking inane questions?"

"I'm sorry, I forgot you don't know what a book looks like. When was the last time you attempted something more advanced than a diagnosing-psychopathy checklist?"

We circled each other, electric tension filling the space between us.

"At least I have redeeming qualities," I sneered. "You surrender the second anything gets too difficult for you. Forgive me for not wanting to talk to a woman who spends ninety percent of her time whining."

Her face twisted in contempt.

"And what redeeming qualities might those be, hmmm? It's certainly not *good humor* or a *charming wit.*"

This woman! It's like she always knew exactly what to say or do to tip me off-balance.

"You 'bout done?" I threw my hands in the air. "Fuck, you're insufferable."

"Better obnoxious and fun than cold and quiet."

"You think I'm cold? Hardly. You just don't get me hot."

Why did I say that?

"Ha! *You* might not get hot, but your dick sure loves pinning me to the mat."

"If it's my dick you want, you should have said that in the first place. Just know I'll still want you to *actually follow through.*"

Her anger surged, and she slapped me so hard my head snapped sideways. The little stones on her ring bit into my cheek. Blood welled on my skin, barely enough to streak down my face.

Jex stood there, stunned, looking at me and at her hand.

I glowered at her. It took every ounce of resistance in my body not to grab her and show her how hot she made me.

I wiped blood from my face and examined it under the dim light.

My gaze fell to her, her wide, green-blue eyes shining with confusion and fear—and openness. None of the attitude. None of the mask she wore for everyone else. Scared and alone and asking me to protect her, even from myself.

Bloodying me, the weakening line between us disintegrating under the weight of misdirected tension, reduced Jex down to her most basic part.

That part was unsure and needed me to answer for her.

It poked the part of *me* I'd locked away from her, the part that wanted to pursue her with a single-minded goal . . .

Enough. I'd held back long enough.

When I surged toward her, she stepped back in surprise. Grabbing her neck, I slammed my mouth against hers, ordering her surrender and doing my damn best to convince her to stop fighting so fucking hard against me.

My essence practically leapt at her, demanding more contact. I forced the threads straining to tie us together to settle, like I'd had to do so many other times in the last few weeks. She might not be ready to complete the pairing, but our essences still keened with it.

For once, I let go and took from her what I'd been dying to since the moment I'd first touched her.

She was mine, and I'd make that clear to her.

Not tonight. Tonight, I'd show her what was possible. Tonight, I'd convince her to try.

I needed her to try.

Having her agree could be enough for me, for now.

Made in USA - North Chelmsford, MA
1371193_9798461714963
05.23.2023 1045